MW00345864

BOOKS BY TIM MCBAIN & L.T. VARGUS

The Violet Darger series
The Victor Loshak series
The Charlotte Winters series
The Scattered and the Dead series
Casting Shadows Everywhere
The Awake in the Dark series
The Clowns

DARK PASSAGE

DARK PASSAGE

a Violet Darger novel

LT VARGUS & TIM MCBAIN

COPYRIGHT © 2021 TIM MCBAIN & L.T. VARGUS

SMARMY PRESS

ALL RIGHTS RESERVED.

THIS IS A WORK OF FICTION. NAMES, CHARACTERS, BUSINESSES, PLACES, EVENTS AND INCIDENTS ARE EITHER THE PRODUCTS OF THE AUTHOR'S IMAGINATION OR USED IN A FICTITIOUS MANNER. ANY RESEMBLANCE TO ACTUAL PERSONS, LIVING OR DEAD, OR ACTUAL EVENTS IS PURELY COINCIDENTAL.

DARK
PASSAGE

PROLOGUE

The dozer scuttled up the trash heap, shoving the bulk along, grinding its way closer to the center of the landfill. Keith jerked the wheel, felt the vehicle wobble over the uneven surface of the garbage heap, its tracks grating and churning.

He glanced at the rearview mirror. Saw the sweat glistening on the puckered skin beneath his eyes. Already he felt that itch, the little rectangle in his breast pocket calling out to him. Not yet, though. Better to get further out to sea first, well away from the office, out toward the middle of the ocean of trash where no one was looking.

The incline grew steeper beneath the bulldozer. Tilted Keith's shoulders back in the bucket seat. He climbed the mound of garbage slowly but surely, inch by inch, like that first hill on a roller coaster.

This was his job, for better or worse. Driving a tractor over a sea of trash known as the Wissahickon Creek Landfill — a giant hole in the ground with 500 feet of mostly shredded Philadelphia County garbage floating atop it. He sailed his lonely vessel out over the mess like a makeshift raft and let the blade shove the swells of trash around so someone else could shred and then compact it all, shove it deeper into the hole.

The pay was OK, but this was a shit job, as far as he was concerned. The smell alone confirmed that. The slop was ripe today — acrid and tangy, some umami punch adding a layer of pungent earthiness. Savory, he thought. Like a few tons of rotting hamburger and mushrooms had been blended in with

1

the usual shit smell.

Smell that rich aroma, he thought, gritting his teeth. His recurring internal joke had never been spoken aloud. It probably never would.

A giant wad of debris rolled in front of him, growing slowly like a cartoon snowball tumbling down a hill. And it was juicy. Like the sun was coaxing sweat out of the trash's paper and plastic skin.

Keith's eyes flicked to the rearview again. Watched the slowly scrolling ski slope of trash there. The office had become a tiny speck. That was good enough.

The box in his breast pocket thrummed with cold current. His fingers reached for it. Found it.

He plucked a Marlboro Red from the pack and attached the filtered end to his lips. His lighter flickered to life. The flame bent into the tobacco cylinder and made a faint sucking sound as it lit.

He drew in a big lungful of smoke. Could only kind of detect the flavor of it with the garbage smell so strong today. Even so, it tasted pretty goddamn good.

He'd been smoking these for twenty-seven years now, since his junior year in high school. "Cowboy killers" people called these particular cigs, presumably since multiple models from the Marlboro Man advertising campaigns had succumbed to the Big C.

What a shame it'd be if the tobacco took me down, Keith thought. Gone way too soon. He had so much shoving around of garbage left to give.

His eyes shifted to the mirror again. The office remained a tiny dot there. He didn't know what he'd expected to see. The boss man, Mike, rocketing up the trash heap to catch him in the act? Mike would have no idea about this violation, a thought that brought the faintest smile to his lips. Sometimes he thought he only enjoyed smoking out on the garbage pile because it wasn't allowed. Strictly verboten.

The other workers wondered how he could even stand to do it, too grossed out by the smell. He'd been working here eighteen years now, though. Had given the best years of his life to this squalid expanse of filth. And time had a way of changing you, hardening you to certain things. The stench had become part of his world, part of him. It simply was. Getting upset about the smell would be like getting upset about the wind or the stars.

He hit the cigarette hard. Felt the smoke swirling in his lungs. Held it there. Savored it.

This time when his eyes slid over to the mirror, he saw something there that made him cough. The smoke sputtered out of him. His foot jammed the brake.

He sat there a moment. Eyes fixed on the image in the mirror. Staring. Not smoking. Not breathing.

The lower half of a body jutted up from the trash heap, everything from the waist down angled awkwardly into the air. Naked. Legs limp and folded. For a second he told himself it was a mannequin, that he was overreacting, but something was wrong with it.

Too bony.

The hip bones looked skeletal. Skin drawn taut over the joints as though no muscle tissue remained. No mannequin existed like this.

And yet something about the shape reminded him of his

daughter, Mia. She was scrawny and frail, just like the girl out there.

Just like her.

He stubbed his cigarette out on the Mountain Dew can he used for an ash tray. Watched the white tube of tobacco bend and crush and then disappear into the wide mouth hole.

He knew it wasn't her. Knew it. He'd seen her this morning. It couldn't be her.

Nevertheless, he climbed out of the vehicle. Felt his boots sink ankle-deep into the sludgy garbage. The smell assailed his nostrils, sharper out here in the open. The stench seemed to cook in the sunlight, some oily vapor that changed in the heat and hung in the air.

He waded over to where the corpse projected from the garbage. Knelt down beside it.

His gloved hands dipped into the trash, went to work digging the girl out. The heavy work gloves disappeared into the junk and reemerged over and over, flinging bits away. Excavating.

The blazing June sun baked the back of his neck. Beaded fresh sweat along his hairline. And the wind blew in haphazard bursts, touched the wet bits of his skin and cooled them some.

Part of him knew he shouldn't be doing this, shouldn't be messing with a likely crime scene. But he needed to see her. Needed to know.

He shoveled away crumpled popcorn bags and crushed paper Pepsi cups from a movie theater. Then he pulled out a tattered blanket, faded blue, scratchy material damp with garbage juice. Next came empty Heineken cans in various states of dented-ness.

His hands kept working, kept digging. He watched them in a daze. Watched the pale skin of the girl's upper body slowly come clear until he reached the milky white flesh of her face.

Purple surrounded her sunken eyes, breaking up the pale sheet of skin. Dainty elfin features formed her nose and lips.

Ghostly.

Angelic.

Beautiful.

Even with her face emaciated so the cheekbones protruded like doorknobs set beneath her skin, she was beautiful.

He stood and stumbled back a step. Choked. Coughed. Felt hot tears in his eyes.

Not Mia. Not his daughter. He'd known it wouldn't be, and yet he found no relief in the revelation.

For this girl — a daughter to someone — had been plucked from this life. Taken. Set afloat in the sea of trash, launched into his reeking world, like another used up plastic object to be doused with piss and shit and garbage juice.

And he knew that this moment had changed everything again, that this world would be forever different for him now. For both of them. She was part of it. Eternally. Like the smell. Like the wind and the stars.

He dug back through the trash he'd thrown. Draped the rough blue blanket over her. He knew it was silly, this overwhelming urge to cover her, protect her. It was far too late for that. But if it had been Mia… well, that's what he would have wanted for her. Someone to give her one last bit of dignity, at least.

Then he hustled back to the tractor to call the office and tell them what he'd found.

CHAPTER 1

The road sliced a clean charcoal line through the forest. Hemlock trees formed a wall on either side of the asphalt, with a sliver of pale gray sky visible overhead. Violet Darger's rental car rocketed through the cleft in the foliage.

She fidgeted in her seat. Shifted from one butt cheek to the other. She'd been driving for almost four hours straight, and she was antsy for the journey to be over.

Her finger found the power button for the radio and turned it on. The chorus of "Take It Easy" by the Eagles blared from the speakers, and just as soon as she'd turned the music on, she turned it back off.

It's been a long drive, and I hate the fucking Eagles.

Darger's gaze slid over to the navigation app on her phone. She was nearly there, anyway. Might as well settle in for the last stretch in silence.

But the quiet had a strange way of amplifying her anticipation. Snake-like tendrils of anxiety squirmed in her belly.

Her mind flashed on the photographs in the file Loshak had sent. Three emaciated bodies found in a garbage dump in Pennsylvania. Two women and a man. One of the women had been wearing a thin tank top and panties. The other had been completely nude. The man was fully clothed in all black and covered in a layer of what looked like dirt or soot unrelated to the trash around him.

The first question was how three people could go missing

without any fanfare until they turned up in the garbage heap.

The second question, the more troubling question, was how they'd become so thin.

Darger lifted her travel cup from the drink holder and took a sip. Her nose wrinkled involuntarily. The barista had been a bit too heavy-handed with the vanilla syrup in her latte. It was a touch over the line in a way that made the sweetness stick to the back of her tongue and throat.

The car rounded a corner, and an ending to the dense cluster of trees appeared in her windshield at last, taking shape in the distance. The opening in the hemlocks grew larger as she sped down the two-lane road. When the trees finally parted for good, the land opened up, spreading out to the horizon on either side. And then she saw it.

Two immense heaps of garbage jutted up from the earth, towering peaks with smaller crests surrounding them that sprawled in all directions like foothills. A breath sucked into Darger's throat and held still there as she took in the display, eyes dancing over the hulking bulges, almost awe-inspiring in their sheer size. A virtual mountain range of trash.

This was the Wissahickon Creek Landfill, one of many large dumps serving the Philadelphia metropolitan area. It was also the location where the bodies had been found.

Small black shapes circled above the two big mounds, swooping and diving. Darger's first thought was flies, but then she realized they must be seagulls, swirling everywhere in the sky in search of fresh meals.

Chain link fence traced the perimeter of the compound, the barrier complete with faint coils of barbed wire spiraling around the top, as though the precious piles of garbage must be protected at all costs.

Darger pulled to the gate and wrestled her ID from her pocket. With a quick glance at her FBI badge, the attendant lifted the arm of the boom gate and waved her through. It wasn't until she was moving again that Darger realized she'd held her breath as soon as she'd rolled the window down to show her badge.

Even still, she hesitated to inhale, worried about what kind of stink might have snuck inside when she'd had the window open. As the seconds wore on, her lungs began to protest.

She finally relented. Took a test sniff. Detected nothing.

Well, that was a surprise.

Maybe it was a wind direction thing. Or maybe the stench would only hit her once she stepped outside. In any case, she kept a steady stream of oxygen moving to her lungs for the moment.

She wheeled into the dirt parking lot, passing dumpsters of various sizes and colors arranged in rows. The tires of her rental gushed through the muddy sand, sizzling over the wetness.

Darger slid into an empty space next to a shitty little office building. The once-white corrugated metal exterior of the place was stained brown like a tooth, smudged with black streaks emanating from the corner of each window. A gull squatted on the roof eating something it had harvested from the massive smorgasbord of trash surrounding them.

Darger's eyes slid back to the massive garbage peaks as she pulled the key from the ignition. A bulldozer scurried up the pile, the yellow vehicle bumping up and down as if it were tottering atop the trash instead of rolling over it. For a moment, she could only marvel at how small the machine looked next to the heaps of refuse.

And then her stomach churned a little at the thought of what other secrets might be buried in all that garbage.

CHAPTER 2

The moment Darger stepped out of the car, the wave of garbage smell hit her — an odor somehow rich and sour at the same time. It seemed to rise into the air like a filmy vapor and cook there in the sun. She wrinkled her nose.

She'd only taken a few steps in the muddy lot when a man in a hazmat suit approached. He was very tall and thin, and the white coveralls fit him awkwardly. Tight in the crotch but baggy everywhere else.

"Agent Darger?"

"That's me."

"I'm Officer Primanti," he said, shaking her hand. "I've got a suit for you right over here. Detective Ambrose and Agent Loshak are already inside the search grid."

Darger followed Primanti over to a canvas tent where he handed her the various pieces of PPE gear. She stepped into the suit first, zipping the Tyvek coveralls up to her neck, and then donning a bright yellow reflective safety vest. Next she traded her regular boots for a pair in black rubber. Primanti helped her fit a respirator over her nose and mouth before pointing to a row of hardhats.

"The helmets are a facility requirement. Anyone going past the crime scene barrier has to wear one."

"They get a lot of trash falling from the sky around here?" Darger asked, her voice muffled by the mask.

Primanti chuckled, shrugging.

"Liability and all that, I guess."

Darger smoothed her hair back and snugged up the strap on the hardhat.

After they each squeezed into a pair of gloves, Officer Primanti lowered his respirator and put his hands on his hips.

"Ready?"

Darger gave him a thumbs up. Primanti nodded once and led her out of the tent and through a gap in a row of police saw horses.

"We have to sort of edge around this ridge here," he said, gesturing to the angled slope of one of the trash mounds. "And you're gonna wanna watch your step. The garbage is awkward to walk on."

That was an understatement in Darger's opinion. Each step was a fresh gamble as she moved up the slope, shuffling from a section that felt like stable ground to another area that buckled and shifted under her weight.

Her arms splayed out to her sides, working to maintain her balance through the rough stuff, and she kept her eyes on the ground as she walked, trying to determine by sight whether her next step would be mushy or firm. She was still watching her boots when she heard a shrill whistle.

She glanced up and realized they'd rounded the far side of the garbage mountain. A cluster of figures huddled in the distance, all matching in their white coveralls and yellow hardhats. One of the suits put up a gloved hand and waved.

And even though the suits made the figures look identical from this distance, Darger knew by the whistle that it was Loshak.

Primanti turned back to face her.

"You think you can make it over there on your own? I have

to get back to my post."

"I'm good," she said. "Thank you, Officer Primanti."

Darger picked her way closer to the group. The inside of her respirator was warm and humid from her breath. She'd been breathing through her mouth since she got out of her car, not sure if the filters in the mask were capable of blocking out the smell or not. The stench was strong enough in the parking lot. She could imagine how much more intense it would be when she was standing on the ragged slopes of Mount Dung.

She trudged through more slop. Feet sinking and squishing. Eyes drifting up now and then to watch the seagulls above as they zipped around, squawking like crazy.

When Darger finally reached the group, Loshak clapped her on the shoulder.

"Hope the traffic wasn't too rough," Loshak said.

"Not as rough as the walk over here," she said. "Less smelly, too."

Loshak chuckled.

"Detective Ambrose, this is my partner, Agent Darger."

The detective lowered his mask to greet her. He was an older black man with a shaved head and a graying goatee.

"We appreciate you coming up," he said.

Their gloves made a faint squeaking sound as the two rubbery surfaces made contact.

"I was just telling Agent Loshak, I've never seen anything quite like this. To have three bodies that we can't even officially label as homicide victims? But then the state of the bodies…" He blew out a breath. "The medical examiner is conducting the autopsies right now, so I've got my fingers crossed he can give us something to work with."

"Any luck pinpointing where the bodies might have come from?" Darger almost had to yell to be heard over the sounds of a nearby bulldozer.

"We're working on it now. Sorting everything in the immediate vicinity of the bodies." Ambrose wagged a finger in the direction of a group of techs in an area marked off by red string. "The techs are all divided into pairs. One person sorts, the other person logs what they find. We're tracking any addresses on mail or paper receipts."

"And you can use that information to track the vicinity the trash came from?"

"That's what they tell me," Ambrose said with a shrug.

"They?"

Ambrose pointed out another suited figure with hair dyed a dark mahogany red about twenty yards away and held up a hand. The woman caught sight of this gesture and approached.

The closer she got, the more Darger realized how tiny she was. Not an inch over five feet, if she had to guess.

"This is Agent Ana Zaragoza from the state crime lab," Ambrose said. "She's really the one running the show."

Zaragoza reached up to adjust a pair of teal cat eye glasses and nodded at Darger.

"Detective Ambrose was telling me you can sort and log the trash to narrow down where the bodies might have originally been dumped?"

"That's right. According to the manager of the facility, they're able to identify the original source down to a single city block in some cases." Zaragoza tapped and swiped at the screen of an iPad as she spoke.

"And that's something they do often?" Darger asked.

13

"Track where their garbage comes from?"

"It's a post-9/11 thing. All municipal waste facilities in the country are required to monitor the incoming loads for the presence of radiation. And when they do detect it, they have to be able to figure out where it came from. So they already have a system in place. I'm just… improving upon it."

Ambrose propped his fists on his hips.

"She's a machine. When I got here after the first body was discovered, I wanted to get down on my knees and weep."

Agent Zaragoza finally glanced up from the screen long enough to roll her eyes.

"I told you already, Clark. Kissing my ass isn't going to get the job done any faster."

"I'm not kissing anything. Just telling it like it is."

"Anyway," Zaragoza said, "If you'll excuse me, I've gotta get back to it."

After the small woman had stalked back over to the bustling techs sorting through the refuse, Detective Ambrose swiveled to face Darger.

"Zaragoza doesn't mean to be rude. She's one of those people with such a laser-like focus that she sometimes forgets the niceties."

"No offense taken," Darger said. "I'll take competence over politeness any day."

Loshak snorted.

"You can say that again."

"Shut it," Darger said, glaring at him.

"Case in point."

The sound of an old rotary phone jangled from somewhere, and Ambrose pulled a phone from his pocket and glanced at the screen.

"This asshole again," Ambrose muttered, scowling. "Captain thought it would appease the mayor to give him my direct number for updates, but now he thinks he's got permission to call me every half hour. Every time I tell him we're still working on it, he gets a little more frantic."

Detective Ambrose stepped away to take the call, leaving Darger and Loshak to stand near the corner of one of the three rectangular areas marked off by red string.

"I'm assuming each marked section represents where they found one of the three bodies?" Darger asked.

"That's right," Loshak said.

"But the assumption right now is that the bodies were dumped together in the same dumpster."

"Right again. I guess the garbage gets spread around quite a bit after dumping. They bring in the bulldozers to situate everything to their liking. So that's how waste from one dumpster can end up spread out over a larger area. At least that's how it was explained to me."

Two screeching seagulls swooped overhead, one chasing the other. Darger squinted at the shapes wheeling around in the air above them.

"I wonder what this looks like to them. All of us down here bustling around in our coveralls."

Loshak craned his neck to look at the two birds.

"Oh I doubt we're much more than small specks of white in a vast sea of trash to them," Loshak said. "Tiny and insignificant."

CHAPTER 3

After several minutes of watching the crew work as an idle bystander, Darger grew impatient. She was beginning to sweat beneath the suit and mask.

"I feel kinda guilty just standing here," she said. "Should we offer to help? This seems like an all-hands-on-deck kind of scenario."

"I offered several times, but Agent Zaragoza was adamant that her people do the sorting, and Detective Ambrose concurred." Loshak shrugged. "Their crime scene, their decision."

"Yeah," Darger muttered, though she wasn't sure what the fuss was all about. This crime scene was already cross-contaminated to hell and back. She didn't see how having a few extra hands aiding in the sorting could possibly make things worse. But the local jurisdictions were always a bit sensitive about the feds horning in on their cases, so she and Loshak generally did what they could to avoid conflict.

Darger watched the crime lab techs sift through the trash and marveled at the full array of colors represented there. A red Dixie cup. An empty jug of Tide detergent in orange. Yellow and green on a crushed two-liter of Squirt. A blue laundry basket. A rainbow of plastic that would never biodegrade.

"Seeing all this stuff kinda makes me tempted to become one of those zero-waste nuts," Darger said. "You know, the people who start using rags instead of toilet paper and refuse to buy anything packaged in plastic?"

Loshak scoffed.

"Rags? Ass rags? Have these people not heard of a bidet?"

Darger chewed her bottom lip.

"I had an apartment with a bidet once, but I was too afraid to use it."

"Afraid? What's so scary about a little bit of water?"

"I turned it on once to see how it worked, and it shot out a jet of water that went all the way up to the ceiling. Seemed like too much power for my comfort."

Loshak wheezed out a laugh.

"Jan and I got into an argument once. She was real particular about recycling everything. Every bottle. Every can. The thing is, you can't just empty a tub of yogurt and toss it in the bin. You have to wash it out. Get rid of all the food residue. A real pain in the ass, right? I went along with it for a while, but at some point, I wondered how many hours of my life I'd already spent washing the garbage and how many more I was willing to give. Was every other family in town washing their garbage so diligently? Not likely. I guess it was around that time I started having my doubts about the recycling industry as a whole. Whole thing doesn't add up."

Darger squinted.

"So what I'm hearing is that you're a terrible person who hates the environment and the children."

"That's pretty much what Jan said when she caught me chucking an empty peanut butter jar. She went off. Told me I obviously didn't give a shit about the environment and was no better than a common litterbug."

"She told you," Darger said, smirking.

"I want to be clear about something: I *do* give a shit about

17

the environment. I give a pretty big shit, as a matter of fact. But it wasn't only about the time wasted washing trash. I'd thought about the logistics of a residential recycling program and realized there was no way they were really recycling everything they picked up. There was too much of it, and they didn't even make us sort it. So you know that for every Jan out there washing each lid and jar, there's two or three jagoffs tossing in empty cans of baked beans without rinsing at all, right?"

"Probably," Darger agreed.

"We were living in Fredericksburg at the time. That's a town of about ten thousand households. And every two weeks the city is picking up sixty to a hundred gallons of unsorted recycling from each one. I should mention that the recycling pickup was built into the contract the city negotiated with the waste company. You could opt-out and arrange your own service from an alternate company, but it was more expensive. I doubt anyone did that." Loshak paused for a moment, adjusting his face mask. "So I did some math. I know not everyone is as diligent as Jan, so let's say only half of those households are actually recycling anything. That's still 300,000 gallons of recycling to sort through every two weeks. And I'm supposed to believe that the waste management company is hiring people to stand around and pick through our nasty garbage just so they can be good little tree-huggers? Not happening."

"You know there's a chance you've thought about this way too much?" Darger asked.

Loshak held up a finger.

"I'm just saying, I knew it wasn't feasible. Not in any way, shape, or form. Even if we were all Jans, they'd still have to go through the process of sorting the various plastics, removing labels, and on and on. So I'd been thinking for a while that this had to be a big scam to make us all feel like we're doing our part to save the environment and all that. Anyway, Jan and I got in a big fight over it. She's yelling about me destroying the planet, and I'm hollering about how I'd love to save the planet, but washing out a peanut butter jar wasn't doing shit in that arena."

"I bet that went over well."

Loshak raised his eyebrows and sighed.

"I should probably mention that this was when Shelly first got sick, so I think the fight was more about venting some of the pent up pressure surrounding all of that. Because when your kid is sick, you gotta put on a brave face. You have to smile when you tell everyone how positive things are looking with treatment, even when inside, you're scared shitless. Anyway, I was so mad after our argument that I halfway considered following one of the trucks after a pickup to see where they went. I could just imagine tailing them back to the landfill and watching them dump the garbage and the recycling right in the same pile."

"Did you?"

"No," Loshak said, shrugging. "I told you, the fight was more about Shelly than anything else. But the point I'm getting to is that a story came out a month or two back about how the whole idea of recycling plastic was a marketing ploy. A lot of what we turn into the recycling places ends up buried at the landfill. See, they knew the public felt kinda guilty about buying all this plastic crap that we just end up throwing out. Because we all know the math. It takes something like a thousand years for a plastic bag to break down. Four hundred years for that Mountain Dew bottle over there. Even the least granola among us don't like that idea. Seems wrong. Wasteful. Stupid. So they sold us this pretty fairytale about how we could recycle the plastic and reuse it over and over. But it's bullshit. They've known since the seventies that recycling plastic would never be viable. For starters, every time they melt it down to reuse, it degrades, so they can only do that once or twice before it's toast. So all in all, less than ten percent of plastic gets recycled. The whole idea of recycling plastic is a PR sham concocted by the petroleum industry."

"Less than ten percent?" Darger asked, gritting her teeth. "Jesus. That's pitiful."

"No kidding." Loshak frowned. "There's probably a special place in hell for the petroleum industry executives. Right next to the people that don't pick up dog shit in public places."

Darger looked out over the expanse of trash and wondered how many tons of plastic were here in this one landfill alone. She felt her blood pressure rise at the idea that people could get away with lying on such a massive scale. It was infuriating. Eventually, though, her mind returned to Loshak's original story.

She glanced over at him.

"So have you told her yet?"

"Told who what?" Loshak asked.

"Told Jan that you were right about recycling being a load of crap."

"No," Loshak said, crossing his arms.

"Good." Darger nodded once. "Don't."

Loshak smiled.

"Not my first rodeo, kid."

CHAPTER 4

Darger scanned the area for Detective Ambrose and found that he'd moved some distance away, standing a little farther down the slop, his feet and ankles submerged in what looked like reams of soggy paper. His phone still pressed tightly to the ear with the rumple of the hazmat suit's hood bunched behind it, and Darger figured he'd been trying to get as far from the sound of the bulldozer as he could.

"Well, I was going to wait for Detective Ambrose to get back before we started talking shop, but you know I can only be patient for so long," she said. "What the hell is going on here? You ever seen anything like it?"

"Can't say that I have," Loshak said.

"Any theories?"

"Nothing solid. And even though we can't say with absolute certainty that we're dealing with homicides, I think we're all thinking it's gonna tip that way eventually. People wouldn't dispose of bodies, multiple bodies, like this unless there was something to hide."

"Right. So, let's assume for now that this is, in fact, a homicide case."

"OK." Loshak pursed his lips. "Well, the fact that we've got a mix of male and female victims kind of skews things away from a serial killer. It doesn't rule it out of course. There are examples."

"Richard Ramirez, Dennis Rader, the Zodiac," Darger said. "But they were always primarily fixated on and motivated by the female victims. The male victims were generally someone who stood in their way."

"Exactly," Loshak agreed. "Multiple victims could also point to a mass killing of some kind. But I don't know if I can think of an example of a mass murderer that killed his victims and then disposed of the bodies. They tend to kill them in an outburst and leave them where they fall, so to speak. More akin to smash and grab robberies. In and out. The higher the body count the better."

"There's also the publicity factor," Darger added.

"Yep. Most mass murderers have an interest in creating a spectacle. You could say the same for the guys you mentioned before. Ramirez, Rader, and Zodiac. They, too, wanted their crimes to be public. They wanted people scared. That was part of the draw for them. But whoever did this was obviously trying to cover it up."

They were silent for a moment.

"I tried the gang angle," he said. "The drug cartels sometimes dump bodies like this, in groups. But we're right outside Philadelphia. Not exactly a hot cartel area."

"And why would a cartel choose a dumpster when there are a thousand remote wooded areas they could have hidden the bodies?" Darger asked.

Loshak scratched under the edge of his mask.

"There's definitely a disorganized feel to all of it. On the one hand, this guy wanted to get rid of the bodies, but then it seems like he didn't do a whole lot of thinking as to the best way to do it. I mean, it seems like dumping them was almost an afterthought."

"Or panic."

"Yeah. Could be that."

"Then there's the condition of the bodies," Darger said. "I know we're still waiting on the full report from the medical examiner, but they sure looked like people who'd been starved to me."

"Me too."

"My first thought when I saw the photographs of the bodies was that case out in California where the parents had tied up and starved their thirteen kids."

"Oh right, I remember that." Loshak removed his hard hat and ran his fingers through his hair a few times before replacing it. "I assumed they must have had a compound out in the boonies or something when I heard the story. And then I saw the pictures. It was a big house in the middle of an upper-middle-class subdivision. Neighbors all around. I couldn't believe the parents had gotten away with the abuse for so long. I mean, some of the kids were adults, right?"

"Several of them were over eighteen, yeah. But they were so malnourished that all the neighbors thought they were much younger. The oldest was twenty-nine and weighed eighty-two pounds. The one who escaped and called 911 was seventeen, but when the police first arrived, they thought she was twelve."

Loshak's mouth was a grim line.

"Almost unimaginable. But I'm glad you brought that case up. It might actually give us some insight into what we're dealing with here. Because honestly, I've been stumped up until now."

"The problem with trying to draw comparisons between that case and this one, of course, is that those were kids being abused by their parents," Darger said. "Even though some of them were adults, there was probably a sort of natural Stockholm syndrome inherent in the situation. The parents could use their power to perpetuate the abuse and get away with it for years. I'm struggling to imagine how you might achieve the same with adults. Maybe you could do it with one, but with several? At the same time?"

Loshak got a sudden gleam in his eye.

"What about some sort of religious cult?" he said. "There's a lot of that going around these days. Cults. The starvation could be a ritualistic activity, a fast, either done willingly as an act of penance or forcibly as punishment."

"Maybe…" Darger trailed off, nodding.

"It could explain the attempt to cover up the deaths. No cult would want it known that three of their members had met rather sudden demises." Loshak heaved a sigh. "But we're getting ahead of ourselves. Let's see what the autopsies tell us, and then we'll piece that together with where the bodies came from, once Zaragoza's team has answers."

Detective Ambrose stalked over, finally finished with his phone call.

"God damn politicians. I got three unidentified bodies and a mountain of trash to sift through, and the mayor wants to bitch to me about optics. What the fuck are optics anyway?"

Ambrose crossed his arms and surveyed the techs bustling back and forth inside the marked grids.

"I'll tell you what, when I was a young detective, I envied the older guys. The ones with seniority got all the respect. All the good cases. The headline cases." He scoffed and shook his head. "Well, now I'm the detective with the most seniority, and you know what? I could happily go the rest of my career only getting the vanilla assignments. None of this weird shit. Trudging around in garbage. Emaciated bodies showing up in landfills three at a time. It's a shit show, and I'm perched ankle-deep in it."

No one spoke for several seconds. They watched the techs dig and sort and log, working hard but barely making a dent in the mountain of trash.

"Anyway, I guess what I'm trying to say is that I appreciate the FBI lending a hand. I figure with everything you've seen, weird shit must be kind of your specialty."

"Yeah... weird is par for the course. But this... this is weird even for us," Loshak said.

"I have to tell you, that is not a comforting thought."

There was a sudden commotion from the far end of the search area. An urgent shout that sounded female.

Everyone froze, all the white-suited figures going rigid at the same time. Except for one. A willowy woman toward the back quadrant of the furthest search grid was waving one arm and yelling something at Agent Zaragoza, but her mask muffled the words too much for Darger to make them out.

Loshak and Detective Ambrose exchanged a meaningful glance.

"Sheeeeit," Ambrose said.

"What is it?" Darger asked. "What did she say?"

Loshak inhaled. It was several seconds before he answered.

"They found another body."

CHAPTER 5

Darger and Loshak followed Detective Ambrose toward the commotion, slogging up the slope. Darger's foot sank into a sludgy section that gripped her up to the mid-calf, her boot coming out slick with what she could only think of as "garbage juice."

As they got close to the tech crew, Agent Zaragoza put her hands up and addressed the gathering crowd of law enforcement. Pretty much everyone working the scene had stopped working and were now huddled along the edge of one of the search grids, trying to get a look at the new discovery.

"I need everyone but Detective Ambrose and myself to stay back so we can keep the integrity of the scene intact."

There was some shuffling and muttering, and then a path opened up for Ambrose, the swells of bunny suits parting. Darger stood on her tiptoes as the people around her shifted, trying to get a glimpse of the body. She was curious whether the newest victim was male or female, but there were too many people for Darger to see anything but more trash.

Agent Zaragoza began issuing orders to her people.

"Mike, can I use your camera to document?" Agent Zaragoza asked a thin man whose head bobbed once. "Thank you. Heather, I need you to mark off this new area, starting from the southwest corner of the previous grid and extending to just past where I'm standing right now. Where's Luis? Come over by me so you can record video with an unobstructed view, please."

Ambrose glanced around until he found Darger and Loshak in the cluster of white suits and waved them closer.

"I'd like the Feds to see this."

Zaragoza only nodded and continued snapping photos of the body.

Loshak shouldered his way through the crowd and Darger followed closely behind him until they'd reached an edge marked by red string. Finally, she could see what all the upheaval was about.

A man's body sprawled there, lying face down, his black-clad figure still partially buried by trash bags, water bottles, and what looked like crumpled balls of newspaper. The garbage covered up the sides of the body and most of the limbs, the head wedged down in the trash, leaving only his back exposed — the image reminded Darger of something she might see at the beach, kids partially burying each other in the sand before running out into the water to wash the grit away.

While they watched, Agent Zaragoza instructed her people as to which pieces of garbage to remove. They worked piece by piece, excavating in meticulous fashion, with Zaragoza snapping photographs at each interval until he was mostly uncovered.

Plastic sheeting swathed his legs, and Darger wondered if he might have been wrapped in it at the time he was dumped. None of the other bodies had been covered or wrapped in anything. She supposed this one could be different, but she doubted it. Everything about these body dumps suggested a lack of planning. Rushed and disorganized.

The techs continued working, revealing a little more at a time. Now Darger could see that the dead man's face was pressed against the side of a crumpled KFC bucket, the folded up red and white cardboard concealing his features.

Like the others, the man was horrifically thin. His clothes — a pair of black pants and a black shirt — looked far too big on the stick-like frame of the body. Spiky bits of skeleton poked against the fabric. Again Darger tried to make sense of the emaciated condition of the bodies and came up with no simple, logical explanation.

"Dressed in all black again," Loshak said from beside her, his voice low and gravelly. "Just like the other male victim."

Darger nodded. She'd been thinking the same thing.

"But not identical," she said. "I think the other guy was in a black t-shirt. This guy's shirt has a collar. Maybe a polo style. And the pants look like they might be black work pants versus black jeans. Still, could be some kind of uniform."

Agent Zaragoza was at the far side of the new grid, crouching down low to get a photograph of the body at a new angle.

"I'm ready for him to be flipped if that's OK with you, Detective Ambrose," she said, straightening to her full height of approximately five feet.

"Ready when you are," Ambrose said.

Zaragoza gave a signal to the two techs who'd been clearing each piece of trash under her guidance. They stooped, each one taking hold, one gripping a shoulder and one clutching at the thigh and hip.

Darger didn't envy them. This body looked more decayed than the others. The skin was splotchy and flecked. Dark gray patches shone here and there where the outer layer of dermis was missing. Even standing a few yards away made her skin crawl.

Flies buzzed around the remains, spiraling, spiraling, a miniature rendition of the seagulls circling the landfill. Their fizzy sounds seemed frantic, excited, a bunch of tiny zippers being pulled endlessly.

On the count of three, the two men heaved the body onto its back. As the face rolled into view, maggots spilled from a hole in the cheek. Darger could sense the crowd around her recoil at the sight, the mob wincing and rolling a step back as one.

It wasn't just the maggots. The face cast an appalling picture even without the insects.

Skin mottled and torn. Lips pulling back from the mouth, exposing all the teeth in a grimace. Nose mashed and sunken in. The whole face looked shrunken and gray and wrong.

There were gasps from the onlookers, and Darger heard someone behind her gag.

"You know it's a bad one when the pros start blowing grits," Loshak muttered.

Darger stared at the body, thinking that it wasn't only the maggots and decay that turned the stomach. It was the obscenity of finding human remains here, in this heap of refuse.

There was a reason death had so many rituals and traditions attached, Darger thought. Embalming. Funeral rites. Eulogies.

Death demanded reverence, demanded awe. Each passing person was a singularity, a unique individual ceasing to exist. Their body was to be honored. Washed. Preserved. Buried or cremated with great care. The various death ceremonies dated back thousands of years, to the roots of human history.

To throw someone out, to literally dump them like trash, was worse than cruel. It was inhuman.

CHAPTER 6

Back in the canvas tent outside the crime scene, a numbness came over Darger as she stripped off her gear in reverse: first the gloves, then the hardhat, the boots, and finally the coveralls. Loshak did the same next to her, neither of them talking. Maybe that cold, blank feeling had gotten a hold of him, too.

After, they stood a moment in the parking lot. A white van from the M.E.'s office was parked with its rear doors open to the curb so the two assistants could more easily load the body bag into the back. In it went, and then the doors folded shut to close the body off from them, the rear of the cargo van feeling very much like an internment chamber in a mausoleum.

Darger and Loshak split up then, each heading to their respective vehicles. Ambrose had spoken to the Medical Examiner, a Dr. Fausch, who would be fast-tracking the next autopsy, and Darger wanted to be there to observe that. She and Loshak had agreed to meet up at the morgue, in the university district, where the examination would take place.

Alone in her car, Darger couldn't help but picture the body again in her mind's eye. So skinny that the elbows and knees seemed to bulge. Limbs looking stretched out and distorted. And then she saw the maggots spilling from the John Doe's face.

An icy shiver ran up her spine, the inside of the car suddenly feeling cool and dank, almost cavernous. It felt striking and strange after all that time out in the open atop the trash heap — the sea gulls swooping and shrieking, the

32

bulldozer engines grating in some off-key harmony. The chill gripped her arms and didn't let go.

It suddenly struck her as very odd that her job was to make sense of these crimes. They would work this case. Gather and examine the evidence, search out the meaning behind these deaths.

But what explanation could possibly make sense of it all?

At a red light several miles from the dump, Darger realized she was still breathing through her mouth. She inhaled through her nose and instantly detected the odor of garbage. The question now was whether *she* smelled like a dumpster or whether the interior of the car had some residual stink from being parked a few hundred yards from Mount Garbage. She hoped it was the latter. This case was going to be taxing enough without having to trot around for the rest of the day reeking of rotten kitchen scraps.

These thoughts were interrupted by the ringtone of her phone. It was the opening riff of a Black Sabbath song, which told her immediately the caller was Casey Luck.

"What's up, Iron Man?" she asked. She'd given him the nickname after he'd had ten screws inserted into his ankle after an arson case they'd worked together the previous year.

"Oh, just having a crappy day and wanted to commiserate with someone who understands the special hell that is desk duty."

"But filing requisition forms and processing background checks is so fulfilling," Darger said with a flat affect.

Luck scoffed.

"At this point, that might be all that's left for me. I don't know if they're ever going to let me get back to field work."

"That's bullshit," Darger said. "If I can claw my way back in, then you have no excuse with your measly injuries."

In reality, his injuries had been anything but measly — aside from the broken ankle, he'd suffered a concussion, smoke inhalation, and severe burns — but Darger had figured out by now that offering Luck sympathy was the opposite of effective. He seemed to interpret attempts to comfort him as pity and responded much better when she took a slightly antagonistic angle.

"It's not the injuries. It's the way everyone looks at me. Like I'm something fragile and pathetic." Luck sighed. "Every time I bring up requalifying for fieldwork, Slevin gets this patronizing smile on her face, and her eyes go straight to my cane."

Darger switched the phone to her other ear so she could adjust the rearview mirror. There'd been a lot of pep talks like this over the last few months. Luck's recovery had been slow and not always steady. She didn't mind, though. They shared a certain bond now that they'd faced a brush with death together.

"Well, who gives a shit what Slevin thinks or how she looks at you?" Darger said.

"She's my supervisor, Violet."

"So what? You think I asked anyone for their permission or their blessing before I came back?"

Luck snorted.

"No."

"It's not Slevin's decision anyway. You don't need her approval to retake the fieldwork exams, so fuck her. After my head injury, the more people looked at me like I was some pitiful charity case, the more I wanted to prove them wrong. Rub their stupid faces in it. You gotta do this the Violet Darger way: Take all the anger and frustration flowing through you and use it as motivation."

"You sound like a sith lord from *Star Wars*," Luck said.

"Good. Jedis are pussies."

Luck laughed.

"Anyway, what you have to do now is focus on what you can do, not what you *can't* do. How's rehab going?"

"It's going. Irma thinks I'm making great progress. She has me doing this exercise where I have to write out the alphabet with my foot."

"Like, with a pen?" Darger asked, imagining Luck clutching a ballpoint Bic between his toes.

"No, just in the air," he said, chuckling. "And it sounds easy, but it hurts like hell. I had tears in my eyes yesterday."

"That means it's working," Darger said. "If your physical therapist isn't making you cry, they aren't doing a good job."

"I'm going to tell Irma you said that. The woman is a sadist. She'll love it." Darger heard the telltale creak of a cheap FBI office chair over the line. "Oh, I almost forgot to thank you for the care package. Jill already tore into the giant bag of gummy bears. Not sure if there are any left."

"Tell her I said hi."

"I will."

In front of her, the right-hand turn signal of Loshak's rental car blinked on and off. They pulled into the parking lot for the Joseph W. Spelman Medical Examiner's Building, a large brick structure across the street from the sprawling VA Medical Center.

Darger pulled into the empty parking space next to the one Loshak had taken.

"So as much as I'd love to keep talking, I have a date at the Philadelphia morgue with a decaying corpse. We just pulled him out of the town dump," Darger said, putting the car in park and pocketing the keys.

"Well, it would be rude to keep him waiting," Luck said. "My break's about over anyway. But thanks for the kick in the pants, Violet."

"Anytime," Darger said as she opened her door and climbed out of the car.

Loshak raised his eyebrows, a wordless inquiry as to who'd been on the other end of the phone call.

"Luck," Darger said, tucking the phone into her bag.

"How's he doing?"

"Oh, he wanted to whine about desk duty and physical therapy."

"Still struggling, eh?"

"Yeah, well, I told him to quit wallowing and do the work so he can get back in the field."

Loshak wheezed out a laugh.

"You must have made such a great counselor when you worked in Victim Services, what with your gentle ways and wealth of empathy."

"Hey, sometimes you need someone to hold your hand, and sometimes you need to get slapped upside the head and told to quit feeling sorry for yourself. Self-pity never did anyone any good."

They'd reached the public entrance of the building, and Loshak paused in front of the door.

"You ready?" he asked.

"No, but we might as well get it over with."

"That's the spirit," Loshak said, holding the door open and gesturing for her to go in first.

CHAPTER 7

Darger and Loshak followed the signs down to the basement of the medical examiner's building, which was artificially bright despite the lack of windows. The floors gleamed, so clean they squeaked under the soles of Darger's boots, and the smell of cleaning solvents was strong here, a bright chemical stench that tingled and almost stung in her nostrils.

They checked in with an assistant at a desk, who told them Dr. Fausch would be with them shortly.

Darger crossed and uncrossed her arms, then tugged at the sleeves of her jacket.

"What's wrong with you?" Loshak asked. "I've never seen you get so jumpy over an autopsy before. You getting squeamish on me?"

"I have no problem with fresh bodies. It's the ripe ones I don't care for. Especially not when maggots spill out like candy from a piñata. Besides…" Darger paused to sniff the shoulder of her jacket. Nothing.

She leaned over and tried to get a whiff of Loshak.

He recoiled as if she were a child with peanut butter hands trying to give him a high five.

"Now what are you doing?" he hissed.

"All that time at the dump threw off my nose. I can't smell anything."

Loshak ducked his head and snuffled at his shirt.

"Huh. Me neither."

"Makes me paranoid that I stink. You know the only thing

worse than *knowing* you stink is thinking you *probably* stink but not being sure."

A door down the hall swung open, and a small man with cropped white hair and round glasses took a few steps into the corridor. He swiveled his head in their direction and cocked his head to one side.

"You're the FBI agents Detective Ambrose sent over, if I'm not mistaken," he said, moving toward them.

"Agents Loshak and Darger," Loshak said, putting out his hand.

"I'm Dr. Fausch." His voice was soft and slightly raspy, and when it was Darger's turn to shake his hand, she found his grip gentle. He reminded her more of someone's grandpa than a guy who sliced into corpses all day.

"Why don't we step into the cold storage room, and I can bring you up to speed," he said. "After that, you're more than welcome to stay to observe the postmortem for your second John Doe."

"As long as we're not in your way," Loshak said.

"Not at all."

He motioned for them to follow him down the hall to a door requiring a key card to enter. Dr. Fausch pressed the ID badge around his neck to a black box mounted on the wall. The door lock beeped and an LED changed from red to green.

As soon as Dr. Fausch pushed through the door, a row of fluorescent lights mounted on the ceiling flickered to life. The room was empty save for a cluster of five gurneys pushed to one side. Both side walls and the entire back wall were made of stainless steel and covered with doors. That cleaning smell was different here, the pickle odor of preservative chemicals joining the fray.

The morgue.

Loshak opened his eyes wide in mock excitement and mouthed, "Yippy!" over to Darger. She had to bite the inside of her cheek to keep from giggling.

"I'll introduce you to your John Doe One and Jane Doe Number One and Two," Dr. Fausch said. "We'll keep them in the negative chambers, probably for the next several weeks in hopes of identifying them and notifying next of kin."

"And if you can't identify them?" Darger asked. "Or no one claims them?"

"They get cremated, and then they go into a cabinet we have for unclaimed remains. We hold onto those for as long as we can, but eventually we run out of room and have to bury them en masse. I don't like doing it, but we only have so much space to store unclaimed remains. And it happens more and more often, it seems — no one to claim the deceased."

Fausch unhooked a clipboard from the wall and ran his finger down to an entry halfway down the page. Then he stepped to one of the stainless steel doors, opened it, and slid the metal drawer out.

The body came out feet-first and was swaddled in a white plastic sheet. Dr. Fausch peeled back the sheet near the face, revealing a gaunt-faced man with a shaggy unkempt beard.

"John Doe Number One. Caucasian. Approximately 25 to 35 years of age. Seventy-one inches in height. One-hundred and seventeen pounds in weight. Brown hair. Green eyes."

He stepped over to the next storage chamber and opened that one as well.

"Jane Doe Number One. Caucasian. Approximately 25 to

35 years of age. Sixty-six inches in height. One-hundred and one pounds in weight. Blond hair. Brown eyes."

Fausch opened a third drawer and introduced the second female victim.

"Jane Doe Number Two. Caucasian or light-skinned Hispanic. Approximately 18 to 25 years of age. Sixty-two inches in height. Eighty-nine pounds in weight. Black hair. Brown eyes."

Darger stared at the three bodies laid out in a perfect row. It was always strange to hear victims identified in such a way that lacked any personality. A list of physical features and demographics, but nothing about who they'd been, what they'd wanted to do in life.

"Can you determine how they came to be so emaciated? And whether or not that was the cause of death?" Darger asked.

"The most likely cause would be starvation, but there are other possibilities," the doctor said. "We saw a fair amount of AIDS Wasting Syndrome back in the 80s, but we tested the three bodies for HIV. All came back negative. There are other wasting diseases, but it would be highly unlikely that four victims would all have it. Another possibility would be some kind of parasite, but again, I found no evidence of that."

Dr. Fausch replaced the clipboard into its slot on the wall.

"All three had empty stomachs and clean bowels, which certainly lends itself to the theory of starvation, or possibly dehydration. But I should tell you, even in a best-case scenario, it's extremely difficult to determine either one as a cause of death with an examination alone. The state of the decedent's body gives us clues, of course. In the case of starvation, we can see the wasting. And with dehydration, we can look at the vitreous fluid analysis to get a clue. But until we know the specific preceding circumstances to the deaths of these three individuals, it's almost impossible to say with certainty."

He glanced over at the nearest body, which happened to be Jane Doe Two.

"She was the first one they brought in. And my immediate thought was a case I had a few years ago. A young girl who'd struggled with an eating disorder for many years. She'd actually been in recovery for some time until she found an internet group of what they call 'pro-ana' activists."

"Pro-ana…" Darger repeated. "Pro-anorexia?"

"That's right. The most extreme among them insist that anorexia is a 'lifestyle choice' and that attempts by family members and medical professionals to intervene is a form of discrimination. They share tips on hiding their weight loss from family and friends, have contests to see who can lose the most weight…"

"Christ," Loshak said.

"There was a criminal investigation. The district attorney wanted to make the case that the group was at fault for the girl's death."

"Kind of reminds me of the Conrad Roy case," Darger said. "He committed suicide, and then they charged his girlfriend with involuntary manslaughter after they found text messages where she'd encouraged him to go forward with it."

"Very similar. Anyway… that's the only recent autopsy I've performed with a similar level of emaciation."

Darger turned to Loshak.

"We never thought about the eating disorders."

"Doesn't explain how they all wound up in a dumpster

together, though," Loshak said.

Dr. Fausch clasped his hands together.

"When I think of these poor souls being so unceremoniously dumped into a local landfill, I can't help but think of photographs from the Nazi concentration camps. My grandmother was just a girl when she was sent to Ravensbrück. She was one of nine children, and she and one sister were the only two who survived. Their parents and seven of their siblings died in the camps. I'd heard it spoken of here and there as a boy. The bad thing that happened to Bubbe. But it wasn't until I was in high school and a teacher showed us *Night and Fog*." The doctor closed his eyes. "I will never forget those images. But they were only that — images. In black and white, no less. When I arrived at the landfill yesterday and saw what they'd pulled from the heaps of garbage, I saw it in the flesh. The absolute disdain for human life."

His eyes fluttered open now, and he gazed at each of them in turn.

"I try not to get too emotionally invested in any one case. A certain detachment is necessary to do this job efficiently, in my opinion. But I do hope you find the person responsible for this."

Darger swallowed.

"We'll do our best," she said, then nodded over at the three bodies still on display. "Any wounds?"

"All three had extensive contusions and bruising. John Doe One had a fractured tibia. Jane Doe One had several broken fingers and a fractured wrist. Jane Doe Two had a few broken ribs. The issue is determining whether those are ante-mortem or post-mortem injuries, given the manner of disposal. If the running theory is correct, the bodies were first deposited into a dumpster, and I doubt the type of person disposing of human remains in such a way is being particularly gentle."

Darger nodded.

"After that, the dumpster itself is emptied into one of the trucks from a height of approximately 18 feet from the topmost position of the dumpster to the bed of the truck, meaning the bodies might have fallen from almost two stories. Then they get carted around town for who knows how long, having more refuse added to the pile. I've seen people throw entire sofas into those big rolling dumpsters, so now imagine something like that landing on one of the bodies. And we haven't even gotten to the landfill yet. Detective Ambrose informed me that they use bulldozers to move the trash around?"

"That's right," Loshak said.

"So you can see how all of these factors contribute to my inability to state whether there were any injuries to the bodies prior to death." Fausch held up a finger. "Save for one."

He directed their attention to Jane Doe Two. He nudged the plastic sheeting aside, revealing an exceptionally thin arm that looked more like it belonged to a child than an adult woman. The doctor lifted the arm and pointed to a ring of bruise-colored flesh around the woman's wrist.

"Is that a ligature mark?" Darger asked, bending closer.

"I believe so. At least, I can't think of anything that might have happened in the course of the body making its way from the dumpster to the landfill site that would have left such a perfect band around the wrist like that."

"But you didn't find any marks on the others?"

Dr. Fausch shook his head.

"No, but Jane Doe Two has something else special about her," he said, parting a section of her hair. "She has a scar here. It's more visible along the scalp, but it runs all the way down to her cheek. I could also see some very old facial fractures. Some sort of traumatic injury. A car accident would be my guess. This reconstruction work was done by a very skilled surgeon."

"Sounds expensive," Loshak said.

"Exactly. Someone got this girl the very best cosmetic reconstruction money can buy. My guess would be in the tens of thousands."

"Which means someone gave a shit about her," Darger said.

Dr. Fausch seemed to blush at the cursing but nodded.

"So now the question is, why isn't the person or persons who paid for the expensive plastic surgery raising holy hell about where their daughter or girlfriend or wife disappeared to?" Loshak said.

"I can't answer that." Dr. Fausch blinked. "But I hope it will help in our efforts to identify her."

"And the others?" Darger asked.

"We work with an excellent forensics team. Dr. Reed, our forensic anthropologist, and Dr. Bertram, our forensic odontologist are experts in their respective fields. Between the two of them, not to mention the various jurisdictions who can use the demographics we've supplied to compare against current missing persons reports, I'm optimistic that we'll identify all of the decedents. It might take some time, but I have high hopes." Dr. Fausch straightened and folded his arms. "There is one final detail to discuss before we head over to the autopsy suite, and that is that when we swabbed both Jane Does, we found spermicidal residue."

"Evidence of sexual assault," Darger said.

"Technically I can only say that there's evidence they came in contact with a condom or other contraceptive containing nonoxynol-9. But it certainly *suggests* sexual intercourse. I know that in your position, you always have to question whether the intercourse was consensual or not when dealing with potential homicide victims. But again, without knowing the circumstances preceding death, I can only say whether or not the evidence before me supports or contradicts a theory."

Dr. Fausch rolled the bodies back into the refrigerated compartments and closed each door with a snick.

"Now, I believe your John Doe Number Two should be ready for us in the autopsy suite."

CHAPTER 8

Back in the corridor, they followed the doctor through the swinging door he'd originally emerged from. An assistant was already in the small antechamber beyond, washing his hands at one of the large stainless steel sinks set against the wall. Dr. Fausch introduced him as Tyrone Vaas. There was a round of head nodding in lieu of handshakes.

While Dr. Fausch scrubbed in, Tyrone directed them to the boxes of gowns, hair caps, booties, and of course, gloves. For the second time that day, Darger found herself swaddled in layers of PPE.

After gearing up, Tyrone took them into the autopsy suite. Darger squinted under the glare of the bright overhead lights.

"That's one thing they always get wrong on TV," Darger said.

"What's that?" Loshak asked.

"When they show morgues and autopsy suites in TV shows, it's always dark and moody. A single spotlight on the body. But this place is lit up like a Christmas tree."

Fausch came in then, adjusting a pair of goggles over his glasses. Tyrone wheeled a gurney laden with John Doe Two's body bag closer to one of the exam tables. On the count of three, the two men transferred the bag from the gurney to the table.

"Not very heavy, is he?" Dr. Fausch asked, then glanced over at the agents. "I got the impression this one is emaciated like the others?"

"Pretty much," Darger said.

Tyrone unzipped the body bag, and a few maggots spilled out and fell onto the table. Darger couldn't help but watch the reaction of Dr. Fausch and his assistant. She didn't care how many times they'd done this, surely maggots still held a certain ick factor. But Dr. Fausch merely bobbed his head toward the wriggling larvae.

"Would you collect a few of our stowaways in one of the entomology vials? They probably already took samples at the scene, but you know I never like to leave these things to chance."

The doctor's voice was calm and completely unruffled as far as Darger could tell. Even as Tyrone scooped some of the maggots into the glass tube, Darger failed to detect even the slightest sign of disgust.

"I see we're going to need to spray this one down before we begin, just like the other three. Let's get a few swabs first."

Tyrone plucked half a dozen sticks that looked like over-sized Q-tips from his cart and passed them to the doctor who swiped at a few different areas on the body: cheek, nose, arms, hands, and legs. He passed the swabs back to Tyrone, who labeled and logged the samples before stowing them back in the cart.

"Can you tell if there's anything unique about the dirt on the bodies?" Darger asked.

"Other than the sheer amount of it? No," Fausch said, peeling back the black plastic of the body bag and peering inside at the remains of John Doe Two. "I'm afraid that's not my specialty, but I expedited the samples from the first three bodies to the state lab for analysis this morning. Sometimes the particular makeup ends up being something they can use to pinpoint a location or source."

Dr. Fausch directed Tyrone to take a few photographs of the body while it was still in the bag before they carefully lifted the body from the bag and laid it out on the table. It looked even smaller than before, all by itself on the gleaming metal surface.

"I've been wondering if maybe the bodies were underground for some time before being dumped," Loshak said. "Like maybe someone buried them and then changed their mind, got spooked or something. So they dug them up and dumped them."

"I'd considered that myself," Dr. Fausch said, "but if they'd been buried, I'd expect to find dirt in the orifices — eyes, mouth, nose. In each case, the deposits are entirely superficial."

He waved them closer to the table.

"Have a look," he said, parting John Doe Two's eyelid with a gloved thumb and forefinger. Darger caught a glimpse of the cornea gone milky white. "In fact, you can even see how the areas around the eyes, nose, and mouth are all a bit cleaner than everywhere else. As if he'd been wiping it off."

Next, Dr. Fausch lifted one of the victim's hands.

"Here you can see there's quite a bit of dirt under the fingernails, which we'll also want samples of." Dr. Fausch took a small metal pick offered to him by Tyrone and scraped some of the grime from under the dead man's thumbnail. "If I had to guess, I'd say they'd been digging."

"Digging?" Loshak repeated. "Digging what?"

"Hard to say. Gardening, perhaps?" Dr. Fausch dropped the under-nail sample into a fresh vial and passed it to his assistant.

"My wife is a master gardener, as it happens. Makes up her own soil mix for her plants, which means hauling a lot of bags of compost, manure, vermiculite, and peat. I've helped her with it a few times, and it makes quite a mess. We dump all the ingredients in the middle of a tarp and then toss it around with shovels and mixing forks to get it evenly blended. By the end, we're both covered in a fine layer of black grit. So… maybe they work in a nursery or a soil mixing facility? The companies like Miracle-Gro and such must be doing what my wife does on a large scale."

Eventually Fausch shrugged.

"But that's speculation on my part. I imagine Marcia Blatch will have more to tell you once she analyzes the samples."

John Doe Two had several more portraits taken before Dr. Fausch asked Tyrone to cut off the garments. As Tyrone sliced up the front of the dead man's shirt, Dr. Fausch leaned in for a closer look.

"Hmm," he said. "That's interesting."

"What?"

"Quite a lot of tattooing on this one. Could be the key to identifying this fellow." Dr. Fausch pointed at markings on the skin of the chest. "We'll get him cleaned up a bit, and then we can get a better look at the ink."

Darger couldn't help but smile at the small grandfatherly man using the term "ink."

When Tyrone had finished removing the clothing, he bagged it as evidence while Dr. Fausch took a few more photos. Then he set the camera aside and used a tool like a kitchen sprayer to hose down the body. The colors of the tattoo became more visible as he worked. It was much more vibrant than

Darger had first realized: bright turquoise, neon yellow, deep purple, and pitch black. Beneath the colored shapes, each one of the man's ribs was clearly visible, the pitted skin dipping and puckering between the bones. Darger shuddered.

She and Loshak approached the table for a better look. The most obvious shapes were yellow lightning bolts, but there was also a triangular purple shape and something round and turquoise.

"What am I looking at?" Darger asked.

"You can't see it?" Loshak asked. "Come over here."

She moved from her position next to John Doe Two's head to a spot closer to his knees. She'd been looking at it upside down and now the tattoo made sense to her eyes. It was a skull-faced wizard in a pointed hat, with flowing hair and beard. He grasped a crystal ball in one skeletal hand.

Darger pulled out her phone and started going through the Pennsylvania Department of Corrections database, which listed known identifying marks of anyone with a criminal history. She typed in various combinations of "wizard," "crystal ball," "magician," "lightning bolts," "skeleton," and "skull" with no luck.

Loshak peered over her shoulder.

"Try 'sorcerer,'" he suggested.

Darger nodded and tried it. A moment later, she shook her head.

"Nothing."

Dr. Fausch directed their attention to the screen of the iPad he'd been using to take photos during the exam. He cycled through a few of the pictures he'd taken of the man's chest.

"If you'd like, I can email these to you right now."

"That'd be great," she said. "We should send these over to Detective Ambrose so he can start circulating them among the jurisdictions in the area."

"Let's see if we can get some people to start canvassing the tattoo shops county-wide, too," Loshak said. "See if anyone recognizes the work. If we can figure out who did the ink, they should be able to give us a name."

Darger looked at the body of John Doe Two laid out on the table.

"And if we can identify one victim, that might lead us to the identities of the others."

CHAPTER 9

After the completion of the autopsy, Darger and Loshak were due for a meeting at the headquarters for the 5th District of Philadelphia PD. They drove through the Roxborough Manayunk area, a part of Philadelphia that looked older and more small-town-ish than the rest of the city. A Jiffy Lube and an Auto Zone were nestled among the modest homes and apartment complexes along their way.

They parked across the street from the building, a pale brick affair that looked like an old middle school from the outside. Inside, an officer led the agents down a narrow hallway to a small conference room with four tables arranged in a square-shaped ring.

Detective Ambrose and Agent Zaragoza stood at one side of the square, ready for the meeting to get underway. Ambrose introduced the other two men in the room — Mayor Gelardi and Captain Dalton, his boss.

Darger craned her neck toward the door, looking for a stream of various uniforms and detectives to come flowing into the conference room, but no such crowd was forthcoming. She was used to bigger meetings with dozens of people from different jurisdictions. But given the fact that all four bodies had been found on the 5th District's turf, she supposed it made sense that it was a smaller group this time around.

They'd had just enough time to stop for Loshak's usual donut offering on the way, but he was turned down by everyone except for the mayor, who chose a French cruller and didn't seem to notice that he was the only one eating, glazed flecks trailing down to dapple his necktie. Darger figured everyone else had been to the dump site and probably didn't have much of an appetite, especially not if they were convinced the stink was still clinging to them the way she was. She had to resist the urge to sniff her jacket again. In front of Loshak was fine, but not here.

"I think we're waiting on Marcia, then," Captain Dalton said. "She's on her way, but she's stuck in traffic. All that damn construction they're doing around the airport. Anyhow, I think we ought to get started without her. She can present her findings on the soil sample analysis when she arrives."

Dalton nodded at Detective Ambrose who cleared his throat.

"OK, well... I guess I'll start by giving a brief update on where we stand at the present moment," he said, smoothing his tie. "We've got some high-res photos of John Doe Two's tattoos, which we're hoping we can use to ID him. I sent Kimmel, Richards, McGill, and Prost to canvas tattoo shops in the city. On top of that, I have our interdepartmental liaison officer getting these photos to the other Philly districts as well as the departments in the greater metro area."

"And how close are we to being able to figure out where the bodies came from?" Dalton asked.

"The waste facility manager thinks we'll be able to narrow it down to a specific location by the end of the day."

Captain Dalton scribbled something down in a notepad.

"Excellent. And what else did we get from the medical examiner?"

Detective Ambrose swept his hand in the direction of

Darger and Loshak.

"I'll toss this one over to our friends from the FBI, since they talked to Dr. Fausch in person and observed the exam on our second John Doe."

Loshak gave a nod to Darger, the indication that she should give the summary.

"Well, I'll give the bad news first, which is that Dr. Fausch wasn't able to pinpoint a cause of death on any of the four bodies. He can't even say for certain that the emaciation was caused by starvation, but he was willing to hedge that it was the most likely cause."

"What about all the wounds?" Mayor Gelardi asked, wiping cruller crumbs from his fingers with a paper napkin. "From the sound of it, the bodies were in rough shape, right? Sounded to me like someone did a number on these folks."

"John Doe Two had a contusion on the back of his head, and the other three had broken bones. But given the manner of disposal, Dr. Fausch can't determine whether the injuries happened before or after death. Most of them, anyway."

"There's an exception?" Captain Dalton asked.

"Jane Doe Two had ligature marks on one wrist," Darger explained. "And since there's not much reason to restrain someone after death, we can reasonably assume she was tied up beforehand."

Darger waited to see if there were any more questions. When no one spoke up, she continued.

"There was also spermicidal residue found on both Jane Does." Darger glanced down at the notes she'd jotted during their talk with Dr. Fausch. "Coupled with the fact that the female bodies were in various states of undress, there's a high likelihood they were sexually assaulted."

"But we can't say for sure," Ambrose said with a sigh. "Like pretty much everything else we've found so far."

Darger turned to Loshak.

"Why don't you give them the good news?"

Loshak leaned against the side of one of the tables.

"Right. Jane Doe Two had some old injuries that required cosmetic surgery," he said, gesturing at his own face. "Dr. Fausch thinks that will help our chances of getting an ID on her."

"Ahh, that *is* good news," Captain Dalton said, rubbing his hands together.

The mayor raised his hand.

"Hold up. Are we really throwing a parade over some plastic surgery and a tattoo? I mean, I expected to come into this meeting and finally get some answers about who these people are and what the hell happened to them. Where are the facts? The hard evidence?" He stabbed a finger into the table. "*Four* bodies appearing in the local dump? People expect an explanation."

"As I explained earlier, Tom, an investigation like this is a process," Captain Dalton said. "We're doing everything we can."

"Oh, I've seen the kind of overtime man-hours your district logs. The question is, with all the running around, with all the people I saw swarming the dump site in their little white suits in the morning news footage, how are we still at zero? Because I wouldn't allow that kind of inefficiency in my office. It's unacceptable."

Detective Ambrose straightened.

"I'll tell you what's unacceptable: some little pissant pencil pusher coming in here and telling us how to do our job. You want to talk about man-hours? About inefficiency? Let's have a conversation about you calling me up every hour demanding an update. But then I guess you don't have anything better to do." Detective Ambrose narrowed his eyes down to slits. "And when you start lobbing accusations, I *know* you're not talking about Agent Zaragoza or her crew, because her people have been knee-deep in filth for going on thirty-six hours."

"I wasn't saying—" Mayor Gelardi started to say, but Ambrose cut him off.

"Do you have any idea what kind of forensic nightmare it is to process a garbage dump? We'd be in the weeds even if we had IDs on the bodies. Because they just keep coming. I keep waiting to get a call that two more corpses rolled out of the trash of their own volition."

The mayor shifted from foot to foot. All the bluster seemed to have gone out of him.

Captain Dalton's voice rang out like a middle school gym teacher trying to referee a heated game of dodgeball.

"That's enough!" When he had the attention of both Ambrose and the mayor, Captain Dalton went on. "Why don't we all take a step back, OK? Tensions are running high. That's understandable. But this isn't productive."

The mayor wore a sour expression on his face, like a kid bitter at being put in the timeout chair. And Darger could see Ambrose's jaw muscles grinding so hard she worried he might break a tooth.

She wasn't sure the dispute between the two men was entirely put to rest, but she was glad that for once, she wasn't the one getting in a spat with the higher-ups.

CHAPTER 10

A somewhat awkward silence followed Captain Dalton's plea for peace, the conference room taking on a hush that made it seem bigger and emptier. It was Loshak who stepped in to fill the void.

"I'd like to point out that nothing about this case is normal. We're all playing it by ear." Loshak thrust one hand into his pocket. "I know it seems like we've got next to nothing to go on right now, but identifying the victims is exactly the kind of thing that will get this investigation rolling. If we have a positive identification, we can talk to family, friends, coworkers. Find out who the person was, where they hung out, who they knew."

Darger backed him up, nodding.

"There's also a good chance that IDing even one of the bodies will cause a domino effect that leads to uncovering the identities of the others," she said.

Loshak went on.

"I hate to use the word 'traditional' in this context, because one thing I've learned in my career is that there's no such thing, but in a more 'traditional' serial killer case, it might take months or even years before anyone even realizes that a handful of separate cases are related. So in that sense, you could say we've got a massive head start."

Mayor Gelardi's eyes stretched wide.

"Excuse me. Did you say *serial killer*?" He turned and stared at Captain Dalton. "Did he say serial killer?"

"We don't know that yet," Loshak said. "I was only using it as a frame of reference, to better put things in perspective. We're talking about being able to identify a group of victims in a matter of days, and that—"

The mayor sputtered and held up his hands.

"And now we're calling them victims? Didn't you just get through telling us that the medical examiner can't confirm the cause of death as homicide?"

Loshak sighed.

"Mayor Gelardi, I was only trying to explain that we have plenty to be optimistic about."

"If that's your idea of optimism—"

Whatever the mayor said next was swallowed up by the commotion of a round-faced woman with curly hair bustling into the room with her arms full of papers, file folders, a laptop case, and a gallon-sized water bottle.

"Ah, Marcia," Captain Dalton said, noticeably relieved for the interruption. "Welcome."

"Oh, I hope you're not waiting on me!" she said, dumping all of her things on top of one of the tables. A collection of pens scattered over the surface, one of them dropping to the floor. "So sorry. I got lost. I'm a bit directionally challenged."

"Ladies and gentlemen, this is Marcia Blatch from the state lab. She's going to present her findings on the soil samples from the first three bodies."

"I need a minute to get set up." Marcia held up the cord of her laptop. "Is there somewhere I can plug this in?"

While Marcia fiddled with connecting her laptop to the projector, Darger replayed the look on the mayor's face when Loshak had said the word "serial killer." She let out a snort that was thankfully only loud enough for Loshak to hear.

"What's so funny?"

"Nothing."

He glared at her.

Marcia brought up a series of charts and graphs on the projector screen.

"I have the exact chemical analysis here if we've got any mineral geeks in the room, but I've found you law enforcement types generally want more of a practical summation of findings, so here goes."

She brought up a photograph of three samples, side by side. Two of them looked the same. They were pale and almost chalky looking. The third was darker and brick-colored.

"Samples one and two are from the two Jane Does, respectively. The third is from John Doe One. You'll no doubt notice the increased chroma of the sample from John Doe. That's a result of a high mineral content, iron oxide mostly. In the geology biz, we call that illuviation."

"How does that happen?" Detective Ambrose asked.

"It's a natural occurrence that happens as water percolates from the surface through the various soil layers, bringing organic and inorganic matter from the upper layers to the lower layers."

Marcia pointed at the paler samples.

"The two samples on the left are highly eluviated," she said, stressing the 'e' sound at the beginning of the word, "which means the soil has been leached of a significant portion of its organic and mineral content. That's why they're paler in color."

"So they're essentially opposites?" Ambrose asked. "Eluviated and illuviated?"

"Mmm… not opposites. More like two conditions that influence one another."

"Is it significant to find the two different types together?" Darger asked. "Or at least on three samples we expected would have the same soil conditions?"

"That's hard to say without knowing how these people came to be covered in the soil in the first place. All I can say now is that this soil," she pointed at the darker sample, "came from a different horizon from the other two. And it was likely at a greater depth."

Darger turned to Loshak, and they frowned at one another.

"Any ideas?" she whispered.

"Well, we talked about the possibility of gardening or maybe working somewhere that mixes soil with Dr. Fausch."

"But if they were mixing soil, wouldn't we expect the samples to be nearly identical?" Darger asked.

"Yes," Loshak agreed. "So then maybe we're back to gardening. I don't know."

Marcia had continued with her presentation and the image on the projector was now some sort of topographical map with different patterns and labels that Darger couldn't make heads or tails of.

"The soil is a mellow brown silty loam with a very smooth texture, almost buttery. The parent material is made up of gneiss and schist, so I can say with a fair amount of certainty that the soil came from this area here, in the central part of Chester county." She pointed at one of the patterned areas on the map. "It's a rather larger area that extends in a general northeast-southwest direction and is known for having this particular type of silky subsoil, which can extend down a number of feet."

Mayor Gelardi perked up at that.

"Chester county… so you're saying the bodies didn't come from within the city," he said, looking positively delighted.

"Well, that's not necessarily true." Marcia quirked her nose. "I'm saying the soil very likely came from outside the city."

"But… I mean, isn't that the same thing?"

"No. The source of the soil can't move," Marcia said. "But people can."

Mayor Gelardi stared at her blankly.

"I think what Marcia is trying to say is that the soil doesn't necessarily tell us where they died," Detective Ambrose explained. "Our stiffs might have picked up the soil from Chester county when they were still alive and then come into the city where they… met their demise. Is that right?"

Marcia nodded.

"My analysis can only say for certain where the soil came from. How they came into contact with it and when they came into contact with it… that's beyond my capabilities."

"Sounds like splitting hairs to me," the mayor said.

A phone began to ring, and Agent Zaragoza immediately pulled it from her pocket and headed for the door.

"I'm so sorry," Zaragoza said. "Please excuse me."

Ambrose raised a hand and redirected their attention to the soil analysis.

"So the best we can say is that they were… digging or otherwise coming in contact with topsoil and subsoil from central Chester county?"

Marcia folded her hands together.

"Exactly."

Detective Ambrose turned to Darger and Loshak.

"What do you think? Does this give any insight from a profiling angle?"

"It might," Loshak said. "But I don't think we're going to get any true clarity until we start figuring out who these people are."

Darger had to agree. So far, they'd only managed to uncover ambiguous details that hinted at certain possibilities but gave them nothing certain. Just like traversing the landfill earlier in the day, Darger felt like the ground beneath the case wasn't completely solid.

Agent Zaragoza came flying into the room, looking more animated than Darger had seen her before. Cheeks flushed and eyes alight, she looked like a kid on Christmas morning.

"We've got it," she said, holding her phone in the air. "We've got it!"

"Got what?" Detective Ambrose asked.

"The dumpster."

CHAPTER 11

The mood in the conference room shifted immediately upon Agent Zaragoza's announcement. The almost dour tone had been shattered, excitement bursting in to replace it, and now Darger found herself bouncing one leg up and down in anticipation. She watched Detective Ambrose crack his knuckles and thought they were all experiencing a similar jolt of adrenaline.

Zaragoza took charge of the projector, bringing up a satellite map of the city. She zoomed in on a four-block section southwest of their current location.

"Keystone Disposal analyzed the waste we sorted through yesterday and this morning and determined it came from one of the eight dumpster pick-ups located in this area."

She marked each dumpster site with a marker.

"The dumpsters on this route get picked up on Thursday, so that would mean they were most recently loaded four days ago. The truck that picked them up made its run through this area from approximately 5:17 AM to 5:35 AM."

"So we'll want surveillance from the area starting at 5:35 AM and before," Captain Dalton said. "The question is whether we can narrow it down from there or if we need to look at the entire week preceding the pick-up."

"I'd get everything I could," Loshak said. "We don't know yet how organized this operation was. If there was some planning involved, I'd say the bodies were probably dumped within a few hours of pick-up. But then there's always a chance that whoever dumped the bodies was just driving around town looking for an ideal place to get rid of them. In that case, it could have been done at any point between the previous pick-up and the most recent."

Detective Ambrose clicked his tongue.

"That's going to be a hell of a lot of surveillance footage to sift through."

"Start with ten PM on the night before pick-up," Loshak said. "If you don't get anything from that time period, expand backward from there, sticking with night time hours. It's unlikely someone would be ballsy enough to dump three bodies in broad daylight, but sometimes I'm surprised at the risks people take. If we still come up empty after checking all the night footage, we'll start looking at daylight hours."

"Who do you want on this, Ambrose?" Captain Dalton asked. "I told you before, you have your pick in terms of who's on your team."

"Caine and McGill are on call. Let's get them in here, as well as Park."

Loshak nudged Darger with his elbow.

"I bet if we drive around and take a look at these dumpsters in person, we can narrow it down further. What do you think?"

Darger nodded.

"Should we tell the others?" she asked.

Loshak's neck swiveled as he scanned the bustling task force around them. Then he tilted his hand in the air.

"Let's see what we can find out. If we get something useful, we'll share."

Darger and Loshak gathered up their things and headed outside. When they reached the parking lot, Loshak pulled his phone out.

"I'll navigate, you drive?"

"You're volunteering to use your phone?"

Loshak brought up the marked map on his screen.

"Jan's been teaching me how to use all the little apps and things."

"Apps," Darger said. "Wow. You know the lingo and everything."

Loshak made a dramatic show of swiping up on his screen, his finger arcing upward in an exaggerated flourish.

"Not to brag, but I'm kind of a pro at this now."

CHAPTER 12

They rolled through the streets of Philadelphia, passing by rows of houses and a series of factories that had been converted into offices and luxury apartments. The outskirts of the older cities on the east coast always seemed oddly quaint to Darger, like you could still see the ghosts of the smaller towns they'd once been as soon as you got out away from the skyscrapers. As they drove under an old stone bridge, she spotted a black and red food truck advertising the "Best Effin' Cheesesteaks in Philly!"

"You know, I don't think I've ever had a real Philly cheesesteak," she said.

Loshak glanced up from his phone.

"How is that possible?"

"Well, I've had cheesesteaks. But it was like… a Chicago cheesesteak or an LA cheesesteak. Not an authentic Philly cheesesteak from, you know, Philly."

Loshak squinted.

"I'm not sure there's anything fundamentally different, honestly." He ticked off the makings of a cheesesteak on one hand. "You got your beef. Onions. Whiz, if that's your thing."

"Come on. I may not have ever had a cheesesteak from Philadelphia proper, but even I know it's not a cheesesteak if you don't get Cheez Whiz on it."

"I'm just saying. Some people prefer real cheese."

"Buncha snobs," Darger said. "It's not like they're trying to pull one over on you. It's spelled out right on the jar. 'Cheez' with a 'z.' It knows it's not cheese. No illusions."

Loshak chuckled and gestured at the upcoming traffic light.

"We should be coming up on the first dumpster in a second," he said. "Right after this intersection."

Darger kept her eyes peeled as they proceeded down the street.

"There's one."

She nodded toward a royal blue dumpster next to a gas station. It was completely surrounded by chain link fence.

"Fenced and padlocked," Loshak said, waving his pen as they rolled by.

Loshak had scribbled a copy of their dumpster map onto a legal pad, and he scrawled a quick note beside the first marked dumpster.

"OK, the next one is about two blocks up and on the left."

"I see it," Darger said a moment later. "It's right off the street, and it's got two flood lights mounted over it."

Loshak jotted this down.

"Noted."

They continued this process until they'd gotten a look at all eight dumpsters, and then Darger pulled into the lot of a Dollar General so they could discuss what they'd learned.

"So we've got two that are locked," Loshak said. "I figure we can cross those out right off the bat."

He drew a line through the two locked dumpsters on his hand-drawn map.

"And the three that had signs saying they're monitored by cameras," Darger said. "Even if the signs are fake, I don't think anyone would risk it."

"Agreed. Scratch those for sure."

Loshak crossed those off the map as well.

"What does that leave us?"

Using his pen as a pointer, Loshak tapped the locations of the remaining three dumpsters.

"Let's see... we've got the one next to Starbucks, the row of dumpsters along the backside of that Little Caesar's, and... the last one is over at that alternative high school."

"Oh right. The one with the big mural of Ed Franklin on the side?"

Loshak blinked and stared over at her.

"You mean *Benjamin* Franklin?"

"What did I say?"

"Ed," Loshak repeated. "You said Ed Franklin. Are you having a stroke or something?"

Darger felt her cheeks flush.

"No, it's just that I used to get Thomas Edison and Benjamin Franklin confused as a kid," she said, chuckling.

If anything, Loshak looked more worried than before. His eyelids trembled.

"What does that have to do with calling him Ed Franklin?"

"*Ed*-ison."

Creases formed across Loshak's forehead.

"I don't know if it's just because we haven't worked a case together in a while, but I don't remember you being this weird before."

Darger rolled her eyes.

"Are we going to go take a second look at these dumpsters or what?" she asked.

"Let's go." He waved his hand in the air. "You're driving."

Darger steered them back onto the street, catching a glimpse of the setting sun in the rearview mirror. Bands of pink and orange streaked the sky, reminding her of the rainbow sherbet she used to get when she was a kid. Was it already that late?

The nearest potential dump site was actually a series of three dumpsters arranged behind a Little Caesar's storefront that backed up to a parking area for a group of townhouses. Darger circled the townhouse lot and then idled near the dumpsters.

"Doesn't look like the lighting is great back here," Loshak said. "Even with the street lights from the parking lot, those trees would probably keep the dumpster on the far end in the shadows."

Darger tried to imagine what it would be like back here in the dead of night. Pictured herself creeping into the parking lot after midnight and snugging up beside the dumpsters. Climbing out and then glancing both ways to check for witnesses. The light from the sodium bulbs would stain everything yellowish. A tainted glow.

She felt the trunk latch thunking faintly as she released it, the struts almost sighing as the hatch swung open. Inside, a tarp or maybe some plastic sheeting would partially conceal the tangle of human bodies. The horribly sinewy limbs. Far too thin. Knees and elbows swollen and jutting. With one last look around, she pushed open the lid of the dumpster and began the grisly work. Hugging the nude body of one of the Jane Does to her chest as she hoisted her over the lip and tumbled the corpse into the gaping maw of the open dumpster.

With a jerk, Darger came back to the present moment, shaking off the chill of the imagined scene. And again she wondered: How? How could someone do such a thing?

She turned her head and gazed out her window, studying the townhouses overlooking the area. They were clean and modern-looking, with steel cable guard railings stretched across each balcony. Next she surveyed the cars in the lot — Subaru Outback, Mazda Miata, Audi A3. All newer models. So it was an upper-middle-class place, if the cars were anything to judge by. A woman watering plants on her second-floor balcony stopped what she was doing and stared down at the idling car, no doubt wondering why someone was loitering in her parking lot.

"Hey. Check this out," Darger said, directing Loshak's attention to the woman watching them from her balcony.

Loshak peered up.

"Ah. Looks like we've got a nosy neighbor."

"You think that's enough to cross this one off the list?"

"Maybe so. In my experience, those snooping types are always watching and listening. Just itching to call the cops on a suspicious-looking character."

They headed over to the Starbucks dumpster next. It was enclosed in plank wooden fencing with a gate at the front, but there was no lock.

"What do you think about the fencing?" Darger asked.

"Could give some cover, but it's also a barrier to deal with."

"Maybe they had a truck. If you stood in the back and tossed them in, you might not even have to open the gate part," Darger said, then studied the traffic. "Pretty busy street, though. Maybe it's quieter at night."

"I don't know," Loshak said. "That's a Walgreen's next door. Sign says they're open 24 hours. Even if things were slow, there'd be no assurance you were going to find a long enough chunk of time to dump three bodies without someone either driving by on the street or bopping into the pharmacy next door."

Darger nodded.

"And there's nothing aside from the fence and the dumpster itself to give you any cover. No trees. No bushes."

"I say we go look at the dumpster at the school. If we can't say definitively it's the one, then we can pull surveillance for these three. But maybe we'll get lucky."

The final dumpster was snugged up against the back wall of Hicks Alternative High School. Water dribbled from a broken downspout nearby, and the moisture had stained the dark bricks green with some kind of slimy moss or algae.

Darger parked next to the dumpster and climbed out. There was a Burger King across the street, which reminded her of a crime scene in Athens, Ohio, where a man they'd called the Doll Parts Killer had once disposed of a body.

"I'm guessing this lot is full during the day, but it's getting toward dusk?" Loshak said, glancing around. "Aside from us, there are only three other cars in the lot. I bet it's a full-blown ghost town late at night."

"And those shrubs growing along that fence shield this part of the building from the street."

As they spoke, the streetlights illuminating the lot blinked on. All of them, except for one. The lamp nearest the dumpster stayed dark. Coupled with the thick tangle of Siberian elm, buckthorn, and honeysuckle that would block most of the light from passing traffic, this small area at the back of the building would be quite dark in the middle of the night.

They both stared up at the dead bulb for a few seconds

before exchanging a glance. No words had to be spoken. They'd made a decision.

"I'll call Ambrose," Loshak said, getting out his phone. "I'll tell him to pull the surveillance and traffic camera footage from all three unsecured dumpster sites, but we should focus on this one first and foremost."

CHAPTER 13

On the way back to the 5th District headquarters, Darger and Loshak stopped off at a local pizza place and ordered enough pies to keep the team that would be going through the surveillance footage fed for at least the first part of the evening. Darger carried the pizza boxes while Loshak manhandled four 2-liters of soda.

When Detective Ambrose saw them come in with the food, he let out a groan.

"Hallelujah," he said. "I haven't eaten since breakfast."

Darger handed him a pizza box.

"Help yourself."

"Don't mind if I do," he said, flipping the lid open and removing a slice. He took a bite and sighed. "I tell you what, standing around that dump really puts a damper on the ol' appetite. This is the first time I've felt hungry since this morning. Maybe that could be the next fad diet. You have to go sift through the trash at the local landfill for a few hours. You never eat again, and the fat just melts away."

At the mention of the word "diet," an image of the skeletal bodies laid out in the morgue flashed in Darger's mind, and again she found herself wondering what was going on with this case.

Her eyes went to one of the detectives scrolling through traffic cam footage, and she hoped tonight they might finally get some answers.

"We've got four different cameras from around the school.

There are two in the parking lot of the school itself, one at the traffic light down the block, and one outside the Burger King across the street," Ambrose explained in between bites of pizza.

"May I?" Darger asked, gesturing at the empty computer chair Detective Ambrose had vacated when they'd come in with the pizza.

"Be my guest." Ambrose took a sip of Pepsi from a coffee mug that said WOKE UP SEXY AS HELL AGAIN. "This is footage from the night before the last dumpster pickup. Figured we'd start there and work backward, like you said."

Darger pressed play on the video file that was already loaded up. It was grainy black and white feed looking down on the Burger King drive-thru window. In the top left corner of the screen, a sliver of the school parking lot was visible, along with one corner of the dumpster.

After watching a few seconds of the footage at normal speed, she sped it up until the cars were zipping through the drive-thru line at a much more rapid pace. She stared at the upper left-hand side of the screen as the seemingly never-ending line of cars slithered past, afraid that if she even blinked she might miss something.

She wasn't sure how much time had passed when Loshak tapped her on the shoulder.

"You're getting kinda squinty over here. Why don't you let me have a turn?"

Darger paused the video and squeezed her eyelids shut.

"My eyes could definitely use a break," she said.

She traded places with Loshak, stretching her shoulders and her neck to try to loosen them up a bit.

A few minutes later, there was a knock at the door, and

Officer Primanti came in with a large box of coffee. He handed the box and a paper sack to Detective Ambrose.

"There's cream and sugar in the bag," Primanti said. "Cups too, if you need them."

"Appreciate it, Primanti." Ambrose set the box down on an empty table at the front of the room. "Why don't we all take five? Have a cup of coffee, answer nature's call, etcetera, etcetera."

Everyone gathered near the table, each person waiting their turn to fill their cup with hot caffeinated liquid.

"You guys ever hear of a cannibal sandwich?" Loshak asked.

Ambrose wrinkled his nose.

"A what?"

"It's a thing in Wisconsin," Loshak explained. "A holiday tradition. You top a piece of rye bread with a mix of raw beef, salt, and pepper. Couple slices of onion on top."

"Well what's the deal with naming it a 'cannibal sandwich?' Kind of sick, if you ask me," Ambrose said. "Me, I prefer my cow no longer mooing when I eat it. Never understood the appeal of raw food. Cave men invented cooking for a reason."

"Sushi's alright," Darger said.

"Nope." Ambrose shook his head. "Raw fish? Forget it. You know, I dated a gal who only ate raw food. I mean, she was vegan too, so she basically only ate sprouts and carrots as far as I could tell. One time she made me try her kale juice. Tasted like something you'd scrape off the side of a boat."

Darger laughed and refilled her coffee. Loshak was already back in the chair scrolling through the Burger King footage again, and she wandered over and watched from over his shoulder.

She was about to suggest that she start going through the video from the previous night on a different computer when something interesting happened on the screen.

"Did you see that?" Darger asked.

"Yeah. Looked like it headed over to the school parking lot, didn't it?"

Loshak stopped the video and backed it up. They watched it again, this time at normal speed.

"I've seen a lot of cars come through the Burger King lot and turn left or right, but this is the first one that clearly goes straight."

"Hey, Ambrose," Darger said. "You should check this out."

Loshak played the video for the detective. After watching it through twice, he put his hands on his hips.

"And the only thing across the street is the school parking lot?"

"Yep."

"How far is the dumpster from the street again?"

"Ten yards, at most." Loshak replayed the clip again, pausing the moment before the car left the Burger King lot. "Not a good angle in terms of getting a license plate, unfortunately."

Ambrose clapped his hands together and addressed the room.

"Alright, I want everybody to bring up the footage you've got from early Thursday morning around 2:45 am. We got a dark-colored sedan, newer model. Looks higher end. Maybe a Lexus or an Infiniti," Ambrose said. "He goes cruising through the Burger King lot, hops across the street, right over to the school dumpster, it looks like. But we can't see the license plate from our angle."

The other three detectives in the room got to work, and Darger followed Ambrose over to observe. They ran through the footage from the other three cameras, but none of them showed a dark sedan.

"He must have taken Rose Street when he left the school lot," Detective Ambrose said, consulting a map someone had scrawled on a whiteboard showing the positions of the various cameras in relation to the school. "If he skirted around the southwest corner of the lot after hitting the dumpster, he wouldn't be on any of the other cameras."

"The question is whether he was avoiding the cameras on purpose," Darger said.

"Shit," Ambrose said. "If he was avoiding the cameras, what are the odds this *isn't* our guy?"

He went back over to stand behind Loshak's computer and peered down at the screen.

"Times like this, I wish we were like the TV shows. You know, where all I have to say is, 'enhance!' a few times, and then out pops a perfect image of the license plate." Ambrose inhaled and let out a breath. "You think he could have three bodies in that sedan?"

"The three bodies we found, yeah. They didn't exactly take up much space, did they? Even if he couldn't get them all in the trunk, he could have had one or two in the backseat."

Ambrose clicked his tongue in disapproval.

"Can you imagine putting a corpse in a ride like that? I mean, I drive a 2012 Passat. Nothin' fancy. And I still wouldn't be putting any corpses in there. Not in the trunk and definitely not on the upholstery. You get some of that stanky decomp smell in the fibers? That ain't never coming out."

Ambrose's phone rang.

"Oh… it's Gilly. This could be good." He answered the call. "Ambrose."

Darger watched Loshak play the video of the dark sedan on a loop. Over and over. Frame by frame, hoping for a magical shift that made the license plate visible.

"Good work, Gill. Yes. Absolutely."

Ambrose ended the call. His eyes were gleaming with renewed energy.

"That was my esteemed colleague, Detective McGill. He thinks he found the tattoo artist who did the ink on John Doe Two."

"We have an ID?" Darger asked.

Ambrose grinned.

"The deceased's name was Stephen Mayhew. And there's more. I guess the tattoo artist was kinda friendly with our guy." He rubbed his hands together, beaming. "He's coming down here now to give a statement."

CHAPTER 14

Ambrose read off the rap sheet of Stephen Mayhew, or "the artist formerly known as John Doe Two," as the detective seemed to delight in calling him.

"DUI. Criminal mischief. Drug paraphernalia. Misdemeanor theft in the third degree, which means whatever he stole was valued at less than fifty dollars. Standard petty crimes of a what I like to call a D.A.K."

"What's that?"

"Dumb Ass Kid," Ambrose explained. "Of course, he wasn't a kid anymore, but... these are pretty mild, run-of-the-mill charges. Nothing violent. Nothing weird. No hard time. Couple fines, community service, drug and alcohol counseling. Doesn't mean he wasn't involved in something more serious. But this doesn't give us much to go off. He also doesn't seem to have any family in the area from what we can tell so far."

"What about this tattoo artist?" Loshak asked. "Any criminal history?"

"Negatory. He's as clean as Clorox. Good work as an artist, albeit as expensive as hell. Huge following on Instagram, too. Anyhow, see for yourself. I just got a text that he's waiting in interview room two."

Gage Medina was a short, fit man wearing a pair of ripped jeans and a tank top that showed off his tattoos. His head was shaved, and Darger assumed it was to make room for more ink, since the back of his neck and head were marked up as well.

Darger and Loshak crowded into the interview room with

Detective Ambrose, and they took turns introducing themselves to Medina.

"Well, Mr. Medina—"

"Call me, Gage, man. That 'mister' stuff sounds weird. Too formal. I feel like I'm back in school at St. Mary's about to get my ass handed to me by one of the nuns."

"Gage, then," Loshak said. "How long have you known Stephen Mayhew?"

"Oh, maybe five years or so."

Ambrose nodded.

"And how did you meet?"

"He was looking for someone to do a big chest piece. I think I was the second or third artist he'd talked to about it. And we hit it off right away. He was a cool dude. Very laid back. Non-judgmental type, you know? A free spirit."

Medina had long dark eyelashes, and he fluttered them open and closed a few times.

"And that's how I try to live, you know? I try to keep a pretty open mind about most things. Judge not lest ye be judged and all that. Plus, I figure, you never know what crazy shit you might experience if you just go with the flow. Like one time, I met this dude named Asher Moon at a gas station in Escondido. Turned out he was this, like, shaman dude. Very spiritual guy. Talking about how, like, everything is harmonics and shit."

Darger immediately pictured a white guy with dreads in some kind of white linen robe.

"He ended up inviting me out to Joshua tree where he was leading this ayahuasca vision quest. There were five of us, and we all took off our clothes and laid down on the rocks and communed with our spiritual ancestors. Changed my whole perspective on shit."

Medina's dark eyebrows knitted into a frown for a moment.

"And just to be clear, Asher's, like, half-Mexican, so it was like… totally legal for him to be in possession of ayahuasca. It's ceremonial or whatever."

"So you're what some might call a free thinker," Darger offered, and she thought she saw Loshak struggling not to smirk beside her. "Not hemmed in by traditional ways of thinking."

Medina snapped his fingers.

"Exactly! It's like, I ain't afraid to admit that I don't know everything, so why pretend like I do?"

"And Stephen Mayhew… is that where you found a common bond?" Darger asked. "He was another free-thinking type?"

"Well yeah. At first, anyway. He seemed very enlightened. We'd talk about the Nasca lines in Peru or the Voynich Manuscript. These ancient mysteries that no one has been able to solve, which is mind-boggling, you know? We have all this technology, all this artificial intelligence we can use to solve shit, but we're still stumped by these things created thousands of years ago. That's just wild to me, man. Anyway, one day Steve came by to pay off the most recent piece I did for him. I let some of my more regular customers pay in installments. So he was dropping off his last payment and mentioned that he was going out into the boonies for this celebration of the full moon with a group he was in with. Asked if I'd be interested in tagging along. I said hell yeah."

"What were they planning on doing?"

"Well, when he first mentioned it, I was imagining some kind of half-hippie, half-hillbilly kegger out in the woods." Medina scratched the side of his head. "I ended up driving us up there, because I guess Steve's girl bailed, and he didn't have his own ride. Anyway, he started telling me more about these people on the way up. Said they had built this community out near Hershey. Self-sufficient and all that. Solar power. Off the grid. Totally green. And I can get behind that, you know? I think the current lack of action toward the climate crisis is criminal. But that's beside the point I guess. What he was telling me sounded pretty cool. The guy that's sort of their leader is big on self-actualization. On stripping away the material trappings of our current society. Of getting back to what matters. Personal connection. Mind-body-spirit wellness. Plus Steve said the women in the group were pretty much all smokin' hot. Like, not just pretty faces. Killer bods, too."

Normally Darger would have been tempted to make a sarcastic remark at that, but something Medina had said earlier had caught her attention.

"You said this group has a leader?"

"Yeah. Dude named Curtis," Medina said. "Steve talked about the guy like he was some kind of messiah."

"Curtis?" Darger repeated. It wasn't exactly the type of name she'd expect from a messiah.

"And did the group have a name?" Loshak asked.

"Mm... something golden. Children of Gold? No... that's not it. Children of the..." Medina shook his finger in the air. "Golden Path!"

"Children of the Golden Path?"

"Yeah. Pretty sure that's it."

Darger glanced over at Loshak. He was obviously thinking what she was.

A self-built community with a messiah-like leader. Sounded like a cult. And they'd already discussed cult behavior once when they were speculating on possible causes for the emaciation. Darger felt giddy but knew she shouldn't get ahead of herself.

"Would you say the group was religious in nature?" Loshak asked.

"Religious… well, see, that has such strong negative connotations for me. My parents were very strict. I went to Catholic school and everything. So my idea of religion tends to be tainted by all that."

"OK, so you drove out to the country for some kind of celebration," Darger said. "What happened when you got there?"

"Well it was great, at first. They were very welcoming. Some of the women took us to this bath house and, like, literally bathed us."

"You and Steve?"

"Yeah. Which probably sounds weird, but it just, I don't know… It felt right. It was like I could literally feel all the bindings of the material world washing away. All the stuff you worry about on a day to day basis — job, mortgage, taxes — gone. A true cleansing. They get all the water right from a creek that runs through the property, and they make their own soap and essential oils. The whole place is like… of the earth. We had this incredible meal at this long table in the middle of a field full of flowers. That's how they bring in cash. I didn't know this until Steve told me, but apparently cut flowers are one of the most profitable crops you can grow. This place is a real working farm. We're talking freshly churned butter. Honey straight from the hives. It was… wholesome."

"At first," Darger said, repeating the words he'd said before. "And then something… unpleasant happened?"

Medina licked his lips and fidgeted. It was the first time in the entire interview that he'd seemed uncomfortable. He'd been leaning back in his chair, but now he sat up straighter in his seat.

"There was this drink at dinner. They called it moon juice. I thought it was just, like, boozy punch. Tasted good as hell. I had like three glasses. Later I found out it had been dosed with psilocybin."

"Magic mushrooms?"

"Yeah. And like, I've done shrooms tons of times. It's great if you're prepared. The right frame of mind, you know? I think it should always be consensual. Sneaking it into a beverage without a warning… that's not cool. You don't know who you're dealing with, you know?"

He rubbed the backs of his knuckles.

"So anyway, once it got dark, they built up this big bonfire and started dancing and chanting. Drums. And they all put on animal masks. Tiger and bear and wolf. All very primitive looking. Feathers and bark and strips of leather. I swear mine had real teeth. Tiger, you know."

His eyes stared into the middle distance, and his voice took on a faraway tone like he was reliving all of this as he told the tale.

"We walked over to this altar, and there was a girl. In this like, pristine white gown. Like something a Greek goddess would have worn. At first she was lying very still. Almost like she was asleep. And then she opened her eyes, and when she saw all of us standing around in masks, she recoiled. Tried to get away. But she was tied down. She started pleading with us to untie her, but we weren't supposed to talk. It was supposed to be very animalistic. Role-playing, you know? Feral and shit. So she could talk, but we could only grunt or growl or scream in response."

He swallowed hard, and his throat clicked.

"And she was pulling at the ropes. Eventually she freed herself and ran. And we all chased after her. Running through the woods. She was laughing then. Or at least, I thought I heard laughing. That part was kind of amazing. There was a full moon, and it felt very visceral. Like maybe what it would have been like to be a prehistoric man, you know? Nomads and whatever. Living off the land—"

"What happened with the girl," Darger asked, more interested in the ritual than what Medina's drugged-out mind had thought of it.

"Well, eventually the group caught up with her. I was toward the back, but when I got there, some of the masked people had surrounded her. And she was trembling. Actual tears in her eyes. And they closed in on her and started tearing at her clothes. They ripped the gown to shreds until she was completely naked. And there was blood, like they were scratching her with real claws or something."

His eyelids fluttered and then steadied.

"They tied her to this post. And she was screaming and crying, and that was when it got to be too much for me. I mean, Steve insisted later that this was all planned, that she was playing a role. It was something she'd signed up for. A ritual. But the fear looked real to me, man. That's not my scene. Like, it's just not. So I screamed for them to stop." Medina shrugged. "I told them I was done. I wanted out. And I guess any of the congregation speaking actual words interrupts the ceremony or whatever?"

Darger waited for him to continue. He reached up and scratched the side of his face, grimacing slightly.

"Things got kinda heated after that. They were pretty pissed that I'd 'broken the circle' or whatever." Medina made air quotes with his fingers. "I tried to tell Steve I only wanted to get my stuff and go. After the cleansing bath, they gave us these robes to wear and took our regular clothes, so I didn't have my keys on me. But… well, I wasn't even supposed to be at this ritual. Steve had sorta snuck me in, and I blew the whole thing. And so he got led away looking like he was going to face a firing squad. A couple of the others tried to corral me, take me somewhere so I could come down from the trip, so they said. But by then I wasn't going anywhere but home. Luckily I'd left my wallet in my truck, and I always keep a spare key, so I just ran to where I'd parked and got the fuck out of there."

He inhaled deeply and seemed to return to the present moment. He made eye contact with Darger and smiled about halfway.

"I mean, I'll admit that I had a bad trip, right? Like, I realized after I came down that it had to all be set up. When we chased her through the woods, the path was very clear. Like, no sticks or rocks to trip over. And then when we caught up to her, we ended up right next to another bonfire with a post and stuff to tie her up. It was like she ran from Point A to Point B.

A planned course. So yeah, I freaked out. But I wasn't prepared to witness something so intense in that state. Steve didn't warn me, you know?"

"Did you go back or see any of the people again after that?"

"Steve came by a few days later. He stopped in and brought me the stuff I'd left. My pants and keys and whatnot. He was pretty angry about me, uh, leaving like I did. Kept saying that he never would have brought me there if he'd known I couldn't handle myself. And that if I would have played it cool, it all would have been fine, which I still think is pretty unfair. But I guess he got chewed out by Curtis and was being punished."

"Punished how?"

"He didn't say. And I felt bad about it at the time. But it turns out I was right, huh?"

Darger shifted in her seat.

"Right about what?"

"About them being into weird shit. I mean… the ritual might have been a big show, but the detective showed me that pic of Steve's body. Pretty gnarly. He was all messed up." Medina sighed. "I don't know what they did to him, and I'm sorry it happened, but I'm, like, glad it ain't me."

Ambrose pulled photos of the other victims out of a manila folder and laid them out. Three bony faces stared up from the tabletop, angled at Medina.

"I know Detective McGill already asked if you recognized any of these others, but I want you to take one more look. Could any of these people be from the Children of the Golden Path?"

Medina's eyes skittered over the faces, twitching forward and back.

"I don't know. That night is kind of a blur now. I mean, the ritual part stands out clear as day. And I remember Steve and Curtis. And the girl — the, like, sacrificial lamb. If these other people were there, I don't remember them. But it was a big group. And it was dark for most of it. And I was tripping megaballs on mushrooms."

Medina snapped his eyes away from the photos and tilted his upper body and face away from them. Uncomfortable, Darger thought, but that would be a normal enough response given the condition of the deceased.

Darger reached out and shoved the photos back inside the folder.

"What's the address of this place?"

"No address. Like I said. It's out in the middle of nowhere. Unmarked two-track off a road that leads to the State Game Lands. Probably the only slice of pseudo-civilization for miles."

"Do you think you could take us there?"

"Nope. Hell no. I can give you directions as best I can, and I happen to draw a pretty mean map." Medina shook his head, eyes wide. "But there is no way I'm ever going back there."

CHAPTER 15

Rain pelted the car, rivulets of wet streaking down the windshield. Cora stared through the beads of water smeared across the glass, fingers clutched around the seatbelt running a diagonal line over her chest. Watching. Waiting.

Her boyfriend, Chase, knocked on the door of the monumental house before him. He stood with his back to her, the porch light shining down on him, his face angled away from her. The shadows grew thicker as they trailed down from the back of his head, which she didn't like.

Stone columns framed the front door of the big house, like something from the cover of one of the *Country Living* magazines her mom always read in the lobby at the dentist's office. One of those stately, immaculate places that looked too fancy for anyone to actually live in. Maybe Joanna Gaines or someone like that might look at home here, but not a real person.

Chase looked wrong standing before this suburban palace, with his t-shirt sleeves cut off and cargo shorts going ratty and frayed at the bottom. The awful barbed-wire tattoo circling around his bicep rippled as he lifted his arm to ring the doorbell and then knock again. He turned his head, and she could see his chiseled jaw for a second, the fresh coating of dark stubble angling into the light. The image reassured her, if only a little.

Thunder rumbled in the distance, and Cora swallowed in a dry throat. They shouldn't be here. The whole neighborhood made her wince, cringe, some knot of discomfort constricting in her belly. She wasn't sure if the hulking home qualified as a mansion or not, but it had to cost something like twenty times the trailer her family rented. Maybe more. She lived a few tax brackets away from this neighborhood, and she mostly figured she always would.

Chase belonged in the trailer park, and so did she. Or at least that's what the world seemed to believe. Her dad had warned her about places like this, about the people who lived in them.

He'd worked thirty plus years at a shower head factory, all of it second shift, so he wasn't home much at any time she was awake. During those rare times when he was there, she remembered a sweaty can of Pabst Blue Ribbon in one hand and a smoldering cigarette in the other, a perpetually defeated look in the purple bags under his eyes. In her nineteen years on the planet, the only thing the old man had really impressed upon her boiled down to four simple words: don't trust rich people.

"Listen to me. Don't go trustin' no rich kids, OK? Don't do it." He jabbed two fingers at her for emphasis, smoke twirling off the cigarette perched between them. "The cake-eaters been taught their whole lives to look out for themselves, to be willing to throw anyone to the wolves if it means savin' their own skin. Loyalty is for suckers in their world. For losers. Like all of life is a damn business decision. A number crunch. They'll smile in your face, big shit-eating white tooth grins, but just you remember that they're never really your friend. Ever."

Her dad, too, readily accepted his lot in life. Worked his shifts at the factory without fail. Considered watching twelve hours of football every Sunday to be a form of enlightenment.

Chase was different, though. He had dreams. Hustling and grinding to lift himself out of the gutter. Making connections. Taking risks. He was looking to move up in that world. A friend had set up this meeting tonight. "A chance to make real money," Chase had called it. He'd sold drugs off and on since Cora had been with him, but only minor stuff. A little weed. A few boner pills here and there.

But this? This was crystal, and while he hadn't been explicit about it, she thought it was going to be a lot of the stuff. More than he'd ever handled before, for sure.

He had even started getting kind of uptight about it. He'd been so quiet on the drive over here, which was out of character for him. But he'd also talked about how this would be their ticket out of the slums, into the good life.

His words had painted pictures of new clothes, nice cars, a house in the suburbs where they could start a family. He'd wooed her with visions of a better life, a better world, right from when they'd first met. Sometimes he could be immature, yes. He was easily hurt and quick to wound her with insults when his pride was punctured. His sense of humor veered toward the juvenile as well, his fart and dick jokes raring up in times and places that embarrassed her.

And yet, being with him inspired her, felt like a true adventure. He made her believe, in brief fits and starts, that her life could be more, greater than the sum of its parts, better than the dreary way of living the world had presented her. He made her think that anything was possible, at least for brief snippets of time.

"All of life is a risk, ya know?" he said. "Like, it don't last forever, Cora. We gotta take some chances. Make some opportunities. Cut a few corners if that's what it takes. Get rich or try dying."

That made her laugh.

"Wait. You mean die trying, right?"

He smiled, that square chin emerging like it always did.

"Nope. Get rich or try dying. That's how I say it."

The front door of the mansion twitched and swung open, bringing Cora's attention back to the world beyond the windshield. At first, there was only light shining in the open doorway.

Then a figure in a cowboy hat jutted into the gap. Aviator sunglasses covered most of his face. Two mirrors that reflected the dark bulk of Chase's shape in them.

Cora's fingers pinched the edge of the seatbelt like crab claws, flexing and releasing over and over. That hollow drumming of the raindrops on the roof of the car persisted. Kept a steady backbeat to Cora's racing thoughts.

The figures on the stoop talked a moment. Then Chase and the cowboy-hatted man turned and looked toward her in the car, and something cold sloshed around in her gut. This wasn't good.

Chase jogged back to the car, a hand cupped over his brow to keep the rain out of his eyes. He popped open the driver's side door and leaned over the seat toward her.

"Come on, babe," he said, not quite looking at her. "He says the both of us should come inside."

"What?" For some reason, Cora didn't want to go in that house. "But why me?"

Chase's eyes danced all over the inside of the car, his gaze piercing empty space.

"He, uh, says he wants to see who he's dealing with. It'll only be a minute."

Cora didn't move. Her eyes slid over to the man in the cowboy hat. He stood there, a cartoonish silhouette, watching them.

She felt a hand on her shoulder. Chase was looking at her finally. Smiling in that disarming way he had.

"Don't worry, baby. He's just one of those paranoid types. Wants to make sure we're not narcs." Chase winked. "It'll be quick. I promise."

Cora held still for a second longer. Then she moved to undo her seatbelt.

☾

The cowboy led them through the house. Saying nothing. His ponytail dangled from the back of his hat and swished slightly as he walked, the heels of his boots clicking on the tiles in a crisp way that almost seemed prissy.

Apart from the overhead light in the foyer, the suburban palace was mostly dark inside. Eerie. Elongated rectangles of light reached through the windows and stretched over the floors. The gloom seemed to blossom off leather furniture in the living room and stainless steel appliances in the kitchen, gathering strength in the corners of each room they passed through.

Cora fought the instinct to reach out and grab Chase's hand. She was scared, creeped out beyond all reason, but some instinct told her to not show any weakness in this place.

They crossed another living space and went through a

darkened doorway into an office. The cowboy had them sit in front of a desk, closing the steel door behind them before he made his way to the chair on the opposite side.

He switched on a lamp shaped like a dragon. It was clearly more a novelty item than something meant to illuminate a room, with all the light shining through orange and red stained glass panels shaped like scales. It reminded Cora of being in a bedroom lit only by night light.

When the cowboy spoke, his words lilted with an indistinct accent — a bastardized Texas drawl that felt clunky and inauthentic, Cora thought. Was he faking it?

"So Rico recommended you." He lowered his aviators to make eye contact, but only for a second. "I respect that."

Chase nodded, something stiff in the gesture that the cowboy seemed to notice.

He leaned back in his chair. Smiled without showing any teeth.

"Well, hell. This all feels a little formal now, don't it? A little stiff. You can relax, boy. I just wanted to chat a minute with you. With both of you. Sort of get to know each other before we get knee-deep in the swamp together."

Cora was suddenly struck by the fact that she couldn't tell how old this guy was. Was he thirty-five or sixty-five? She searched for hints. Age spots on his hands or the hint of crow's feet protruding from the edges of the aviators. But the way the gauzy shadows swirled behind the desk made it impossible to tell.

"This is a risky kind of business, you understand?" he was saying. "Gotta make sure everything is clear up front. Clear as crystal."

"Absolutely," Chase said, his head nodding nonstop like a bobblehead figure.

"But I'm getting ahead of my own self. First of all, let me get the goods out. Let's let everyone involved see what we're talkin' about here."

He stood. Walked around the desk to a filing cabinet along the wall next to Chase's seat. Opened the top drawer. Moved things around inside. Bulky objects clanged against the steel body of the case.

Cora swallowed. Something about the metallic clinks and clunks made every hair on her body stand on end, made her shoulders crawl upward until her collarbone touched the sides of her neck. They shouldn't be here. It was all wrong.

And then a wave of embarrassment came over her. Always such a scaredy-cat, such a baby. Ridiculous. Nothing was even happening here. Nothing scary, anyway. Chase knew how to deal with these kinds of people. He wasn't like her dad. He'd done this before.

The cowboy turned and looked over his shoulder, a sheepish grin curling the bottom half of his face.

"Shoot. Could use an extra set of hands here. Wanna help me out?"

Chase hopped up. Bounded two steps that way.

The long blade came out of the drawer slowly. Gleamed a second in the strange reddish glow of the dragon lamp. Jumped then. Lurched to life.

It jammed into Chase's gut just as he got within arm's reach.

Chase's forward momentum stopped. A faint wet sound popped from his lips.

The cowboy thrust the knife several times. His body looking taut and wiry as he hurled himself into it. The mirrored sunglasses making his eyes look insectile, blank and unreadable. That almost sheepish grin never leaving the bottom half of his face.

Cora shrank back in her chair. Her mouth moved to scream, but no sound came out.

The knife punched into Chase's abdomen nine or ten times. Sliding in and out with ease. Lisping out wet slurs with every entry and exit. Whispering sibilance.

Cora couldn't move. Couldn't breathe. Mouth and eyes opened wide. All the way.

Finally Chase buckled forward. Gasping and whimpering. Bending at the waist. He toppled like a felled tree. Flopped onto hands and knees.

Runnels of blood pulsed out of him. Slapped and puddled on the tile floor in front of him. Wet sounds babbling with each throb.

The cowboy strode around behind him while he was still on all fours. Ripped the knife across Chase's throat. Shoved his bleeding body to the floor.

Cora came unglued from the chair. Scrambled for the door. Twisted and yanked the knob. It moved about a millimeter toward her before it stopped.

Locked.

No. Jesus, no.

Her hand scrabbled over the cool steel surface. Fingering the seam where the door met the frame like a hamster pawing at the glass wall of its cage.

She turned. Saw the cowboy's silhouette stalking toward

her.

And then words came out of her. Spilling from her lips without her thinking them first. Surprising her as much as him.

"Please. Whatever Chase did. Whatever… I had nothing to… I know it's a business thing, and I won't tell anyone. I promise I won't. It's business."

The cowboy stopped abruptly a few feet shy of her. Blood dripping down from the knife dangling at the end of his arm.

He stood there. Stared. Motionless.

And then a laugh hissed out of him, wet between his teeth.

"What on earth do you think is happening here, darlin'?" he said, his voice deep and oddly calm. That Texan accent seemed to have faded away. "Cause I got a feeling you have no idea entirely."

He lurched for her then, that wiry body knifing over the space between them all at once.

His arm lifted. Shot out for her.

His fingers clasped her by the hair on the back of her head and pulled her close.

CHAPTER 16

The first thing Darger wanted to do when she walked into her hotel room later that night was to collapse directly onto the bed. But phantom whiffs of garbage stench continued to plague her. She dared not risk contaminating the bed with the stink.

Instead, she dropped her bags inside the door and headed for the bathtub. She turned on the taps and watched the water slap against the smooth porcelain surface of the bottom of the tub.

A standard assortment of miniature bottles stood in a row next to the sink. Shampoo, conditioner, shower gel, bubble bath. Darger lifted the bottle of bubble bath and sniffed at the open lid. It was a very floral scent, which wasn't Darger's favorite. Reminded her of potpourri and grandmas. Then again, anything was better than the smell of rotting garbage.

Darger paced from the edge of the bathtub to the door of her room while the tub filled. She was simultaneously exhausted and completely jacked up on adrenaline. Her mind had been whirring since the interview with the tattoo artist. Had she and Loshak been right about the cult angle? Darger wondered if Stephen Mayhew's emaciation was the result of the punishment he said he'd earned after bringing Gage Medina to the ritual. Could they be starving people who angered the leader? Broke the rules?

But she was getting ahead of herself again. They'd find out what was really going on with The Children of the Golden Path tomorrow morning, when she and Loshak drove out to talk to

Curtis, the mysterious leader of the group.

For now she needed to wash off the grime from a morning spent in a landfill and hopefully find a way to relax enough to sleep. Today had been a long day, and she doubted tomorrow would be any different.

Darger slid her jacket off and held it to her nose, trying to determine once and for all if the lingering smell was real. Nothing and then… maybe? Perhaps it was only a memory thing. Garbage heap PTSD. She wondered how people worked in that every day, knee-deep in all that waste, trudging through it, trucking it around. Did they just get used to it?

She slipped into the scalding water and tried to clear her head. That worked for about thirty seconds, and then an image of the emaciated bodies appeared in her mind. And instead of pushing it away, she let her brain puzzle over it again. Tried again to make some sense of it, working at the edges of it, like she might make some leap about the missing pieces if she kept cycling through the whole mess in her head.

Her contemplation was interrupted by the sound of her phone ringing. She squinted across the bathroom at the buzzing device. It was past midnight. Who could be calling at this hour?

Could be Loshak, having some epiphany in the middle of the night, she thought. Well, he'd have to wait. Her phone was at the opposite end of the bathroom counter, and she wasn't ready to get out yet.

She took a deep breath, inhaling the perfumed steam from the bath. Her phone blipped. A text message this time.

Someone calling and texting after midnight seemed like it could be important.

Damn it.

Darger hurried through the rest of her bath, washing her hair, and then wrapping it and the rest of herself in towels.

She released the drain plug and hobbled over to the phone, wet feet slapping against the tile floor. She dried her hands and swiped at the phone. She had a missed call and a text from Luck. So... nothing relating to the case.

She went back to the tub and watched the last of her bathwater spiral down the drain.

Damn it all.

She dressed in a pair of joggers and an old t-shirt. Rain pattered against the window as she climbed into bed, her skin still radiating heat from the hot bath water.

Lying there in the stiff hotel sheets, she opened the text from Luck.

Luck: I told Jill I was commandeering the last of the gummy bears you sent. Dad Tax. And then this happened.

There was a video attached, and Darger clicked to play it.

Jill with her cheeks puffed out like a chipmunk, gummy bears spilling from her mouth.

"You're going to choke!" Luck said, laughing so hard the camera shook.

Jill tried to respond, but her words were garbled and unintelligible because of the gummy mass in her mouth. This only made the two of them laugh harder. The video ended.

Darger chuckled softly to herself and found herself wondering what it would have been like to have a dad like Luck. Someone who was there. Someone who gave a shit. Someone you could laugh to the point of tears with over some gummy bears.

Dark Passage

She set her phone on the bedside table and turned out the lamp. Settled her head back onto the pillow.

In the darkness, her mind wandered back to trying to solve this morbid puzzle. The images flashed through her head. Starved bodies. Dumpsters. Tattoos. Weird cults.

Tomorrow they'd know more, she reminded herself. They'd drive out to the cult grounds and ask some questions. She felt a twinge of excitement just thinking about it.

She didn't think she'd be able to sleep, but less than two minutes after the lights went out, unconsciousness pulled her under.

CHAPTER 17

The cowboy dragged Cora back out into the halls of the murky house, a handful of her hair in one hand and the knife in the other. He gripped her hard enough to slant her head at an odd angle away from him, chin tilted upward, neck stiff. Pain radiated from the back of her scalp where the hair was pulled rigid, stinging in strange flickering patterns like an electrical current circulated in the pale skin there.

Even with the hurt and fear, she focused. Eyes darting everywhere. Seeing everything. She needed to take in her surroundings. Note the details. Mentally record the floor plan. If any kind of escape became possible...

They shuffled down the hall, moving vaguely toward the glow of the foyer light in the distance. Cora's eyes widened at the brief glimpses of the door she could make out from the corner of her eye. Freedom was so close, even if it did her no good.

Then they veered left, passed through the kitchen again, those stainless steel appliances once again huddling in the shadows around them. Bulky shapes in the dark.

The cowboy kicked open a door set into the back wall of the kitchen. That prissy looking boot rising and thrusting. Then he leaned into the darkness beyond the doorway and flicked a light switch.

The fluorescent glow took a second to arrive. The bulbs humming and buzzing as they came to life.

And then the wooden staircase took shape, leading down

into a basement.

Cora's eyes went wider still. *The cellar. Not good.*

She stopped her feet just shy of the threshold. Refused to walk forward.

He changed his grip on the back of her hair. Jerked her in front of him and thrust her forward with a lifting motion.

"Walk or fall," he said. "Like I fucking care."

The sensation of being pushed and lifted at the same time reminded her of being in a mosh pit, totally at the whims of the surging crowd around her.

His new grip was lower on her head, moving down toward the scruff of her neck. The pulled hair stung more sharply here, but as a trade-off she'd regained the ability to angle her head downward. That helped her see enough to place her feet from step to step, avoiding that face first plunge to the smooth gray concrete floor below.

At the bottom of the steps, they veered to the left. The fluorescent bulbs buzzed louder here. Shimmered splotches on the matte gray paint coating the floor.

The basement was vast and clean. Industrial. Machines lined the walls. Commercial grade embroidery machines or sergers, Cora thought. She didn't know what to make of that.

The cowboy moved up beside her, and she turned to look at him for the first time since they'd left the office. What she saw made her gasp.

His ponytail had slipped down, half falling out of the back of his cowboy hat. It now looked like it sprouted out of his lower neck. A wig? She didn't know what that could possibly mean, but the image creeped her out worse than before.

He seemed to sense her gaze and fixed the hat. Sliding both

it and the wig back up with a single motion. Something he'd done before, she thought.

She struggled then. Threw her head forward. Tried to rip free of his grip while he was distracted.

He ground his knee into her back. Wrenched her shoulders backward with both hands. The blade now touched the skin along her larynx ever so faintly. He forced her down to the ground that way, his touch taking her straight to the floor.

She squirmed. Tried to buck and almost swim her way away from him.

One kick to the ribs sucked all the fight out of her. The steel toe of the boot pounded into her side with a sound like a meat tenderizer flattening a chicken breast.

She curled up into a ball. Eyes squeezed shut. Breathing. Watching a yellow light flicker at the bottom of her field of vision.

"Almost wouldn't respect you if you didn't at least try," he said. "Once is enough, though. Try it again, and I'll give your throat the same deal ol' boy upstairs got. Slashing prices, you could say. I'll give you a second to get your wind."

When she opened her eyes a few beats later, he gestured for her to stand. She got to her feet.

They walked to the far corner of this industrial space, his hand now wrapped around her arm. Fingers warm.

Her heart thundered in her chest. Blood roared in her ears. But what could she do? The image of the blade punching into Chase's gut replayed in her head, then the blood slapping down at the tiles, red puddles spreading over the floor.

When they neared the back corner of the room, the cowboy reached out a leg. Kicked at a squat wooden end table. A rustic, heavy-looking thing. The piece of furniture slid out of the way, inching over the floor with each kick, and she realized that it had a piece of wood attached to the bottom, painted to blend with the floor.

A hole in the concrete took shape as the table moved aside. It was slightly bigger around than a manhole on a city street.

Jagged cement formed the outer ring where the basement floor had been chiseled away, and the light reached down far enough to make some of the sandy dirt of the walls visible before the shaft running into the floor sheared off to blackness.

Cora froze. Stared. Blinked a few times, half expecting the hole to vanish, reveal itself as some figment of her imagination, replaced with that smooth gray-paint finish of the floor made whole again.

It didn't disappear.

Her eyes edged deeper into the vacancy. Tried to pierce that emptiness. She couldn't see the bottom, only a black hole that trailed down into impossible darkness. A fucking chasm hiding in the bottom of some suburban home.

The image made her skin crawl, but she couldn't look away.

She wanted to run. Fight. Scream. Kick.

But she only stared down into the wound in the concrete, into the void beyond.

And then the cowboy took a step toward her. Rough hands caught her high on the back, barely wider than her shoulder blades, and gave her a good hard shove. It tipped her top half toward that shadowy breach in the floor.

And she fell into nothing.

CHAPTER 18

The plunge into darkness ended abruptly. Cora slammed down to what felt like packed sand, motes of bright light exploding in her field of vision. Instinct had managed to blunt the impact with her outstretched arms, partially breaking her fall with her hands and then elbows, something she realized only after she'd landed.

Her torso, on the other hand, smacked down hard. Pain flared in the center of her abdomen, and she felt her breath ripped from her chest. That imploded feeling seemed to suck her ribcage inward, freezing her lungs into two tightened balls. Immobile.

She blinked in the darkness. Lips spluttering. Eyes bulging.

She tried to draw breath and couldn't. Patted her hands around the floor of this pit, found the sand compacted and gritty and solid as stone.

When her wind came back, her chest hitched and a big breath lurched into her. She smelled the dirt then. Earthy and dry. It overwhelmed this space, filled her nostrils.

She glanced up at the circle of light beaming down from the hole in the basement floor. Tried to estimate how far she'd fallen. Ten feet at least, maybe more like fifteen. Jesus. She was lucky nothing was broken. She flexed her fingers and wrists then, just to make sure. Everything moved as it should, sore but whole.

Still, she watched the glowing jagged breach above, that mouth that opened into the basement. No sign of the cowboy.

She didn't know if that was good or bad. Didn't know what was happening here.

It was almost like she remembered to panic then.

A surging tide of terror flooded her skull. Delivered an urge to scrabble away from the basement opening, whether it made sense or not.

She propped herself up on her elbows, then pushed onto her hands and knees. A sharp ache radiated from her sternum with each movement, tendrils of pain spiking outward from that epicenter.

When the lights began to click on around her, she stopped moving and blinked again. Stared down the manmade shaft etched into the dirt, watched the lights flicker on one after another. The passage just kept stretching out, elongating, each bulb illuminating deeper and deeper until it reached beyond her view.

It wasn't a pit. It was a tunnel.

What the fuck?

Who digs a tunnel under a house?

She wasn't sure she wanted to know the answer to that question.

Metallic sounds drew her eyes back toward that concrete mouth above. A ladder now protruded through the hole in the basement floor, and the cowboy climbed down it in a hurry, boots pinging against the aluminum rungs.

Her legs pushed off the dirt floor then. Found traction. Launched her into a wobbly run.

Her gaze probed deeper into that manmade cave before her. It was the only place to run, the only place to hide, the only place to go.

The section directly beneath the basement had been about fifteen feet high, but the circular tunnel tapered down to perhaps eight feet as it trailed away from the house. The hand-dug cave was vaguely circular, and she had the sense of moving slightly downhill as she ran.

She leaned into it. Pushed herself harder. Made it perhaps twenty feet down the passage before her toe caught on a rough spot.

She crashed back to the ground face first. Chin bashing and scraping on the sandy surface.

Pain flared inside her head. The coppery taste of blood rushed to fill her mouth. She'd bit her tongue.

And then he was on her. Callused hands grabbing her and snatching her by the hair again. She could smell his body now, something like leather mixed with a sharper sweaty odor.

This time his hand gathered a fistful of hair at the crown of her head and yanked straight up.

She scrabbled to her feet. Hot tears stinging her eyes. Beading along her lower lashes and blurring her vision.

He pulled her a few paces deeper into the tunnel, veered right into a broader chamber there.

She didn't see the cage until she was being shoved toward the open gate on the front of it. It was a dog pen, she thought. Small. Its spindly steel frame barely thicker than wire.

Her hands shot out. Grabbed the sides of the opening. Fought to keep herself out of it.

He clubbed her in the side of the head, a quick jab right over her ear. She saw stars for a brief moment, but that was enough.

Her grip faltered. She shot head first into the dog crate, face pressing into the steel grid at the back, and her limbs sort of folding up under her like an accordion.

From there, she sank down. Found a fleece blanket laid out on the bottom of the cage and more blankets bundled in the corner.

The cowboy latched the crate, and then snapped a thick padlock on the hasp. His tongue darted out to wet his lips.

"There you go, little lady," he said. "You'll find blankets. A pilla in the corner. Free room and board, you could say. All the amenities."

He patted the top of the cage a few times as he stood.

"Do you grok what's happening here yet? Do you want me to explain it?"

She struggled to untangle herself. Barely had enough room to get turned around in a crouch.

"See, we didn't have too much interest in your boyfriend. Whole thing was a ruse, right? To get *you* here."

She blinked hard, and the warm tears streamed down her cheeks at last.

"See, uh, Chase, I don't figure he knew what he had. Didn't fully appreciate you. Me? I'd never take you for granted. Can't wait to spend more time together. But for now I have a, uh, prior engagement, you could say."

He took a few steps toward the ladder just barely visible in the distance, gauzy clouds of dust billowing up next to his boots, shadows swirling everywhere around him. Then he stopped and turned back.

"You know what? You can go ahead and wait here. Just, you know, make yourself at home."

That brought a snicker out of him. He climbed the ladder

and pulled it up after himself, the aluminum grating against the chiseled concrete along the edge of the hole and then disappearing into that circle of brighter light.

She stared at that hole. Let her fingers lace around the slender bars of her cage.

The lights snapped out. The darkness encroached. Thickened around her like soup. Only the faint glow of the tunnel mouth offered any illumination. A weak beam spilling downward from the jagged opening, not even strong enough to reach all the way to the floor.

The end table slid back over the hole. Scuffing over the concrete. Cinching closed that circle of light like a solar eclipse until it was snuffed out.

The quiet intensified as soon as the darkness became total. It rang hollow in her ears, brought with it a memory of her wind getting knocked out, that imploding, empty feeling seeming to happen in her ear drums now instead of her chest.

She listened. Thought she might be able to detect his footsteps trailing away or a closing door. Something. Anything.

But the concrete foundation must have been too thick for anything like that. She heard nothing. The big nothing. That screaming silence sucking in her ears.

She breathed at last, inhaled two lungfuls of the dark. And then she heard and felt her breath come pluming out of her. It provided some small relief. The sound of her own breath proved to some panicked part of her that the world was still out there in the dark, that reality persisted, that she persisted, in the face of the gloom.

The smell grew stronger in the dark, the dusty, earthen tang of the exposed dirt walls on all sides of her cage. She could feel its arid touch in her throat. So dry. Stale.

She stared in the direction where the tunnel lay as though something might appear there. A beacon of light in the distance. Anything.

The black nothing gaped back at her.

CHAPTER 19

The next morning, Darger and Loshak met in the lobby of the hotel for a quick breakfast before the long drive into the Pennsylvania boonies. The continental breakfast bar didn't seem too awful, though Darger thought the chafing dish of scrambled eggs looked a little dicey.

She poured two cups of coffee from the dispenser while she waited for a bagel to toast. Loshak selected a single serving cup of orange juice from a bucket filled with ice and held it up.

"OJ?" he asked.

"Sure," Darger said.

Back at their small table, Loshak smeared butter and strawberry jam on a croissant.

"So there's been a small change of plans," Loshak said.

"Oh yeah?" Darger asked.

"Detective Ambrose called me right before we came down to breakfast," he said. "He thinks they managed to track down a family member for Stephen Mayhew. An aunt. He wants to be there when she comes in to do the body identification so he can interview her. See if she recognizes any of the other victims."

Darger shrugged and swallowed a mouthful of bagel.

"Maybe that's a good thing."

"What?"

"Just the two of us going in. We don't know how jumpy these Children of the Golden Path people are going to be. Are they the peaceful hippie types or the gun-toting anti-government type?" Darger sipped her coffee. "Personally I hope

114

they're the gun-toting type. I hate the smell of patchouli."

Loshak chuckled.

They finished up their breakfast and went outside to the car. As they passed through the front doors of the hotel, Darger chugged down the last of her orange juice and tossed the cup into a nearby garbage can. She couldn't help but envision the journey her cup would take after that. From the can here to a dumpster out back and then into a truck and hauled to perhaps the same landfill they'd been wading around in yesterday.

"You mind if I drive?" Loshak asked, dangling the keys to his rental from his thumb and forefinger.

"Not at all."

Darger followed Loshak over to where he'd parked and climbed into the passenger seat.

"So Ambrose talked with Marcia Blatch this morning. Our soil expert," Loshak said. "He wanted to know if the soil samples taken from the bodies would be consistent with the location of the Children of the Golden Path compound, especially considering Gage Medina said the place is a working farm."

"And?"

"She said the location of the compound is known to be acid shale and sandstone. In other words, all wrong for our samples."

"Maybe they haul it in," Darger said. "You can buy a truckload of dirt from any landscaping supply or hardware store."

Loshak started the car and put it in gear.

"Something to inquire about, for sure. If we can figure out a way to ask The Children about it without tipping our hand."

"Right," Darger agreed.

"The detective also had a chat with the Chief of Police out in South Londonderry Township this morning," Loshak said as he steered them onto the road. "Gave him a heads-up that we'll be poking around in his neck of the woods today."

"Gotta watch those toes," Darger said. "Did he have anything to say about The Children of the Golden Path?"

"He did. And Ambrose asked if they'd have any trouble from the group, and the chief said individual members have been picked up for minor things like vending without a permit and hitchhiking, but nothing major. The only time they've been called out to the compound itself was for a noise violation for some music festival they put together. Said they generally keep to themselves and have thus far been well behaved."

Darger searched "music festival South Londonderry Township PA" on her phone and found a few articles about it.

"Aww man," Darger said, disappointment oozing from the words.

Loshak turned on his blinker and merged onto the highway.

"What is it?"

"It's a folk music festival. Acoustic guitars. Bongos. Tie-dye." She held up one of the photos of the festival. "I can practically smell the incense and body odor just looking at these pictures — that sort of pungent cheese-going-bad smell of a hippie out too long in the sun. My nose can't get a break. First the garbage, and now this."

Loshak laughed again.

"Anyway, the chief said the townsfolk in the area seem to have mixed feelings about the group. Some figure that as long

116

as they're peaceful and not bothering anyone, they don't mind them hanging around. Others are more distrustful. The group comes into town to vend at the various farmer's markets and whatnot, and they hand out pamphlets and fliers for their events and retreats, and I guess some folks don't like the idea of The Children trying to recruit from the local population."

"Sounds like standard small-town shenanigans," Darger said.

"Yeah. Ambrose also asked if the chief had heard anything about the group fasting for religious purposes or otherwise. He said he had no knowledge of anything like that. The chief added that they seem fairly fit on the whole, but he owed that to the vegetarian diet and manual labor."

Darger did some further searching and found a website for The Children at WeAreTheGoldenPath.org. It looked a bit outdated, but there was a bio for Curtis.

"Oh yuck."

"What?"

Darger read the bio out loud.

"'A world-renowned master of shamanic healing and body-mind mechanics, Curtis is believed to be a reincarnated Hataɫii named Aditsan, which means 'one who listens.' A hataɫii is a powerful healer in Navajo culture.'" She stopped reading and snorted. "Do people actually believe this crap?"

"There's a photo of him?"

"No."

"What's your guess on demographics?"

"Let's be real. Any guy named Curtis who calls himself a shaman is *definitely* white."

"Alright, how about a little wager?" Loshak asked. "Do you

think his holiness has dreadlocks or a manbun?"

"Neither," Darger said. "Jesus hair and a beard. I'll stake twenty bucks on that, any day."

Loshak squinted.

"Well, Jesus hair can be put into a manbun, so I guess I'll take dreads," Loshak said. "Anyway, as for how anyone can believe it? There are people who believe the earth is flat, and that the world is being run by a secret cabal of lizard people. All things considered, this is far less absurd."

CHAPTER 20

They'd been on the highway for almost half an hour when Loshak turned on his blinker.

"I'm gonna gas up before we get on the turnpike," Loshak said, changing lanes so he could take the next exit. "Might as well grab some snacks, too. We're gonna be on the road a lot today."

"Good idea."

They pulled into a gas station a few blocks from the highway.

"Ohhh look," Loshak said, feigning excitement at the words written across the windows of the convenience store. "Soft drinks, souvenirs, and sundries. I *love* sundries."

Darger went inside while Loshak stayed behind to pump gas. She went straight for the coffee. The monotony of the road was already starting to make her sleepy. Apparently the small cup of coffee she'd had at breakfast wasn't going to cut it. After filling a large size coffee, she grabbed a water, some jalapeno flavored potato chips, and a bag of Red Vines.

Loshak met up with her at the counter. Along with coffee and water, he'd grabbed a Coke Zero, Doritos, and a Hostess strawberry pie.

While they waited in line, Loshak nudged Darger with his elbow and nodded at a coin-operated penny-flattener next to the cash register. One of the options was a souvenir penny featuring Benjamin Franklin's face.

"Look, it's your pal Ed Franklin."

Darger sighed.

"You're never going to let that go, are you?"

Back in the car, they consulted the route ahead.

"It's pretty much a straight shot down I-76," Darger said, using her finger to trace the path from their current position right outside of Valley Forge to the wilderness surrounding a small tourist town called Mt. Gretna.

They drove on down the turnpike, much of it appearing as a narrow corridor through the trees. Here and there a small town or overpass interrupted the walls of green, but mostly it was road and trees and sky for as far as the eye could see.

"So how do they do it?" Darger asked eventually. "How does someone like this Curtis fellow manage to convince a bunch of people that he's a reincarnated Navajo healer?"

Squinting, Loshak thought about it for a moment.

"You know, people like to assume that these cult types must be geniuses. Master manipulators. But it's like what I say about serial killers. In my opinion, they get much further on boldness than anything else. On taking risks that might fail massively. More often than not, the reason they get away with it isn't the result of being so damn brilliant. It's because the people around them don't want to rock the boat."

"Reminds me of Ted Bundy wearing a cast and asking women to help him carry a briefcase. Some women got a bad feeling and refused to help him, which probably says something about how convincing he was," Darger said. "And yet there were other women who went right along with it, probably because they worried that refusing to help would be impolite."

"Exactly. The other thing is that a lot of these guys don't start their cults from scratch. They sort of co-opt another

120

group. There was a group of Hare Krishnas a few hours from here, out in the hills of West Virginia, led by a guy named Keith Gordon Ham. He was a prime example of that."

"You talked about him in your class on charismatic cult leaders at the Academy, right?" Darger asked, trying to recall the details.

"That's right. Ham started by insinuating himself amongst the followers of Prapbupadha, who was the original Krishna guru. Within a year of becoming a disciple, Ham was already fiddling with his teacher's devotional system, trying to add little bits of Christianity to make it more appealing to Americans. He was obsessed with trying to make the Krishna stuff more approachable to Westerners, and I think it was because he knew it'd be easier to gain followers that way. The more familiar he could make it, the easier he made the pill to swallow, and the more people he could pull into his circle of control, yadda yadda. Anyway, the Krishnas weren't stupid. They saw it as a power grab and banned him from teaching in any of their temples for a while."

"A while," Darger said. "Too bad they didn't just boot him right then. Wasn't he the one that ordered several followers and dissidents to be murdered?"

"We never actually proved it, but that's the theory. Though my guess is that Ham would have found another way. Whether he simply formed his own temple or searched out another group to siphon off of." Loshak changed lanes to pass a slow-moving semi truck. "Jim Jones wasn't much different. He pretty much openly talked about using established church groups and well-known religious figures to gain followers for himself. Of course, he said he did it to 'demonstrate his Marxism.' But I think any political ideology he might have had was always twisted up with his desire to control large groups of people. David Koresh? Same deal. The Branch Davidians had been around for almost thirty years before he came waltzing in and usurped control."

"What about Heaven's Gate?" Darger asked. "Didn't they mostly recruit using pamphlets and advertisements?"

Loshak nodded, frowning.

"That one always puzzled me. Here's this group making absolutely wild claims about aliens and space ships with absolutely no evidence. And people are signing up left and right." Loshak rubbed at the stubble under his chin. "But I've been doing some research on the followers of QAnon lately, and I think there might be some similarities there. Bold claims, presented as secrets 'they' don't want you to know. Truths we can't tell just *anyone* because they wouldn't be able to handle it. They're not enlightened enough. Or they've been brainwashed not to see, yadda yadda."

"You say that a lot when you're talking about cults," Darger said. "Yadda yadda."

"Well, that's what it is, isn't it? A bunch of meaningless words that sound deep and interesting. But there's never any substance." Loshak shrugged. "My point is, I think that can be very appealing for some people: feeling like they're one of the few who are 'in the know.' It makes them feel superior and special. And I guess buying into the philosophy, no matter how batshit it might be, is a small price to pay."

Darger took a sip of coffee and then replaced the cup in the holder.

"Maybe instead of being the exception to the rule, what

Heaven's Gate really proves is that different techniques work on different people," Darger said. "Co-opting an existing group works for a guy like Ham or Jim Jones, because they're kind of preaching to the choir, so to speak. They've already got a group of believers. On the other hand, there are plenty of people out there still searching for something. Something to believe in. A place where they belong. And the Heaven's Gate types can speak to this big secret no one wants you to know. I think that would be very appealing to someone who's maybe drifting a little. Here's someone telling you, 'Oh yes. There's more. And it's not what everyone else thinks it is. You can be one of the chosen that gets to know the truth.'"

"Pretty much," Loshak said.

"It's the next part that makes less sense to me." Darger rested her skull against the headrest. "When the followers have to prove that they're worthy by renouncing all worldly possessions and agreeing to do everything their leader says. I mean, it makes sense to me in theory. I've seen people blindly follow something or someone enough times to know it happens. But on a personal level, I don't understand it at all. When someone tells me what to do, no matter what it is, there's a part of me that always thinks, 'Fuck you, now I want to do the exact opposite.'"

"Really?" Loshak's face was a mask of feigned surprise. "I never would have guessed."

Darger rolled her eyes.

"The trick is that the cult eases them into it," Loshak said. "In fact, they rarely do a hard sell. I heard a sociologist give a talk about cult recruitment tactics once, and she joked that a used car salesman comes on stronger than a cult at the first meeting."

Darger smiled at the comparison.

"They're craftier. More subtle. They have to be. They're asking for a lot more than your money. They want you to hand them the reins to your entire life, in a sense. Imagine if right off the bat they told you, 'We'd love for you to join our group, but first you have to cut out all relationships with anyone outside the cult.' Most people would walk."

Darger chuckled.

"What?"

"Well, the cults are always led by a man, and it's only a matter of time before he decides it's his religious duty to have sex with everyone in the cult. So I was imagining that being part of the hard sell. 'You can't see your family and friends anymore, and also I'm going to need to bone you.'"

Something like a laugh burst from Loshak's lips.

"I mean, Jim Jones was having sex with men *and* women in the congregation. And then The Source Family guy decided he needed fourteen wives."

"Father Yod," Loshak said.

"That's him. Then there's David Koresh. Charles Manson. And if I recall correctly, Ham was accused of molesting children that lived on the Krishna compound."

"True. But there's one fly in the ointment of your theory." Loshak waggled his eyebrows. "Marshall Applewhite."

"Which one is he again?"

"Heaven's Gate. He was a proponent of celibacy."

Darger crossed her arms over her chest.

"Well, you know what? Fuck that guy. He messes up all our theories." She made a fart sound. "Who needs him?"

Loshak held up a finger.

"Eh, it's part of the profiling game, isn't it? There's always one that spoils the pattern."

"Like Dennis Rader being married and having kids and leading a 'normal' life?" Darger said. "Not the normal serial killer backstory."

"Exactly—"

Darger could tell Loshak was about to say more, but he was interrupted by the sound of his phone ringing.

"It's Detective Ambrose," he said, glancing at the screen and then back to the road. "You wanna get that for me? Our exit is coming up, and I don't want to miss it."

"Sure," Darger said.

She plucked the phone from the center console and answered the call.

"Agent Loshak's phone," Darger said. "How can I help you?"

"Is that you, Agent Darger?" Ambrose asked.

"It is."

"This is Ambrose. Have you two seen this shit in the Inquirer?"

"No."

"Hold on," Ambrose muttered. "I'll text you the link."

Darger's phone blipped. She kept Loshak's phone pressed to her ear and opened the link Ambrose sent, which led to a news article that mentioned an unnamed source who speculated that the landfill bodies might be the work of a serial killer.

"Where'd they get this?"

"No idea," Ambrose said. "And of course *I* know that this

didn't come from you. But the mayor? He's not convinced. I just wanted to give you a heads up. He might try to make trouble in DC if he can figure out who to call. He's not very connected as far as I can tell, but he's crafty, and he's mean. I didn't want you or Loshak to be blindsided if he decides to throw his weight around."

"Thanks," Darger said. "We appreciate the warning. Have you talked to Stephen Mayhew's aunt yet?"

"Not yet. I'm at the morgue as we speak. She should be here any minute."

"We're getting off the turnpike now." Darger checked the map on her phone again. "Should be at the location Gage gave us in twenty minutes or so."

"Give me a call when you're done," Ambrose said. "Let me know how it goes."

Darger promised to do so and hung up.

"Well?" Loshak asked. "What happened? Sounded like some kind of bad news."

Darger read the pertinent quote from the Inquirer article and explained that the mayor assumed Loshak was the unnamed source. She couldn't seem to keep the smirk off her face as she spoke.

"You think this is funny?" Loshak asked.

Darger held her thumb and forefinger about a quarter-inch apart and squinched one eye shut.

"A little."

They'd reached the line of toll booths off the turnpike exit, and Loshak pulled into a lane marked "Cash Only."

"You better hope the mayor doesn't make too much trouble for me," Loshak said, rolling his window down. "Trouble for me is trouble for you."

Darger handed him a fist full of quarters.

"How so?"

The quarters clanged into the toll collection bucket, and the boom gate rose to let them pass.

Loshak swiveled his head over to deliver a pointed look.

"Because you don't have any other friends aside from me at the Bureau."

Darger chortled and sat back against her seat as they rolled through the gate.

"Touché."

CHAPTER 21

The road to The Children of the Golden Path compound
twisted back and forth through the trees and up and down hills
and ravines, a serpent of asphalt winding through the
Pennsylvania countryside. Darger hadn't seen a house or even a
driveway for at least ten minutes when she checked the GPS
and found they were closing in on the area Gage Medina had
described.

"Should be coming up here on the left," Darger said.

"Was that it?" Loshak asked as they passed a barely visible
gap in the trees.

"I don't know. Maybe?"

Loshak slowed the car and executed a tight U-turn. They
rolled slowly back to the narrow track, which was little more
than two dirt slashes etched into the foliage. About a hundred
yards in, the path bent out of sight.

"What do you think?" Darger asked.

"I guess we're about to find out," Loshak said as he
wrenched the wheel and steered them onto the rugged drive.

The weeds tinkled and dragged at the undercarriage of the
car. Rain had etched washboard-like ruts into the surface of the
trail. The tires juddered over the uneven surface, and Darger
found herself bouncing one way and then the other.

She kept an eye on the GPS on her phone as they crept
along through the forest. They'd gone nearly a mile down the
drive when a fence took shape through the trees. Twenty feet of
vertical chain link with barbed wire coiling around the top.

128

They rounded another curve, and then Darger spotted a large gate with a small shed beside it.

"You think the high-security fence and guard post come standard with the Doomsday Cult Starter Kit?" Darger asked.

"Only the deluxe edition," Loshak said. "The standard issue is your basic six-foot fence and a simple gate with a padlock."

"I thought we were dealing with hippie types. Since when are hippies into barbed wire and boundaries and..." Darger caught sight of the man inside the gate house. "...and shirtless men with assault rifles?"

The man guarding the gate was probably about Loshak's age, but in worse shape, which made him seem older. He had a tangle of reddish hair and a graying beard. As they approached the fence, he stood, keeping the rifle clutched tightly to his bare potbelly and pointed at the ground.

The rest of his body came into view as he rose from his lawn chair. Too late, Darger realized he wasn't just shirtless. The man was completely naked, and she couldn't help but notice that the carpet matched the drapes.

Darger half-gasped, half-giggled at the Lil' Smokey set in a thatch of red pubes like an acorn in a bird's nest.

"You act like you've never seen a naked man wielding an AK-47 before," Loshak said drily, which only made Darger giggle harder.

Loshak rolled down his window.

"What's yer bidness?" the naked man asked.

"We're here to see Curtis."

"Curtis don't have any visitors on the roster today, and I don't know you, so that's a no."

With a sigh, Loshak reached into his jacket and pulled out

129

his badge.

The naked man scowled at the ID for a beat before hocking a loogie into the grass.

"Feebs," he growled. "Shoulda known you'd come sniffin' around here sooner or later. Always think everythang's your business, doncha?"

"We're only here to talk," Loshak said. "We have some questions about a man named Stephen Mayhew. You know him?"

The naked man frowned. His jaw worked up and down like he was chewing on the question. Without a word, he swiveled back to the guard booth and picked up a walkie-talkie from the chair set beside the door. He muttered something into the black box, but it was too low to hear.

They waited.

Naked Guy had a bit of a back and forth with whoever was on the other end of the radio, his unblinking stare never leaving Loshak's car. After a minute or so of this, he came back out.

"Curtis will see you," he said. "You gotta park here and walk in, though. We try to keep motor vehicle traffic to a minimum inside the gates, else the road in gets all tore up and muddy. Over there is good."

He waggled a finger to a place just off the driveway where the grass was matted flat. Loshak put the car in gear and steered it into the makeshift parking area.

They stepped out into the breeze and the sun. It felt good to be out of the car. Darger stretched. Insects chirped everywhere, a many-voiced sound that never let up.

Naked Guy approached. Darger noticed for the first time that the only item of clothing he wore was a pair of work boots.

No evidence of even socks. His eyes zeroed in on her holster.

"You'll have to surrender your firearms before I can let you in."

"No can do, pardner," Loshak said. "That is quite literally against federal regulations, and I figure you know that. Do we look like fresh-out-of-the-Academy rubes who would actually fall for that?"

The naked man's top lip quivered, and then he grumbled something unintelligible. He turned on his heel and stomped back into the booth, various body parts jiggling and shaking. There was a mechanical whir, and the big gate began to slide out of the way.

"It's about a mile and a half up the road," Naked Guy said, gesturing with his rifle. "Can't miss it."

They started down the dusty track, and Darger was thankful for the canopy of trees that kept the way shaded. A walk like this in the city would have been a nightmare, with all that concrete and metal absorbing the heat and reflecting it right back at you. They would have been baking.

Even with the benefit of the shade, Darger felt beads of sweat forming along her brow and the back of her neck after a few minutes. Loshak tugged at the collar of his jacket, and she was glad she'd left hers behind.

They'd been walking for about ten minutes when the trees on the right opened up, revealing rolling hills in a patchwork of dazzling colors — red and purple and orange and yellow. The flower fields.

Darger paused, her eyes studying the near-perfect rows of plants.

"I still think it's an awfully big coincidence that the cult our dirt-covered corpse came from happens to have a working farm."

Ghostly white shapes flitted along the tilled paths, and it was a moment before Darger realized they were women in white dresses tending the plants. The breeze shifted and she caught a snippet of someone singing.

"But it sure is peaceful out here," she admitted. "Looks like something from another century."

"Yeah it's all wholesome and old-timey until they re-enact a human sacrifice under the full moon, right?"

Darger snorted.

"You think they starved Stephen Mayhew as punishment for bringing along an outsider who interrupted their fake ritual?"

"I don't know. It sounds far-fetched, but then so does finding a bunch of malnourished bodies in a landfill." Loshak wiped the back of his neck. "Anyway, I guess we're about to find out."

They moved on down the driveway, veering away from the fields and deeper into the trees again. The wind kicked up, causing branches to creak overhead.

Their footsteps carried them up a slope, and when they crested a low hill another clearing came into view. This one was situated directly in the path of the drive, and Darger saw a scattering of small buildings — cabins and yurts and even some tents. A plume of smoke arose from a small fire near the center of it all.

Darger opened her mouth to comment on the seemingly random assortment of buildings when a blood-curdling scream stopped her in her tracks.

CHAPTER 22

Darger and Loshak made eye contact for a split second, as if to confirm with one another that they were indeed hearing what they thought they were hearing.

A woman screaming bloody murder. Shrill sounds ringing out from the bottom of the hill. Pained or terrified or both.

Without exchanging a word, the agents took off running toward the awful noise. The ragged sound of the woman's voice made the hair on Darger's arms stand straight up.

Beside her, Loshak drew his weapon. Darger unholstered her Glock as well, keeping it pointed at the ground as she ran.

They drew up on the camp, and Darger spotted people milling around the camp fire at the east end of the clearing. She caught a whiff of fried onions and saw coils of smoke and steam rising from a skillet. She glanced around and saw smiles on most of the faces. Heard the sing-song lilt of upbeat chatter.

Surely they could hear the woman's agonized cries? She and Loshak had noticed the wailing from all the way back down the road. These people seemed totally oblivious to it.

Her mind whirred, searching for an explanation. And the simplest answer was that the sound of someone screaming was common enough that they'd all learned to ignore it.

That thought sent another wave of chills through Darger's flesh. For now, she needed to focus on finding the woman and putting a stop to whatever was happening. The people around the fire, as disturbing as their apathy was, didn't seem to be any kind of threat.

Darger's lungs began to burn as they crossed the last stretch of road, hot and cold and stinging in her chest. She could hear Loshak huffing for breath alongside her.

She followed the screams to a small modular shed tucked beneath a copse of chestnut trees on the west side of the camp. They sprinted to the door and paused outside, both crouched beside the entrance.

The screaming had taken on a strangely rhythmic quality now. The woman let out a long, drawn-out wail, and then there was a pause.

Another long wail.

Pause.

The sound seemed sharper this close up. Even through the walls of the small building, it was piercing.

Loshak was positioned on the side of the door closest to the handle. He gestured that he'd open the door and allow Darger to enter first.

She gave a nod to indicate that she was ready.

Loshak took a big breath, shoulders heaving. In one fluid motion, he turned the handle and shoved the door wide.

Darger entered low and swept the room, swiveling the Glock in front of her, eyes scanning everything.

One, two, three, four people sitting on the floor in the small space. Three women and a man. Their legs folded up beneath them, the lotus position or something like it, Darger thought.

"Hands," she said. "Let me see your hands."

The screaming cut off suddenly and a pile of pillows on the floor shifted, thrashed as though this collection of cushions was coming to life.

Darger squinted at the shambling heap and realized she'd

counted wrong. There were five people in the room.

The pillows bulged around a woman in a floral dress on the floor, laying in the fetal position. Her red and splotchy complexion told Darger that this was the one who'd been screaming.

The woman spun around. Sat up. She had red-rimmed eyes, but she didn't look in pain or injured. Wasn't bleeding. Wasn't even being touched by anyone. The woman clutched one of the pillows to her chest and stared at Darger, a confused expression on her face.

Darger lowered her weapon and sensed Loshak do the same.

"What's going on in here?" Loshak said. His voice still had a little edge of adrenaline in it, but it already sounded more unsure than authoritative.

"Uh, maybe you should tell us who the heck you are, first," the man asked. There was a lilt in his voice, the tone of each sentence going up at the end, almost as if he were asking a question. "Like, you can't just burst in here."

Darger studied him. His sandy hair was styled in dreadlocks, and he wore a white t-shirt that was so dirty it looked as brown as a rotten apple. Darger had a feeling she was about to lose her bet with Loshak. Why hadn't she picked dreadlocks?

"I'm Agent Darger from the FBI. This is my partner, Agent Loshak." Darger flashed her badge. "We heard screaming."

"Uh, yeah," Dreadlocks said, mouth agape. "This is the Primal Scream shed, bruh. What did you expect to hear?"

"Primal..."

"Scream." The voice came from behind them.

Darger turned and found another man standing in the door frame. He had shoulder-length blond hair and a beard roughly two shades darker.

"You must be our visitors from the FBI."

"Curtis, man," Dreadlocks said. "They just, like, burst in and totally harshed the vibe. Citrine was really making some progress, too. I could hear the past-life trauma in her screams."

Darger had to bite the inside of her cheek to keep from smiling. So Dreadlocks wasn't the cult leader, after all. And Curtis was looking pretty Jesus-y. Loshak owed her twenty bucks.

"It's alright, Sonny. The interruption was my fault. I fully intended to meet our guests, but I got held up in the kitchen with Juniper. Another plum butter incident. You know how she is." Curtis smiled, but there was a tension there. "Coming upon our camp and hearing screaming, well… they probably thought poor Citrine here was being tortured."

Everyone but Darger and Loshak chuckled at this.

Curtis let his gaze sweep the small room before locking on Darger. He had pale blue eyes. Clear and intense.

"I understand you have questions about Stephen," he said. "Why don't we let this little group get back to it, and we can go somewhere… *quieter* to talk."

The group tittered again, and Darger wondered if Curtis had brainwashed them all into thinking he was funny. She didn't think mere narcotics, even in copious amounts, would be enough to explain laughing at these comments.

"Lead the way," Darger said, and then she and Loshak followed Curtis out of the shed.

CHAPTER 23

Cora curled up in a tiny ball in her cage, wrapping herself in the blankets as best she could. Down there in the dark, she had very little sense of how much time had passed. Hours? Days?

Despite it being the middle of June, there was a permanent chill in the underground space. And a dank earthen smell that reminded her of the cellar at her grandpa's house.

Adrenaline kept her awake for a time. She couldn't stop worrying that the cowboy would return, and she didn't want to be caught unaware. But eventually she grew tired, and there was nothing to do there in the dark but close her eyes and nestle a little deeper in the blankets.

Sleep came in brief shards and fragments. Dreams flitting through her head off and on, mind-made images breaking up the endless dark with vivid color and shape.

She dreamed of Chase, her imagination reanimating him just as he was. Dark stubble speckled his jaw, drawing stark the chiseled lines of his square chin. He squinted and smiled and drove them down endless city blocks in his piece of shit Toyota, cigarette smoke spiraling around his head like a gray halo. He chain-smoked and talked about all his big plans. His schemes and impossible dreams. About how they'd spend all the cash — champagne and lobster and gold-plated everything.

He talked about a better life, dreamed out loud of a better world. Talked about an escape from the dreary way of living they'd both been born into.

Maybe that was why she'd loved Chase despite all else. He'd

dared to dream of a way out of the trailer park hole, dared to fight back against what had felt like a certain fate — brutal poverty meant only to span another generation through them. Everyone else she knew seemed so ready to submit to that force, resigned to let the preexisting way of things bend them to its will, slot them into their place in the world like being poor was some destiny or birthright. But Chase had fought against it like hell.

Then she dreamed of the knife entering Chase's gut. Punching home and retracting. Sliding in and out with such ease. Wet scraping sounds that whispered and hissed.

His blood spattering the tile, runnels of red winnowing into the grout lines as the puddle spread ever outward from the point of impact.

It couldn't be real, but it was.

When she woke, she wept. Hot tears drained down to touch her chin, seemed to make the skin of her cheeks soggy.

The loss had finally caught up with her, overtaken the sense of shock that had numbed and awed her mind to the point of blankness at first. But now it hurt, and the pain only seemed to grow.

Grief was the mind grasping along the edges of a hole, she thought — the hurt of trying to understand an absence like it was an object.

Cora scooted forward in her cage. Wrapped her fingers around the cold metal of the frame again. Thin bars. Smooth to the touch, that glossy black enamel coating them, which she remembered but could not see in the dark.

Her fingers reached out. Stretching toward the latch. Finding that thick bulk of the padlock dangling from the ring of metal there.

She could touch the lock. Feel the different smoothness of its brushed metal. Push it so its hooked shank pivoted against the hasp, hear it slap back against the body of her pen. But that was it.

She pulled her fingers back inside the cage. Breathed. Blinked and then stared into the dark around her, feeling that faint sting of her eyes straining against the blackness.

She closed them. Held still. Focused on her breathing until it cleared her mind.

Her chest rose and fell for a while, and finally, she let her mind reach out. She listened to the silence beyond the sounds of her respiration, listened to the space stretching out around her, somehow calmed instead of panicked by that awareness now.

Space. Stillness. The world beyond her being, beyond her tiny physical form, beyond these walls. So much space.

The stillness seemed to grow, inside of her and outside of her. She drifted in it. Found peace in it.

Her eyes snapped open when she heard the woman's voice in the distance.

"Are you there?"

CHAPTER 24

Outside the shed, they paused briefly to make formal introductions before moving on. Curtis was younger than Darger had imagined. Maybe thirty at the oldest. A little taller than her, but shorter than Loshak. His lean arms were deeply tanned. He wasn't handsome, but he wasn't ugly, either. Physically, he was what Darger would describe as a Ted Bundy type. Normal-looking, possibly deceptively so.

His body language seemed to adjust as they moved out into the open. Whatever tension Darger had detected in him inside the shed quickly giving way to a calm, assertive way of carrying himself. For better or worse, that put her somewhat at ease as well.

Curtis ushered them further down the two-track road, past more of the small buildings. A man with graying hair squatted on the front steps of one of the cabins strumming an acoustic guitar that was badly out of tune. Two women sat near him, one braiding the other's hair and swaying to the music.

"This area is really the backbone of our community. It all started right here. When it began, there were only ten of us with a handful of tents, an outhouse, and a communal fire." He stretched his arms wide. "And in just a few years we've built this."

There were two more men and four women clustered around another fire pit. One of the women wore a baby sling with a sleeping infant tucked inside. Darger was starting to notice a pattern here. A much higher ratio of women to men.

"I truly regret that your first taste of the camp was the Primal Scream shed," Curtis was saying. "It must have been jarring. Then again, sometimes that's exactly what we need. A shock to the system."

"If you're sincerely worried about first impressions, I'd maybe address the naked man with the assault rifle guarding the front gate," Darger said.

Curtis threw back his head and laughed. His teeth were straight and white, with prominent canines.

"I only hope the confusion back at the shed won't color your view of this place. As you can see, we're quite a peaceful lot." Curtis thrust his hands into the pockets of the linen pants he wore. "It's just that we all need outlets. We keep ourselves so bottled up out there in what I call The Material World. All the rules. The formalities. The mores. It's quite stifling. But I don't need to tell you that. I'm guessing the FBI is its own universe of codes and regulations. Meetings and interviews and evaluations. And sometimes, don't you just want to scream?"

"Who doesn't?" Darger asked. "Though I find I get a lot of dirty looks whenever I scream at the meetings."

Curtis chuckled.

"Well imagine if there were somewhere you could go in every office. A place to blow off steam. To release some of that animal aggression, so to speak. Because that is what we are, after all. Underneath the suits and the fancy cars and the official-sounding job titles, we're not so different than a band of chimpanzees. The only thing that truly separates us is that we *pretend* we're something else. Chimps don't pretend. Tigers don't pretend."

The narrow road wound through a patch of untouched

forest and up a small hill.

"Animals are more honest, really. Arguably more sane. We're trapped letting our thoughts dominate our lives. Giving credence to every passing notion. Is Bob going to get the promotion over me? Should I have bought the LS instead of the ES? Does this outfit make me look fat? It's exhausting."

When they crested the rise, Darger saw that the trees gave way to another clearing, which held another field of flowers and a row of three commercial greenhouses.

"Speaking of titles," Darger said, "what's yours? What do the people here call you, as their leader?"

He laughed.

"They call me Curtis. And I'm not the leader."

"No?"

"Of course not. That would suggest I'm above the other members of our community, and that's simply not true." Curtis squinted up into the sky. "I'm not into titles. A title is nothing but a label, and a label is a limitation. But I suppose if I was pushed to answer the question, to satisfy that uniquely human obsession to categorize, I'd call myself a… spiritual guide."

Darger resisted an urge to roll her eyes. The whole spiel had the sound of a practiced speech. A way of seeming disarming and non-threatening. It fit with what Loshak had said about cults in the car. The soft sell over the hard.

They followed Curtis to a large pole barn with dark gray metal siding situated a short distance from the greenhouses. The sun glinted off a grid of solar panels on the roof. Curtis opened a door on the side of the building and ushered them through.

After the pastoral scene outdoors — people clustered

around fires and strumming guitars — the level of activity inside the barn was staggering.

There were dozens of wooden tables set up in the space with a person at each station engaged in some element of packaging flowers. Trimming, stacking, tying the stems into bundles. Darger watched a woman in a white peasant dress pass an assembled bouquet to another table where a woman in a green tunic wrapped them in a plastic sleeve.

At the far end of the assembly area, the packaged flowers were piled into boxes and loaded on a dolly. A man pushed one of the dollies through a doorway closed off with the kind of clear plastic strips she associated with refrigerated rooms. She supposed it made sense that they'd keep the flowers chilled.

The space was filled with a sharp green smell similar to cut grass with a faint floral note. Unlike the leader's stream of B.S., Darger found this scent quite pleasant.

A few of the women were singing some folksy-sounding song in three-part harmony. They actually sounded pretty good, Darger thought, especially a capella. But the acoustics of the space also made it sound a little eerie because of the way the echo sort of shuddered in the air and bounced off the concrete floor.

There were other sounds, too. The metallic snip of shears cutting stems. The crinkle of plastic. The rumble of a dolly over the floor.

"Our business has grown over 800% in the past year," Curtis said, the corners of his lips now stuck in a smile. "We mostly sell to the local florists, but we're selling directly to the public now in a few farmer's markets as well, and every Sunday we have a booth at the Headhouse Market in Philly."

Darger couldn't help but notice how easily he'd slid from spiritual talk into business talk — a man who kept his eyes on the prize.

There were a few office-type rooms built into one of the shorter sides of the barn, all with windows looking out on the flower processing area. Curtis led them over to one of the office doors and pulled it wide. Just as Darger stepped inside, a woman with a tablet in hand bustled out of a neighboring office.

"Sorry to interrupt, Curtis, but I need a quick signature on this purchase order," the woman said.

"Of course." He turned to Darger and Loshak. "Please go in and make yourselves comfortable. I'll be right in."

The inside of the office was fairly slick, especially compared to the rustic nature of the rest of the camp. Darger glanced up at the polished tubes and ducts winding around above — industrial and clean in that modern office way. Loshak glanced back toward the door and leaned in so he could keep his voice low.

"I think you should take point on this," he said.

"You sure? You're the expert on charismatic cult leaders."

"Well, I was thinking about what you said earlier. By the looks of the population around here, I think you're more his type."

Darger raised her eyebrows.

"I mean, look around. It's basically the opposite of a sausage party here," Loshak said.

Squinting, Darger took on a philosophical tone.

"What *is* the opposite of a sausage party? A breast fest? A clam jam? A vagina soiree?"

"I'm reporting you to HR," Loshak said with a snort. "This is a toxic environment."

CHAPTER 25

Curtis closed the office door behind him when he entered, muffling the cacophony of work sounds out on the main floor. He crossed the room and paused next to a mini-fridge.

"Can I offer you a water or kombucha? We make the booch from scratch right here on the farm."

Darger couldn't help but remember Gage Medina's story about unknowingly drinking the psilocybin-laced "moon juice" at the ritual. And while she doubted Curtis would do something as reckless as dosing two federal agents, she simply didn't trust him.

"No booch for me, thanks," she said.

Loshak declined as well, and Darger thought he was probably thinking the same.

Curtis helped himself to a bottle of urine-colored liquid, taking several gulps and then making an exaggerated *ahhh* sound at the end. He sat behind his desk and studied the bottle for a moment.

"Kai was a stockbroker on Wall Street. A successful one, too, but absolutely miserable. Then he came here and discovered he has an innate talent for fermentation. Kombucha, sauerkraut, pickles... you name it. He's our resident Brew Master." He took another sip. "We attract a diverse crowd. We have a Rhodes scholar. A former CEO of a Fortune 500 company. A New York Times best-selling author. A very well-known contemporary artist. You'd probably recognize his name if I told you, but he came here to get away from that, so...."

He waved his hand, as if that would dispel any lingering curiosity.

"A lot of our community is made up of people who excelled in all the material ways of life, and yet found themselves searching for something more. For their deeper purpose."

"And they found that here?" Darger asked.

"Well, I can't truly speak for what they've found, as each person's journey is their own. As unique as a snowflake. But I like to think that being here has given their lives more meaning. I know it has for me."

"So is there some bar for acceptance?"

Curtis paused with the kombucha bottle an inch from his lips and frowned at her.

"Excuse me?"

"It's just that your so-called diverse crowd seems heavily skewed toward people that have experienced some sort of material achievement. Academics, CEOs, best-selling authors. Do you only let in successful people, or...?"

The corners of Curtis' eyes crinkled.

"We don't think of it as letting people in or keeping them out. There are no gatekeepers here."

"Aside from the nudist with the AK-47," Darger said.

Curtis laughed.

"Ahh, such wit. Ozzy is a rare breed. Believe it or not, he has chosen that role for himself, entirely on his own. He feels that's his place in our community. A watchdog of sorts. He's a former marine, so I suppose it makes sense. That training gets imprinted deeply. Wired into the brain. He's a protector. That's his calling. That's why he took the chosen name Osmund. It means, 'divine protector' in Old English."

Darger didn't need to look at Loshak to know what he was thinking. Giving new names to your followers was practically Cult Leader 101.

"Was the nudity imprinted as well, or is that less of a calling and more of a hobby?" Darger asked.

Curtis raised an eyebrow.

"Does it really make you so uncomfortable?"

Darger shrugged.

"Gun out. Dick out. Unkempt thatch of pubes." She sighed. "Call me old-fashioned, but I prefer a guy that leaves a little something to the imagination."

"How is it that we've come to find our true selves so obscene?" Curtis asked, shaking his head. "The idea that any part of the human body could be seen as inappropriate or vulgar is... absurd. It is part of us. It is who we are. Anyway, lest I get too philosophical..."

Darger wondered just how philosophical Curtis might get on the subject of Ozzy's junk but decided she didn't want to know.

"Suffice it to say that Ozzy's nudity is his choice," Curtis continued. "I did ask him about it once, and he said that most people would be put off by the gun alone, but he figures a naked man with a gun is, and I quote, 'whole different banana.'"

"From what I saw, 'banana' seems a bit generous," Darger said.

A wolfish grin spread over Curtis' mouth.

"But we're getting off-topic. You asked about whether we have a bar for acceptance. The answer is that we welcome people from all walks of life. Rich, poor, Ivy League-educated, high school dropouts, Catholics, Jews, Muslims, atheists."

"I see. I guess you didn't mention any of your poor dropouts before," Darger said.

"I'll admit to using some of our more illustrious members as paragons. Examples to hold up to the outside world. Not because I think they have more worth, but because I know how outsiders think. They think we're preying upon the weak, the meek, the lost. We've even been accused of brainwashing by some of our more unenlightened critics. That couldn't be further from the truth. These people aren't feeble or defenseless. These are free thinkers. Fighters. Brilliant minds. Talented creatives. And they're all fiercely independent, or they wouldn't be here. Our community represents the full spectrum of humanity."

Darger leaned back in her chair, twisting so she could see out the window overlooking the flower sorting room.

"Yeah? Because I kinda noticed that there's one particular type that makes up a lot of your... flock."

Curtis' eyelashes fluttered in a show of innocence.

"Oh? And what type would that be?"

"Young. Attractive. Female."

Curtis flashed his teeth, the grin from before returning.

"Are you sure you're not projecting?"

"Projecting?"

"Well, you're a young, attractive woman yourself."

Darger snorted and rolled her eyes.

"Ah. You're shy," Curtis said, an annoyingly smug look on his face. "Unexpected. I didn't mean to embarrass you."

"What makes you think I'm embarrassed?" Darger asked,

returning the smug smirk.

"Well, I want to be clear, I wasn't hitting on you before." Curtis spread his hands wide. "I'm just a believer in radical honesty."

"Are you now?"

"Yes. Does that frighten you?"

"Oh yeah. I'm absolutely terrified."

"You use sarcasm as a defense mechanism quite often, do you know that?"

"And you use rhetorical questions to keep people on the defensive. Preemptive strikes to assert control over conversations." Darger fluttered her eyelashes. "Do you know that?"

For a split second, Darger saw Curtis' mouth tense. She didn't think he liked how this discussion was playing out.

His eyes flicked over to Loshak.

"Agent Loshak," he said, his face serene again. "You've been awfully quiet."

"You mean I get a turn? Goody," Loshak said. "Why don't you practice some of that radical honesty, and tell us about the full moon celebration that went off the rails a few months ago."

"Ah." Curtis adopted a troubled-yet-thoughtful expression. "That was regrettable. A lapse in judgment on Puck's part. Unfortunately, not his last."

"Puck?"

"That was Stephen Mayhew's chosen name."

Loshak nodded.

"What did you mean when you said he had a lapse in judgment?"

"We don't normally allow outsiders to partake in some of

our more… arcane activities. We have many feasts and festivals in which the public are welcome, or special guests by invitation. The full moon feast is open to guests, for example, but they are supposed to leave before the midnight ritual, which is meant for initiates only. Puck, God bless him, allowed an outside guest into our sacred space. Dressed him in one of our costumes and brought him to the midnight ceremony. As I said… it was regrettable."

"Because an outsider saw one of your freaky little games?" Loshak asked.

Cocking his head to one side, Curtis clicked his tongue.

"'Freaky' is a rather pejorative term, don't you think?"

"We were told you chased a girl through the woods. Held her down and tore off her clothes," Darger said. "Sounds violent. And more than a little rape-y."

Curtis sighed.

"It's not real. It's nothing more than the same play-acting every child partakes in. Cops and Robbers or Cowboys and Indians, if you'll excuse the culturally insensitive reference. The sacrifice is only in a symbolic sense. Like what you heard in the Primal Scream shed. The screams are real. The pain behind them is real. But the external expression is essentially a performance." Curtis tapped his chest. "We never harm anyone here."

"The witness we spoke to said the girl in the sacrificial role wasn't a willing participant," Darger said.

"The tattoo artist, you mean." Curtis sniffed. "That's part of the ritual. Have you ever heard of LARPing?"

"What-ing?" Loshak asked.

"Live action role-play," Darger said.

"Ahh, see," Curtis said, folding his hands on his desk. "Agent Darger is familiar with it. It's similar to a more traditional role-playing game like Dungeons and Dragons, except it's played in real life. The players adopt characters, wear elaborate costumes, construct detailed back stories. It brings a sort of magic to it, to have everyone committed to this alternate reality. In some ways, our rituals are like a LARPing campaign, and most of us get very into our roles. Tansy's role was to play the Sacrifice, and the Sacrifice is most convincing if some of her fear is real. But we take consent very seriously here, and I assure you she was a willing participant."

Curtis stood.

"Have either of you read *The Golden Bough*?" Curtis asked, not bothering to wait for an answer. "So much of our modern-day culture and religion is based on ancient rituals that were absolutely pervasive across all of humanity. The fact that folklore from completely separate cultures has always shared so many themes is indicative of how concepts like sacrifice and resurrection are part of our DNA."

While Curtis talked, he meandered over to the door to the office. Darger had to crane her neck to keep her eyes on him.

"Creating these stories and myths has always been so central to mankind and civilization. It's an outlet for us. A type of therapy, if you will."

Curtis opened the door and thrust his head out.

"Tansy?"

A girl with curly blonde hair stopped trimming a handful of zinnias and turned to look at Curtis.

"Could I borrow you for a moment?"

She set down the flowers and came to the door.

"Do you remember the full moon celebration that went awry?" Curtis asked.

Tansy's cheeks went pink, and she smiled slyly.

"Of course."

"Were you harmed during the ritual?"

"I mean, I got a little scratched up running through the woods barefoot, but I barely noticed. I was having too much fun."

Darger couldn't help but think of her as a girl, even though she was clearly in her twenties or possibly older. It was something about the dress and the doe-eyed way she looked at Curtis. Children of the Golden Path had been an apt choice of names, Darger thought.

"Fun," Curtis said, glancing over to make sure Darger and Loshak had heard. "And were you coerced into performing in the ceremony in any way?"

The girl physically recoiled, frowning.

"No. I volunteered." She blinked at Darger. "Everyone wants to play the Sacrifice. It was an honor to be chosen. Some of the others were even jealous."

Darger knew the girl meant some of the other *women* were jealous. She doubted any of the men here would be eager to play the victim of a sacrifice.

Curtis nodded.

"It's a bit like getting to be 'it' when you play Hide and Seek, isn't it?"

The girl giggled.

"It's exactly like that!"

"Thank you, Tansy," Curtis said. "You can go back to work now.

The girl inclined her head before she turned to leave, a subtle bow, and Darger couldn't help but think of the dutiful servant of some Lord or Lady in medieval times. But they were all *equals* here. Curtis had said so himself.

Curtis closed the door, sliding back around to the chair behind his desk. When he was seated again, he crossed one leg over the other.

"Don't you remember what it was like to play those make-believe games as a child? To lose yourself in the fantasy? That's what we're trying to recreate in the rituals. That absolute surrender to the role. I think we shed a great many things from childhood unnecessarily, and we end up craving those things as adults. An outlet for feelings and urges deemed unacceptable by 'polite society,'" he said, making air quotes with his fingers.

Darger was growing tired of Curtis' little sermons.

"Let's talk about Stephen Mayhew."

"Very well. What would you like to know?"

"He was a… what do you call these people?" Darger gestured toward the windows looking out on the work area. "Your followers? Your flock? Your congregation?"

"I don't call them *my* anything," he said. "It's you who've decided I'm some sort of leader. I'm merely a vessel for universal truths. As for what I call 'these people.' I call them my family, because that's what they are. My brothers and sisters."

Darger resisted an urge to ask how many of his so-called sisters Curtis had slept with.

"So Stephen Mayhew was one of your brothers?" Darger asked. "I assume only the fully initiated get the shiny new name."

"He was."

"Did he live here?"

"For a time. We have a somewhat fluid group. Many of our brothers and sisters only come to visit. They have jobs and lives and other more traditional families. Some of our people live in the tents you saw in the warmer months. We make room where we can when the weather turns, but sometimes it's impossible to house everyone here in the sanctuary." Curtis made a vague gesture with his hand. "There's a trailer park outside of town. More recently, Stephen had rented a trailer there with a few of our other family members."

Darger stared at Curtis, hoping Loshak would sense what she was doing and would stay quiet as well. She wanted Curtis to squirm in the silence for a few seconds.

She counted to five before Curtis' curiosity kept him from remaining his cool, collected self.

"Is something wrong?" he asked.

"Well, I've been using the past tense this whole time when asking questions about Stephen, and you haven't corrected me. It's like you already knew he was dead."

CHAPTER 26

"Are you there?"

The girl's voice echoed funny as it traversed the tunnel to find Cora. It was sharp, a little strident, as if the speaker knew she had to make herself heard over some distance.

Goosebumps rippled over Cora's skin, a cold prickle assailing every pore. She tried to speak, to respond, but the words seemed to clamp her throat shut.

That detached female voice sounded down the shaft again, perhaps slightly weaker and thinner this time.

"Are you there?"

Cora's body trembled as she lifted her voice in response. Ribs quaking. Palms flushed with icy tendrils.

"Yeah. I'm here."

The voice wavered when it asked the follow-up question, going thick with emotion.

"Are... are you real?"

Cora fought back the urge to laugh as her mind immediately thought of what Chase would say in this moment, the most immature, inappropriate joke possible: *Real as a fart attack.*

"I'm real," she said, surprised to hear the smile in her voice now. "My name is Cora."

A long silence filled the space before the girl answered.

"I'm Lily."

Cora licked her lips. Her mind raced over the implications of another girl being down here, presumably stuck like she was, somewhere deeper in the tunnel. A pile of questions riffled through her brain like a deck of cards, so many of them.

"They trapped you here like me? In a cage?" she asked, wanting to confirm that first and foremost.

"Yeah. A dog crate, I think."

"How long have you been down here?"

The silence stretched out again.

"I don't know. What day is it?"

Cora thought about that for a second. The night had passed by now, she thought, though the night never really ended down here in the dark.

"Wednesday morning by now, I think."

Another pause, longer than before.

"No. Like, what date is it?"

"The 16th."

"I mean… what month?"

Cora gawked at the black nothing. Felt her eyes go wider and wider until they stung. Watched pink splotches form in her vision and flit across the void before her.

"It's June."

"Oh."

The girl fell quiet again for a few seconds before she repeated what Cora had told her.

"June."

Cora laced her fingers around those thin bars again. Braced herself for the answer to her question. Tension drew all the cords in her shoulders taut, made those slabs of muscle that formed her upper back stiff.

The darkness felt palpable now. Cool and thick around her, touching her everywhere, enveloping her.

"Guess it's been almost two months," Lily said, her voice sounding somewhat hollow now. "Feels like it's been longer than that. And shorter, too."

Cora didn't know what to say to that. Her face felt numb. Her fingers curled tighter around the bars that held her here.

"I remember Easter," Lily said. "Right before I got... Right before they brought me here, I mean. I remember eating Easter dinner with my parents earlier that day. My parents are religious like that a couple times a year, you know? My mom made brisket."

Cora took a second to process what she was hearing. Easter. That had been in early April, she thought... over two months ago. Just as Cora was about to reply, Lily shushed her.

"Did you hear something?" she whispered.

They both listened for a few seconds. Nothing.

"The sound travels funny here. Ricochets around, I think. Sometimes you can hear things from far away and then not hear something just next to you."

They were quiet again for another few breaths. Then Cora asked the question she didn't really want to ask.

"What do they... do to you?"

Lily sighed, a breathy sound that fluttered in the space between them.

"They get you out when they want you," Lily said. "And only when they want you."

Cora swallowed. Closed her eyes. Tried to push down the roaring of the blood in her ears.

Something clicked somewhere in the distance, and the sound shuddered down the tunnel. The reverberation almost seemed to shiver and swell in the air, like the wavering chime of a struck bell. The noise had been metallic and familiar, Cora realized. Someone closing a door? It was hard to be certain.

"Quiet now," Lily said, her voice almost a whisper now. "I think someone is coming."

The pitter-patter of footfalls gritted in the sand and echoed down the shaft of dirt.

CHAPTER 27

There was another long pause, but this time it was Curtis who had gone silent.

"Puck, er... Stephen is dead?" he asked, and to his credit, he seemed genuinely surprised. "You're certain?"

If it was an act, he was quite good at it. He'd even gone a little pale, if Darger wasn't mistaken.

"We assure you, Stephen Mayhew is quite dead."

Now Darger brought out the photos. Placed the glossy rectangles between them until the images of the emaciated body surrounded by trash occupied the surface of Curtis' desk.

"Oh my dear God," Curtis muttered, looking ill. "What happened to him?"

"We were hoping you could tell us."

"I don't... I've never seen..." He glanced up at Darger. "Why would you show these to me? These are horrible. Please take them away."

He shoved the photos back at Darger. She gathered them up and returned them to the manila folder in her bag.

When Curtis had recovered, he took a deep breath.

"I use the past tense because Stephen had left the family." He let his eyelids flutter closed. "Or rather he'd been *asked* to leave, to be completely forthright."

"Because of what happened at the full moon ritual?" Darger asked.

"No." Curtis frowned. "That was a minor offense, really. I had a lengthy discussion with Puck regarding his indiscretion,

160

but he ultimately hadn't caused any harm. He interrupted the ritual, of course. Broke the reality. But that was only spilled milk."

"So why did you ask him to leave?"

Curtis paused again. His eyes moved to Darger's bag, where she'd tucked the folder of photos. He was remembering what he'd seen in those pictures, she thought. Weighing whether to divulge private cult matters to two outsiders in the name of justice for a former member, perhaps. The grave images must have done their trick, because he didn't consider it for very long.

"We discovered he'd been bringing illicit substances into camp, and that is… strictly forbidden."

"What kind of substances?"

Curtis tapped his fingers against the desk.

"Crystal methamphetamine." Curtis sighed. "This is a judgment-free zone. I don't cast aspersions on drug users, but drugs tend to shut down the very senses required to make a true connection with others, which is a key component to what we do here."

Darger couldn't help but wonder if Curtis actually didn't like drugs because they competed with him for control of all of those minds.

"What about the moon juice?"

"Pardon?"

"We were told there was some kind of beverage with psilocybin in it at the full moon feast."

"Only enough for a microdose. More therapeutic than anything."

Darger crossed her arms.

"What our witness described sounded like more than a microdose."

"Well, he wasn't supposed to drink any. The ceremonial wine is for initiated members only. And they all know what to expect." Curtis sighed. "Puck's tattoo artist friend drank the wine without knowing what it was and came into the ritual without proper orientation. Even with the initiated, we discourage them from drinking the wine if it's their first time. That kind of experience coupled with a psychoactive substance, even a small amount, can have disastrous results for the unprepared. And the man's reaction was a perfect illustration of that."

"Who was Stephen close with?"

"You know, when we first started, everyone knew everyone. But as we've grown, I have to say that natural cliques and groups have developed. I worried about it at first. Reminded me of being in high school. But then I realized it's simple human nature. You gravitate to those you share a common bond with. A kinship. After all, you can't help when you feel that connection with someone, can you?"

Darger didn't like the way he stared into her eyes when he said this. Almost like he was trying to hypnotize her.

"Anyway, Stephen was part of a group who called themselves the degenerates."

"The degenerates?"

"I know it sounds harsh, but it was something they came up with themselves. They were all former addicts and alcoholics. That was their common bond. And I do think they helped each other through some things." Curtis' face tightened. "At least for a while."

Darger pulled the other photos from her bag.

"I have some more photos I need you to look at. I should warn you, they're… similar to what you saw before."

She laid out the morgue photos of John Doe One and Jane Doe One and Two.

"Do you recognize any of these people?"

The color drained from Curtis' face.

"My god. How many are there?"

"These three and Stephen. So four total."

Curtis' hand shook as he pointed first at the photo of Jane Doe One and then at Jane Doe Two.

"These two."

Darger sat up straighter.

"You know them?"

"If I saw these photographs out of context, I'd say no. But given that you found them with Stephen?" He let out a shaky sigh and then turned in his chair. "Here, I'll show you."

CHAPTER 28

Curtis swiveled in his chair and pulled a leather-bound book from one of the shelves behind him. It was thick and landed with a thud on the desk. When he flipped it open, Darger saw that the pages were filled with photographs. Various events and daily life around camp. Professional looking, too.

"Juniper is an award-winning photographer." Curtis winced. "But there I go bragging about my family again. Anyway, she puts together a book like this for the camp every year. A visual history."

Pages swished as he riffled through them, finally pausing on one halfway through the book. He spun it around and handed it to Darger.

In the photo, the sun shone down on a small group sitting together at a picnic table. Three women, two men. They had plates of food before them, and one of the women had flowers in her hair.

"That's Puck on the far left."

Darger was startled to see how normal Stephen Mayhew had looked not so long ago. He wasn't a particularly large man, but he also wasn't the gaunt skeleton they'd pulled from the garbage heap.

"The woman beside him with the marigolds in her hair is Trinity. That was on their joining day."

Trinity was of average height and build, looked to be in her late twenties, and had blonde hair and blue eyes. A dead match for Jane Doe One.

"Joining day?"

"The equivalent of a marriage here." His finger jabbed at another face. "That's Celestia sitting beside Trinity."

Celestia had a mop of curly red hair and an abundance of freckles dotting her skin. Not a match for Jane Doe Two, who'd had dark hair.

"And her?" Darger asked, pointing to the third woman.

She was small and dark-haired and wore a pair of oversized glasses with black frames.

"That's Amaranth," Curtis said, and she heard an emptiness in his voice now. "I think the two women you found are Trinity and Amaranth."

"How about this other fella," Loshak asked, knocking a knuckle against the second man in the photo. He lifted his eyes to look at Curtis. "You think he could be our other John Doe?"

"I don't think so. The John Doe's height is listed as 71 inches. That's what... five-feet-eleven?" Curtis shook his head. "Worm is quite short. No more than five-five or five-six, if that."

"Worm?" The name didn't have the same hippie-esque flare the rest of the cult names had.

Worm had an arm slung around Amaranth, and Darger thought the girl looked a little like she was recoiling from his touch. There was the slightest tinge of discomfort in her smile, like she'd realized a spider was crawling up her leg right as the photo was taken.

"But there's an easy enough way to know for sure," Curtis said. "Does your John Doe have a gold tooth?"

"No," Darger said, suddenly noticing a strange glare over the man's mouth in the photo.

"Well, Worm does. He's rather proud of it. Told quite a tale about how he'd lost the tooth in a fight with some Hell's Angels. Said he took three of them on and managed to steal one of their bikes, and all he had to give up was the one tooth."

Darger got out her phone.

"Do you mind if I take photos of this for our records?" she asked.

"Be my guest," Curtis said.

Darger snapped one shot of the full photograph and then close-ups of each individual face.

"When was the last time you saw those three," Darger asked, handing the book back. "Puck, Trinity, and Amaranth?"

Curtis closed his eyes.

"The incident with the drugs was just after the Spring equinox. So it would have been the last week of March. Puck was asked to leave immediately. When he left, Trinity went with him. Given that they were joined, it wasn't wholly unexpected. Amaranth stayed on a bit longer, but she was very close to Trinity. They were practically inseparable. Ultimately, she decided to leave as well. She was gone perhaps a week later."

Darger made note of the dates.

"What about Worm and Celestia?" Loshak asked. "Can we talk to them?"

"Celestia is in India on a spiritual retreat," Curtis explained. "The thing with Puck and the drugs created quite a fuss around here. A rift in the family, if you will. We thought it was best she get some distance. I can provide you information on how to get in touch with her. As far as I know, she hasn't spoken with any of them since their departure, but I suppose it's always possible she'd been in contact with them without my knowing."

Curtis scribbled a phone number and brief instructions on a piece of paper and passed it to Darger.

"Just one request?"

"Yes?"

"Could you wait a few hours before you call her? I'd like her to hear the news from me, if possible." Curtis brushed a lock of Jesus hair from his face. "I really think the person you should talk to is Worm, though."

"Is he around?" Loshak asked.

"Well, I think there's been a misunderstanding," Curtis said. "Worm wasn't a member of our family."

"No?"

Curtis folded his hands in front of him.

"Worm did odd jobs for us. Contract work. Had some carpentry skills. And he had a truck, which was helpful for bringing in manure and compost for the fields and the greenhouse."

"Did?" Darger asked. "As in past tense?"

Curtis swallowed and stared up at the ceiling.

"When we confronted Stephen about the meth, he admitted that he'd gotten it from Worm. Worm had been warned about such things once before. He hadn't brought in illegal drugs before, at least not to my knowledge. But he'd been caught sneaking alcohol and cigarettes in for people. As he wasn't actually a member, he was banned outright. Stephen was told that if he could prove himself contrite and enter a rehab program to get clean, we'd discuss welcoming him back. But I don't think he was interested."

Curtis let out a breath that caused his shoulders to deflate.

"They're really dead? All of them?"

Darger nodded once.

"I'm sorry."

Tears collected at the corners of Curtis' eyes.

"I don't know how I'm going to break the news."

Darger waited a few moments for Curtis to collect himself before asking her next question.

"So does this guy have a name aside from Worm?"

"I'm sure he did, but I didn't know it."

"It didn't strike you as odd that he called himself Worm?" Darger knew it was a stupid question, given the circumstances. Everyone here called themselves by a new made-up name. What was one more?

"Sometimes people have troubled pasts. It's not in my nature or my interest to pry where they don't want me to. Especially with non-family members."

"What if it meant he was hiding something?" Darger said. "He could have been a criminal with a violent past."

Curtis narrowed his eyes.

"Do you not believe that people can change?"

"No," Darger said flatly. "People changing? I'll believe that one when I see it."

"Well, I suppose we have a difference of opinion then." Curtis rubbed a callused hand over his mouth. "I got the impression he was a bit of a drifter. He seemed intrigued by what we've built here. He came to many of our functions. But he always stayed on the fringes. I'm not sure I had any conversations with him directly, now that I think about it."

Curtis' eyes brightened.

"You know, if you want to know more about Worm, Sandy

is the one you should talk to."

"Sandy?"

"She's our master gardener. She's the one who keeps all of this going. It was her idea to turn this place into a flower farm."

"OK, but before we do that, can you tell us the real names of Trinity and Amaranth? I assume you knew that, at least."

"Of course."

Curtis opened a drawer and pulled out a Macbook Pro. He propped the screen upright and turned it on.

"We have a database with member information. Emergency contacts and the like. This should only take a moment." He clicked a few buttons. "Here we are. Stephen's contact was an aunt. Rosemary Mayhew."

"We've been in touch with her already."

"OK. Let's see. Trinity's birth name was Courtney Maroni. Her contact is a sister. She lives in Idaho, if I recall correctly. They weren't close. Trinity had a troubled background. Broken family. Abusive stepfather. But here's her sister's phone number in any case," he said, grabbing a small pad of paper and scribbling the digits. "Then we have Amaranth, formerly Bailey Harmon."

When he finished copying down Amaranth's information, he handed Darger the paper.

"This is a local number," Darger said, recognizing the area code.

"Yes, she grew up here in Pennsylvania. One of the suburbs outside of Philadelphia, if I recall correctly." Curtis tapped the pen against his palm. "Her parents came to one of our festivals, I think."

"You don't discourage them from seeing their family of

origin?"

"Of course not. Not if they're healthy relationships. But a great many families are not. They're toxic," Curtis said. "Society acts like family should always get a pass, but I think that's a terrible message. That we should accept abuse from the very people who should give us unconditional love? Absurd."

Darger's mind puzzled over the fourth body for a moment — another dead male, definitely not Worm.

"You would have mentioned if anyone else had gone missing from your... family... recently?" she said. "It just seems odd that three of our four bodies came from here."

"Given what you've told me? Of course I would have said something if that were the case. But no one has gone 'missing,' and I can't think of anyone I know who matches your John Doe."

Darger glanced over at Loshak, who gave a slight nod.

"Let's go see what Sandy can tell us about Worm."

CHAPTER 29

He hurried through the tunnel. Felt his feet tilt that little bit deeper with every step.

Multiple copies of his shadow fluttered around him, a version of him cast from every single light bulb strung up along the wall. The bulbs buzzed endlessly, faint and high-pitched. The sound reminded him of the deer flies that used to swarm him in the summers as a kid, clusters of them orbiting his head and matting themselves in his hair.

He was late. Again. Instinctively his hand sought the left hip pocket of his cargo pants, fingers wriggling into the opening, seeking the smooth plastic shell of his phone to check the time.

No phone there, of course. Cowboy would never allow that.

Instead, he had the walkie talkie in the opposite pocket. He fingered the button just to hear it crackle and click. He'd never actually used the thing. It was for emergencies only.

Anyway, if he hurried, maybe no one would know how late he was. So long as it never got back to Cowboy...

He picked up the pace again. Weaving around the curves. Turned sideways to sidle around some support beams. Instinctively tongued the back of his front teeth, something of a habit.

The place where the tunnels transitioned to the caves rushed toward him. The dirt walls sheared off abruptly up ahead, that rocky mouth opened wide, ready to devour him once again.

The sand crunched under the tread of his work boots one second, and then he'd transitioned to the stony floor of the caves, and the sound changed to a dull clap that rang out against the rock walls.

He always felt a shred of relief upon reaching the natural rock. Never quite trusted the engineering that went into Cowboy's tunnels the way he did mother nature.

Still a long way to go, though. He fished his water bottle out of the cargo pocket of his pants. Tipped it to his mouth. Sipped.

Christ, he hoped no one else was down there yet. The explosives guy, especially. Total prick, that one. Always grinning that sadistic smile. Wheezing out laughs at everyone else's suffering. The little fucker would positively delight in letting Cowboy know about his tardiness. Tattling. Snitching. Anyway, the prick usually didn't work the early shift, so maybe there was hope. Hell, he wouldn't even think about working the early shift himself if the pay wasn't so damn good.

Climb down into a hole to rove around under the ground and dig and blast and excavate first thing in the morning, sometimes into the middle of the night? Hell no.

For $1,500 a week, though? Hell yeah.

He was a little over halfway toward the $44,000 he needed to buy that used 2005 Dodge Viper from a dealership in Chicago. His dream car dating all the way back to his high school days. Convertible. Copperhead orange. Only 21,000 miles on it, despite its age. Practically mint condition.

And once he had it? Well, Rhonda would have no choice but to take him back, would she?

As he rounded another bend in the cave, his vision started to get hazy. Clouds seemed to spread from the glowing light bulbs hung up above him like gauzy halos, but he blinked a few times, took another drink of water, and it went away.

A little too much Jim Beam last night, methinks. He chuckled softly to himself at the thought, listened to the whispery sound shimmy around as it ricocheted off the walls. Knowing he had to work another shift on a short turnaround, he'd slept in the compound last night — the small cluster of cots Cowboy called "the barracks." He'd chugged Jim Beam to kill the time, to slow down his higher brain, perhaps to knock himself out more or less. *Well, whatever. You work for a crazy weirdo, and you spend eight to fourteen hours a day underground, buddy. Gotta blow off some steam somehow. Hell, taking a few toots of bourbon is better than going on a killing spree, ain't it? OK then. So maybe drinking a lot of bourbon ain't so bad, either.*

Another laugh wheezed out of him. Sizzled between his teeth. Puffed out of his nostrils.

The air grew colder around him as he worked his way deeper into the caves. The chill slowly saturated his arms the way it always did, gripped the meat of his triceps and spread from there.

His eyes traced along the wire running from light to light along the top edge of the cave as he walked. The bulbs flickered faintly, brightening and darkening subtly like a candle's flame, something you only noticed if you were paying attention. He wondered, not for the first time, how long this project had been in the works before he got here. Months? Years?

Some people have too much damn money.

The cave opened up into a vast chamber then, growing wider and taller at the same time like he'd stepped into a living room with a high ceiling. Moss climbed the walls in this portion of the caverns. Glistening green.

The lights only reached part of the way up, so the ceiling of the chamber was swathed in shadows. Silhouettes of stalactites hung there like giant bats. That used to give him the creeps when he first started, but now the open air of the cavern always felt like a relief. He couldn't remember when that change had occurred, but he was glad for it.

Moving to a small rack along the wall, he pulled a hooded sweatshirt off a hook. Slid it over his neck and shoulders. It was cold against his torso, made his skin tighten at its chilly touch, but his body heat went to work on it right away, softening the cold and slowly flipping it to warmth.

Multiple tunnel mouths gaped on the far wall, giving several choices for leaving this big chamber. He walked that way, chose the second from the left. Ducked into the smaller opening and crouch-walked into the shadows there.

This one was a bitch.

As the cave winnowed down to its narrowest stretch, he had to get on hands and knees and then onto his belly. Feeling that tube of rock squeeze around his ribcage always made his skin crawl.

He got down, felt the cold earth immediately transmit its chill through the fabric of the sweatshirt, through his skin, instantly getting at the meat of him. He wormed forward. Slithered over the icy rock.

He could feel the walkie talkie in his pocket as he squirmed, his pants pulled taut around it, its hard edges digging into his hip and thigh. He blinked hard as the rock seemed to squeeze around his back, constrict around his shoulders. Flinched at its touch.

Too damn tight.

He fixed his gaze on the small circle of light ahead, that narrow opening to freedom, and that made him feel better. For a second the light disappeared as he wriggled down a dip — a moment of darkness that always took his breath away — but then it bobbed back into view as he breasted the next rise.

When the tunnel opened up again, he got to his hands and knees to crawl again. Soon, he could stand once more.

He always felt warmer and lighter once he'd exited that tight gap. Like he'd left some kind of baggage behind. Squeezed away some of life's heaviness to carry on lighter than he'd been before. He'd traversed the darkest part of the passage, and now he moved deeper into the stillness.

Almost there.

Today's dig site had undergone blasts recently, so he'd mostly be clearing away debris into one of the side chambers, a task he often worked solo, especially since so many of the other workers had quit in the past few months. He didn't mind it.

The stillness was the one thing he liked about working underground. Things seemed alright when he was down here alone. Nothing in his head. The world above ground stressed him out, made him feel trapped. It was like all the layers of rock and dirt between him and the outside world somehow blocked that feeling out and made the real world meaningless for a bit. He found a peace in it, a sense of intense freedom. Funny how that worked — some sections of the tunnels were about as spacious as a coffin, and yet this was where he felt free.

Once again his eyes traced along the string of lights hung along the right-hand side of the tunnel. He always thought that it looked like an oversized string of Christmas lights — the spacing and proportions adjusted, of course, as though he were made miniature when he stepped underground and the bulbs were still full size.

His eyelids fluttered. The lights suddenly seemed to swirl before him, the whole string of them tilting impossibly upward.

He stopped. Closed his eyes.

The gritty backbeat of his footsteps cut off beneath him. The silence stretched out.

The usual stillness of the cave persisted around him, but his world still tilted and lurched inside, even with his eyes closed. Wooziness roiled in his head.

Instinctively, he flexed his hands. Found them numb, a little weak. He balled his fingers into fists, but he couldn't hold them that way for long.

Jesus. Maybe way too much Jim Beam, but…

He didn't actually let the thought form all the way, didn't let the fear that this was something more, something worse, congeal into a concrete fear in his head. Because he'd read a book in school once that talked about how miners used to take canaries down into mines with them in the old days, because sometimes digging underground could unleash pockets of toxic gas. But Cowboy had always assured them that the air down here was clean, that they tested it regularly. So he made sure those ideas stayed abstract, distant.

He took a step. Felt his legs wobble underneath him, those usually sturdy limbs gone rubbery in this moment.

Right away he squatted down. Didn't want to fall in here and brain himself on a jagged piece of stone.

He chugged water. Put his head between his knees and

breathed. Eyes closed. Mind blank. He focused only on the wind filtering in and out of him.

Probably just dehydrated. He took another big drink of water. Felt the cool of it touch his tongue and tumble down the drain of his neck. That emptied the bottle. He wished he'd grabbed another one from the mini-fridge in the barracks.

In any case, his mind seemed to be steadying.

He opened his eyes. Blinked a few times.

The world remained steady before him. Constant. Reliable. Solid as the stone it was.

He stood up, and his legs, too, felt stronger. He took two steps forward. Slowly. Carefully. So far so good.

He stabbed his tongue into the back of his front teeth again. They felt cool to the touch.

And then the lights snapped off around him.

The cave plunged into darkness.

CHAPTER 30

They followed Curtis out of the office and out through the flower processing room. Darger had to shield her eyes from the sun when they emerged from the barn.

Their shoes crunched over the gravel path that led to the entrance of the nearest greenhouse. A fan came on as soon as Curtis opened the door, some automatic mechanism that kept the climate of the greenhouse constant.

The air was heavy inside and smelled of the forest, leafy and crisp and green.

Just inside the door, Curtis stopped.

"Could you wait here for a moment?"

"Sure," Darger said.

She and Loshak watched Curtis zig-zag around rows of tables holding trays of plants in various stages of growth. Some were only seedlings, others were bursting with flowers.

There were three women at the far end of the greenhouse, transplanting starts into larger pots. They were just as quick and efficient at their work as the people in the flower packing area. This was obviously a task they'd done many times before.

The one Curtis pulled aside was a squat older woman with leathery brown skin from years spent under the sun. Unlike most of the women in the camp, who seemed to favor hippie-ish garb, this one wore a chambray work shirt and denim cut-offs.

Curtis leaned close and whispered something in the woman's ear, then pointed at where Darger and Loshak hovered near the door. The woman nodded.

"Sandy will be with you in one moment," Curtis said when he'd returned to them. "I've instructed her to answer any questions you may have about Worm."

Darger wondered if that meant that she was under specific instructions to *not* answer questions about anything else.

"And again, if you could leave out anything regarding the passing of Puck and the others? The loss of three of our members is going to hit the family hard, and I'd like to be the one to deliver the news."

Always the need for control, Darger thought. She imagined Curtis hurrying back to his office to start composing whatever sermon or eulogy he'd deliver to his "family." Then she felt a little guilty. Surely even charismatic cult leaders felt grief.

"We'll try not to mention it," she said.

"Thank you." He reached for something in one of his pockets and handed Darger a business card. "And in case we don't speak again before you leave, here's a card with an email and phone number where I can be reached, should you have any further questions."

"We appreciate that," Darger said, making a show of passing the card off to Loshak, who tucked it in his jacket with a smirk only she saw.

"I can't say it's been a pleasure, given the news," Curtis said, shaking each of their hands. "But I do hope we meet again."

He said that last part as he stared into Darger's eyes, and she couldn't break the eye contact fast enough. She waited until he'd left the greenhouse before she allowed herself to fully relax.

"This might be our chance to inquire about the soil details,"

Loshak said, keeping his voice low. "But we'll have to tread lightly."

Darger nodded but couldn't say anything because Sandy was approaching.

She took off a pair of work gloves and shoved them down into one of the back pockets of her shorts.

"I'd offer to shake your hand, but I've been up to my elbows in compost all morning," she said. "I'm sparing you, trust me."

They introduced themselves, and then Darger dove in.

"Curtis told us you could tell us about Worm."

"Ah yes. Worm was my jack of all trades." Sandy winced. "I expect Curtis probably told you about the drugs? A shame about that. We first hooked up with Worm because we needed someone to operate a backhoe when we were putting in some irrigation lines. Hired him for that job, and it turned out he was a fairly handy guy in a lot of ways."

"Did you know his real name?"

"Nope. Sorry." Sandy crossed her arms. "He's kind of a squirrelly guy, actually. Maybe that shoulda been his name instead. Squirrel."

She let out a chuckle that sounded forced to Darger's ears.

"What about where he was from?"

"Afraid I don't know that either," Sandy said with a shrug. "All told, Worm was only really around for eight months or so. I wish I could tell you more, but Curtis was pretty clear about cutting ties with him after the whole debacle."

Sandy was smiley and polite, but Darger got a sense that she was holding back. And the closed body language — crossed arms, torso angled slightly away — told her that Sandy might be too defensive to give them anything.

Darger was still considering how she might get Sandy to open up when Loshak cleared his throat and spoke.

"So how did you pay him, if you didn't know his name?"

Sandy froze, her eyes on the ground.

"If he was an employee, you'd need a W-2 on file for tax purposes," Loshak went on. "Even if he was an independent contractor, he'd need a 1099. Both would require a legal name, an address, and a social security number."

She'd been trying to figure out a way to ease Sandy out of her defensive shell, but she supposed Loshak's method of attempting to crack her open like an egg might also work.

When Sandy remained dumbstruck, Loshak filled it in.

"You were paying him under the table."

"It was my idea," Sandy blurted. "Curtis didn't know. No one else did."

"Oh, I think Curtis knew." Loshak put his hands on his hips and widened his stance. "Otherwise he would have gone looking for the paperwork so he could give us Worm's name. But he knew there wasn't any paperwork on Worm, so he brought us over to talk to you."

Sandy's short grey-blonde hair fluttered as she shook her head from side to side.

"But it's my fault. I'm telling you, Curtis… he wants everything done by the books. I'm the one who paid Worm in cash. It was my choice. My decision. If anyone has to go down for this, it's on me."

"Look, we're not interested in any of that," Loshak said. "We only want to know more about Worm."

Sandy swallowed.

"What do you want to know?

"Anything and everything you can tell us about this guy. You really didn't know his real name? Not even a first name?"

"No. I swear it."

Loshak nodded.

"Did Worm have any physical features that stood out? Tattoos? Birthmarks?"

Sandy stretched her mouth into an exaggerated grin and pointed at her teeth.

"Has a gold tooth, right up front."

"We got that. What else?"

"I don't remember any birthmarks. He's a real short guy. I'm 5'2", and I don't think he was more than an inch taller than me," Sandy said.

"What about the type of vehicle he drove? Curtis mentioned him hauling material for you."

"A Toyota Tundra. Black." The words seemed to tumble out of Sandy's mouth in a desperate cascade. "Newer, but not brand new. Like the last four or five years or so."

"Did he ever say where he lived?"

"No," Sandy said. "But he wasn't too far from here, because he could usually show up within an hour of me asking for help. And one time he said he was part owner of a cattle ranch. But I don't know if that was true."

"Why?"

"I got the sense that a lot of what Worm said was a story he was making up about himself. I'd say he was lying, but I think he kind of believed it a little bit. Like a kid playing make-believe who eventually starts thinking it's real. He was always claiming to have done this or that. It was like if you brought any old subject up, he couldn't resist claiming to be some kind of expert

182

on the topic." Sandy picked at the dirt caked under her fingernails. "Claimed to know Tai Chi and be a black belt in Jeet Kune Do."

"Never heard of it."

"It's the martial art philosophy created by Bruce Lee. The thing is, I dated a gal for years who was a Tai Chi instructor, and the stuff I saw Worm doing wasn't like any Tai Chi I've ever seen. I don't like to throw around accusations about things that are none of my business, but I think he was faking it."

Sandy stuck her hands in the pockets of her shorts.

"And there was more. We have a guy here, Thorn. He studied Shaolin Kung Fu in China. So Worm was always razzing him. Saying that Jeet Kune Do is superior to Kung Fu. That even the master Bruce Lee recognized the limitations of practicing set forms over practical fighting skills. And it wasn't like a one-time thing. Every time Worm saw Thorn, it was like he couldn't resist bringing it up. So one day, Thorn suggested they have an exhibition match. Just for fun, you know? So we made an event out of it. Scrounged up some gym mats and cleared a space in the flower sorting barn. Lotus was a referee. And they start the match and go at each other, and Thorn is, well... quite frankly he was kicking Worm's ass. It was kind of pathetic. Just like the Tai Chi thing, I suspect the Jeet Kune Do was all bull. He didn't know anything. And I think Worm knew everyone was starting to realize he was full of it. And he panicked. I swear I could see the switch flip in his head. That moment he said to himself, 'Oh no... I'm being made to look a fool.' So he tapped out. Said it out loud. 'I submit.' Thorn dropped his guard. Put his hands together to bow, and Worm sucker-punched him. Cold-cocked him right in the face. Busted his nose. Blood everywhere. Made a real scene. I mean, this was supposed to be for fun. And then he tried to claim that this was a method in Jeet Kune Do called The Fakeout. A legitimate tactic for beating an opponent since Jeet Kune Do is all about real-world combat."

"Sounds kind of sociopathic," Loshak said.

Sandy made a face.

"I don't know about that. Though I suppose I had kind of a soft spot for Worm on account of how he reminded me of my boy. Brian. Died of an overdose eight years ago. Had a wild streak, that one. But he meant well."

"So he was prone to exaggeration," Loshak said. "What else?"

"Well, he was real shy around the women. I was in the bathhouse once when he came in. He was just giggling up a storm. Blushing and tittering like a schoolgirl. Most guys try to play it cool, but he was like... well, a little kid."

Sandy smiled suddenly.

"Real sweet tooth, too. We grow everything we eat, so it tends to be pretty rustic. Low sugar. We have bees, so we get honey, but Curtis encourages a well-balanced diet. Vegetarian and no processed shit— er, stuff. Worm always had sugar on him. Cookies or candy bars. He'd bring me treats, seeing as how I don't get off the compound much. He really seemed to like those little elf cookies."

"Elf cookies?"

"The Keebler ones with the chocolate filling? He always seemed to have a package of those in his truck."

"And you haven't seen him or had contact with him since he was banned from the camp?" Darger asked.

"No ma'am." Sandy shook her head. "I do have a phone number, but I have to tell you, he used burners."

"Did he say why?"

"He kind of implied that he did covert work for some government outfit on more than one occasion. Something about excavation work, I think. Said, 'You never know who might be listening.' And something about how he had to keep a low profile so as to not blow his cover."

Darger raised her eyebrows.

"Did you believe that?"

"Heck no. No offense to the guy, but like I said, he's squirrelly as hell. And frankly not very smart. Like the bout with Thorn. We all saw what he did. I don't know how he could think he'd get away with it. The drugs, too. He didn't cover his tracks at all. Once we found out there was meth in camp, it wasn't hard to figure out where it came from. Guy has impulse control problems, is what I'd say," Sandy said. "That's how the counselors always put it when I'd get called in for the trouble Brian was stirring up at school, anyway."

She led them over to a desk situated in one corner of the greenhouse. There was a small organizer next to a landline telephone. Sandy flipped through the pages and pulled out a loose scrap of paper.

"This is the last number I had for him, but like I said, this one's a good two, three months old. And he'd give me a new one about once a month or so."

The interview was winding down, but they hadn't had a chance to do any digging on the matter of the soil. Darger knew she'd have to be careful, but Loshak wasn't the only one who could be clever.

Darger turned and let her gaze wander over the rows of plants.

"My mom is an avid gardener," Darger said. "Always tinkering with her bed of annuals. Do you have any secrets I could pass on? A particular soil blend?"

It was mostly a lie. Her mother sometimes planted a few pansies or petunias in a pot on her deck, but to call her an 'avid gardener' was a Worm-level fabrication.

"Where's she located," Sandy asked. "Your mother?"

Darger wondered if Sandy was about to call her bluff.

"Outside of Denver."

"Ah… well, you know the soil in each place is a unique beast. I don't know much about that area. If you live in a place with naturally good soil, that's always a bonus. That's what we've got here. Fabulous dirt, really. We don't do much to it other than amend with a bit of compost."

"So you don't… truck in a special soil or anything like that?" Darger asked.

"Gosh no. I mean, if you're a home gardener that might be feasible. Doing raised beds and the like. But I'm a big proponent of sustainability. Permaculture. Crop rotation. And that means that an organic flower farm on a scale like this almost has to be done in-ground with what the good Lord gave us. And a bit of help from mother nature, of course." Sandy gestured to the rows and rows of pots. "We do all our starts in a soil-less mix. One part peat moss, one part vermiculite. Then we'll add some amendments as we go, depending on the particular plant. Compost, kelp meal, limestone."

Darger peeked over at Loshak. He gave a minute shrug. Another dead end on the soil angle.

"Well, we appreciate your help," Loshak said.

They thanked Sandy, and then she and Loshak headed out for the long walk back to the car.

CHAPTER 31

His wide eyes stared into the black nothingness. He blinked a few times. Realized he couldn't tell the difference between blinking and not.

The darkness was complete. Overwhelming. Awe-inspiring in a terrible way.

He pulled out the walkie talkie. Fingered the button. Spoke into it.

"Lights just went out down here. Over."

His voice sounded calmer than he felt. He was thankful for that.

He stared at the blackness in front of his face where he knew the little device must be hovering, clutched in his fingers.

No response. Shit. Where was everybody?

His breath hitched in his throat. Sounded louder now in his ears. Spilling out of his mouth. Rapid and shallow. Panting like a St. Bernard.

He tried the walkie again. His voice cracked this time.

"Anyone there? Got a, uh, minor situation down here."

Nothing.

Nothing.

Nothing.

Shit. He needed to stay calm.

He shoved the walkie back into his pocket and squatted down like before. Ran his fingers along the smooth rock floor of the cave. Felt its cold leach into his skin right away. Even so, he placed both palms flat against the earth.

Getting low made him feel more in control, for some reason. Touching the rock with his hands helped even more. Reminded him that he was tethered to the solid ground, that he himself was solid.

Had someone turned off the lights intentionally? It seemed unlikely. Could the power be out? Maybe. But there were supposed to be automatic generator backups. He supposed the cause didn't matter right now. Getting back to the light switches did. Or just getting the hell out of here altogether. That sounded better to him.

Still, the blackness devoured all form in the cave. Sucked reality into its hole.

He closed his eyes. Thought it was better, somehow, to not stare into the void.

The darkness underground was more total than any he had ever witnessed before. He sensed that it would unstitch the seams of reality if he let it. Leave only a dark hollow where the world used to be. A black hole swallowing the universe.

Empty space. Worse. Nothingness.

His heartbeat thudded in his ears. That crooked muscle banging away in his chest. Squishing hot blood all through him.

He remembered to take a deep breath, and his chest shuddered. Ribcage fluttering like raven wings. After a few more deep breaths, it got better.

With the first wave of panic receding, he detached one hand from the floor. Fumbled it along his belt to find the flashlight there. It was a small LED thing, hardly bigger than a cigar, but bright as hell.

He found the narrow tube. Lifted it. Aimed it at the dark in front of him like a loaded gun and clicked the button.

Nothing.

He clicked it again. The tiny percussive sound pierced the stillness.

But the light didn't come on.

Jesus fuck.

These LED bulbs lasted years, so it couldn't have burned out. Maybe the batteries?

He shook his head as though trying to shake the fresh wave of panic away. And a thought hit him.

Maybe the lights were like a strand of Christmas lights wired in a series. If one burned out, the whole strand went dead. And maybe the outage hadn't affected one of the separate strings of lights behind him.

He shuffled to turn himself around. Face the other way.

The black was just as endless that way. Just as impossible, impenetrable, utterly complete.

He stuck a hand out. Needed to feel the solidness of the wall to reorient himself.

But his hand flailed at the nothing. Fingers raking empty space. There was no rock wall next to him. Nothing but the cool stale air.

His heart clambered up into his neck. Perched itself there all aflutter like a hovering bat beating its wings.

He spun to the left. Finally his hand found the rock wall. Verified it was still there. But it wasn't where he'd expected it. More of an obtuse angle than the perpendicular one he'd expected, and he realized that he'd already lost track of which way he was facing. He didn't know which wall this was.

How many times had he turned searching for the wall? A full 360 degrees? More? Less?

The darkness made it impossible to be sure.

Christ.

He swallowed hard. Heard his throat clack. Cold sweat beaded along his hairline, and he mopped at it with the sleeve of his sweatshirt.

He stood then. Stumbled forward a few steps. Then reversed himself and shuffled that way, the soles of his boots scuffing against the rock floor.

This was the way back, wasn't it? Back to that narrow passage.

He imagined the rocks squeezing his shoulders again, cold stone snugging tight around his ribcage. There'd be no circle of light to crawl toward this time. Nothing to reassure him. Only that infinite black sea sprawling in all directions.

If this was even the right way. *Goddamn it.*

The wooziness touched off in his skull again. Swirled around and around and around in that bone bowl where his brain sat.

He sat down. Plopped flat on his ass. Tried to slow his breathing which had crept back up into that canine pant. He focused. Wrestled with his quivering chest for control of his lungs.

But it was too late for all of that.

The black world started spinning around him. Whooshing noises filled his ears like flies swooping everywhere around him, like a fan blade spinning in his skull.

He grasped after the walkie talkie again. Failed to get his fingers into his pocket. They kept sliding away from the open flap, missing the mark. Motor skills all clumsy and inarticulate like he was drunk.

Breath hissed out of him. Hot on the back of his front teeth. He was unconscious before his head hit down on the rock floor.

CHAPTER 32

Darger and Loshak retrieved their phones from Naked Ozzy and headed back down the winding dirt drive, but it was still over ten minutes before Darger could get a strong enough signal to call Detective Ambrose.

"According to Curtis, Stephen Mayhew got booted from the Children of the Golden Path at the end of March after they caught him dealing meth. And when he left, two female members went with him." Darger checked the names Curtis had given her. "He identified Jane Doe One as Courtney Maroni and Jane Doe Two as Bailey Harmon and gave us emergency contact numbers for them. I'll text them over when we hang up."

"What about John Doe One?" Ambrose asked.

"Curtis claimed not to know him. But he did suggest we talk to someone named Worm." Darger sighed. "The only problem is that he was the one supplying Stephen Mayhew with drugs, and no one's seen him around since then."

"Still, two more vics identified, and a new lead. Not bad for a day's work," Ambrose said, and Darger could hear the relief in his voice. "What kind of vibe did you get there? You think The Children had something to do with all this?"

"Not sure. If we can tie all the victims to this group, it'd be too significant to downplay, but I think it could get more complicated as we continue the investigation."

"Well, I'll have someone run through our database and see if they can find anyone that's used the name 'Worm' as an alias in the past," Ambrose said. "Worst case scenario, we have to go door to door for every Toyota Tundra owner in the state."

"Let's hope it doesn't come to that." Darger pinched the bridge of her nose. "Did you get anything from Stephen Mayhew's aunt?"

"Not much. They had a falling out some years ago. I guess he had a fairly rocky childhood. Dad ran off early on. Mom shacked up with various nefarious characters who didn't always treat Stephen or her very well. She went to jail for a while for passing bad checks, and Stephen ended up living with the aunt for a year or two in high school. So she said she felt some closeness to him. A motherly affection, she called it." Ambrose sighed. "But I guess a few years back, when he was heavy into drugs, he came around once and stole some stuff from her. She told him flat out that if she saw him come around again, she'd call the cops. Hadn't seen him much since then. She did say he left a note about nine months ago on her door. Apologizing for the theft and some other things. Said he'd found a new purpose, etcetera, etcetera. Mentioned the Children of the Golden Path. She was pretty upset that he died before they could formally bury the hatchet."

Darger watched the greenery on the sides of the road whiz past in a blur — a mess of leaves and stalks and branches all woven together tightly on this rural stretch.

"Did she know anyone else from the cult? Or any other friends of his?"

"The best she could offer was a guy down the street Stephen was friendly with when he was a teenager, but the guy moved down south five years ago. He's a band teacher in Kentucky now, and as far as the aunt knew, he and Stephen haven't been in contact for years. Anyway, I'll give you a call back if we make any progress with any of this."

Darger thanked him and hung up. After texting the contact information for Bailey Harmon and Courtney Maroni to Detective Ambrose, she tucked her phone away and shifted in her seat so that she was angled more toward Loshak.

"What do you think?" she asked. "Do the Children of the Golden Path have something to do with all this?"

"It's an awfully big convenience that at least three of our four victims came from there," Loshak said. "And I'm not put at ease by the fact that the two living people making up the little clique — Worm and Celestia — are notably absent."

Darger remembered the way the cult leader had blanched when she'd told him Stephen Mayhew was dead.

"And what about Curtis? Was it all an act?"

Loshak adjusted his grip on the steering wheel and shrugged.

"The guy practically told us himself that he's an actor. All that stuff about role-playing during their rituals."

"He did seem to recover from the shock fairly quickly," Darger said. "But I expected more secrecy."

Loshak made a dismissive grunt.

"It's all part of the grift. 'Look how open I'm being. I'm a free spirit. I have nothing to hide.' All things considered, we only saw a small part of the camp. Only talked face-to-face with a handful of their members. Who knows what they could be hiding?"

Darger nodded.

"I don't think he liked that we saw the Primal Scream shed." She recalled the tightness in his facial expressions. A wariness in his eyes. "He was all smiles on the outside, but I sensed some tension underneath."

"Oh yeah," Loshak said, chuckling. "I think it pissed him off that he didn't have absolute control over what we saw of the camp and how we saw it, start to finish."

They passed a billboard for a restaurant offering "American fare in a historic stagecoach stop and inn from the 1750s!" at the next exit.

"What do you say we stop off for some vittles?"

"I never say no to vittles," Darger said.

Loshak grinned as he turned his blinker on and took the next exit.

"And I'm paying, seeing as you won our little wager fair and square."

"You're quite chipper for a guy who just lost a bet," Darger said, squinting over at her partner.

"I may have lost the bet on Curtis' hair, but I was dead right about his reaction to you. He was positively smitten."

Darger scoffed.

"Only because he saw me as a perfect addition to his little collection." Darger attempted to mimic the cult leader. "'Are you sure you're not projecting? Oh, you're shy. Unexpected.' What a douchebag."

Loshak chuckled.

"Is that all it takes to win people over?" Darger asked. "Compliments and a vague suggestion that they're 'understood?'"

"At their core almost everyone wants to feel valued, appreciated. *Seen.* And if they aren't getting it, then someone like Curtis can take advantage. Fill that void. Give them the sense of specialness they crave. He tosses it out there like a fish hook on a line, right? Judges how you react. Someone like you might scorn his attempts. But that's fine. Sooner or later, he'll get a bite. And when he does, he already knows what bait to use next time, right? A little ego-stroking."

The car trundled through a pothole in the restaurant parking lot, and Darger braced one elbow against the door to steady herself. The Stagecoach Inn was an old two-story stone house situated beside an antique mall.

Inside, the place was decorated with old collectibles and gingham tablecloths. The hostess seated them at a two-top near the front windows that looked out on Main Street. Darger stared out at the grid of brick buildings clustered around the only traffic light in town. Probably the whole place had been built during some mining or logging boom.

"So is that the soft sell?" Darger asked as she perused the menu. "Curtis gets you on the hook with all of his flowery words. His understanding, then he makes it clear that the reward is conditional. That you only get it if you become part of the group. Join them. Follow their rules. Change your name. Dress in the homespun hippie clothes. Play your role."

"Pretty much," Loshak said.

When the waitress came to take their order, Darger ordered one of the daily specials: chicken fried chicken. Loshak opted for the hot turkey sandwich.

"I can't believe anyone falls for it," Darger said. "How do they not see they're being manipulated? That he's only telling them what they want to hear? He pretends he's challenging people to think differently, but he's really just dangling a carrot of specialness in front of people and dressing it up like some sort of difficult spiritual choice. Won't they do the very hard work of accepting how special they are? The rub is that they only get the carrot by joining this little society and allowing themselves to be molded however he sees fit."

"It helps that he's pretty good at it." Loshak shrugged. "He has his shtick down pat."

"No shit," Darger agreed. "Dude had an answer for everything. Which is a red flag, in my opinion. Real people stumble. They contradict themselves. They change their minds. Especially when they're being grilled by two FBI agents. He was way too cool."

Their food arrived then, two steaming masses of various textures slathered in gravy.

As soon as the waitress left, Loshak leaned forward and said in a stage whisper, "I'm not sure there's enough gravy here. Should we call the waitress back and ask for more?"

Darger snorted and picked up her fork.

CHAPTER 33

Darger hadn't eaten much the previous day, not after the stomach-souring experience of trudging through the landfill. It felt good to have her appetite back. And even better to be sating it with a plate full of wholly unhealthy comfort food. She didn't think Curtis would approve of such decadence, which made her enjoy the food that much more.

She and Loshak were about halfway through their meal when Darger's phone rang.

"It's Ambrose," she told Loshak before taking the call.

The detective wasted no time filling them in on what he'd found.

"I just talked with Courtney Maroni's sister. She had the standard family-member-of-an-addict story. Not unlike Stephen Mayhew's aunt, really. Gave Courtney chance after chance and got burned every time. She did feel like her sister's stint with the Children cleaned her up, but she was pretty jaded overall. Didn't seem too upset or surprised that her sister was dead. She gave me the mom's number, and she was even worse. She says that she hasn't seen her daughter in years. She has six kids, worked her fingers to the bone for them, and as far as she's concerned, once they turn eighteen, she's off the hook. And I quote, 'So whatever Courtney's done, it's none of my concern.' Damn near hung up on me before I could break the news." Ambrose's tone turned sarcastic. "I tell you what, Agent Darger, sometimes this job is such a delight."

Darger considered the few times she'd been in a similar

position.

"The gift that keeps on giving," she said. "Any luck with the emergency contact for Bailey Harmon?"

"I've tried the number three times. No answer." Ambrose sighed. "We traced it to a local address. I sent some unis over to see if anyone's home. They happened to see the next-door neighbor out watering her garden and asked around about the Harmons. She said they've been on vacation for the past week or so. She's been feeding their cat. Anyway, they're supposed to get back tomorrow. I had them give her my number so she can call when they do get home."

Darger felt a familiar impatience in her gut but reminded herself that only a few hours ago, they hadn't identified either Jane Doe. This was progress.

"What about our mysterious friend Worm?" she asked. "Find anything on him?"

"No. We went through the alias database. No one claiming the nickname Worm. I can't imagine why." Ambrose let out a single huff of laughter. "I'm going to assign a group to start combing through the DMV records. I made copies of the photo you sent. I'll have them compare that to the driver's license photos of anyone who owns a newish black Tundra and hope we can find ourselves a short white dude with a gold tooth somewhere in the mix."

"We don't know how long he's had the tooth, so we should bear that in mind when looking at driver's license photos," Darger said.

"Good point. I'll make note of it." Ambrose yawned. "As for me, I'm calling it a day. I've been going non-stop for three days straight, and I'm afraid if I don't show my face at home, my wife's liable to run off with the mailman. You and Loshak should get some rest, too. We'll reconvene on the morrow."

"We'll see you then."

Darger hung up, filling Loshak in as they finished their meal.

"I can't say I'm disappointed at the notion of having a few hours off," Loshak said. "I think I might take a little nap when we get back."

Darger took a sip of her iced tea.

"I just hope we're able to track down this Worm guy. Sounds like someone who might be able to give us the real dirt on the cult. Pun intended."

"Yeah." Loshak scratched his chin. "Might be too late though."

Darger paused with a forkload of mashed potatoes inches from her mouth.

"You think he's dead?"

"Well, we've got Stephen Mayhew, known for breaking various cult rules. Causing a ruckus, if you will. He shows up dead along with his lady and her closest friend. That doesn't bode well for the guy that supplied him with the drugs, does it?"

"Does that mean you think the cult is responsible for the deaths?"

"I'm not saying anything for sure," Loshak said, pausing to sip his iced tea. "It's one possible theory."

"Why the girls?"

"Well, the girls would be my first guess if I was trying to figure out who Worm and Stephen were selling drugs to, for one. They did call themselves the degenerates, after all. Maybe

Curtis wanted to make an example of them. Or maybe it was someone else at the cult. Sometimes they task out the grisly deeds to some kind of enforcer."

"Like the naked guy rocking the AK?"

"Right. And maybe the goal hadn't been to kill anyone. Only a bit of light torture, you know? But they took things too far. They wouldn't want to disrupt their peaceful little lovefest, now would they? Not to mention however much cash they've got rolling in from the farm business. So they cover it up. Drive the bodies out to the city and dump them."

"That still doesn't explain the dirt on the bodies." Darger sawed off a piece of gravy-drenched chicken cutlet. "And as much as I think Curtis is a complete tool, I can't picture him tying people down and intentionally starving them to death. Or ordering-slash-allowing someone else to do it."

Loshak pointed at her with his fork.

"Yeah but can you picture anyone doing that?"

Darger pondered this.

"Leonard Stump, maybe."

Loshak waved the fork in the air, dismissing this.

"That's because you already know the things he's capable of. That's what we're always up against, isn't it? The heinous things we see. The terrible violence. Trying to picture any average person you meet doing any of those things is… it doesn't make sense. It never really makes sense until after. And even then it's usually somewhat academic at best. We can dress it up with motive and whatever, but at the end of the day, a lot of things we've seen don't make any sense. Billions of people live their lives going out of their way to never intentionally cause harm. And then we have these others that torture and rape and kill."

Loshak gazed out the window, chewing silently for a moment. Finally, he swallowed and turned back to her.

"Unless you're one of them, I don't think it can ever really make sense."

CHAPTER 34

He woke up coughing. Facedown on the rock floor of the cave. Breathing dust.

His eyelids fluttered. Opened. Found nothing but the same featureless black wall of darkness hung up all around him.

He lay there a second. Blinking and breathing. The whooshing was still there in his head, but it was fainter than before.

His face was hot, despite having been pressed into the icy cavern floor for who knew how long. That seemed wrong.

He brought his fingers to his cheeks, found them feverish to the touch. It reminded him of being drunk. Or drugged.

Could there have been something in the water? That wouldn't make sense.

He sat up. Patted the ground around him. The same cold stone sprawled in all directions, dipped and cratered like acne-scarred skin.

Again, he tilted his head upward. Looked where the string of lights should be glowing — or at least where he thought they should be. Not that it mattered as only the dark gazed back at him, unblinking.

And then it hit him that he could use the string of lights to orient his direction in the tunnel by touch, if he could find them and feel them. He smiled at the thought, grinning in the face of the endless black void.

The lights had been on his right-hand side when he was heading out toward the dig site. They should be on his left if he wanted to head back toward the big cavern and the light switches and, eventually, the barracks.

He stood. Mind reeling through all of these options as he felt along the wall. His arms went up over his head. Fingers brushing at the knobby contours of the cold rock.

He reached up and up. Stood on tiptoes. In his memory, the lights were low enough to touch, not quite to the height of the ceiling. He wondered if he could even touch the ceiling here.

He reached straight up. Felt empty space above his head. He'd have to jump, but he hesitated. Making any sudden movements in this darkness felt wrong.

He'd have to keep the jump short and tight. Wasn't quite willing to dare a full vertical leap. He counted to three and pogoed.

The split second of being untethered from the ground was strange. Terrifying. Lost in the abyss. He had a sudden memory of being a kid, maybe eight or nine years old, and going down to the basement for something. He hadn't turned the lights on. Hadn't thought he needed to. He'd walked up and down these stairs a thousand times. But he'd miscounted the steps. Lost track of where he was. Thought he'd reached the basement floor when really there was one last step. He'd kicked his foot out, expecting to feel solid ground but found only empty space. The same panic he'd felt then came to him now. He flailed in the dark. Desperate to touch anything in all of this emptiness.

And then his fingertips brushed against the ceiling. The surface was rough and gritty. He landed back on his feet and wondered at all the fuss. He was fine, see? He could do this.

His second bounce was more confident, and he was able to press his palms almost flat to the stone surface above.

OK then. That settled things. He had to be able to reach the lights. He just had to find them — a task that should be dead easy but was far more difficult in the absolute gloom.

His hands worked up and along the wall, petting and caressing as if the rock walls that encased him were some sort of show dog with papers.

Feeling. Stretching. Afraid that if he moved too hastily, he'd miss them somehow.

Finally his wrist bumped a bulb, and his fingers moved to the socket and cord connecting it to the rest. He stood for a second with his fingernails adhered to the plastic coating on the cable.

Relief flooded him. His chest loosened. Breath coming easier. He could feel the tension release in his temples and the corners of his jaw.

He'd managed to get turned around in a matter of seconds — the lights turning up on the opposite wall from where he thought they'd be. The dark was no joke, but for now, he'd outsmarted it.

He thought of the Dodge Viper again, that copperhead orange enamel gleaming in his imagination. Hell, screw Rhonda. He'd have better options once he was tooling around in his Viper. It was a convertible, after all, so the girls could pretty much fling themselves in head first, their panties spontaneously shooting off their bodies as they did, making a *thwop* sound as the fabric vaulted off their legs as though fired from a T-Shirt cannon.

He chuckled at the image, at the sound, the wind of his breath whistling against his front teeth.

Then he started trekking back the way he'd come, letting

his fingertips skim along the wall. His footsteps scuffled and gritted against the stone, echoed funny in the tight quarters.

His mind flashed to the place where the large cavern formed that cathedral-like openness in the midst of all this underground rock. He tongued the sharp edges of his teeth as he thought about what that'd feel like. Walking into that wide-open space. Trying to find his way out among all those cave mouths, all those possible paths. A lot could go wrong in there.

And then he thought about how, in order to reach that chamber, he'd have to crawl through the spot where the cave got tight. He imagined the way it always closed around him like a coffin. Pressed its cold rock against his shoulder blades. Gripped his chest tightly enough to constrict his breath.

He swallowed, and a juicy sound emitted from his throat. Sounded loud in the quiet, almost comically cowardly in his ears.

He stopped. Took a few deep breaths.

He snaked the walkie talkie out of his pants pocket. Thumbed the button to try it again.

"Is anyone up there? I'm stuck in the dark down here."

Still no response. Thinking about it now, the crew had really thinned out in recent weeks. He'd rarely seen some of the regulars, though at first he'd assumed they were just working different shifts. He didn't know what to make of that.

And then a picture flashed in his head. A memory. He saw the current dig site as he'd last seen it. Rubble piled into wheelbarrows. Shards of stone still littering the ground. That wounded concave place in the wall where they'd freshly blasted out more rock.

The camera in his mind panned toward one of the walls

and zoomed in, and he saw then what it was showing him. A curved glass shape hung from the craggy surface, set beneath the string of lights. Motionless.

He turned around. Picked up the pace as he headed deeper into the caves. He knew now what he needed to do.

CHAPTER 35

Cora huddled in her cage, wrapped in one blanket with the other spread underneath her. She listened for a long time but heard nothing else in the distance. No more clicks. No echo of shambling footfalls. Just the quiet.

A dull fear still thrummed in her chest, rippled over her skin in creeping waves now and again. It wasn't the panicked terror she'd felt when she'd watched Chase bleed out upstairs, or when the cowboy had dragged her to the basement and thrown her down this hole. This was a creeping dread, a lingering sense of powerlessness, of defeat.

In digging out the blankets rumpled in the back of the cage, she'd found a gallon milk jug partially filled with water and drank. The cool water felt good on her lips, on her tongue, in her throat. Something about that simple act of drinking brought with it a sense of normality, reassuring.

She took another sip now. Wiped a dribble off her chin. Held the plastic jug up and shook it gently, trying to gauge the water level.

The jug hadn't been full when she'd found it, and now it was down to just under halfway. She'd need to conserve going forward. Make it last.

She wanted more than anything to raise her voice. Project it down that gaping tunnel before her. Say something else to Lily. Ask her the first of the several thousand questions clanging around in her head, probably.

Somehow, though, her voice wouldn't quite leave her

throat. The words quivered there, prickling on her vocal cords, like the string of a crossbow drawn taut in her larynx, ready to let its bolt fly. Her lips even moved, but for some reason the language wouldn't budge.

It was too soon, maybe. She didn't want to rush it. The other girl would know better when it was OK to talk again, when it was OK to breathe again. She should follow Lily's lead.

She rolled over from her side to her back. Felt the hard metal of the bars dig into the flesh along her spine, those rigid wires trying to draw creases into her skin.

The blanket draped over her was heavier — wool, she thought. The one underneath was fleece, softer and thinner. Working together they made her neither comfortable nor warm, but they were better than nothing.

She listened to the silence. The quiet seemed to grow whenever she paid attention to it. Elongating. Stretching out into something stark and striking. Something vast. Uncaring. Unknowable.

This time, her voice slipped out before she could even think to stop herself. It chimed like a bell in the stillness, clear and bright, shattering the silence.

"Lily?"

The sound trailed away. Trembling then gone. Swallowed by the tunnel.

No response.

Her heart hammered in her chest. She licked her lips. Tried again.

"Lily? Are you awake?"

Again the quiet plucked her words from the air. Devoured them.

Dark Passage

The silence intensified. Made her skin crawl on her arms and legs, cold settling over her until her limbs were numb with it. Made her mouth drop open and suck shallow breaths.

Lily wasn't responding.

CHAPTER 36

Ambrose called the next morning, Darger's phone buzzing against the table right as she and Loshak were finishing up their breakfast.

"Just got the call from the Harmons' neighbor. They pulled into the driveway about twenty minutes ago. I figure by the time we get over there, they'll have had a chance to settle in a little before I ruin their day."

"We'll meet you there," Darger said.

She hung up and shoved the last third of her lemon poppy seed muffin into her mouth.

"You're allowed to eat in the car, you know," Loshak said, raising one eyebrow as she washed the huge mouthful down with the remnants of her coffee.

"This is more efficient," she said when she'd swallowed enough to be able to speak again.

"It's more something, that's for sure."

She dusted the crumbs from her hands and stood.

"You ready?"

Loshak blinked.

"You're awfully eager for someone who's on their way to inform a family of a loved one's horrific death."

"I can't change that their daughter is dead. But they might be able to tell us something that helps us figure out who did this."

Twenty-five minutes later, they arrived outside the Harmon home, a red brick colonial house with neatly trimmed hedges lining the front walk, located in the middle-class suburb of Elkins Park.

Detective Ambrose was already there, parked on the street across from the house. Loshak pulled into the spot behind him, and the three of them climbed out.

"How's the DMV search going?" Darger asked.

"Slow as molasses," Ambrose complained. "Apparently they've been having tech issues over there all week. Every few hours their database goes offline, and we have to wait while they reboot everything."

They followed Ambrose up the walk. He paused a few feet from the front steps and pointed at two small impressions in the concrete walkway.

"Shit. Will you look at that?"

The markings in the cement were handprints, and underneath, two names in the messy scrawl of children. Chris and Bailey. Ambrose cringed.

"Let's get this over with."

He proceeded up the steps and across the porch to the door. Three percussive thuds rang out as he rapped his knuckles against the wood frame. A few seconds later, the inner door opened. A woman nudged the screen door open a few inches. She had dark hair and eyes. A middle-aged version of the girl Darger had seen in the photograph.

"Yes?"

"Mary Harmon?"

"Yes."

"I'm Detective Ambrose with the Philadelphia police. These are my friends from the FBI, Agent Darger and Agent Loshak. Bailey is your daughter, is that correct?"

"Well… yes. What's this about? Is Bailey in some kind of trouble?"

"I think we'd better come inside."

She held the door open, and they filed into the house. Darger caught a whiff of cinnamon, and she imagined Mrs. Harmon in the middle of baking some muffins when they'd come knocking.

"Is your husband at home?"

"Lance?" Mrs. Harmon called out. "Could you come out here, please? A policeman and some, um, FBI people are here. They say it's about Bailey."

She directed them into a formal living area with two leather sofas facing off beside a fireplace. "Could I get you something to drink?"

There was a chorus of no-thank-yous as all three of them declined.

A tall, thin man entered from the other side of the room. He had gray hair and wore small round-framed glasses. Ambrose repeated the introductions from earlier.

"What's going on?" Mr. Harmon asked, frowning and taking a seat on the couch.

He seemed more openly concerned than his wife, who'd put on a cheerful mask as soon as Ambrose had told her he was police.

"When was the last time you saw Bailey?" Ambrose asked.

"Oh… two months ago," Mr. Harmon answered. "Maybe three?"

Mrs. Harmon jumped in.

"And you know, Bailey has had her troubles in the past, but she's changed. All of that is behind her. She's changed. So whatever might have happened, however you think Bailey might be involved, well… I'm sure it's some kind of misunderstanding." Mrs. Harmon's hands fluttered about as she spoke, like a pair of nervous birds. "Are you sure I can't get you something to drink? Not even a bottle of water?"

"No, Mrs. Harmon. And I think you should sit down for what I'm about to tell you."

The woman lowered herself to the sofa beside her husband.

Darger braced herself. This was the part of the job that every law enforcement officer she'd ever spoken to said was their least favorite. Notifying family that the worst possible thing had happened. A loved one, gone forever.

Ambrose fussed with his tie and took a deep breath.

"We found some remains."

"Oh my God—" Mrs. Harmon muttered.

"We believe they belong to your daughter."

Mrs. Harmon began to sob softly. Mr. Harmon reached out and rubbed his wife's back.

"What happened?" Mr. Harmon asked.

"We're not sure yet," Ambrose said. "The particular circumstances have left a lot of questions for us. That's partly why we're here. And you'll have to make an official identification at some point, of course, but for now—"

"Will we have to go to California to do that?" Mr. Harmon asked.

"Sorry? California?"

"Well, isn't that who notified you?" Mr. Harmon asked. "The California State Police or…?"

"I'm afraid you've lost me." Ambrose glanced over at Darger and Loshak. "As I told your wife, I'm from Philadelphia

PD. My colleagues here are on loan from Washington D.C. by way of Quantico, Virginia. I'm not sure why law enforcement from California would be involved."

Mr. Harmon blinked.

"Are you saying the remains you found were here? In Pennsylvania?"

Mrs. Harmon stopped crying so abruptly it almost looked like someone had pressed a pause button on her face mid-sob, her eyes going wider.

"Yes," Ambrose said.

Mr. And Mrs. Harmon exchanged a look, and Darger noticed both of them relax. Mrs. Harmon actually let out a little chuckle.

"Well, we can tell you right now that there's certainly been some kind of mistake."

"How's that?" Ambrose asked.

"Whoever you found, that can't be our Bailey. She's not in Pennsylvania."

"No?"

"No. She's out in California. With Bo."

"Who's Bo?"

"Bo Cooke. Her ex… well, I guess he's her boyfriend again now. There's been a lot of back and forth on that over the years, but…" Mrs. Harmon waved her hands in the air. "Never mind all that. Honey, is the letter still in the credenza?"

"It should be."

The couple bustled over to an antique desk in the front entryway and started rifling through the drawers, murmuring to one another as they did.

"These are all bills."

"Try the second drawer."

Ambrose let his eyes slide over to the agents, but they were no help. Darger was equally confused and could only shrug.

"Here it is," Mrs. Harmon said. "Oh, and then there's the postcard. Where did we put that?"

"I think it's in the kitchen with the rest of the mail we brought in," Mr. Harmon answered. "I'll go grab it."

Mrs. Harmon returned to the living room and handed Ambrose an envelope. He studied the front. It was addressed to the Harmons and had been postmarked about six weeks earlier.

Ambrose pulled out a brief handwritten note on a piece of stationery with a pink rose motif, careful to only touch the very corners. When Ambrose finished, he passed the letter to Darger, and she held it so that she and Loshak could both read it.

"Mom and Dad-
You won't see me for a while. Bo got a special assignment in California, and I am going with him. I know you will worry and that is why I didn't call to let you know. I can't tell you much about it, but I'll be well taken care of. I hope you can trust me that I'm making the best decision for myself. Bo will be paid a lot of money for this job but he will be very busy so I might not be able to call but I will try to write again. I'll see you soon and tell you about my adventures.
-Bailey
P.S. Pet Tonks for me."

Mr. Harmon came in and handed over a postcard featuring the HOLLYWOOD letters in Los Angeles. This one was postmarked just four days prior.

"This came while we were on vacation."

The note on the back of the postcard was brief.

"Enjoying the sun!
-Bailey"

"And you're sure this is your daughter's handwriting?" Ambrose asked.

Mrs. Harmon let out a giddy-sounding laugh.

"Well, of course!"

"And this Bo guy she went out there with," Ambrose said, dangling the postcard by one corner, "could you describe him for me?"

"Oh, let's see." Mrs. Harmon's gaze floated up to the ceiling. "He's two years older than Bailey. Light brown hair. Lean and kinda tall, though not as tall as Lance. So maybe six feet? And I believe his eyes are green."

Darger felt the hair on her arms stand on end. Her description was a dead-on match for John Doe One.

"What kind of work does he do exactly?"

Mrs. Harmon glanced over at her husband, biting her lip.

"They were very secretive about it, to be honest. Some kind of gig with this reclusive millionaire. Sounded like a Howard Hughes type. So rich he'd gone a little cuckoo, you know?" Mrs. Harmon squinted. "I think he was some kind of inventor."

"No, I thought it was oil money," Mr. Harmon said.

"Whatever it was, he demanded a certain amount of confidentiality, apparently."

"That's why the letter didn't really worry us," Mr. Harmon

218

explained, and then his smiled tightened. "Well, aside from the fact that she was going out there with Bo, who hasn't always been the best influence."

Mrs. Harmon patted her husband's knee.

"It's not really fair to blame Bo."

"No. It's not," he said, sighing.

"There are some things we should explain about Bailey." Mrs. Harmon cleared her throat. "She was top of her class all through middle and high school. Straight As. We thought she'd be valedictorian. And then... there was the accident."

Mrs. Harmon's chin began to quiver and her husband took over.

"Bailey was in a car accident with some friends. A bad one. Five girls in the car. Bailey was the only survivor."

Shaking her head, Mrs. Harmon whispered, "She had so much guilt. It changed her."

"It wasn't only the guilt," Mr. Harmon said. "She also suffered a traumatic brain injury. They weren't sure she'd be able to walk and speak for some time. They were wrong about that, thank God. But after... her personality was different. She was a quiet, well-mannered girl before the crash. After? She was much more impulsive. She started partying. Doing drugs. I'm not denying that the shock of losing her friends was part of that, but the compulsive behavior came out in other ways that didn't seem to have anything to do with the guilt. She started shoplifting, for example. Silly little things. I think the first time she got caught, it was for some pens. Those... gelly roll pens or whatever they're called. She stole a seven dollar pack of pens when she had a twenty in her wallet. There was simply no reason for her to steal them other than that she *wanted* to."

Darger cleared her throat.

"I'm sorry if this is a strange question, but did the accident require any surgery?"

"Oh yes. She had extensive cosmetic surgery. The whole left side of her face was crushed."

If Darger had any lingering doubt about Bailey Harmon being their Jane Doe Two, this had erased them.

"Anyway, we've done what we've can. Sent her to rehab twice. Four different therapists. Nothing worked for long. Not until she found The Children of the Golden Path."

"She talked to you about her experience there at the, uh… camp?" Darger had to stop herself from blurting out the word "cult."

"Oh yes. The progress she made there… it was like seeing the old Bailey," Mrs. Harmon said.

"That's why we were so upset when she told us she'd left." Mrs. Harmon's hands squeezed into fists. "I begged her to go back. I even called Curtis, but he said—"

"You know Curtis?" Darger asked.

"Oh yes. We talked to him in-depth when she invited us to the Harvest Festival last fall. We had to know how he did it. And of course we wanted to thank him for giving our daughter back. The idea that she'd leave was… worrying."

Mr. Harmon folded his hands tightly in his lap.

"Frankly, without that stability, we were certain she would fall right back into her old habits. But she assured us that everything would be fine. Bo had this new job and all…"

"Was Bo a member of The Children?"

"I don't think so," Mrs. Harmon answered. "Bailey mentioned that he'd once referred to Curtis as a snake-oil salesman. That made her quite angry."

"Did you meet any of her friends from there? Trinity or Puck?"

"Oh yes. Bailey refers to Trinity as the sister she never had."

"What about a man named Worm?"

Mr. Harmon's jaw tightened.

"He was there. At the festival. Personally, I didn't care for the way he looked at Bailey."

Mrs. Harmon chuckled.

"He thinks that about every boy who's *ever* looked at Bailey. She's always been a daddy's girl."

Darger noted the use of present tense. At some point, Ambrose was going to have to break the news. Again.

"Tell us about Bo," Ambrose said. "And about this job."

"They've had an on-and-off thing since high school. And he's not a bad kid. Just has a bit of a wild streak. Maybe didn't have the best role models growing up. A rough family background."

Mr. Harmon reached up and adjusted his glasses before he went on.

"As for the job, we know almost nothing. Bailey couldn't even tell us who it was for. Always referred to Bo's boss as Mr. Big."

Mrs. Harmon suddenly held up a finger.

"You should talk to Danny Jessop. That's Bo's best friend."

"What would Danny know about any of it?" Mr. Harmon asked.

"Well, that time Bailey and Bo came around, when you were fishing with Roger, Danny was the one who dropped them off. I got the impression that they'd come straight from the Mr. Big job because Bo was absolutely covered in filth."

Beside her, Darger sensed Ambrose's spine stiffen.

"Looked like he'd been digging foxholes or some such thing."

Mrs. Harmon chuckled at the memory, and then her smile faltered.

"But… I'm sorry. We've already told you that the… *remains* you found can't be Bailey so… well, what are all these questions about?"

Ambrose pulled his phone out.

"I'm very sorry to do this, but I need you to look at this photo." He entered his lock screen code and swiped at the screen. "I should warn you, it's fairly graphic."

Darger knew without looking that it was one of the autopsy photos of Jane Doe Two. Her stomach clenched, and she had an urge to bolt from the room, to save herself from having to watch this family's grief unfold before her. But she couldn't do it to Ambrose, and she couldn't do it to the Harmons.

And so she sat very still while Mr. and Mrs. Harmon looked at the photograph of their dead daughter and watched as their world fell apart.

CHAPTER 37

The first thing they did after leaving the Harmon home was to huddle in Ambrose's car and find what they could on Bo Cooke and Daniel Jessop.

After some typing and swiping, Ambrose pulled up the driver's license photo of Bo Cooke on his phone. He held it up toward the agents in the backseat.

"What do you think?" he asked, flipping back and forth between Bo Cooke's driver's license photo and the morgue shot of John Doe One. "Looks about right to me."

The fleshy face in the license photo wore a stupid grin that seemed almost obscene transitioning to the grimace on the emaciated corpse, but Darger agreed it was Cooke, as did Loshak.

"I'll text Detective McGill and see what he can dig up on this Bo Cooke," Ambrose said, tapping out a message with his thumbs. "In the meantime, why don't we drive over to see if young Mr. Jessop is home?"

Darger and Loshak got in their car and followed Ambrose to the west side of Elkins Park. Daniel Jessop's address was listed as a second-floor apartment in Thornberry Estates, a fancy-sounding name for a rather low-rent looking complex. From the street, it was all cracked stucco and dead grass and a parking lot pocked with potholes.

They climbed the exterior stairs that led to the upper floor. The walls were dark gray and marked by sloppy looking graffiti tags. Darger could see the layers and varying shades where old spray paint had already been covered more than once.

Ambrose banged his fist against the door of apartment 2B. There were no peepholes on these units, but each door had a sidelight covered by a curtain. Jessop's was dark.

Darger glanced across the small covered breezeway and noticed the curtain on his neighbor's sidelight shiver slightly. One sliver of a girl's face peered out at them before the curtain flicked back into place.

Ambrose rapped his fist again, but after several minutes with no response, it was clear Daniel Jessop either wasn't home or at the very least wanted them to think so.

Darger gestured at the neighboring apartment.

"Maybe we could ask if the neighbors have seen Jessop around recently."

"Good idea."

They moved over to the apartment with the lit window. Ambrose's knock was slightly less forceful this time.

They waited long enough that Darger worried the girl wasn't going to answer the door, but eventually they heard the sound of scuffing feet and then a click. The door swung open.

The girl was maybe twenty-five. She wore hot pink sweats, and her hair was pulled into a messy ponytail.

"Any chance you're friendly with Daniel Jessop next door?"

"Why?" She toyed with the zipper on her sweatshirt. "Is he in trouble?"

"Not at all. We just want to ask him a few questions," Ambrose said.

The girl crossed her arms, hugging herself. She was skittish, this one.

"Well, I haven't—"

Darger took half a step forward.

"Actually, we're doing somewhat of a wellness check on him. We have reason to believe Danny might be in danger."

It wasn't totally untrue, since several people in Danny's circle were now dead.

The girl's defensive posture softened slightly. She dropped one arm and went back to fiddling with her zipper.

"Danny? In danger?" The girl looked comically worried now. "I guess he hasn't been around in a while. Is he OK?"

"How long is a while?" Darger asked.

The girl shrugged.

"Three weeks, maybe? He asked me to get his mail for him." She gestured to a thick stack of envelopes and catalogs on a small table beside the door.

"Did he leave a way for you to get in touch with him?"

The girl pinched the collar of her hoodie tight to her neck.

"Well yeah, but he said it was only for emergencies."

Darger put on her most disarming smile.

"What's your name, hun?" Darger asked.

"Leslie," the girl said. "Zlotnik."

"My name is Violet. I work for the FBI."

The girl's eyes went wide. She mouthed the letters F-B-I back to Darger, possibly without realizing she was doing so.

"We're worried that some very bad people might be looking for Danny, and we want to make sure that we find him before they do." Also not technically a lie. "I'd say that qualifies as an emergency."

Leslie swallowed.

"Well... he, uh, said if I really needed to get in touch to call The Red & Black — that's a bar he goes to sometimes — and I should ask for Patricia and leave a message for him."

"OK, here's what I want you to do. I want you to call the bar, ask for Patricia, and tell her you need Danny to meet you there this afternoon. Tell her it's a matter of life and death. Ask if she can arrange that."

"Oh God, this sounds so serious," Leslie said.

"It is. It's really important that we find Danny. Today."

The girl's hand shook as she pulled out her cell phone and made the call. Leslie relayed the message to Patricia, whose voice was loud and shrill on the speakerphone.

"Hold on a minute, Leslie. I'll text him now and see if he can come." There was a long pause before Patricia returned. "Danny says one o'clock. That work for you?"

Darger nodded to Leslie.

"Yes," the girl said. "That's fine. Thanks."

When she hung up, she gazed up at Darger.

"Was that good?"

"It was excellent. Thank you."

"And Danny's not… I mean, you're not going to arrest him or something, are you? I'd feel terrible if I got him in a lot of trouble."

Darger put a hand on the girl's shoulder.

"You're helping Danny," she said. "Trust me."

"So am I done?"

"Actually, if you could come down to The Red & Black with us, to help us identify Danny, that would be a great help," Darger said.

"Oh. Um, sure," Leslie said. "Just let me go grab my glasses real quick. I don't have class today, so I didn't put my contacts in."

When Leslie had disappeared deeper into her apartment, Ambrose turned to Darger.

"You think we need her for this?"

"No, but if she has another way of contacting Danny, we don't want her to tip him off. Sounds like something spooked him if he took off for three weeks," Darger said. "Better to keep her close until we have him."

"Good point," Ambrose said. "I'm gonna go down to the car and put in a call for some backup on the bar. Bring her down when she's ready."

He turned to go and then paused to rub his hands together.

"I feel like the pieces of this are finally starting to fall into place."

CHAPTER 38

The air seemed to grow colder as he wove his way deeper into the tunnels. The chill made him shiver slightly, made him feel vulnerable. He'd always liked that coolness before. Usually he was working down here, body heat swelling to match the strain of his labor. Now he wanted to pull up the hood of his sweatshirt, but he didn't dare cover his ears.

He kept going. Jabbed choppy steps into the void. Pressed face first into that abyss.

He pictured the lantern again as he'd last seen it. It hung on the wall near the end of the cave where the digging still persisted in fits and starts. Glass and metal. Shaped roughly like an hourglass.

He was pretty sure it was an old carbide lantern like the miners used back in the day. As far as he knew, it was there partially as a backup light source and partially as a decorative touch. Cowboy loved ranting and raving about the old coal mines in the region, like even now he pined for the days of child labor and black lung.

Little twinges of giddiness roiled in his gut as he thought about the lantern. Tried to picture the glow coming to life. Beating back the shadows once more.

Something clacked and scraped in the distance, loud sounds that fluttered in the cave around him, seemed to come from everywhere and nowhere all at once.

He flinched. Shuddered. Put up his hands as though the reverberations might leap for his face, for his throat.

Then he stopped. Held his breath. Listened.

Nothing.

Must have been the echo of his own footsteps bouncing around. Swooping back at him like a boomerang to damn near scare the cream cheese out of him.

His heart punched in his chest again, chugging along at top speed.

Jesus. A little jumpy, aren't we?

He started forward once more. Could admit it now — the sound had startled him pretty good, wrenched the thoughts clean out of his head, left him shaky.

He tried to think of the Viper again to center himself, a reminder of why he was putting himself through all of this. He pictured himself riding around with the top down, Rhonda riding shotgun, both of them sporting sunglasses, wind batting their hair around, his hand gliding up her thigh. It helped a little.

The cave floor bent upward beneath his feet. He climbed the slope, knowing he was close now, close to the end, close to the lantern.

He worked both hands along the wall. Patting and feeling in the dark, his touch covering a broader swath of cave wall than before. The lamp would be there soon enough, and he didn't want to miss it.

The smell grew stronger as he neared the freshly blasted area. Dustier. Earthier. More pungent. Maybe that made sense, being that they'd exploded a fresh round of particles into the air not so long ago. He wondered how long it took for all those tiny pieces to settle, for the cave to return to its dormant stillness.

Another scraping sound made the hair on the back of his neck stand up. He whirled, pretty sure it had come from somewhere behind him, that whatever it was had been close.

"Hello?"

His voice rang down the long tunnel. Wavered as it traveled away from him. Oddly high-pitched. He willed it to sound stronger and deeper when he spoke again.

"Is someone there?"

No response. Only the quiet.

His skin kept crawling. Wriggling. Tightening around the musculature of his body. His scrotum shriveled up into a walnut.

He struggled to control his breathing. Wind pushing at his lips. Sucking into his chest. Hissing and sounding wet against his teeth.

He backpedaled a few paces. Brought his fingertips back to the wall.

Someone was there. Close. Looming in the dark. He didn't know it for a fact, but he felt it. Sensed it.

Just keep going. Find the lantern.

Both of his hands found the wall again, skimming over it with urgency now. Broad sweeps of his arms left and right like he was beating his wings out of time at it.

And then his wrist knocked into something. Tinkled out a metallic chime.

His fingers moved to the source of the noise, found a bulbous protrusion jutting out of the wall. So smooth compared to the rough rock face he'd touched for so long. His fingertips squeaked faintly on the glass globe, found the metal of the ventilation cap cooler than either the glass or rock. The thin arms of the frame arced downward from that, feeling angular and skeletal.

He managed to detach the lantern from its hook, metal scraping metal as he did, the sound so loud in the quiet it made him grimace. He held it up by the handle with one hand while the fingers of his opposite hand swooped around underneath it, clawing at the empty air there. At last they found what they sought.

The small box felt so solid in his hands. More substantial than it had any right to. Just holding it made him feel incredible.

A pack of kitchen matches dangled from a string tied to the bottom of the lantern. He remembered seeing it there so many times, wondering if any of them would ever use it.

He snaked his wrist through the handle and let it hang there like a clunky bracelet while he drew a match. Scraped it along the ribbed strike plate along one side of the cardboard box.

The match rasped and flared to life. A stuttering burst of light exploded from the chemical tip, orange and blue and white, and as he lifted the tiny wooden stick, that tremoring fit of flashes somehow congealed into a single teardrop of orange flame.

He watched the blaze a second through slitted eyelids. Found himself almost incapable of comprehending its brightness after stumbling around in the dark for so long.

His throat got tight as he stared at it. The spiky ball of fire seemed like the most beautiful thing he'd ever seen. Almost felt like it might make him cry.

He ducked the flame toward the lantern and lit it. Watched

the small orange glow strengthen within the glass dome. He shook the match out, threw it on the ground. Then he held the lantern up to look around the dig site.

The way the light and shadow danced over everything seemed foreign. The textures of the rock, the shape and contour of everything, it all seemed different than he'd remembered it — the scale, proportion, something was off. Crazy how fast he'd gotten used to the dark, had forgotten what light was like.

He turned. Held the lantern up higher to let the illumination spill all the way down that slope trailing away behind him.

The cave floor looked like papier-mâché in the half-light. Blemishes disrupted the surface. Lumps and dips and cavities and hollows twisting the stone into something singular, something detailed to a level he never could have held onto in his memory.

The walls, too, held the same idiosyncrasies, as did the periodic stalagmites and stalactites growing like rock icicles out of the floor and ceiling respectively. His eyes crawled over it, soaked in the details, watched the way moving the lantern even slightly seemed to shift it all, change it all.

He didn't see the shadowy figure nestled among the stalagmites a few feet away until it lurched at him.

CHAPTER 39

Darger rode over to The Red & Black with Ambrose and Leslie Zlotnik, with Loshak following behind. They wove down city streets through some vaguely industrial neighborhood, older brick buildings occupying much of the scenery with a few sickly-looking trees sprouting up from the concrete here and there.

"This is it?" Ambrose asked as they rolled past the bar.

It was a fairly standard dive bar, dark brick with blacked-out windows. A glowing neon Miller Lite sign gave off pale blue light just next to the door.

"I mean, yeah, I guess," Leslie said. "I've never actually been inside myself."

Ambrose gave an almost imperceptible nod to the men in the unmarked car already sitting on the place. There was ample parking on the street at this early hour, and Ambrose chose a spot across from the bar with a clear view of the front door. Loshak eased into the space behind them.

Maybe twenty minutes passed with only one customer entering the place — a heavyset woman who was very much not Danny. As the hour approached, Darger couldn't stop checking the clock on the dash and comparing it to the one on her phone. She noticed Ambrose doing the same.

A few minutes after one o'clock, Leslie perked up. Following her line of sight, Darger saw a figure approaching the bar. The man had his hands thrust in the pockets of a pair of ripped black jeans. The hood of his black hoodie was pulled up over his head.

"Is this him?" Darger asked, realizing that the man was dressed very similar to their two John Does.

Leslie squinted.

"I think so."

As the man reached the door of the bar, he paused with one hand on the handle and glanced around, as if worried he was being watched. When his face angled toward them, Leslie nodded.

"Yeah," she said. "That's Danny."

"OK. You're gonna sit tight, alright?"

The girl nodded again.

Darger and Ambrose climbed out of the car. A moment later, Loshak joined them. They moved on the building, their little pack splaying and building speed like dogs on the hunt.

Loshak reached the front door, gripped the metal handle and paused there a second.

"You ready?" he said to Darger.

"Yep."

He opened the door then and held it aside.

Darger led the way through the front door. She could feel Loshak just a few paces behind her.

She let her gaze sweep the room. The place was dimly lit, with most of the light coming from a collection of old neon beer signs on the walls. Heineken. Yuengling. Budweiser. It took a second for her eyes to adjust.

Then she saw him.

Danny hunched in a booth in the back corner of the place. His dark figure looked like a shadow against the harsh gleam of the rainbow lights reflecting off the glossy tabletop before him.

His hood was still pulled up, too, which wasn't exactly an inconspicuous look.

At the movement of the front door, he turned and glanced over at them for half a second before returning his focus to fidgeting with a bottle PBR.

"Two o'clock," Darger said.

"Yep," Loshak said. "I see him."

"I'll take his side of the booth. Block him in, keep him from bolting."

"Let's go," Loshak said.

They moved on him. Darger tilted her head toward the floor, made sure not to look at Danny or his table. She set her shoulders like she was going to walk right past him. Only once she was right there, close enough to touch him, did she slide into the seat beside him.

Danny's mouth popped open at this sudden invasion of his personal space by a complete stranger.

"Hey man, this seat is… like… taken."

"Daniel Jessop? Violet Darger. FBI," she said, reaching into her jacket for her badge.

Danny's eyes went wide and wild.

"Oh fuck!"

Quick as a squirrel, he hopped up onto his seat, did a skittering run over the tabletop, and hurdled the other side of the booth.

Darger and Loshak exchanged a quick glance before taking off after him.

Danny careened to his left, ducking into a hallway that led to the bathrooms according to the signage. Darger and Loshak pursued him down the dingy passage. Ahead of them, Danny passed both bathroom doors, turned a corner, and disappeared from view.

By the time Darger reached the bend, Danny had just pushed through a door at the end of the corridor marked "FIRE EXIT ONLY" in bright red letters. The warnings slowed Danny not at all. He burst over the threshold in one motion, bending at the waist as he flung the door aside and then righting himself.

The hooded figure zipped into the back alley, really moving now, lifting his knees higher and higher. They were going to lose him.

A dark shape darted out from the side of the building. An arm in a navy suit jutted out from the side and caught Danny in the neck.

The kid hit the limb barrier at full speed and tipped backward, feet kicking out from under him all at once like he'd been chopped in half. He slammed to the wet asphalt, shoulder blades hitting first, then the rest coming down in a heap.

Darger blinked. Taking it in faster than she could process it.

Ambrose had clotheslined Danny. They had him. The detective leaped onto the kid to hold him down.

Darger and Loshak shot through the door. They drew up on the mass of limbs and torsos.

Danny was flailing and screaming under the bulk of Detective Ambrose like a trapped cat.

"Motherfucker! Get offa me!"

"Calm down, son," Ambrose said, but Danny wouldn't listen. He just kept fighting and howling. "If you don't settle down I'm gonna have to restrain you."

Darger and Loshak held Danny as still as they could while

Ambrose got out the zip restraints. Some of the fight went out of the kid as soon as he was bound. They hoisted him as a group and set him on his feet.

"I haven't said anything to anyone, OK?" he said, and Darger thought he sounded like he was on the brink of tears. "You don't have to do this."

"Do what?" Ambrose asked.

"Whatever, man. I swear, I won't say anything."

The back door of the bar had let out to an alley and a small parking area, and Ambrose started dragging Danny toward the street. There were two women in athletic gear jogging down the sidewalk when they reached it. As soon as Danny spotted them, he immediately began to struggle again.

"Help! Help me! They're going to kill me! Call the police!"

"Fool, who do you think we are?" Ambrose asked.

The jogging women froze a few yards away, and one of them already had her phone out. Ambrose whipped out his badge and showed it to the women and then to Danny.

"Wait. You're cops?"

Danny relaxed for a beat, but then he went rigid again.

"Well I don't know nothing about nothing!"

"No? How about your friends Bo Cooke and Bailey Harmon?"

Danny flinched and swiveled his head away, an obvious move to avoid eye contact.

"I don't know no Bo or Bailey."

"No? So it wouldn't bother you to find out that they're both dead?"

Danny's eyelashes fluttered.

"What? No." He shook his head. "You're just saying that."

Ambrose said nothing. He only stood and stared at Danny, hands on hips.

"They're dead?" Danny asked.

"Yeah."

"Fuck," Danny whimpered. "I mean, I *knew*. But... fuck."

"We're gonna need to ask you some questions." Ambrose raised his eyebrows. "If I take those restraints off, you won't run, will you?"

"Look, I'll tell you what I know, if it's even worth much, but can we go somewhere else? Like, off the street? I need protection."

"Sure," Ambrose said, removing the zip ties from Danny's wrists. "We'll go down to the station. Ain't nobody gonna touch you there, OK?"

Danny stopped.

"Are you going to put me in a cell?"

"A cell? No. We'll go sit in an interview room. I can get you a soda, and we'll just sit and talk."

They walked a few more steps.

"Are there windows? In the interview room, I mean?" Danny asked, frowning.

"Windows? Uh, no."

Danny's face twitched.

"And I probably can't smoke in there, can I?"

"Nope."

Danny stopped again.

"Can we talk somewhere outside? Please?"

"I thought you wanted to be off the street. You said you wanted protection."

"Yeah, but... I don't want bars or locked doors or anything

like that."

Ambrose glanced at Darger, but she was just as baffled as he was.

"OK, fine. Name a place, my man."

"There's a park down that way." Danny pointed down the street. "We can talk there."

CHAPTER 40

Two blocks down from the bar was a small municipal park with a fountain in the center. Sparse pine trees clustered along a snaking flagstone pathway with weather-stained park benches sprinkled along the route. Ambrose let Danny get a few paces ahead of them as they passed through the park gates, and then the detective turned and murmured to Darger.

"Go easy on 'im. He's right on the edge."

Darger nodded.

Danny led them over to the fountain and perched on the concrete edge. The fountain was dry, non-operational, its pale innards stained with dark brown streaks and tendrils of what looked like a rusty fungal growth. As soon as he was seated, Danny's right leg began bouncing up and down, a nervous expulsion of energy.

"So who did you think we were?" Darger asked as she lowered herself beside him.

"Huh?"

Danny pulled a pack of cigarettes from his pocket and lit one with a butane lighter shaped like a hand with the middle finger extended.

"When you ran. You didn't think we were the cops because you told those people to call the police. So who did you think we were?"

Danny blew out a stream of smoke but didn't answer.

A woman pushing a baby stroller entered the park, and Danny's head whipped around to face her. His leg stopped pistoning. He stared at the woman for several seconds before apparently deciding she wasn't a threat, and the jouncing of the leg began anew.

Darger decided to take a different approach. Something less direct.

"Were you one of the Children, too?"

"The what?"

"The Children of the Golden Path," Darger said.

"Oh... right. That was the cult group that Bailey and them got into? Nah, man. They told me you have to be like, abstinent or whatever. No sex and no substances? They even tell you when to eat and when to crap. If I wanted that, I'd go back home and live in my ma's basement."

He smirked and ashed his cigarette into the fountain.

"You called it a cult. Is that what your friends called it?"

"Hell no. They were totally gaga about the guy that ran it. I swear, even Stevie talked about that dude like he had a hard-on for him, you know? I joked about that once, actually, and Steve did *not* think it was very funny."

"This is Stephen Mayhew?"

"Yeah."

"And did you also know Courtney Maroni?"

"Sure. She was Steve's girl."

"Did you meet them through some event they had at the camp?"

"No, I never went to any of that crap. Like I said. They have all these policies. No smoking. No drinking. Sounded lame." Danny took a long drag off his cigarette. "I only met Steve and Courtney after the lot of them got kicked out. I mean, can you fucking imagine? Even after this messiah dude boots them from his little paradise, they all still worshipped him. Fucking brainwashed, man."

"So where did they go after they got kicked out?"

"Bailey went where she always goes when the shit hits the fan. Straight back to Bo." Danny shook his head. "I always thought she was trouble, man. I told Bo that once. I waited until one of the times they were broken up, otherwise he probably woulda kicked my ass. But he didn't listen. If Bailey hadn't come back here, we never would have ended up—"

Danny suddenly stopped talking.

"Ended up what?" Darger asked.

Danny's eyes narrowed to slits.

"Do I *have* to talk to you?"

"Legally? No. But Bo and Bailey are dead. And so are Stephen and Courtney."

"Fuck," he whispered, his shoulders deflating.

"I think you know who did it. Or at least suspect someone." Darger leaned in a little. "I know you're scared, Danny. But if you tell us what you know, we can put a stop to this."

Danny jabbed a knuckle into his eye to wipe away a tear.

"I ain't scared."

A silence followed, and Darger didn't immediately rush to fill it. She let the chirping of the birds in the pines cleanse the air for a few seconds.

"You were all working together, is that right? For some mysterious billionaire?"

Danny's eyelids stretched wide.

"This isn't a trick, is it? Like a test or whatever? You don't, like, work for them or something?"

"You want to see my badge again?"

"No. It's just... you don't know what it's like." Danny shivered and rubbed at his forearms. "I wake up in the middle of the night all sweaty, and I'm back there."

"Back where?"

"Underground."

Now it was Darger who was fighting off a sudden chill.

"Underground, doing what?"

He swiveled his head around so he could look her in the eye.

"Digging."

CHAPTER 41

The shape leaped out of the shadows. Reaching for him.

He stumbled back instinctively. Threw his arms out to the side, the lantern tipping and lurching in his hand.

The sphere of light shining out of the glass globe swung wildly around the enclosed space. The glow surged up the walls and crashed back down like a tidal wave. It made all the shadows stretch and bend and jerk as it moved.

His backpedaling feet snagged on knobby protrusions on the cave floor. Gravity pulled at him, wanting to take him down. But he kept upright, kept moving away, retreating.

As the dark figure stepped into the open, he saw the knife in its hand first. The long blade angled out of the shadows, its steel gleaming in the orange light.

And then the rest of the shape seemed to follow it into the brightness. Entering the light as though appearing there, becoming real there.

The familiar cowboy hat sat atop the head. Perched there like it might pounce. The mustache darkened the lip beneath the mirrored aviators, mouth sneering. The western cut shirt adorned the torso, the bolo tie dangling just shy of the collar.

It was Cowboy. That was plain.

His mind reeled at this revelation. *Why would Cowboy want to kill me?*

Cowboy stalked toward him, shoulders faintly hunched, arms splayed at the sides. Something aggressive in the way they swayed back and forth, the knife wagging in a vaguely serpentine zigzag.

Cowboy smiled. An evil grin splitting the flesh above his chin. And something there made the whole picture make sense for the first time.

He gasped. A single hiss escaping his lips.

Then his back butted up against the dead-end wall of the dig site. He turned. Stared a second at the sheared off stone face before him.

Impossible. Overwhelming. Impenetrable rock. Hundreds of feet thick from this point, according to the geologist's report they'd looked at when planning the blasts.

Nausea gurgled in the center of him. Tottered against the walls of his stomach.

His eyes traced a crack up the rock face. A crease that drew a stark black line in the sandy looking stone. If only he could peel it apart. Crawl inside there.

"Nowhere to run now," the voice behind him said.

Boots scuffed on the rock floor behind him. Jerky.

He turned just as the knife swooped for him. Tried to dodge it. Failed.

The metal plunged home into his belly. A cold spike entering the center of him, the meat of him. Shoved in up to the hilt.

He stood up straighter for a split second, and then he hunched over the wound, over the outstretched arm still jamming that knife into his torso, trying to twist the blade.

They were close now. He and the man killing him. Face to face. Intimate.

That leering mouth hissed out a laugh. Insane. Tongue flicking out to wet the lips.

The knife jerked out and slammed into him again. Slurping and whispering.

And coldness spread outward from the wounded place now. Icy tendrils worming into his muscles, undulating like tentacles. The chill overtook him from the inside out. Permeating. Saturating. Puddling and sloshing and gripping until the chill laminated his sheening skin.

The knife eased out of his belly, wet and shiny. Trembling in the red hand that held it.

It sprange to life again. Slashed across his chest.

He weaved to his right. Attempted to evade it a beat too late. Felt the sting as it opened more of him. Etched another line of agony into his flesh.

His eyelids fluttered. Wet. Then going blurry, out of focus. The knife swooped for him yet again.

He ducked. Flinched. Whimpered faintly.

The tip of the weapon jabbed at his cheek. Pierced it. Then scraped across it like a cat claw.

Another seam torn open in his skin, his body coming asunder.

Bright flashes of pain pulsed in multiple places now. Searing. Thrumming.

He slumped to the stony ground. Knees hitting first. Then he tumbled to his side.

The cold feelings got bigger as he touched down. The cave happy to receive the last of his body heat. Endlessly hungry for it.

He held up his arm as though to defend himself. But that dark figure wasn't there anymore. The silhouette had stepped back. Motionless now. An observer.

Dark Passage

He brought the hand to the gaping hole. Cupped at the wet there. And he tried to curl in on himself. Knees tucking up toward his ribcage. Fetal position. Like folding into a ball might keep him together, might hold the life inside of him a little longer.

The blood drained from his torso, sluicing through the fingers clutching his abdomen. Red puddled on the rock floor. The dark pool slowly advancing away from him in all directions, his life pumping out onto the bedrock. Returning to the earth.

The footsteps trailed away a few steps. Echoed funny in the cave.

And no real thoughts came to him as he bled out. No words in his head. Only a feeling of loss, of shock and grief and some vague sense of remorse for the time he'd lost, for the time he'd wasted.

He blinked. Stared out at nothing. Fuzzy light and shadow. Flecks of bright and dark that refracted everywhere around him like a kaleidoscope.

The cold took him quickly.

CHAPTER 42

"Digging for what?" Darger asked.

"Man… I signed stuff, you know? They said there'd be repercussions if they found out I was talking about what I did." Danny pulled another cigarette out and tucked it between his lips. "This is all supposed to be top secret, you know? The whole reason I've been hiding out is because I was worried what might happen if they found me and thought I'd been talking."

Darger looked from Loshak to Ambrose. They seemed as baffled as she did by what Danny was saying.

"OK," she said. "Let's talk about 'they' then. Can you tell us *who* you're hiding from?"

"Shit, man." Danny lit the cigarette from the middle finger on his lighter and inhaled. "I don't know if this is such a good idea. Me talking to you."

"Four people are dead," Darger said. "You seemed fairly convinced you're in danger. We want to help you, but we can't do that if you don't tell us what happened. Who were you doing this hush-hush secret work for?"

Danny closed his eyes.

Finally he said, "Cowboy."

Ambrose blinked and leaned forward.

"Did he just say a cowboy?" By the look on the detective's face, Darger could tell he thought Danny was out of his mind. "You on something, son?"

"Not *a* cowboy. Just Cowboy," Danny said, gesturing with

the cigarette. "That's the dude's name."

"Oh yeah?" Ambrose chuckled. "And is that a first name or a last name?"

"I mean, I figure it's a nickname. On account of him always wearing a cowboy hat and boots. And those nuthugger Wranglers. Just picture a Joe Exotic looking dude, OK?" Danny shook his head. "Look, I don't know his real name. That's what I'm trying to say, man. You think I'm paranoid? This dude is next level. Walks around with a bulletproof vest on half the time."

Darger filed that little nugget away for later.

"How'd you meet him?"

"Bo hooked me up. Said he was getting paid good money under the table to do some construction work. Had all these stories about the dude he worked for. Wild stuff. Like one time he paid for all the seats at the movie theater so no one else would be there for the new *Star Wars* movie. Said he wanted to enjoy the cinematic experience free from interruption. Always had a big wad of cash stuck down in his boot. One time he tipped a waiter at Steak 'n Shake with a hundred-dollar bill because the guy gave him extra malt powder in his chocolate malt."

Darger let Danny talk, not wanting to stop the flow of information now that the floodgates had been opened.

"He told us how he tried to cook up various new drugs when he was our age, thinking maybe he'd discover the next hot club drug. Tried the banana peel thing."

"Banana peel thing?" Darger asked.

"It's an old hoax from back in the 60s," Loshak explained. "Some guy claimed that if you scraped the pith off a bunch of banana peels and smoked it, you could get high."

"Well I guess Cowboy tried it, except he used fresh banana peels," Danny said with a shrug. "Made like a smoothie out of it. Said it didn't do anything but make him shit about ten gallons of liquid. But according to him, the nutmeg trip was wild. Said he put on a movie and something got messed up, like the sync between the sound and the visuals were off, and he became convinced that he could hear the future."

He ashed the cigarette.

"Also, the guy is obsessed with coconut water. Drinks gallons of it. Said he's considered moving to somewhere tropical just so he could get his coconut water straight from the tree. He tried planting some here but they died." Danny paused to pick a bit of loose tobacco off his lip. "Bo said they went out to eat once, and when the waitress offered him water, he scoffed. Said there are like eight thousand beverages in the world — many of them delicious — why would anyone choose to drink water? That's one thing I can say about Cowboy. Dude was generous. Didn't skimp with food or booze or dru—"

Danny stopped short.

"Drugs?" Darger asked. "Four people are dead, Danny. We don't care that you did some blow once. Keep going."

"OK, yeah. So Cowboy uh… he's kind of a drug dealer on the side."

"On the side of what?" Ambrose asked.

"However he makes all his money. Oil, I think? Or maybe fracking?" Danny sighed. "I don't know. There are a lot of stories, and it's hard to know what's rumor and what's not, you know? Anyway, he has this philosophy. Kind of anti-government, I guess you could say. He doesn't think anyone should have a right to tell you that you can't imbibe of substances. Sells drugs as like, his civic duty or something."

Ambrose scoffed.

"Hey man, I'm only telling you how he thinks, OK? I'm not saying that he's not full of it." Danny scratched the side of his head. "Anyway, I'd been hearing stories about this guy for weeks. So when Bo told me they were looking for more guys, I was like, 'Hell yeah. Where do I sign up?' Worst fucking mistake I've ever made, man."

"You keep saying *they*," Darger said. "Who else was there aside from Cowboy?"

"I guess they used to have a bunch of people working down there, but by the time I got involved, he had a small crew working for him. Me. Bo. Stevie. Worm."

Darger pointed at her teeth.

"Gold tooth?"

"Yeah. That's him." Danny grimaced. "He dead, too?"

"We don't know."

"Oh fuck me. If they're all dead, it means I'm next. Do you understand?"

"Why? Why would this Cowboy guy need to kill you?" Darger asked. "What were you doing for him exactly?"

"I don't even know! That's the fucked up part. They kept us in the dark about everything. I don't even know where we were working because he'd blindfold us and drive us in."

Darger wanted to stop, to have a moment to process all of this bizarre information, but she couldn't. She had to keep pressing forward.

"They blindfolded you?"

"Yeah. We'd all meet up at this Arby's over on West

Baltimore Pike, and Cowboy would pick us up in this big diesel pickup truck. We'd climb in, and they'd hand out blindfolds. Sometimes I'd fall asleep, and that was better, because otherwise it felt like the ride took hours. But I timed it once, and it was only about forty minutes."

"Then what?"

"We'd get to the place. They'd pull in and park inside this garage. And I say garage, but this place was huge. Like the kind of thing you could park a semi inside. Once we were in, then they'd undo the blindfolds. No windows, and the door into the house itself was always locked. From the garage, we could go down a flight of steps and get into the basement, which was sort of a barracks for us workers. Hot tub. A few cots. Cooler full of beverages. He had all this stuff stored down there. Furniture and just shelves of stuff. Old lamps. Statues. Pieces of an old pipe organ from some church. And in one corner, there was just this… black hole in the cement. That was the tunnel."

"And that's where you were doing the digging?" Darger asked.

Danny nodded.

"I fuckin' hated it down there. The tunnels were rigged with lights and shit, but it was still creepy as hell. Cold and kind of damp all the time in parts. They'd done a lot before I got there."

"A lot of digging, you mean?"

"Yeah. I mean, it's hard to guess how long this tunnel was, but it had to be hundreds of yards. Maybe a mile. Most of it real narrow but with some wider chambers cut out and shit here and there. It hooked into these caves, and we were mostly working at pecking out some rock during my time. I never knew what for, and we didn't make much progress. It's slow going, trying to blast that shit out and haul it away."

"And they never said what the tunnels were for?"

"No. It was made pretty clear that we weren't to ask about the whats and whys. And there were certain shafts of the tunnel that were off-limits. Course there were rumors amongst us diggers. And by that I mean me and Bo and Steve. Steve said it hooked into the Philadelphia County Sewer system, but I had my doubts."

"What about Bailey and Courtney? Were they digging too?"

"Nah. Bailey bitched a lot about that, because she knew how much money we were making and wanted in on some of the action."

"And how much was that?"

"Fifteen-hundred a week. Cash. Always rolled up in a rubber band."

Six grand a month, Darger thought. Not bad.

"Cowboy had opinions about what kind of work was appropriate for women, though," Danny went on. "They came over sometimes and hung around in the barracks while we worked. I always thought it was odd that Bo and Stevie would go along with that. Especially with the way some of the guys looked at Bailey. But they were so weird after spending time up in that cult. Always talking about how you have to let each person choose their own path. And that a partner isn't property. I said that's all fine and good until some creep like Worm is checking out my girl's ass and makin' little innuendos all the time. At some point, a line has to be drawn, you know? All I know is that if that was my girl, I woulda been all up in that guy's grill."

Darger nodded.

"So what happened that made you leave?"

"To me, it was a construction job that paid well. And that was good enough, for a while, despite all the weirdness. But eventually, it started to get *too* weird. Like no amount of money is worth... Look, I guess I assumed the whole deal was to run drugs. I'd read an article about that. The drug cartels had this half-mile-long tunnel that ran across the border from Mexico into San Diego that had been used to smuggle thousands of tons of cocaine. Then they had another three quarter mile one that they used for El Chapo to escape from prison. I figured with everything else, that kind of thing made the most sense."

Darger considered explaining that Pennsylvania was nowhere near the US border but decided it was better not to interrupt.

"Anyway, one time Stevie said he heard voices down there. Women's voices. I didn't like the sound of that. And then the next time I was down there working, the power went out. It was only for like ten minutes. One of the generators they use to power some of the equipment ran out of gas... Have you ever been in pitch black before? Absolute darkness, like you can't even see your hand in front of your face? That was scary enough. But then I realized that as soon as the lights went out, I'd completely lost track of where I was. I was stuck down there, I don't know how far down. And I'm telling you, that ten minutes felt like ten hours. And then I heard... something. I thought it was crying, maybe? But almost like part animal. I don't know. It could have been my own imagination for all I know. I was flipping out down there in the dark, I won't deny that."

"What happened after that?"

"They were all apologetic about it, but…" Danny hacked up something and spit it on the ground. "Anyway, I didn't tell them, but that was it for me. Between the idea of getting stuck underground, and the weird noises, I was done. I got the hell out, right? Next thing I know, Bo is incommunicado. No one's seen Bailey or Stephen or Courtney. All of them just — poof — gone."

Danny got fidgety again, eyes darting around everywhere like a weirdo in a Cowboy hat might be watching even now.

"OK," Darger said, taking it all in. "So you don't know Cowboy's real name. Don't know where he lived or where you were doing the work. What do you know? You mentioned a truck. Do you remember what kind?"

"Like a… Ford F-350. The one with the extra rear wheels that bump out on the sides."

"License plate?" Ambrose asked.

"What do I look like? Sherlock Holmes?"

"What about a custom paint job? Something like that?"

"It was white. Pretty plain. Kept it clean enough to eat off of, but I don't remember it being all that particular other than that."

Darger clenched her jaw. In many ways, they'd made tremendous progress, and yet they had almost nothing to go on when it came to trying to find this Cowboy guy.

"What about other things… did he wear a fancy watch? Were his boots custom made?"

"No. I mean, I don't really know fashion or whatever."

Grasping now, Darger tried to rattle off any rich person thing she could think of.

"Did he have a boat? Some kind of collection? Did he

smoke cigars?"

"No, but he was really into bourbon…" Danny paused, thinking. Then he snapped his fingers. "What's the name of that guy that always falls asleep?"

"A narcoleptic?"

"Nah, man," Danny said. "He grows a long beard and goes bowling."

The only answer Darger could think of was Jeff Bridges, and she figured that couldn't be right. Thankfully her partner was better at speaking dingbat than she was.

"Rip van Winkle," Loshak said.

"That's it! Old Rip van Winkle. Cowboy went on and on about this bottle he had. Called it 'Ol' Rip' like it was a person. Said one day, when we finished up the job we were doing, he'd take it down, and we'd all party with Ol' Rip. He showed it to us once. Kept it in this fancy carved box lined with velvet, swaddled in there like a baby. Said it cost him like two grand. But he had this other kind that he bought on the regular. Like, by the case. Hold on…"

Danny pulled a phone from his pocket. He scrolled through a photo gallery for a few seconds and then held it out, showing off a selfie of himself and Bo Cooke. Each of them held a bottle of Heaven Hill bourbon in their hand.

"That's you and Bo?" Darger asked after jotting down the specific name of the bourbon in the photo.

"Yeah. Sometimes after we were done working, Cowboy'd be in a good mood. He'd want all of us to hang around. Chill in the hot tub. Get shit-faced. Party, you know? And I wasn't complaining. He'd send Worm out for food and whatnot. This night here, he only had one bottle of Heaven Hill left, and so he asked Worm if he'd picked up the order he put in earlier in the week. Worm said he hadn't had a chance to stop by the liquor store to get it." Danny shrugged. "But Cowboy wanted Worm to go get it, and right now. Said the clock was ticking since he'd have to drive over the state line to pick up the order, and the store would be closing in less than half an hour. They got into kind of an argument about it. Worm was in the hot tub and didn't wanna get out, I guess. He kept saying that we could share what was left."

Danny's eyes got that faraway look of someone reliving a memory.

"So Cowboy set the bottle of bourbon on this big ass dragon statue he had down there, went up to the house, and came back with a baseball bat. Didn't say nothing. Just lined up the shot and smashed the bottle to bits. Said now they were plum out of Heaven Hill, and Worm knew how he got when he didn't get to properly unwind on the weekend. Worm was pissed, but he jumped up outta that hot tub real quick and got his ass dressed."

Danny inhaled, coming out of the dream-like state.

"Me and Bo wanted to take off after that. Cowboy could get kind of agitated when he did coke. Like mood swings or whatever. He'd be laughing his ass off, and then he'd go quiet and stare at you real intense." Danny crossed his arms. "And just so you know, I never did any of that. I stick to strictly legal substances."

"I'm sure you do," Darger said, waving him on. "Keep going."

"Well, we asked Stevie to take us home, and that got Cowboy even more agitated. Said the party was just getting started. Ushered us into this back room in the basement where he had a little theater set up — a projector and those red velvet curtains and a popcorn machine. He put on some old porno movie. Like from the 70s, I'd say. And it wasn't like normal porno, where the cable guy comes in and ends up banging the two roommates. This was like a few different ladies dancing naked on stage and doing weird routines. Like one of them could shoot stuff out of her nethers, and a different one was squirting milk from—"

Darger held up a hand.

"I think we get the idea."

"After a while, Cowboy got quiet and did the staring thing. Started asking us weird questions. Like, had we ever thought about how the world needed a reset. That certain people are natural leaders. Made to dominate the rest, keep the sheeple in line, but that things right now are out of balance because all the wrong people are in power. He said that some sort of apocalyptic event was an inevitability, so anyone with half a brain should be planning for that, because we'd need a certain number of people to repopulate the planet after. And then some shit about a prison planet." Danny's mouth formed a scowl. "It was uncomfortable as hell. Even if the porno he'd put on hadn't been that weird shit, the stuff he was talking about..."

"Did you connect his talking about an apocalypse to the digging?" Darger asked, wondering now if the whole case could be explained this simply. Someone with paranoid delusions attempting to build an underground bunker for the apocalypse he was certain would come. But why kill four people? And why starve them first?

"Not really. I was more focused on trying to get the hell out of there," Danny said. "But then Worm got back with the bourbon and Cowboy calmed down. Said we should each take a bottle and call up the girls and really make a night of it."

"And what about—"

Danny straightened suddenly and let out a gasp.

"Oh god."

Darger followed his gaze over to the entrance of the park. There was a group of four elderly women speedwalking in windbreakers and sunglasses and a teenage boy throwing a stick for a Dalmatian, but Darger saw nothing that should have alarmed Danny.

"What's wrong?"

Instead of answering, Danny jumped to his feet and took off at a sprint in the opposite direction.

"Danny, wait!" Darger said, hopping up and going after him.

Danny was faster than he looked and had an uncanny ability to slip through gaps in a crowd. He reached the street that bordered the far side of the park and ran straight across without looking for traffic. He made it to the other side unscathed, but Darger had to stop for a city bus. By the time she reached the sidewalk on the other end, Danny had disappeared inside the farmer's market.

"Shit," she muttered when she reached the pavilion.

The place was packed. A bustling horde of people haggling over produce and flowers and candles. And Danny wasn't in sight.

Ambrose caught up with her then, breathing heavily and wiping sweat from his brow.

"He's gone," she said. "We lost him."

"Eh, I figure we got the bourbon thing out of him. That's something."

"I guess," Darger said, pausing to catch her breath. "What spooked him?"

"An extended cab truck rolled by. It was silver, not white. But I guess in his paranoid state, his mind saw what it wanted." Ambrose gestured back at the park. "Come on. Loshak's looking up the Old Rip van Winkle right now, seeing if we can use that to trace our guy."

CHAPTER 43

He fixed his hat and then hunched over the body. Careful to keep his feet wide of the red puddle surrounding it. The wetness on the rocks looked glassy and dark in the soft light of the lantern.

Was he dead yet?

He gazed down at the torso. Saw no rise and fall of the chest. And the blood had stopped flowing from the wounds.

He shuffled a little closer, still stooped over. Hissing breaths spouted from his nostrils as he moved. Almost sounded like silent laughter. Maybe it was, he thought. Maybe it was.

He poked at the corpse with the tip of his blade. Speared it along the collarbone.

No response.

His free hand reached down for the corpse, fingers curved like claws. He squeezed the cheeks between his thumb and forefinger and lifted the face. Turned it toward him.

The flesh was still pliable, going cool now, but still warm, all things considered. He looked into the eyes. Or tried to.

Another hissing breath spurted from his nose. This time it was definitely laughter.

The dead man's peepers were pointed in different directions now. One angled up and to the right. The other pointed straight down. He looked like a broken Howdy Doody doll or some creepy thing from a thrift shop.

Jesus. Wrong place at the wrong fucking time, hombre.

Those pinchy crab fingers released the cheeks. The skull

plopped down in the blood with a slap and a slurp, splashed a little.

He knelt down fully now and took his blade to the fleshy skin just along the jaw.

CHAPTER 44

Cora tried to extend her cramping legs, but the cage was too small. No matter how she contorted herself, she couldn't stretch her aching muscles. No relief.

Her water was gone now. She tilted the jug to her lips anyway. Tried to spill any remaining drops into her maw. If even one droplet fell, she couldn't feel it on her tongue, which now felt like a microwaved sponge had been shoved into her mouth.

"Lily!" she hissed, taken aback by the shrill intensity in her voice.

No response. Never any response.

She'd almost believe that she'd imagined Lily now, that her panic-warped brain had created a voice to keep her from succumbing to the silence all around. But she was pretty sure the girl had been real, had been there, even if she wasn't now.

Another flare of pain shot up from her feet into her calves like a bolt. The cramps clenched the muscles as hard as they could. Made her toes curl.

She gritted her teeth. Twisted within her nest of blankets. Lay down flat on her back and tried to stretch her legs into the opposite corner.

It didn't help much.

Little puffs of frustration came out of her nose now. A staccato wheeze. She knew if she didn't reel that in, it'd mean more tears, and she didn't want to waste water that way. Not any more of it, at least.

She closed her eyes. Forced herself to take a deep breath — in through her nostrils and out through her lips. Slowly. And then another deep breath and another.

She wasn't sure how long it'd been now. Two days or maybe three, she thought. She'd slept for a lot of it, though the rest didn't seem to do her any good, leaving her eyes feeling sandy and stinging.

It didn't help that the sleep was always fitful. Populated with violent dreams. Knives piercing abdomens. Throats cut. Blood spilled.

Stab. Slash. Thrust. Slice.

Chase taken away from her. Plucked from this plane and thrust into oblivion.

She rubbed her legs. Fingers pinching at the sore muscles though the massages only seemed to hurt, never seemed to help.

The ache had gotten in deep. Settled into the meat of her legs and neck. It wouldn't just go away.

She stopped rubbing when she heard the noises.

Little pops echoed down the tunnel in staccato bursts, sounding hollow.

Footsteps.

Someone was coming.

CHAPTER 45

Darger walked the snaking trail back toward the dry fountain. As soon as she saw the scowl on Loshak's face, she knew it wasn't good news.

"Tracing the bourbon isn't going to be as cut and dry as we first thought," he said, fiddling with his phone.

Darger was impressed with how much progress he'd made using his phone since being back with Jan. There was a time when she could barely get him to answer a simple phone call, let alone use the internet on the damn thing.

"So is it not that rare or what?" Ambrose asked.

"Oh no. It's rare. It's so limited that you have to enter a lottery every year to even have a chance of buying a bottle directly from the distiller."

"That's even better," Ambrose said. "We just need the names of the lottery winners."

Loshak grumbled.

"He didn't get it through one of the lotteries."

"How do you know?"

"Because the distillery sells the bottles at MSRP, which is nowhere near the two grand Danny said he paid. That means he most likely bought it second-hand." Loshak sighed. "He could have bought it anywhere. There are websites that sell it. And there are groups of collectors that do private sales amongst one another."

"In other words, harder to track," Darger said.

"Hard, but not impossible." Loshak set his phone down

beside him. "It'll take more time than we were probably initially thinking, that's all. And we still have the truck Danny described. The Arby's they met up at. We've got leads."

Darger clenched her fists, digging her fingernails into her palms. She glanced in the direction Danny had gone.

"I wish he hadn't taken off like that. We could have asked him a few more questions," she said, talking more to herself than anything.

Ambrose shook his head.

"Kid was in a state. Only time I've ever seen a witness that jumpy was either paranoid schiz or a tweaker. Though I suppose I can understand," he said. "You ever been underground?"

Darger considered the question and remembered a family trip to Glenwood Caverns.

"I did a cave tour once, but I was so young I remember the pictures more than the actual experience."

Ambrose nodded.

"Makes you feel small. Powerless. Like an ant. Imagine being in one of those tunnels and worrying about what happens if it collapses?" He shrugged. "Then all your friends end up dead, and you're convinced that you'll be next. I guess I'd be on edge, too."

"Speaking of caves, you know the first doomsday cult in America took shelter in caves right here in Philadelphia way back in the 17th century," Loshak said. "The Cave of Kelpius in Fairmount Park. They called themselves a few different names including 'The Mystic Brotherhood.'"

Part of Darger's mind had been wandering while Loshak spoke, and now she whipped her head back around to face him.

"Wait a minute. Maybe it's not the Rip van Winkle that's the key."

"Huh?"

"Maybe it's the other stuff he drinks..." Darger got out her notes, checking the name of the other bourbon Danny had mentioned. "According to Danny, Cowboy regularly buys Heaven Hill Bottled-in-Bond by the case. I'm guessing it's not quite rare enough that someone buying a single bottle would necessarily be traceable. But a case? And we know, at least once in the last few months, that Cowboy sent Worm out to pick up a case."

"And that it wasn't in Pennsylvania," Ambrose said. "Danny said Worm had to cross the state line to pick up the order. Liquor stores in the state of Pennsylvania are run by the state. So my guess is that he can pick up a case for cheaper if he buys out of state."

"So we need to start talking to all the liquor stores near the state line," Loshak said.

Ambrose was already pulling out his phone.

"I'll call the station and have them put a list together."

While Ambrose made the call, Darger sat down next to Loshak.

"What do you make of all of this?" she said. "I thought this case was weird at the beginning. But the deeper we go, it just keeps getting weirder."

"Can't disagree with you there." Loshak absently mussed his hair with one hand. "We've got starved bodies. A cult. A missing handyman named Worm. An enigmatic billionaire known only as Cowboy. And he's hiring people to dig tunnels under his house. Possibly as some kind of nuclear bunker. Or possibly to run drugs to the Mexican border."

Darger snorted.

"Don't forget the part about how much he's paying. If Danny, Bo Cooke, Worm, and Stephen Mayhew were all getting paid $1500 a week, that's over twenty-thousand a month. And Danny seemed to believe there'd been a bigger crew at some point in the past."

"You know, the first thing I thought of when he started talking about the tunnels under the guy's house was this thing out in Maryland," Loshak said. "There was this kid — very bright, but more than a little eccentric. He was also obsessed with the notion of some kind of impending apocalypse. Roped some guys into digging out a bunker under his house, though I don't think he hid the purpose. Anyway, it all came out because there was a fire in the kid's basement and one of the guys digging ended up dying."

"Christ," Darger said. "I mean this kid sounds mentally ill."

"Yeah. But you think this Cowboy guy sounds completely sane?"

"Good point." Darger crossed one leg over the other. "But why the secrecy? Blindfolding the people he brings in to dig just seems... odd."

Loshak shrugged.

"A lot of these end times types are convinced that part of the deal will be fighting off all the people that didn't see it coming. Didn't prepare. So maybe he's covering his bases. Making sure no one knows too much about his underground refuge."

Loshak cocked his head to one side before he went on.

"Or maybe they stumbled on something they shouldn't

have. Sounds like this Cowboy guy has all manner of odd and outright illegal things going on."

Ambrose strolled over, tucking his phone back into his jacket.

"You two in the mood to do some phone banking?" he asked. "I can offer to repay your help with a gourmet meal of lukewarm pizza and a Dixie cup of Pepsi."

"Make it a Dixie cup of Coke, and we're in," Loshak said.

CHAPTER 46

The first thing Ambrose did when they reached his station house was to get someone from the state liquor control board on the phone to have them look into any orders for a case of Heaven Hill BIB in any of their stores. The representative called back and informed them that no such orders had been placed in any of their stores.

"What we expected," Ambrose said. "But I had to check anyway, just in case."

They went back to their other task, which was pulling the numbers for all liquor stores within half an hour's driving distance from the Pennsylvania state line. They came up with a list of 164 stores and divided it amongst themselves.

Hours passed as they made call after call. Sometimes the calls were quick — many of the liquor stores were small mom and pop affairs. If it happened to be the owner who answered, they could often tell Darger off the top of their head whether they'd ordered a case of the Heaven Hill recently since they were responsible for putting in all the orders with the supplier. So far, the answer had always been no.

Other stores were chain affairs. Darger would be put on hold and connected with a manager who had a lot of questions. Explaining that she was an FBI agent was usually enough to get them to check their logs. And still she struck out, again and again.

A few minutes after five o'clock, Officer Primanti came in with a tall stack of pizza boxes in his arms.

"Primanti," Ambrose said. "My man."

He took a slice of pepperoni and mushroom from one of the boxes and took a bite.

"You wanna know why Primanti is always running these little errands? Bringing us coffee and pizza and whatnot?"

"Why?"

"He wants to be Homicide, one day. I told him the best way to do that is to kiss a little ass now and then." Ambrose clapped Primanti on the shoulder with a free hand. "But our boy here is a Grade A Brown Noser. He takes sucking up to a whole new level."

Primanti blushed.

Ambrose's phone rang, and the jovial expression on his face soured as soon as he saw who it was calling.

"Fucking mayor again. Jesus wept."

He ducked into the hallway, and Darger couldn't help but notice that Primanti seemed relieved. She gestured to her work station.

"You wanna do some real homicide work?" she asked. "Make some calls while I eat?"

"Really?" Primanti's eyes glittered with eagerness. "Sure."

Darger handed him her sheet and gave him a quick rundown of what to say.

When Ambrose came back in from his call, his eyes immediately zeroed in on the pair.

"Did you pull a Tom Sawyer on Officer Primanti?" he asked, crossing his arms. "You get him to whitewash your fence?"

"It's good experience."

He snorted.

"Is he paying you for the pleasure, too?" he said, chuckling.

Darger finished her pizza and took the seat next to Primanti. He was still on a call, so she took the next number on the list.

The manager of a store named Veni Vidi Vino put her on hold for a solid ten minutes, only to click back on the line to say they didn't have any receipts for a case of Heaven Hill.

"Sorry," the woman said.

"Thanks for your time."

Darger hung up and grabbed another slice of pizza. She took a bite and chewed as she dialed the number for Lasko's Liquor and Spirits, located in Brandywine, Delaware.

Darger repeated the words she'd said a few dozen times now, explaining that she was an FBI agent looking for a store that had sold a case of Heaven Hill sometime in the last six months or so.

"One second," the girl said, and Darger was glad when she didn't put her on hold. "Oh yeah. Here it is. About four months ago."

Darger sat up in her seat, heart thumping.

"Can you tell me if the same customer has ordered a case before?"

"Mmm… yeah. Pretty regularly. Every four to six months, it looks like. Going back… years. Wow. I guess they know what they like."

"Great. I'll need the name and address on the order."

"Of course," the girl said. "Do you have a pen?"

There was a little yelp from the girl, and then a man's voice came on the line.

"Who is this?"

"My name is Violet Darger. I'm an agent with the FBI."

"Is this a joke? Some kind of crank call?"

"No. I'm working a homicide case with Philadelphia PD. If you'd like, you can speak with the lead detective."

"Philly PD? What's that got to do with us? We're located in Delaware."

"I understand that, but we really need to locate the person who bought that case of bourbon and—"

"Yeah... I don't think I should be handing out this kind of information to some random person over the phone. Doesn't sit right with me."

"This is for a homicide investigation, sir. I'm only asking you to do the right thing. The easy way, you could call it. But if you want our task force to come down with a warrant and make a scene by seizing all your computers and paperwork in front your customers, we'd be happy to oblige."

The line went silent for a beat, and then the man's voice came back, all the piss and vinegar from before having drained out of it.

"Keith Heider. 377 Hidden Valley Lane, Glen Mills."

When Darger went to thank him, he'd already hung up. That was just as well, she thought.

She repeated the address to the others in the room.

"How far is that?" Darger asked.

"Not far at all," Ambrose said, pulling out his phone. "But this time we're definitely going to need a warrant."

CHAPTER 47

Keith "Cowboy" Heider's house was nestled at the end of a
suburban cul-de-sac in an area utterly sprawling with them.
The home was largely indistinguishable from the others in a ten
or so block radius. Large and modern. Slate vinyl siding butted
up against pale stonework. Curving asphalt driveway that led to
a massive garage. The landscaping was mostly comprised of
small trees and neat shrubs in the front and taller pines in the
back, with a row of spiky exotic grasses thrown in to accent the
borderline between the two spaces.

Looking at the Google Maps satellite view of Walden
Woods gave a dreary grid-like impression of this place. Little
boxes dotting the streets in neat rows, turning to loops and
whorls like fingerprints when it came to the symmetrical
subdivisions like this one. All of them looked packed in tight
on the satellite image, like a mouth full of teeth, but in person
the homes had more space than Darger had been expecting.

Her rental car was parked across the street, set on a
diagonal from Heider's place, and she angled her head that
way. Her eyes flicked to the rearview, where the two other
unmarked cars were, then slid back to the house.

Loshak sat in the passenger seat, crunching on chips from a
tiny bag of Doritos.

"What's with the fun-size bag?" Darger said, not breaking
her gaze from the house. "Packing a sack lunch these days,
Agent Loshak? I kind of figured you'd be all about your AARP
discount or whatever. Hitting the diners. Chatting up the

274

waitresses of a certain age."

Loshak dug out another handful of neon orange chips.

"I got these from the vending machine at the station," he said. "And you call yourself a detective?"

Darger snorted out a laugh.

"You want me to keep reading this guy's bio?" Loshak said, after downing a few more chips. "Or would you rather continue busting my balls about my admittedly *wee* bag of Doritos?"

"Can you start over?" Darger said, still chuckling at wee. "I was kind of focused on the house."

Loshak sighed and let the bag of Doritos plop down on his lap. He fumbled to scroll up on his phone, using his pinky finger to avoid touching it with any of the digits stained orange with nacho cheese powder.

"OK. Keith Heider, 38 years old. Alias Cowboy. He served in the Marine Corps way back in 2001. Got kicked out nine months after he enlisted. Bad conduct discharge. We're still waiting on the official records for the details on that, but the current speculation is that it was drug-related. Makes sense to me."

Darger's gaze flitted from window to window up at the house as Loshak spoke. Based on the white truck parked in the driveway, they had hopes that Cowboy was home. But they wanted to get visual confirmation of his presence before they called in the SWAT team. An early raid could tip him off that they were onto him, send him on the run. The task force higher-ups all agreed on that point — they wanted to be absolutely certain they got him on the first try.

"Anyway," Loshak went on. "Heider worked as a contractor for a couple of years after that, the bulk of it in Western

Pennsylvania. He mostly oversaw the construction of prefab homes. By all accounts, he was a moderately successful local businessman in the Allegheny County area. Sponsored a Little League team for a few years. Showed up in the newspaper for a few other charitable events. Real man of the people type. Nothing noteworthy in terms of a criminal record. A couple speeding tickets. No other priors."

Loshak ate a single chip, crunching, chewing, and swallowing before he went on.

"From there, he kind of falls off the map. We've got nothing as of about 2009. No known address for a seven-year period. His business had been shuttered by that time, possibly for quite a while even before then based on his tax returns, which he abruptly stopped filing in 2005. Then in 2016 he shows up in the paperwork in multiple shell corporations we're still digging into. A couple of those are filed in Pennsylvania, six more in Delaware, all reporting serious income — eight figures annually for a few. Problem is, with the crisscross of companies and paperwork, we don't know where the money is coming from."

Darger's phone vibrated from inside her pocket. The display screen said, "Luck." She swiped left to ignore it.

Loshak crunched more chips, looking from the phone to Darger. It looked like he wanted to say something, but he didn't.

Movement at the house caught both of their attention then. Darger sucked in a sharp breath, and Loshak's next Dorito stopped shy of his lips.

A flutter of light and shadow filled one of the window frames in the upstairs of the house. At first the movement was indistinct, some indecipherable shifting of a silhouette.

"That's him," she said, her voice coming out breathy and quiet. "It's gotta be."

"Are you sure?" Loshak said, still holding that chip about two inches from his mouth.

Then the cowboy hat drifted into plain view, held there in the center of the window frame for a few seconds. As he moved his face up toward the window, Darger could make out the chrome sunglasses beneath the hat's brim — a pair that instantly made her think of Elvis Presley and Guy Fieri. Looking lower, she saw the horseshoe mustache, dark bristles bending down from his lip all the way to his chin. Then he turned, and his ponytail trailed out behind him like a scarf.

A single laugh puffed out of Loshak involuntarily.

"Well, the kid was right about one thing," he said. "This guy really does look like Joe Exotic."

CHAPTER 48

Darger kept her eyes on the house while Loshak called it in to Ambrose. She could hear every word the detective said as Loshak's phone was turned up so loud.

"Judge signed the warrant twenty minutes ago, so that's all ready to go, and the SWAT boys are ready to roll. On their way as we speak," Ambrose said, sounding even more chipper than usual. "Give it another fifteen minutes, and we'll be ready to kick this shit heel's door down before he has any clue what's happening."

Good, Darger thought. We'll just keep an eye on the house until the SWAT unit gets here. Easy peasy.

"Cavalry is on the way," Loshak said after he hung up.

"So I heard," Darger said. "Do you always keep your phone volume cranked like that?"

Loshak's eyes shifted back and forth like the silver balls of a Newton's Cradle as he answered.

"What? Yeah. Wait... no. Wait... I don't know. What do I say here so that you don't make fun of me for being old? Like... uh... maaaaybe."

Darger opened her mouth to respond, but Loshak cut her off.

"Blah blah hearing aid. Blah blah AARP discount. Blah blah early bird special at the Old Country Buffet. That good enough? You want to go on and run it into the ground? Really give this dead horse a good and thorough flogging?"

Darger stared at him for a long moment before she

278

responded.

"You're going to damage your hearing is all I'm saying," she said, keeping her voice smooth and sincere. "And how would you enjoy your Bing Crosby records after that?"

Loshak shook his head. They were silent for a while, and then Loshak spoke up again.

"My dad had all those Herb Alpert and the Tijuana Brass records when I was a kid."

Lights flicked on at the front of the house. Two sconces, one on each side of the front stoop, flaring to life. Darger's eyes went wide.

"Had some Jonathan Winter comedy records, too. And one time—"

"Shh!" she cut Loshak off. "Something's happening."

The big steel slab of the front door swung out of the way then, the murk of dusk shifting around it. A figure stepped through the gapped place.

Cowboy stood on the front porch, looking ganglier than Darger had expected. Long-armed and scrawny of limb. Shoulders slightly stooped. The bootcut jeans and distressed denim shirt paired with the standard cowboy boots and hat made him look like a country singer walking out on stage, or maybe someone dressed as Toby Keith for Halloween.

He keyed a number pad to lock the digital deadbolt on the front door before strutting his way over to the driveway. Ponytail whipping and bouncing.

"Oh, shit," Loshak said, his voice drifting down toward a whisper. "Is he leaving? Should we grab him now?"

Darger's lips moved, but she couldn't answer. She could only watch.

When Cowboy reached his truck, he opened the driver's side door and kicked one cowboy boot up onto the nerf bar. But just as his body touched the threshold of the doorway, he stopped dead. Froze there. Motionless for the length of three heartbeats. The dome light reflected little glowing spheres in his sunglasses.

Darger held her breath as he slowly craned his neck. His head swiveled to face her. Stopped there. Stared straight at her. His horseshoe mustache twitched.

"What the fuck?" Loshak said in a whispery falsetto. He scrunched down in his seat as though that might help conceal them.

Everything held still for a moment. The whole world gone quiet, gone motionless.

And then Cowboy bolted back for the house. Didn't even bother to close the truck door. Just ran. Boots clapping against the concrete of the front walk.

Darger's fingers fumbled for the door handle. She climbed out and gave chase. Blood thrumming in her ears.

Footsteps fell in behind her as she darted across the street, Loshak and the officers from the unmarked cars, she knew.

Just as she reached the driveway, the front door opened, and Cowboy disappeared inside.

CHAPTER 49

Darger zipped across the concrete walk. Vaulted up onto the stoop. Launched herself through the gapped doorway, a forearm knocking the door out of her way.

The foyer opened before her, and Darger slowed, drawing her weapon and pointing it at the floor. Observing. Listening.

High ceilings yawned overhead. Slate tiles tapped out brittle ticks beneath her footsteps. She paced across the space and stared into the house beyond, gun drawn.

Multiple potential pathways lay before her. A den to the right with a back hallway stretching out from there. A staircase leading up next to that. And the kitchen straight ahead.

If Cowboy was moving somewhere near, she couldn't hear it over the sound of her heart thudding in her chest.

Her mind raced. He could be destroying evidence right now. Why else run for the house instead of jumping into the truck?

She clenched her jaw. Fought down the urge to bound ever forward. Forced herself to wait there on the precipice of the living room.

Loshak and the others filtered through the door right behind her, two detectives and a couple of plainclothes officers joining her partner. They drew up alongside her place at the edge of the foyer, and then everyone looked at one another.

They communicated with hand signals and nods, Loshak taking point. He motioned to them one by one, ordering each individual toward one of the doorways with a wave of his hand.

From there, they fanned out and pressed deeper into the house. Two of the officers veered right into a den that led to a back hallway. Another pair took the staircase next to that, veering up and out of sight.

Darger proceeded straight into the kitchen alongside Loshak, each of them winding around one side of the island. Their footsteps were careful. Quiet. Darger's eyes scanned everything.

Shiny concrete countertops gleamed gray under the pendant lights, and a hulking stainless steel sink made a canyon-like vacancy in the center of the counter, seemingly fit for a restaurant. Shaker cabinets faced outward from the walls above and below the counters, the matte finish a muted blue like flax. Small appliances squatted in strategic locations: blender, coffee grinder, espresso machine, juicer.

The entire wall ahead was comprised of three industrial-sized refrigerators set side by side. A fourth fridge sat in the corner next to those, with glass windows like a convenience store soda cooler revealing endless Tetra Pak cartons of coconut water inside, lined up in neat rows.

Loshak lifted one hand from his Glock to point at the closed door opposite the Vita Coco display, and Darger nodded. She knew what he was thinking right away.

They edged toward the wooden door. Darger got there first and pulled it open.

The basement steps trailed down from the open doorway. Light streamed up from the chamber below. She could hear his boots clicking down there.

He was in the basement.

Darger raced down the steps. Eyes locked on the smooth

concrete of the floor below.

At the bottom, she wheeled to her left, lifted her gun.

He was there. Hunched over a large piece of furniture, arms wrapped around the dark bulk, trying to shift its weight. His feet kicked at the floor behind him, heels of his cowboy boots scrabbling and sliding over the smooth concrete floor like hooves. He torqued his hips. Hurled himself into the piece of furniture. His ponytail jerked and flopped along with his strain, swishing over the back of his shirt like a brush.

"Freeze! FBI!" Darger said.

Her gun floated up into her field of vision, the sight lining up with the curved place where his ponytail connected to the back of his skull, just along the brain stem.

Cowboy struggled with the bulk in his arms for another second, scraping it over the floor. Then he dove for the concrete, belly slapping hard against it, arms and legs clambering to push him forward. He tried to slither into the narrow gap in the floor next to the end table. The tunnel.

"Freeze!" Loshak said, shuffling up next to Darger.

Cowboy's head disappeared into the breach, his cowboy hat knocked off by the bottom of the table, tumbling down beside him. He crawled forward, but his shoulders caught there, jammed between the bottom of the end table and the jagged concrete edge. Stuck.

He wriggled. Tried to use serpentine motions to worm his shoulders through the tight space.

"Grab his legs," Darger said, holstering her weapon and diving for the wiggling idiot.

She clutched one ankle, and Loshak grabbed the other. Together they yanked him free of the hole.

His emerging skull somehow reminded Darger of a turtle head poking out of its shell.

They pulled him straight back. Legs lifted up. His top half still facedown on the floor.

He lurched to grip the edge of the hole, fingers catching the lip, arms quivering as he tried to pull himself toward the gap.

But the agents wrenched him free and kept backpedaling. Watched him claw at the concrete, fingers curled into talons, fingernails scraping over the smooth cement.

When they were well clear of the hole, Darger leaped onto his back. Thighs straddling his ribcage.

She yanked one of his arms behind him and bent the hand up toward his shoulder blades, felt the limb grow taut until it quivered. She hurried to work the first loop of the handcuffs toward his wrist. Snapped it into place with a metallic click.

"Be-itch!" he said, suddenly aware of what was happening.

He kicked. Flailed. Bucked his hips and arched his back. Tried to throw her. Every tick of his body language screamed out a toddler-like tantrum. Ponytail whipping.

"Be-itch! Be-itch! Be-itch!"

Darger held on. Clenched her thighs tighter around his middle and felt this flexing cluster of muscles going wild beneath her. Thrashing around. A bronco at a rodeo.

One of her hands gripped a wad of his shirt up near the scruff of his neck. The other arm reached out for balance, drifted in the air beside her.

This close, the stench of too much Stetson cologne rolled off of him in waves as though the pores of his skin were secreting it. Sharp and faintly soapy. Something familiar in it, Darger thought. Maybe sandalwood.

She watched the cuffs whip back and forth from his wrist as she held on. Thought about when she might be able to grab the loose side and get them on his other wrist.

All at once he went limp beneath her. Let his head and arms go slack and sink to the smooth concrete. One big breath made the ribcage between her legs puff up, and then the air came seeping out, reducing him, smaller and smaller.

Darger jerked his hands behind his back once more and cuffed the other wrist. He didn't resist.

Then she climbed off him. Stood. Took a few deep breaths. Eyes never leaving his heaving back, that ponytail jutting from the back of his head, his face turned away from her.

Loshak helped her turn him over so he was sitting upright, each of them scooping beneath an armpit, and Darger braced herself for a second round of struggling, feet set wide, core tensed.

But he kept his head down. Lips pouted. Chin quivering ever so faintly which made the bottom of his mustache flutter. He looked like a scolded child about to cry.

The other officers had made their way down to the basement by now, and they all watched this from the bottom of the steps. Held rapt there. Quiet. Hesitant, it seemed, to move fully into the room.

"What a piece of work," Officer Primanti said, shaking his head.

That seemed to break whatever spell had held them at the threshold, and they all came over and surrounded Cowboy. Trying to get a better look, Darger thought. One of them ripped his silly chrome sunglasses off, and they all observed him in silence for a beat.

"Jesus Christ," one of the officers said. "Dude really *does* look like Joe Exotic. Except, like, really sad."

With the suspect secure, Darger crept over to the piece of furniture he'd been struggling with. Saw the grooves in the floor where the thing had gouged the concrete.

Then her eyes drifted lower, to the open place in the floor.

The hole into the tunnel seemed to remove any lingering doubt. This was their guy — Keith "Cowboy" Heider.

Darger stepped closer. Peered down into the dark tunnel, a black hole, and shuddered. She wondered what horrors must lie down there now. Waiting in the dark for the light to lay them bare.

"Well... we got him," Loshak said behind her. That pulled her out of the gloom, drew her back to the light. "It's been good to work another case with you, Agent Darger."

She turned around and headed that way. Saw the crooked grin on her partner's face. Then she saw his raised hand next to that, though it took her a second to realize what he wanted.

She gave Loshak a high-five, feeling a little weird about it.

The other officers seemed downright giddy now, huddling over their sad Joe Exotic, faces aglow with triumph.

CHAPTER 50

By the time they were ready to perp-walk Cowboy up the steps and out of his home, the full brunt of the police force had descended upon the scene.

Agent Zaragoza appeared, barking orders at no one in particular about how she wanted the interior search conducted, voice lifted so all could hear. Meanwhile, Detective Ambrose talked with the SWAT team about regrouping for the impending raid of the tunnel below.

Crime scene techs swarmed through the house in disposable white coveralls — bunny suits. They flitted like moths from room to room. Cameras flashing everywhere. Evidence logged and bagged. Excited voices tangling over each other.

Darger walked behind Cowboy as they mounted the basement steps. When they reached the top, she gripped his upper arm and guided him through the mess of law enforcement toward the front door.

He still seemed listless. Stoop-shouldered and silent.

The scene swirled around Darger. She felt some kind of hyper-awareness kick in. Every detail made sharp. Vivid. Like her mind was recording this, needed to collect every sensory detail.

The way his boots clicked and echoed over the floor. The strobe of a camera flash. The faint scent of almonds.

She gripped Cowboy's arm tighter as they rounded the corner in the kitchen, and the foyer came into view. Her eyes snapped to the front door and danced around its edges. She was beyond ready to pass through it, to load him into the back of a patrol car and get him to an interrogation room. Aching to fill in the rest of this story.

The answers were close now. Finally.

Three paces shy of the home's entrance, Cowboy's arm started to shake in her hand. She squeezed tighter still, thinking he was maybe going into shock and might grow woozy or faint.

The full convulsions began after that. His body quaked. Wrenched free of her grip. He shook back and forth in place, violent shudders. Limbs jerking and kicking.

Darger gazed into his face. Saw a blankness in his eyes. An utterly vacant stare, focused on nothing. Then they rolled back into his head, and he tipped backward and went down.

He crashed flat onto his back. Body thumping down. Writhing. Chest popping.

Foam pulsed from his open mouth. Froth heaping there and spilling from the corners, looking like lacy beer suds where it clung to the rim of his mustache.

"We need an ambulance!" Loshak said, his voice sharp with tension.

The room had gone still. Hushed.

All those swirling crime scene techs and detectives and SWAT team members turned their heads this way. Held their breath and watched.

"We need to turn him on his side," Darger said. "So he doesn't choke."

Loshak knelt beside her and helped her roll the seizing man off his back.

His torso flexed and released from the middle out, flopping

the rest of him like a salmon out of water. His skull cracked against the tile over and over, looked like it was trying to pound his ponytail into the floor.

The skin of Cowboy's face had gone cherry red now. More and more froth spilled out of his lips. Small choked sounds coming out along with the foam now. And still his eyes strained upward so that Darger could see only the whites.

Then he stopped. Limbs slowly settling into place and holding utterly still.

No more tremors. No more foam. No more strangled sounds coming out.

All those watching hesitated. Blinking. Waiting.

Darger glanced at Loshak. He nodded, and they eased him onto his back again.

Loshak leaned over and pressed his fingers to the side of Cowboy's neck. They looked ghostly white against the strange red skin. He held them there for what felt like a long time. Pulled them away at last.

"He's dead."

CHAPTER 51

Darger stood in the front yard and watched the EMTs through the open doorway. They hoisted Keith "Cowboy" Heider's limp figure from the foyer floor, shifting him up and into the open flaps of the body bag. The zippered edge yawned like a mouth, curled around him like lips, the black plastic swallowing him.

His face jutted from the gap. His eyes were still open. Those exposed whites pointed up at nothing.

And then the zipper mended itself over top of him. The pull tab climbed up from his feet. Passed over his body. And finally dead-ended above his head. The black plastic closed, blotted him out for good.

"Did you see how red his skin got?" Loshak asked.

Darger blinked, startled from her thoughts.

"What?"

"His skin. Looked like a boiled lobster. It's a sign of cyanide poisoning," Loshak said. "The Nazis loved cyanide. The SS soldiers carried little capsules on their person. Better to commit suicide than be captured, right? Just crush the capsule between the molars, swallow the concentrated poison, and be whisked away to oblivion before the enemy could torture you for information."

He shook his head before he went on.

"Heinrich Himmler killed himself in custody that way. Leonard Lake did the same when he was arrested. Had the capsules sewn into his clothes. Took him a few days to actually die, though."

Darger's palms felt icy. Fingers numb. She rubbed her hands together, but it didn't help.

One of the paramedics tapped his shoe on the footswitch of the gurney, and then the two of them lifted the bed frame until the folding support legs extended and locked into place beneath. With the gurney at full height, they wheeled it through the door and down the walk.

It was late now. Almost dark. Thick gray hung everywhere, like the color had been drained from reality as the day gave way to night.

It wasn't cold, but Darger shivered nevertheless. Something about seeing death up close, seeing it rip someone from the mortal plane so quickly, had shaken her, even if the victim in this case wasn't someone who probably deserved much sympathy.

The paramedics loaded the body into the back of the ambulance and closed the doors, one after the other. Then they climbed into the front seat and slowly pulled away from the curb.

No siren. No twirling lights. They just drifted away.

A hand grabbed Darger's shoulder, startling her. She turned to find Detective Ambrose, a grave look on his face.

"We've got something you should see in here."

CHAPTER 52

Ambrose led Darger and Loshak to a guest bedroom at the back
of the house — a small space with dark blue walls and darker
wood details. There seemed a tighter cluster of crime scene
techs swirling here, their vinyl bunny suits crinkling as they
jockeyed around each other for position, snapping photos as
always.

Darger's eyes scanned the decor first. A mahogany dresser
and similarly dark bedside table surrounded the twin-sized bed,
its bedspread dominated by dark purples and reds.

Across the room, she finally saw what Ambrose wanted to
show her.

A bookcase had been swung away from the wall, revealing a
hidden doorway behind it. Thick darkness lay beyond that
rectangular opening. Too thick, Darger thought. Utter darkness
hung like a blanket on the other side of the door frame.

Then a camera flash lit up the space, and Darger
understood.

"A hidden room," Ambrose said, knifing between some
techs to get to the door. Darger and Loshak followed.

"Did you have to pull on one of the books to get it to
open?" Loshak said, but Ambrose didn't respond to his joke.

"Seems our boy — our recently deceased Cowboy, I should
say — was big into amateur photography," the detective said.
"An enthusiast, you could say."

They stepped into a darkroom for developing analog
photographs. An acrid chemical smell filled Darger's nostrils

right away, the fumes stinging faintly in her eyes. Ambrose dismissed the tech snapping photos and flipped a light switch just inside the door.

Red light lit the space. A dark glow like wine illuminating all that stood before them.

Various trays of liquid lay in front of them. Shallow sinks, more or less, indented into a workbench. Photos hung on a clothesline in the opposite corner of the room, but they were faced away from Darger, forming four white rectangles from her point of view. Blank.

Ambrose moved to the line. Reached up with a nitrile-gloved hand and plucked one of the photos free. Then he turned it for Darger and Loshak to see, not quite offering it to them.

In the photograph, a naked woman posed on all fours, perched on what looked like a cheap motel room bed. The gaudy floral print of the blanket beneath her combined with the wood-paneled wall seemed to suggest it was taken years ago, but the fact that it was recently developed seemed to suggest otherwise.

"Alas, he was more of a pornographer than an artist," Ambrose said, clipping the photo back on the line. "He had a sensitive aesthetic eye for, you know, boobs. Quite prolific, too."

Ambrose shot a pair of finger guns at a stack of something in the corner of the room. Darger turned. It took her eyes a second to make sense of what she was seeing.

Photo albums. It was a stack of photo albums slightly taller than her. It had to be thousands of pictures.

She picked one up and riffled through a few pages. Naked

flesh gleamed up from the glossy photo paper, all of it tinted blood-red by the darkroom light.

Fresh faces made eye contact with the camera lens, seemed to stare right into the viewer's gaze. A new face adorned every page or two. So many different girls.

Not just thousands of pictures, Darger realized. Thousands of girls.

"There were even more," Ambrose said. "A whole 'nother stack of photo albums just like those. The techs are processing a big batch of them now."

Darger's eyes drifted from face to face. Tried to read the expressions. Some of the girls looked nervous, but others didn't.

"Do we think these were taken consensually?" she said, turning her head to Loshak.

Her partner crinkled his brow.

"Some of them maybe," he said. He gestured to the stack of photo albums. "But this level of output speaks to intense compulsion. Obsession. I would expect the behavior to escalate. What starts as an amateur porn habit grows into something else, right? Into whatever led to those bodies in the landfill. Into whatever we'll find in the tunnels, I suspect."

Commotion outside the darkroom pulled all eyes to the doorway.

Agent Zaragoza materialized in the strange red light of the room, her face positively glowing under the bunny suit hood.

"He left something for you, Ambrose." She handed Ambrose a manila envelope. "Found it in a locked drawer in the big oak desk in the office."

The detective ran a gloved finger over the sealed flap, then turned the thing over.

Black sharpie ink scrawled spiky text on the front of the envelope.

Open in the event of my death. -K. Heider

CHAPTER 53

Ambrose carefully sliced open the envelope with a box cutter. The angular blade made a zipping sound where it slit through the manila paper.

He parted the flaps, and they all peered into that gaping yellow maw.

Inside was a single DVD-R. The gray Memorex label looked matte silver and speckled on one side, and the bottom of the disc gleamed little rainbows where the light touched it.

Ambrose dumped it into his hand and turned it over. The disc itself had no writing on it.

"Is there a DVD player where we could watch this?" he said, his eyebrows lifting as he regarded Agent Zaragoza.

The hood of the bunny suit wrinkled as she nodded.

"Out by the flat screen in the living room."

They all filed out to the front of the house then. The group of law enforcement seemed to grow into a crowd following along behind them, whispering and gesticulating. Everyone wanted to see.

Agent Zaragoza knelt before the TV and fingered the button to turn it on. The blank screen turned red, and the Roku logo flared in the center of the screen.

Ambrose popped the disc into the DVD tray beneath the flat screen. Then he fished the remote off the coffee table and hit play.

The screen went black for a second, and everyone in the room held still and silent. Darger could hear her own pulse.

And then Cowboy's face filled the screen, an arrogant smirk curling beneath the horseshoe mustache.

The image of foam frothing from his mouth and wetting that very mustache flashed in Darger's head right away, making her faintly queasy. Her hand clutched at the front of her jacket just beneath the collar. Pinched it closed.

Cowboy scooted back from the camera, his arm falling away from where he'd clicked it on. The grin on his lips bloomed into a full-blown smile, big bleached teeth exposed.

Then he looked into the viewfinder a second. Straightened his hat and sunglasses. Ran his fingers over his mustache as though smoothing it down.

"Look, here's the deal," he said into the camera. "My name is Keith Heider, and if you're watching this, then I'm probably dead. Pretty bad case of chomping on a couple cyanide capsules, right? This here video is, uh... Shoot, this is my damn manifesto, I guess you could say."

He turned his head. Took a deep breath. Then he looked back to the camera and went on.

"I got family, right? A sister. Nieces and a nephew. I just want to explain myself here. Lay out the whole, uh, explanation. Maybe that'll absolve my family of some future suffering. I hope so. They deserve no blame for what I done. No blame at all."

Cowboy lit a cigarette. Leaned back in his chair.

"We've built something. Dug something. Excavated. I'm sure that's been discovered by now. I won't belabor the engineering feat of it all."

He licked his lips. Breathed smoke.

"I have a certain taste in women. A certain... uh... fetish, I

297

guess you'd call it. I've never had a lot of trouble getting girls. Even before all my crypto investments went cuckoo-bananas, I could go out to a bar and get a girl to spread her legs for me, you know? Not a problem, bucko. Wasn't always the prettiest girl in the place, but good enough..."

He ashed his cigarette, the smoldering tube pounding against a grooved spot in the ashtray next to him.

"But over time, and I don't know exactly when it happened, I started wanting something more. I mean, there was something missing, I guess. The satisfaction was fleeting. No fulfillment. Getting a girl is one thing, you know? But keeping her? Keeping her is something else altogether."

He smiled again. Pushed his sunglasses back up onto the bridge of his nose.

"See, I wanted to keep a girl. Not like a relationship where she chatters my ear off and tries to get me to go shopping for window treatments or on family outings or some such nonsense. No, no. I wanted to bring her out when I wanted her. Put her away when I didn't. Not a relationship. Possession. It became like the ultimate desire. The most erotic thing I could think of. I get that it's, like, a control freak type of deal or whatever. Wanting to keep a girl in a little cage down in a damn tunnel or whatever."

He shook his head.

"But a man don't decide what he wants. He just wants it."

He stubbed out his cigarette and lit another.

"And then it grew from there, I guess. Wanting to keep a girl has a way of turning into wanting to keep two. Or three. Or eight."

Little puffs of laughter jetted from his nostrils, bringing

smoke with them.

"When you want something bad enough, long enough, hard enough, pursuing it stops feeling like a choice. Starts feeling like a goddamn crusade. Manifest destiny and whatever the hell. Every beat of your heart thrums with it. Every breath you take is only to get you one step closer to that edge. The point of no return, you know?"

He thumped his cig against the ashtray again.

"So I guess I've been willing to lose everything for this all along. Willing to risk it all. To the point that I carry around little poison pills on my person, OK? We all die, though. Every single one of us. Death was always part of the equation, always part of the deal. Better to accept it quickly than to rot in prison. So I promise you, I'll have no regrets right up until that final breath."

He fell silent for a few seconds.

"Better to chase a dream, man. Better to live a while."

Abruptly he moved to the camera, lifted his hand into the frame, and shut it off.

The screen went black.

CHAPTER 54

Cowboy's voice played in Darger's head as she strapped on her Kevlar vest and slid on her helmet. Little snippets of what he'd said echoed in her skull, sounding close. Intimate.

"Not a relationship. Possession."

His words made her hands go icy. Made her flesh crawl.

"A man don't decide what he wants. He just wants it."

With her body going cold and numb, she didn't feel like she was still here, in this suburban home swarming with law enforcement. Didn't feel like she was just around the corner from where a man had ridden a couple of cyanide pills into oblivion, limbs flailing, mouth foaming.

Instead, she felt alone and hollow, sucked inside herself. Ghostly. Held still somewhere cavernous and cold, somewhere far from any road.

She had to shake herself out of that state, she knew. Like right now.

She glanced over to see Loshak adjusting the chin strap of his helmet. The black vest already swathed his torso, the same as hers.

They were gearing up to follow the SWAT team into the tunnel, bringing up the rear of the underground rescue raid. She needed to stay sharp, needed to be ready for whatever might be down there.

The primary hope of everyone involved was that they'd find the girls he kept down there, and that they'd find them alive. Darger swallowed a lump when she thought about the alternatives, her eyelids fluttering.

Please let them be alive.

((

Darger watched two of the SWAT team members as she got ready. One of them took off his helmet and tucked it under his arm, a movie star haircut spilling out from beneath the hard shell as he did — hair so blond it almost looked yellow. He looked remarkably like the actor who'd played Jamie Lannister on *Game of Thrones*.

"What do you think the holdup is this time, DeBarge?" he said to the officer standing next to him.

His friend was adjusting his vest, loosening the straps and pulling the shoulders of the thing back, then re-tightening everything. He was doing this more out of boredom than anything, Darger suspected. All the SWAT guys had been geared up and ready since before any of them had stepped foot off the truck.

"You know how it works. They need to yell at us for fifteen minutes before they send us in there. Standard operating procedure."

Jamie Lannister turned his head toward Darger then. Squinted his eyes down to slits. A smile slowly spread over the bottom half of his face. He whacked his buddy on the shoulder.

"That's Violet damn Darger over there, DeBarge."

"Who?"

"Violet. Darger. The profiler who helped catch the Doll Parts Killer in Ohio. Read a newspaper once in a while."

"Oh yeah," DeBarge said, nodding and smiling.

The Kingslayer stuck his large hand out to Darger, and she

shook it.

"I'm Hendrix. This is DeBarge. We're big fans of your work."

Loshak came closer then.

"Oh, hey," Hendrix said, his movie star hair twitching back from his eyes as he saw the second agent. "You must be, uh, Agent Lorshak."

Loshak, too, shook his oversized hand, smiling. Darger thought he would correct the officer's pronunciation of his name, but he didn't.

"You ever heard of a little someone called Zakarian the Barbarian, DeBarge? Cause this guy singlehandedly took him down. Shot him right in the face."

Hendrix retracted his hand from Loshak's and proceed to pantomime a dramatic execution with a finger gun, complete with mouth sound effects, his arm whipping back from the imaginary recoil.

"Jesus, Hendrix. Give it a rest," DeBarge said. He turned to Darger as he went on. "He's always like this before a raid. Obnoxious, I mean. And it's not all that different from how he is on a normal day, but I think the adrenaline makes him extra annoying."

Hendrix scoffed.

"Someone has to keep things loose around here. We can't all be as uptight as you are, DeBarge. He's a real professional. You want me to tell 'em how constipated these raids make you? Guy gets all dried out from it. As soon as we're done, like clockwork, he rockets toward the nearest toilet, lifting his legs like Usain Bolt, sweatin', but he can't go. Sits there for like 45 minutes at a stretch. Said it's like trying to shit petrified wood for the next few days." He rubbed at his belly. "Thick oak branches turned to stone in the gulliver."

They bickered on like that for a while, and Darger felt her chest loosen some. Something about these quarreling partners had brought her back into the moment. And as ridiculous as it was, she was thankful for it.

((

Once they were all strapped up, Darger followed Loshak down the basement steps to where most of the SWAT team waited, ready to breach the hole in the concrete once and for all. The two agents stood on the wooden landing at the bottom of the stairs, staying back from the crowd of the black-clad raid team.

The adrenaline had all the SWAT guys fidgeting in place. Bouncing on their toes. Rocking their weight from foot to foot. Adjusting their grips on their AR-15s. It was like none of them could keep still.

While the team leader barked at them, Darger focused on one member of the squad. His breath was fogging up the inside of his helmet and clearing over and over, a small cloud misting one side of his visor.

That kind of stressed excitement was somehow contagious, Darger thought. Like the epinephrine seeped out of their pores, spritzed itself into the air, infected all who came near.

Stimulation. Provocation. Blood lust.

Then the team leader's speech built to a crescendo. He waved an arm.

And the SWAT team lurched forward as one. Edged closer to the ragged hole in the concrete. The furniture had been cleared away, laying the circular vacancy bare.

The SWAT officers dove in one after another. Sliding down a rope that'd been looped over an I-beam and draped down into the void rather than using the ladder they'd set up for exiting the hole once the raid was over.

The word *spelunking* rang in Darger's head as she watched them zip down the line. Swallowed whole by the basement floor.

The crowd kept surging that way. Tightly packed bodies inching, pressing, shifting forward. A wave of humanity crashing toward that side of the basement, funneling into the floor like they were spilling down a drain.

Darger recognized Hendrix and then DeBarge shooting down into the chasm — one wearing a clever smile, the other looking gravely serious.

Loshak stepped down from the landing to the concrete floor. Darger didn't want to follow his lead, but she did.

She did not, she realized, want to go down into that hole. Did not want to step off of this plane and disappear into that portal into the dirt. Her chest got tight when she thought about it, sharp tendrils of electric current spiking through the meat of her forearms, radiating outward from her hands.

No, she didn't want to do it. But she would. For the girls that may be down there, she would.

Once all the SWAT officers had gone down, Ambrose waved them through, smiling faintly beneath the glare of his faceguard.

Darger grabbed the rope, hooked one foot in, and swung out over the pit. She could feel her eyes go wide as she looked down into the open space where more floor should be.

Then she descended. Thrust downward. The rope loose

against her palms. Airy. Skimming past.

The light changed around her. That hard edge where the concrete ended and the earth began darkened beside her, snuffed out the fluorescent glow of the basement above.

Her feet touched down on the dirt floor. Knees bending. Ankles flexing.

She stood. Craned her neck to take in her surroundings fully, eyes dancing from the ceiling to the walls and back again.

The circle of light above, the hole in the concrete, looked somehow wrong — an escape hatch hung out of reach. Below that, sheared off dirt formed the sidewalls. There was a slight gradient to it, the darker soil toward the top slowly giving way to a pale sandstone shade as it worked its way down. A crooked tree root snaked through one section to her left, looked like a bulging vein in the tunnel wall.

Finally, she let herself gaze down the long shaft ahead — the tapering dirt cylinder where the SWAT officers jogged onward even now. Lights dotted the way, a string of glass globes set along the upper right-hand side of the tunnel, forming intermittent bars of light that couldn't quite beat back all of the darkness.

The SWAT team's flashlights joined those bare bulbs, twirling over the wall, beams swinging everywhere in front of her.

Loud clangs drew her head to her left. Metallic. Piercing.

Loshak climbed down the ladder, his shoes pinging against the aluminum rungs, the feet of the thing gritting against the floor, kicking up dust. When he reached the bottom, he turned and smiled at her.

"I know what you're thinking," he said, lifting a finger. "But

I'll have you know that I only took the ladder because I'm too damn old for the whole gym class rope thing. Too, uh, what's the word… rickety."

"I was actually wondering why I didn't take the ladder," Darger said.

But her eyes were already locked on the tunnel ahead again, looking at the way it pinched tighter as it proceeded from here. She shuddered, her shoulders shimmying back and forth.

"You alright?" Loshak said, his voice going softer.

She took a breath.

"I'm fine. Let's move."

CHAPTER 55

Darger had only trod a few paces when the tunnel went crazy in front of her.

Shouts erupted first. The voices were sharp. Excited. Maybe scared. The emotion in them made the hair prick up on the back of her neck.

Next the twirl of the flashlight beams on the wall, too, seemed to intensify. The beams swung wildly. Stabbed and slashed everywhere. Something frantic in their motions.

Darger's gaze stretched down the tunnel. She squinted. Tried to make sense of the tangle of lights, of all the loud noise.

She realized that the SWAT team had stopped ahead of her. All those black-clad officers seemed to be packed in tightly, leaning toward something ahead, jostling against each other some, but not advancing any longer.

"They must have found something," Loshak said.

They picked up the pace, quickly drawing up on the mob. Sporadic shouts still rang out among the throng, and now Darger thought she understood one of the words.

She elbowed her way through the crowd, finding the throng here oddly rigid. Everyone stood straight up, their chins tucked, their bodies tense. It felt like picking her way through a cluster of statues.

And then she broke through the last row. Reached the front of the crowd and stopped dead.

In the passage before her, she saw exactly what she'd feared she would.

307

The image sucked the breath out of her chest. Held the muscles around her ribcage utterly taut. Made it feel like her lungs were imploding.

The officers had formed a semi-circle around it. Kept some three or so feet shy of it out of instinct. That made sense, Darger thought. She, too, hesitated there a moment, held in the safety at the edge of the crowd, staying an arm's reach away until she was able to take a breath again.

Finally, she dared to get closer. Edged that way with choppy steps. Knelt next to it.

A body sprawled in the center of the tunnel, laid out on its back in the dirt. The skin of its face had been cut off.

CHAPTER 56

Within minutes, a few of the bunny-suited crime scene techs were swarming the tunnel just as they had up in the house — as above, so below. They snapped photos of the grisly corpse, grim expressions etched onto their features as they manned the cameras.

Darger couldn't take her eyes off the body for long, her gaze perpetually drawn back to that naked butchery where the face used to be.

The skin had been peeled off from the forehead down to the jaw — the whole face reduced to red stringy musculature and bulbous eyes set in a skull. The patches of exposed white bone looked stark against the red tissue, and the face itself seemed oddly small having been stripped of its flesh. Frail and gaunt. The shallow chin looked utterly out of proportion with the neck and shoulders below.

Most of the blood had gone tacky and dull, but the face still sheened in a few places. It glittered where the forehead had been stripped down to curved bone along the hairline. Sparkled at the thicker muscles at the corners of the jaw.

They wouldn't know exactly how long the body had been down here until the medical examiner got to work, but based on the shiny places, it couldn't have been all that long.

Darger felt Loshak at her side. Both of them stared at the body now.

A face without skin looked vaguely industrial, Darger thought. Red sinew wired the cheekbones to the jaw like the suspension cables of a bridge. Angular bone jutted here and there like the metal struts along a factory ceiling.

For Darger, the nose was somehow the most disturbing element of all of this. What remained of the flayed cartilage looked like lumpy gristle. And the nostrils appeared bigger than before. More exaggerated. Two pits in the center of the face. It made this body look more animal than human.

Below the nasal cavity, the exposed teeth glistened, permanently grinning now. But that wasn't the most significant detail there — a tooth was missing. The front left incisor had been cut out.

"They checked him for a wallet. Didn't find anything," Darger said. "You notice he's dressed all in black, like the others?"

Loshak nodded.

"I think we found the elusive Worm," Loshak said. "I mean, why else cut out that tooth? Had to eliminate a possible identifying feature."

"That would only delay the inevitable, though, wouldn't it?" Darger said, her voice sounding hollow. "If anything, it only made it more obvious that this had to be Worm."

Loshak shrugged.

"I figure once the landfill bodies hit the newspaper, ol' Cowboy went into damage control mode. Panicking. Had to tie up any loose ends. He was probably waiting to dump the body later tonight, under cover of darkness."

"That would make sense."

Chatter behind them broke up their conversation.

The SWAT team was lining up again. Ready to press on. Ready to see what other terrors this dark passage held.

Dark Passage

Darger tried to steel herself for whatever came next.

CHAPTER 57

Darger's skin grew taut as she plunged forward in the tunnel. Her legs felt wobbly beneath her. Nervous liquid thrashed in her belly.

She forced herself to focus on the dancing lights of the SWAT team ahead. They drifted and jerked and flitted around like fireflies. Traced glowing lines on the tunnel walls.

Loshak kept quiet as they proceeded, probably sensing Darger's claustrophobia-induced nerves. He shuffled along beside her, his footsteps scuffing at the sand like a crunchy drumbeat.

They kept going, descending gently, weaving around the support beams set in their way. Soon they reached the point when the dirt gave way to stone, the manmade section of the tunnel connecting to an underground cave.

At this development, Darger's skin tightened further, and her whole body suddenly felt clammy. She tried to shake the feeling off.

They moved into the stone passageway. The craggy walls kept their distance for now, but Darger could only imagine that the cave would get tight in places. Squeezing. Crushing. She shuddered again, her shoulders jerking harder this time.

"You sure you're all right?" Loshak said. "I don't think it's absolutely necess—"

"I'm fine. Let's just keep going."

Something in the flashlights changed ahead then. That cluster of fireflies widened. Spread like a puddle. It confused

Darger at first, but as they strode closer, it all became clear.

They'd reached a large cavern. It felt like the space had expanded here, asserted itself, some act of will pushing the rock surfaces back in all directions. The ceiling grew higher above them, gnarly stalactites hanging down.

All told, the chamber was about the size of the sanctuary of a small church, mostly flat along the floor with some crevices making divots here and stalagmites jutting up there.

The SWAT team had stopped, the whole group milling around again, like a pack of dogs not quite sure how to proceed. That nervous energy seemed to resurface in their body language right away. It was like whenever they weren't charging forward at something, they didn't know what to do with themselves, and Darger wondered how true that was for most people in life, herself included.

The squad leader hopped up on a raised shelf in the rock and yapped fresh commands at them with his raspy voice, but Darger couldn't focus on his words. Not after what she'd just noticed.

Five small cave mouths led out of this space, and some of them looked tight. Very tight.

The SWAT team lurched back to life. Divvying up. Smaller groups headed for the various passages open before them.

Darger tried to take a step forward, urged her legs to keep moving, but she could only stand there, eyes locked on those narrow passageways cut into the stone.

Loshak turned and grasped her by the arm.

"If the caves are getting to you, there are ways up top you could be more useful. I overheard Agent Zaragoza mention that they'd found deeds for at least five other houses owned by

Cowboy's shell companies. A couple of them are within a few blocks. You could go take a look, maybe help figure out exactly what was going on here. Believe me, there are more than enough of us down here to handle whatever we find."

Darger thought of the girls that may be down here. *May.* She didn't want to leave them, even if she knew Loshak and the others were more than capable of taking care of things.

But then she stared into one of the smaller cave openings before her. Watched two SWAT members get down on their bellies to wriggle through a passage about the width of a coffin.

She looked back at Loshak and nodded her head.

CHAPTER 58

A tranquil suburban landscape rolled past outside the rental car's windows — picket fences, stone veneers, sweeping driveways with basketball hoops tucked off to one side.

Something about the juxtaposition made Darger's jaw clench. Here was the peaceful, idyllic surface, but she'd gotten a glimpse of what lurked beneath the facade. She imagined the people in these homes learning what was happening a few blocks from here, down in the dirt.

A cartoonish voice sounded in her head.

My God! What will the people at the country club think?

She blinked and involuntarily pictured the foam growing in the hollow of Cowboy's mouth, spilling over the sides of his lips. Shuddered again.

The second property owned by Cowboy was less than a mile from the house on Hidden Valley Lane. Another suburban home nestled amongst all the other little boxes. No different from the rest, at least viewed from the photographs she'd found on Zillow. The dark brick facade was a deep, almost chocolate shade, and the big front door was cornflower blue. Darger wondered what might lay inside those walls, though. Horrors? Banalities?

Information, she hoped. Evidence that would cement the story of what exactly happened here, what exactly this maniac had been up to.

She took a left into the cul-de-sac. The green lawns sprawled ever wider here, vast expanses of manicured grass separating the homes from the asphalt and each other. Colorful bursts of landscaping jutted up everywhere along the brick and stone structures. Lilacs and rhododendrons and magnolia trees, wagging their leafy limbs in the breeze.

Darger parked in the driveway outside the Ash Avenue house. Scooped Cowboy's oversized key chain from the passenger seat and clutched it in her fist as she traversed the pale sidewalk to the front door.

It took a while to find the right key, but when she did, the blue steel door swung aside. She stepped into the house. The security system squawked, but she punched in the code one of the techs had already tracked down via the company and silenced it.

A potpourri scent wafted about the foyer. Something cinnamon in the odor, Darger thought, almost like pumpkin pie spice.

She closed the door behind her and stood in the dim entranceway for a moment, facing the open passageway into the house proper, letting her eyes adjust to the low light inside.

The quiet swelled in this place. Some hushed feeling coming over Darger as she stared into the grand living room beyond the foyer, a cavernous room with naked wood beams stretching across the ceiling. She felt immensely aware of the empty space here, a little in awe of it, as though she were standing in some famous cathedral instead of a house in the suburbs owned by a recently deceased psychopath.

Her gaze shifted over vases and paintings and elements of decor at odds with what she knew about Cowboy. It was all a little modern. Clean lines. Muted colors. Minimal. Like something she'd expect to see in an upscale hotel room.

Finally, she took a step forward. Watched as the rest of that mammoth living room came into view to her right.

Button tufted leather furniture perched around the space, its shiny exterior the color of mocha. Glass masks covered the center of the wall above the fireplace — crude, almost featureless faces, all tinted different shades of translucent green and blue. Abstract paintings hung in recessed spots in the walls, built-in displays for this strange art that mostly looked like red and blue smears to Darger.

She paced across the room, footsteps clacking on the tile and echoing around the yawning enclosure. No flat screen mounted on the wall here. No point of focus save for perhaps the decorative masks. It seemed like one of those rooms set up for display only, staged, a space no one had actually lived in. Maybe it was.

Thick wood slabs formed lintels over each doorway leading out of the room, this rustic detail matching those exposed beams overhead — pale timber with grain etching darker lines all over it in warped concentric circles. She passed under one of them, moved into the kitchen beyond.

Stainless steel appliances faced off here. The gleaming quartz of the countertop coating the island separated the fridge from the stove and dishwasher. A farm style sink was situated opposite that, a copper behemoth set deep into the counter.

She kept moving. Slipped into the hall past the kitchen.

And the faintest prickle of goosebumps settled onto the backs of her arms as she entered the back half of the house.

She slowed. Took more care with her steps, moving heel to toe to stop her footfalls from clapping and echoing.

She listened. Heard nothing.

Was she being paranoid? Cowboy was already dead after all. The villain captured and then dispatched, so… She could just call out, couldn't she? See if anyone was here? A guest perhaps? A tenant seemed unlikely, but it was possible.

Still, that faint twinge of suspicion didn't die back. She trusted her instincts. Crept further down the hall.

The first door was open to her left. Thin berber carpet, gray with black flecks, lay beyond the chrome strip of the threshold here. Getting closer, she found a small exercise room with an elliptical machine. Mirrors hung on the wall. More red and blue smear paintings.

A large rust-colored object out the window caught her eye. She passed the exercise machine to get a better look, using her fingers to pry open the slats of the blinds and peeking through.

A huge metal statue of a vulture sat on a cactus in the back patio, its wings spread in a threat. Somehow it was tacky and impressive at the same time — finally something in this house that seemed to properly express Cowboy's eccentric tastes.

Chunky brickwork formed a grand outdoor space around the vulture centerpiece, with what looked like multiple grills built into the brick wall and another stainless steel monster of a grill that almost had to be commercial grade. There was a flat screen mounted under the awning, too. *Wouldn't want to miss a key third down when you're out cookin' an entire cow's worth of beef on your numerous grills.*

Turning back, Darger crossed the hall to the next open doorway. She peeked in at a ritzy looking office. A sturdy oak desk dominated the floor space, the tall back of a high end office chair protruding from the opposite side of it. Behind that, leather bound books filled floor to ceiling bookshelves. It looked like something from a cheesy lawyer commercial on TV, one of those guys in a loud suit pointing at the screen a lot and asking if you've recently been injured in an automotive accident. *Better Call Saul!*

She started to smile at the thought. Then her eyes snapped back to the desk without her telling them to.

A bowl sat in front of the office chair. The neon orange shade of Kraft Macaroni and Cheese practically glowed against the white ceramic. It was half full, with a fork still jabbed into noodles. A bottle of ketchup sat next to the bowl, and looking closer, Darger could see that someone had squirted ketchup into the macaroni.

Something told her to go closer, so she stepped into the room, drawn toward this bowl of pasta as though by way of tractor beam, her eyes never leaving it. She didn't know what she intended to do until she reached a hand out and touched the side of the bowl.

It was still warm.

Darger's scalp prickled.

Someone had been here minutes ago. *Jesus.* Had they heard her come in and abandoned their meal? Were they hiding somewhere inside?

And then the sound of a flushing toilet crashed down the hall, the sucking noise of the water spiraling down the drain somehow strident in the quiet house. Jarring.

Darger unclasped her holster and drew her gun.

CHAPTER 59

Loshak knelt to get a closer look at the oblong puddle on the stony cavern floor. It was dull. A little cloudy. But there was no mistaking that metallic tang that stuck in your nostrils. It was definitely blood, and a lot of it.

"We figure this would be where our, uh, faceless man met his demise," a mustached crime scene tech said. He kept his voice low, perhaps out of a kind of reverence for what had happened here. "No sign of his flesh, though... the removed skin of his face, I mean. Nor the, uh, tooth."

Loshak nodded once, and then the tech drifted back as though to give the agent some space.

Cowboy had moved the body a great distance and left it not far from the basement entrance to the tunnel. That was plain. The question was why.

Was he planning to dump it somewhere, the same way he had the others?

That had been Loshak's instinct upon finding the body, and it still probably held the most logic. Something about it didn't sit right with the agent now, however. He kept thinking about what Darger had said. That while at first glance cutting the man's tooth out would conceal a potential identifying feature. But it also hung a lantern on it.

Maybe he wanted us to find the body. Wanted us to think... what?

The burden of that unanswered question settled its bulk onto Loshak's shoulders, onto his neck. Made him tense up like the culprit behind all of this wasn't already chilling in a locker at the county morgue.

Loshak stared into the matte pool as though it might offer him answers, tried to stare through the filmy surface. It looked burgundy against the rock, like a dark red wine.

CHAPTER 60

Darger eased her head out into the hall, right shoulder pressed into the side of the doorway. She gripped the gun with both her hands, its barrel pointed at the terrazzo floor.

Two closed doors faced her from the left side of the hallway. Based on sound, she was pretty sure the bathroom was the one further down from her, past a console table sporting decorative crockery.

Her focus sharpened on the door — a thick plank of solid oak, smooth and pale, separating her from the sound of the toilet tank refilling. She let her gaze drift down to the tarnished brass door handle, thought about whipping it open to get the upper hand here, but her gut told her to wait.

The odds were still high that this whole situation was harmless, even if the adrenaline coursing through her system told her otherwise. Cowboy could have a friend or tenant staying at this property, even if it wasn't registered as an official rental property. He certainly seemed the type to conduct as much business as possible off the books.

The spray of a running faucet sounded from behind the door now. Whoever was in there was washing his or her hands. They'd come out any second now.

Darger swallowed and stepped fully into the hallway. Felt her pulse pounding in her temples. Felt a little flutter of lightness in her belly.

She lifted her weapon. Aimed at the door. Ready for him. The knob turned. The door swung open.

A small man appeared there in the opening. His eyes widened as they flicked up to her, to the gun in her hand.

Darger barked at him.

"FBI! Hands in the air!"

He flinched backward in a stutter-step, brought the hardcover book in his hand up as though to protect himself. A thick George R.R. Martin tome hovering over his heart.

Darger stepped forward, sucking in a big breath that she hoped didn't look as shaky as it felt. Her eyes scanned the guy up and down, trying to figure out how he might fit into all of this.

And then he jolted forward and flung the hardcover book at her face.

Darger ducked. Off-balance. The dragon sigil on the cover glinting as the book whooshed over her head.

The man lurched into the hallway and raced away from her. Zipping down the corridor. Darting like a cat. His bare feet slapping at the smooth surface of the floor.

Darger recovered her footing and trained her weapon on his back, but he'd disappeared around the corner — one quick cut like a juking running back, and he was gone.

She stared at the empty hallway for a second. Listened to his footfalls racing away. Blinked twice. Then she followed.

In that flash of a second, as he'd hurled the book at her, she'd seen enough to finally start making sense of things:

When his lips pulled back in a strained snarl, a gold tooth gleamed at the front of his mouth.

CHAPTER 61

Darger swung herself out into the intersection of the hallway where Worm had disappeared, feet set wide, her gun pointed in front of her. She gritted her teeth. Peered into the gap.

Clear. Another empty section of hall stood before her, the walls populated with more muted art. He was gone from view, but she could still hear his footsteps somewhere in the distance, thumping along at a rapid fire clip.

Damn it. These houses are too fucking big.

Her heart thundered in her chest, but her voice came out clear and strong.

"FBI! Come on out, Worm. I just want to talk."

Her mind whirred, trying to make this new puzzle piece fit.

We'd figured him for a potential victim. But victims don't generally throw big ass dragon books at law enforcement. And if this was Worm, then who the hell was that down in the tunnel with his face peeled off?

She set the questions aside for a moment and listened. Let her eyes drift down the hall. The path before her ended, leaving a corridor running to the left that would take her back toward the front of the house. It sounded like that was where he was headed.

She turned around. Ran back the way she'd come. Hoped she might be able to cut him off.

The oak doors blurred past alongside her as she rocketed toward the sound of the footfalls. She pushed herself harder, picked up speed.

When she exited the hall, motion caught her eye to her right. It was him.

She stopped. Got into her stance. Hoped that the sight of her standing her ground with her gun drawn would stop him in his tracks.

"Freeze! Down on the ground! Right now!"

He kept moving. Didn't even flinch at her words or acknowledge them in any way. Oblivious.

Her finger trembled against the trigger guard. Slipped off into the empty space in front of the trigger. Hesitated there. Unsure of whether he posed a threat or not. Was he on drugs? Why didn't he obey?

He hurdled the back of a big sectional, knees partially buckling as he tromped onto the seat cushion. And then he hurled himself off the sofa and dropped low, scrabbling on all fours into the kitchen. Disappearing behind the large bulk of the island.

There were sounds. The clatter of silverware and other kitchen implements being tossed on the floor.

And then the noises cut out. Silence.

She crept forward a few steps. Her gun now quivered in her grip, and she could feel the sweat of her palms slicking the weapon.

Her vision stayed trained on the hard line where the quartz of the island sheared off, eyes sliding up and down that angular plane, searching for any signs of movement in the space beyond the counter's edge.

A revolver lurched up over the lip of the counter. A little Saturday Night Special, gleaming steel, hovering there above the quartz.

The bottom of Darger's stomach dropped out. Mouth suddenly dry. Eyes opened all the way.

A gun. That's what he'd been running for.

His hand squeezed. Finger flexing against the trigger.

The gun barked. Bucked. Snorted flame.

Darger dove onto her belly.

CHAPTER 62

Loshak strode across the large chamber — the main chamber of the cavern as he thought of it — watching the various tunnel mouths set in the wall before him. After Darger left, he'd watched all the SWAT officers file down those tunnels, the glow of their flashlights flickering over the walls, slowly going smaller and then disappearing as the deeper darkness swallowed them up. Then he'd made his way down to the bloody smear. Getting back, he was anxious to find out what information had come streaming in while he was away.

Now his eyes shifted to Ambrose who paced back and forth just shy of the tunnels along with a few other detectives from the task force. The big detective had a radio in his hand, alternately holding it out to listen and then bringing it to his mouth to speak. Loshak made his way toward the head of the task force, figuring he'd be the first to find out about any updates they might be getting from the various caves.

Multiple radios squawked all around as he got closer. Chatter burbling in unison on them. Deep voices and sizzling static emitted from the small speakers and bounced around the cavern, the echoes shivering in the dank space.

Loshak didn't mind the radio babble. The staccato patter almost had a calming effect for him after a while — radios provided background noise to perpetually fill the silence in tense moments like this one. It wasn't unpleasant, even if he could only make out bits and pieces of what was being said.

"Got a cage of some kind here," one voice said. "Looks like

a dog pen, but it's empty."

"Moss everywhere out this way," another voice said. "Big bushy clusters of moss hanging down off the walls. Soggy and scraggly as hell. Jesus. Almost looks as unkempt as DeBarge's pubes."

Loshak recognized that one — the one who'd called him Lorshak. A couple of the detectives snickered, but Ambrose's brow furrowed. He brought his walkie up like he was going to scold Hendrix for tying up the line with jokes, but then he stopped himself.

Another deep voice crackled out of the radio.

"We're clear in tunnel three. Just empty cave this way. Tight as hell part of the way, and then it dead-ends. We'll start making our way back."

Just as Loshak neared Ambrose, frantic chatter burst from the radio. Voices strained into something high and tight. Nervous and jittery. They were talking too fast for Loshak to understand any of it at first.

Then he could.

"She's still alive."

CHAPTER 63

Darger skidded over the slick tile floor on her chest and rolled onto her back. Pointed her Glock at the island. Finger trembling on the trigger. Ready to squeeze.

Her eyes squinted down to slits. Watching for his head to poke out from behind the cabinetry under the quartz countertop. Flicking to one side and then the other.

He didn't show. Didn't make a sound.

Keeping the gun in front of her, she pushed up into a crouch. Gaze still jumping over the gleaming surface of the island, waiting for him to emerge.

She stayed low. Backpedaled into the mouth of the hallway she'd just vacated.

A rivulet of sweat drained down from her hair, touched the skin behind her ear.

Eyes still locked on the kitchen, she tilted her head to the right. Caught sight of the doorway into the exercise room in her peripheral vision, a dark rectangle in the corner of her eye. She ran for it.

Gunfire cracked behind her. Two shots that echoed sharp and shrill off all the hard surfaces.

Drywall burst over her head. Bullets gouging the wall, spritzing white powder into the air. One of the smearing-looking abstract paintings went crashing to the floor.

She ducked into the doorway of the exercise room. Flattened her back against the wall.

Then she held her breath. Listened for the sound of

footsteps, either fleeing or coming closer. Heart punching in her chest. Eyes blinking rapid fire.

When no footfalls came, she edged into the doorway. Peeked her head out.

He squatted in the narrow passageway between the island and the fridge. Gun arm raised. One eye squinted shut.

His arm jerked. He fired again.

The wood of the door frame exploded inches to her left. Splinters flung from the shattered jamb.

She pulled her head back into the room.

Another round pinged off a door hinge, the sound of metal striking metal impossibly sharp and brittle at this proximity.

And then his gun clicked. Empty. The unmistakable sound of a dry firing revolver.

Darger leaned out with her gun drawn just in time to see him vanish into a doorway on the back wall of the kitchen. Heard the clatter of his bare feet pounding down wooden steps.

The basement.

She ran.

CHAPTER 64

Darger sprinted down the hall. Reached the doorway as he lurched to his left at the bottom of the steps, moving out onto the smooth gray concrete of the basement floor. Again he vanished from her narrow field of vision.

She darted down the bare wooden stairs, taking them two at a time. Ready to shoot. Ready to tuck and roll. Ready for anything.

More and more of the basement came into view to her left as she descended. Huge and clean and mostly empty floor space. The sprawling floor was splotched with the oblong reflections of the fluorescent bulbs above, a row of them trailing deeper and deeper into the space.

A workbench emerged. Tools hung up on nails above it meticulously. It looked practically unused, as most everything in this house did.

She reached the floor at the bottom, and Worm was there, across the vast basement floor from her. He careened around a steel support beam jutting out of the exposed floor joists above, his back to her. Sprinting away, arms and legs churning.

Darger felt her feet snap to a shoulder-width stance beneath her. Training and instinct taking over now.

Once more she raised her gun. Aimed. Arm muscles tightening. Hands and wrists ready to squeeze off the shot that'd take him down. Already certain beyond a doubt that her aim would be true.

She didn't hesitate. Darger pulled the trigger.

And then Worm dove face first into nothing. Disappeared into a gaping hole in the basement floor.

CHAPTER 65

Darger gasped. Felt the shock physically as a prickling of her scalp, a numbness in her cheeks, her jaw dropping open.

And words pounded in her head, keeping time with the speed metal rhythm of her heart.

Another tunnel. Another hole etched into a basement floor. How many?

She sidled up to the edge of the hole. Peered down into the void where the concrete was wounded, where the soil lay open.

Her breath hissed in her nostrils. Those words replayed in her head over and over.

Another tunnel. Another tunnel.

What the goddamn fuck?

A ladder rested at the lip of the jagged opening. And the lights within the tunnel were on. Yellow light oozed down from a string of bulbs, formed glowing puddles on the sandy layer of earth.

That strand of lights trailed away out of view, and she saw no sign of Worm down there. Gone already, to be certain. Running deeper and deeper into the underground shaft. Listening, she thought she could hear his footsteps, a tiny pattering and scuffing of his bare feet at the dirt floor, echoing funny, but the tapping was ultimately too faint for her to be certain.

She tucked her gun in her holster and pulled out her phone to call it in. Icy fingers worked at the touchscreen. She scrolled past Loshak's name on the contact list and found the number she meant to call.

With the prospect of cell coverage underground spotty, she called the task force hotline. One of the dispatchers answered.

"This is Agent Darger requesting backup at 8901 Ash Avenue. We've got another suspect to deal with in the Heider case."

Darger listened to her pulse in her ears as she explained that Worm had fired at her, and that she'd watched him dive into another basement tunnel. The dispatcher asked all the routine questions, and Darger answered what she could.

Then her mind snapped back to the moment when Worm's gun had clicked. Out of ammo. She'd expected to watch him move through the doorway leading toward the foyer. Instead he bolted the other way, vaulting himself down the basement steps.

There had been nothing between him and the front door. So why would he do this? Run for the basement, dive for the tunnel?

Darger's mind drifted as the dispatcher talked on the line. Eyes spearing empty space, the voice in her ear going quieter and quieter until she'd tuned out reality entirely.

Words she'd overheard at the mouth of the other tunnel echoed in her head. "For all we know, there could be miles of tunnel here. Connecting to natural cave systems. Weaving around like interstate traffic loops under half of the damn county."

There could be an escape route, even multiple, for all she knew. Why else would Worm run for the tunnels instead of the front door?

"Wait at the scene, Agent Darger. Backup is on the way."

Darger closed her eyes before she answered.

"I'm going to give pursuit," she said, her body already trembling at the thought of descending into that dirt tunnel. "The suspect is unarmed and barefoot, and I want to keep eyes on him if I can. There could be any number of escape routes from here."

The voice went quiet on the other end of the line for the duration of a few heartbeats.

"But I've already—"

Darger hung up the phone and took a breath.

Then she lowered herself into that concrete mouth in the basement floor.

CHAPTER 66

Loshak's heart thudded in his chest as the girl locked in the tiny dog cage came into view. That hollow sound of blood squelching in his ears drowned out his footsteps. Still, he could feel the dirt gritting beneath his feet as the passage had transitioned from rock back to manmade tunnel this way, something that brought a new sense of horror all on its own.

Christ. How many tunnels did they dig? How long will we be down here, poking our flashlights into the dark?

He drew closer to the officers standing over the cage, slowing some.

The details of the dog pen sharpened, the black lines of the metal enclosure growing stark, the thick padlock coming clear on the hasp, and then the dark shape inside winnowed into focus.

A girl. So skinny he could see the shape of her hip bones protruding clearly even at a distance.

One flashlight's beam shined onto her face smudged with dirt, on the long eyelashes knitted closed there. Ghostly shadows formed in the pitted place beneath her brow, in the hollows under each of her cheekbones.

She was so still, Loshak thought at first the voices on the radio had been wrong. Was certain this girl was dead.

But then he noticed the very faint rising of her chest. Every inhalation lifting the blue and white chevron afghan draped over most of her.

"First girl — here — is breathing but so far not responsive.

336

We're waiting on a pair of bolt cutters so we can get her out," the SWAT officer standing next to the cage said. Then he gestured to the tunnel leading past him. "But there's another one. Further down there. That one's conscious."

Loshak managed to pry his gaze away from the comatose girl. He kept moving. Feet shuffling beneath him. That accelerated beating of his blood still emanating from his chest and pulsing in his ears.

A small chamber opened up to one side. A gap in the dirt wall.

And then he saw the second cage tucked off to the left. More SWAT officers knelt there. Talking to the girl within.

She looked so scared. Eyes wide and wet and blinking in rapid bursts. Her fingers wound around the wiry bars of her cage to the degree that they could, clutching like she was scared to let go.

"Bolt cutters will be here any minute, and we'll get you the hell out of there," one of the officers said to her.

Loshak pulled up to stop next to the cage, heaving for breath a little. He stared at the girl locked inside.

"They tell me your name is Cora?"

She met his eyes. Hesitated. Nodded.

"Do you know how long you've been down here?"

Her voice came out in a croak.

"Two days. I think. Maybe three. Ran out of water yesterday."

He glanced back, hoping he'd see whoever had the bolt cutters on the way. They had to get this girl out of this cage.

He turned to face her again, squatting down low in an attempt to be at eye level with the girl, which was pretty much impossible given the tiny dimensions of the crate.

"I don't want to press — we need to get you above ground and get some fluids in you — but you wouldn't happen to know what all was going on down here?"

She thought about it. Shook her head.

"But Lily did."

"Lily. That's the girl down a ways?"

Another nod.

"Is she OK?"

Loshak waffled a second, not sure if he should sugarcoat it for her. He told her the truth.

"She's breathing. We haven't been able to wake her up so far, but…"

Cora's gaze fell to the dusty floor then. Her eyes looked faintly wet. Loshak could imagine exactly how the tears would brim along her bottom eyelids if she weren't dehydrated.

"She's been down here… a long time. When I got here, she didn't even know what month it was."

Again, Loshak looked back the way he'd come, anxious to see someone with the tool that would free this girl. When he saw the way behind him was still empty, he decided enough was enough.

He swiveled on his heels to face the nearest SWAT officer.

"Do you have a baton?" Loshak asked.

"What?"

"Your police baton," Loshak said. "Give it to me."

His tone and the way he stuck out his hand left little room for argument. The man tugged the club from his tactical belt and handed it over.

Loshak made eye contact with the girl in the cage.

"Can you back up a little for me, Cora?"

She blinked and then scooted toward the back of the cage.

"This is going to be loud," Loshak said, and then he brought the club down on the padlock.

The first blow glanced off the side of the lock, but the second struck true. The small hook cleaved away from the bottom of the lock, breaking clean, the lock releasing.

Loshak yanked the shank from the hasp. He ripped the door out of the way and stepped back.

The girl crawled out. Slowly. Hands and knees drawing her out onto the dirt floor on shaky limbs. As soon as she was all the way out, her chin puckered and trembled, and actual tears spilled over her cheeks at last.

CHAPTER 67

Darger's heart thundered as she swung her first foot down into the breach, kicked out in the empty space, trying to reach the ladder.

Even with the cold underground air reaching up from below, sweat leaked from her temples. Drained down her cheeks. Glued her hair to her forehead. She reached one set of fingers up to wipe the sweat away, smearing it around above her brow.

Finally her toe hit the solid metal it sought. She mounted the ladder and started climbing down.

Each aluminum rung pinged like a popping kernel of popcorn as her foot found it, and the whole ladder bobbed up and down with her shifting weight. She started slow and picked up speed.

Those sheared off dirt walls surrounded her as she made her descent, the tunnel enveloping her. The soil smell was thick in the air, pungent and earthy.

Her feet touched down on the grainy floor of this underground passage, the soles of her shoes rasping as she shuffled a few steps from the ladder. Her eyes flicked up to that opening in the concrete, and some deep instinct begged her to race up the ladder again, to scurry back to the safety above ground.

Instead she moved into the tunnel. Cold wind sucked into her throat. And she fumbled to get her gun free from its holster, hands going shaky again.

Dark Passage

She pressed forward. Gun clenched in both hands and pointed at the ground. The sound of her own blood thrummed in her ears.

The broader opening beneath the basement tapered, the tunnel walls seeming to close around her with every step. A dirt tube growing tighter and tighter. Cinching like a sphincter.

But the path only went one way. Nowhere for him to hide so far, no way for her to lose track of him. She needed to keep going.

Her eyes stayed trained on that well-lit tunnel ahead, the glowing shaft sliced into the dirt. She saw no movement there, no sign of life. It bent into a curve up ahead, with everything veering out of her view at that point. The sight of it twisted her gut into knots, the unknown section of tunnel laying beyond it somehow both desirable and awful. She simultaneously wanted to get there as soon as possible and utterly dreaded reaching it.

She pushed herself. Picked up the pace. Not too worried about her footfalls crushing and grinding at the dirt, the sound of them reverberating against the walls around her. She was armed, and he wasn't.

She squeezed the gun tighter in her grip. That was what gave her the edge here. She needed to close on him now, press that advantage while she had it.

When she reached the bend, she still couldn't see him. Just another section of blank tunnel ahead. Hollow. Vacant.

Again, she forced herself onward. Dialed up the speed until her pace morphed into a jog.

It occurred to her that this dark passage was now veering downward at a sharper angle. Descending. She gulped at the thought, a fresh wave of chills crawling up her spine, cold shuddering through her.

But she pushed the fear down and kept going. She just had to keep moving.

A snippet of his scuffing feet sounded somewhere up ahead. Harsh and scratchy. The sound fluttered strangely down the hall, echoed around like a living breathing thing, a panicked bird flapping everywhere, flapping everywhere, trying to find a way out.

It gave her some confidence, though. Now she knew he was still up there somewhere. Not so far away after all.

She broke into a run, plunging deeper into the hole.

CHAPTER 68

Ahead, the dirt walls of the tunnel widened slightly and then dead-ended against a craggy rock wall. Brown and gray swirls almost seemed to decorate the stone, the multicolored bands distinguishing it from the flat sandy monotone of the dirt. Darger's eyes moved lower on the rock face, following the strand of lights again.

A hole yawned in the center of the wall, and a stony passage carried on there just as the tunnel had. It looked shorter and narrower than the manmade dirt shaft she was currently in. The knobby rock surface seemed foreign, almost menacing compared to the smooth dirt walls. But the lights glowed there just the same.

Darger ignored the lurching liquid of anxiety in her belly and maintained her speed, racing for that cleft in the rock. She still couldn't see him up ahead, but he was closer now. She could feel it.

She passed through the threshold without slowing, stepping into the cave. The grainy sound of the dirt tunnel floor under her shoes gave way to the clap of limestone.

Right away the air grew cooler around her. Thicker. It gripped the backs of her arms with a chill that reminded her of a dank basement, formed goosebumps that rubbed against her sleeves as she ran.

She smelled a swampy odor for a second, the overwhelming stench of pond scum making her nose wrinkle, and then it was gone. She knew what it meant. There was moisture down here somewhere, and the thought disturbed her.

The cave seemed to curve more than the tunnel did. Bending and dipping, its lines all crooked. That reduced visibility. Made her uneasy.

And then something caught her eye on the wall ahead and to the right. Glinting.

Hair. Glistening strands of hair in a dark cluster a few inches beyond one of the light bulbs, wet with sweat.

Her breath caught in her throat. A little moan seeping out of her.

She lifted her gun. Hands shaking from the adrenaline and the cold. Forearms flexing. Eyes dancing over those gleaming tendrils.

But it wasn't hair.

Moss hung down from the wall here. Dripping wet tufts of it that looked like long green beards dangling off the rock's surface at first. The clumps grew thicker and thicker as she proceeded until the whole wall to her right was covered in green and beige, the barrier turned organic and soggy, that multitude of beard-like masses coagulating into one. The strand of lights snaked right through the plant life, glowing bulbs protruding from the mess of fibrous green.

A dripping sound emerged. Water seeping into the cave, she figured. Draining down that wall of moss. Some of it gathering in puddles somewhere that she could hear but could not see for the moment.

She kept going. Kept running. Kept taking deep breaths of cold cave air, feeling it spiral deep into her lungs, her body slowly chilling from the inside out.

The dripping sound grew louder as she moved. More

urgent.

Another bend moved her up a small rise and away from the moss, a development she was thankful for. At first.

And then she saw the sheening black surface sprawling ahead.

Her stomach clenched, all internal valves clamping into taut, trembling knots.

The cave opened up some, and an underground lake filled the large chamber before her. The water lay motionless and eerie. Its vast black surface darkled, looked opaque from her point of view, faintly glittering in a dotted line where the glow of the light bulbs touched its rounded edge.

Some garbled H.P. Lovecraft quote flared in Darger's head then. Something about the black seas of infinity, about how mankind's small minds weren't meant to voyage far.

She pushed it away. Kept going.

She followed the thin pathway off to one side of the black expanse where the strand of lights still dotted the wall, her eyes tracing along that line where the stone and water met.

The stagnant water was so close, within an arm's length. She could trip here and fall in. Get sucked down into the dark. Who knew how deep it was, how cold it was? She shivered even thinking about it. Didn't want to find out.

An oblong tunnel veering up and to the right took her away from the lake, away from the moss. Those knots in her abdomen loosened some as she climbed, her breath coming easier again.

The slope gradually leveled out as she proceeded, though troughs of dark water persisted off and on, running alongside her path like drainage ditches scooped out along the shoulder of a country road.

The cold had saturated her limbs and was working on her face now. Her cheeks had gone half-numb, the tip of her nose turning to ice.

Worse, the cave seemed to be narrowing around her. The walls closing in.

She had to turn sideways and sidle through one section, arms up, hands pressing into the wall, rock protrusions jabbing her in the back and belly as she moved. She kept her eyes on the light in the gap ahead, the place where this bottleneck relented.

When the cave widened again, she saw his dark figure just ahead of her.

CHAPTER 69

Darger sprinted now, the fresh jolt of adrenaline popping in her head like a champagne cork, bright electricity thrumming behind her eyes, coursing through her veins, pushing her ever forward. She pumped her arms, watched the Glock rise and fall in the right side of her field of vision.

His small figure grew larger as she ran. She was closing on him rapidly now. Good.

The silhouette hobbled down the declining passage before her. His bare feet clearly bothering him on the rocky terrain, adding strange bounces and hitches to his running motion, something panicked and choppy about it like someone running on hot coals.

The ground seemed more uneven as she accelerated. It dipped and sloped and cratered beneath Darger's feet, tilted her ankles at odd angles, threatened to roll one or the other. She could only imagine how much worse it'd be without shoes, those serrated rock edges knifing into the flesh with every step.

Still, she didn't slow. Kept gaining on him. Pressing her advantage now, once and for all. Ready to finish it.

Slowly details populated the silhouette before her. His shadow seemed to become real, become solid, before her eyes. The bristled texture of his close-cropped hair faded into view, the banded red collar of his black t-shirt, the small Dickie's logo on the back pocket of his work pants.

He craned his neck around, must have heard her getting closer. His wide eyes peered at her. Wild and panicked. Mouth hanging open like a panting dog.

Then he swiveled forward again and picked up speed. His running motion became even more frantic.

She gritted her teeth. Pushed herself harder. Faster now. Faster, faster.

She zipped toward him. Bounding like a predator. Breath hot against her teeth. Closing.

He glanced back once more. Tongue now lolling out of his mouth. Chest heaving.

His foot caught on a protruding shelf of rock. Momentum flung him forward. Laid him out flat so he looked like Superman for a second, and then he crashed down into the rocks.

He tried to catch himself with his arms out in front, take the brunt of it with his hands and elbows, but the force pushed right through. Bent his arms down under his belly as it wrenched him forward. He skidded over solid stone, whole body throttled by the bumps and divots, arms and limbs and torso convulsing. When the skid finally ended, he started dragging himself to his feet.

Darger raced up to within about ten feet. Then she got her gun on him. Arms trembling in front of her again.

"Freeze," she said, her voice sounding wet from the reverb here. She was sucking wind, but so was he.

He'd just gotten his feet under him, but now he looked up at Darger, stared down the barrel of her gun. His hands went up in slow motion.

"Any moves now, and I'll shoot. I promise you that."

She inched closer. Cautious.

Blood wept from the point of his chin. Drizzled fat droplets onto the rocky floor of the cavern. He slow-blinked at her a few times, appearing meek. Again reminding her of a dog, though this time a scolded one.

His eyes drifted away from Darger to the wall ahead of him and went a little blank.

When she'd edged within five feet of him, Worm lurched. He went straight at the wall, as if he thought he might launch himself through the rock.

Darger squeezed the trigger a beat late. Missed. The crack of the gunfire rumbled, the report made piercing in the enclosed space. Spiky in her ears.

The bullet ricocheted off the rock and whizzed around, ringing and shuddering.

Darger wheeled to point the gun at him again.

That was when Darger saw the gray metal electrical box mounted on the wall, wired into the strand of bulbs illuminating the tunnel.

Worm hung from the box, latching onto it like a monkey. Body taut. Bent arms quivering. It looked like he was trying to do a pull up. All at once, he yanked down on the lever protruding from the side of it. Hard. It snapped like a broken twig.

Then the lights winked out all around them.

CHAPTER 70

Darger breathed in the dark. Blinked. Gaped at the black nothingness.

His feet scuffed next to her. Skin scraping against grit and stone. And then he was on her.

She squeezed the trigger, but it was too late.

He'd grabbed her from the side. Tipped her forward. Jammed her arms down toward the ground.

The orange muzzle flash lit both of them up. A momentary burst of brightness bucking and lurching between them. She could see her round fired into the rocky cavern floor, and then the dark swallowed everything again.

She twisted free of his grasp. Shuffled backward off balance. The soles of her shoes rasping over the rock.

She swung the gun back to where he'd been. Moved her finger to the trigger.

Pressure found her hands. Raked the gun away from her. Pried it from her fingers. Tumbling. Clattering to the hard ground.

No.

She lurched after it. Chased the sound. Flailing forward into blackness.

And she kicked it. Felt her toes swoop into the hunk of polymer, fling it scraping away over the rock.

No. No. No.

His arms grappled around her. Squeezing. Constricting around her ribcage like two snakes. His hands fumbled upward, rigid things clutching at her sternum, at her chest, at her collarbone. Seeking her throat.

She got her feet wide, made some space, and threw an uppercut. Fist heaved upward between them.

She felt her knuckles bludgeon his chin. Flipping his head straight back.

And his arms lost some of their strength. His grip on her loosened. Uncinching.

She followed it up with a hook. Legs stepping into it. Hips and shoulders dipping to give the shot leverage, shifting all of her weight forward.

Her fist clubbed the side of his jaw. Wrenched his head away.

He let her go. Stumbled back.

And it felt good. Unloading all of her aggression through her fists.

She stalked forward a couple of paces. Then she remembered the gun and changed course.

She got low. Clambered toward where she'd last heard the weapon on hands and knees. Feeling along the ground. Reaching into the darkness.

So dark. Confusing. She could be going the wrong direction by now. But she trusted her gut.

Her fingertips brushed at cold protrusions and puckered indentations in the stone. Breath wheezing in and out of her lips. Mind whirring, lurching, spitting out panicked snippets over and over.

Where is the fucking gun?

And then his foot found her face. Kicked her in the teeth. Launching her up and backward.

Bright motes of light exploded behind her eyes. Blinding. Turning to pink splotches that floated everywhere.

She floated backward into the blackness. Arms flailing. Disoriented.

When she hit down, it took a second to make sense of things. She'd flipped from her hands and knees into a crab-walk position. Kicked ass over tea kettle. Skull still ringing from it.

She scrabbled to her feet and ran.

CHAPTER 71

The paramedics loaded Lily onto a stretcher and carried her out of the basement. Once they were upstairs, they transitioned her to a gurney and hooked her up to an IV. One of them wiped some of the dirt from her eyelids and cheeks with an antiseptic wipe, her skin looking paper-white against the rim of crud that remained.

She looked peaceful if a little grim, Loshak thought, as he trudged alongside the procession. And his mind couldn't help but leap into the past, to the image of his own daughter laid out in the casket, far too young.

The cancer had seeped the life from Shelly. Drained it from her cheeks and chin first, the cherub-like roundness of those last remnants of baby fat growing ever more lean, ever more gaunt. Bony. Skeletal. Then the rest of her went frail, turned her old before her time.

The process worked slowly at first — a subtle thinning. It went faster toward the end.

Until she wasn't herself anymore. Not really.

She'd been just ashy skin stretched over a skeleton by the end. Emaciated down to all hard angles. Gray and cadaverous even before she passed.

When he sat in the hospital room, all he wanted was to be able to tell her it would be OK, that it would all be OK. And he couldn't.

In the casket, she'd looked more serene. They'd worked their mortician tricks. Brought back some color. Restored some sense of fleshiness to her face.

And part of Loshak had wondered, even as he looked upon his dead child's visage, whether they'd shoved cotton into the mouth to plump the cheeks, whether they'd injected something to give the brow and chin and lips some substance.

But another part of him had accepted the image they'd made. Her suffering was over after all. Only the memories remained. Why question the white lie laid out here? Who did the skepticism serve?

The gurney thumped over a grout line in the tile floor, and Loshak snapped back to the moment. His eyelids fluttered, and he refocused on the girl sprawled beside him.

He wished so badly he could ask her about the case, ask her about exactly what Cowboy was up to. And yet, his concern in this moment leaned away from the endless quest for information that comprised his career. He just wanted her to be OK.

Her eyes peeled open. Blinked. Swiveled everywhere.

Loshak's heart leaped. Pounded at the bony bars of his ribcage. When he tried to speak, to say something to her, his tongue felt glued to the roof of his mouth.

He'd expected some surprise or panic in the moments after she woke up. Expected her to be alarmed at the sudden change of scenery, even if it was for the better. But that peaceful look remained on her face.

Loshak gripped her hand, and her eyes rotated to meet his. She smiled faintly, and a lump shifted in his throat. He wanted to ask her about fifteen different questions at once, but those would come later. For now, he would tell her it was OK.

"We got him," he said, his voice coming out shaky with

emotion. "We got the guy who did this to you. Cowboy is dead."

She blinked hard. Twice. Sucked a gasp in between her lips. "What about the other one?" she said, her voice cracking.

Loshak swallowed again, found it more difficult this time. "The other?"

"His partner." Lily blinked hard. "Worm."

And the word echoed in Loshak's mind.

Partner.

CHAPTER 72

Darger ran. Knifed forward into the darkness. Jaw clenched tight.

She held one arm out in front of her, hand scooping at empty space, doing something of a doggy paddle there. The fingers of her opposite hand traced along the wall of the cavern to keep her from losing her way. Feeling was all she had for navigation now, so she used it.

She tried to stay light on her feet. Flexing heel to toe. Avoiding friction with the rock surface as much as she could. All sound echoed here, strengthened by the repetitions, piling up into something impossibly loud and big in the dark that swooped and careened around on bat wings.

Now his bare feet would be an advantage, she realized. Easier to stay soundless. To sneak up on her. Picking his way over the rocky terrain.

A big breath rushed into her and made her lungs quake. The cold wind roiled in her chest.

Even her breath seemed loud here. Huge and obnoxious. Rasping puffs shuddering around her in the stillness, shivering through the air.

She focused on the wall, on the feel of it against her hand. Chilled rock brushed her skin. Smooth. It reminded her of tracing her fingers along a row of lockers back in school. Barely touching the cool metal while her mind wandered.

She stopped a second. Held her breath. Listened for his footsteps, for his breath, for any sign of him.

Nothing.

Her hand fumbled into her jacket for her phone. Clutched it within her pocket. But she stopped herself short of pulling it free.

She didn't dare light it up here. Not yet. The glow would be visible up and down the tunnel like a flare, would lead him straight to her. For all she knew, he had her gun now. She couldn't risk exposing her position until she was sure he wasn't near.

Anyway, the phone might not work down here, under the dirt, encased in thick rock. Probably wouldn't, she thought. If she could find some kind of shelter, some enclosed space in the craggy wall that might conceal her, she'd try it.

She stumbled on, feet catching on knobby bits of rock now and again, planes of stone jutting up like shelves. They sent her tumbling forward, and then she'd stab a leg into the ground and catch herself over and over. Moving on. Trying to stay quiet.

Mostly she kept her eyes closed. Felt somehow less bewildered by the dark that way, less intimidated by it. Hands endlessly patting against the wall.

She felt pretty certain that she was moving uphill, away from the lake, away from the house, deeper into the cave. The sloping pathway below seemed to suggest that, moving on an incline. Or so it felt in the dark. Water would funnel downhill. Race for the lowest spot, which must be that lake and those wet troughs along the way there.

In any case, she hoped she was moving away from the lake. If this passage eventually connected to the caves the police were already searching — and she suspected it did — then she was heading for a certain kind of safety. Maybe Loshak or Ambrose lay at the end of this underground path.

If he was headed the other way, back toward the house, hopefully the backup she'd requested would be there already. Waiting for him above that hole in the basement. What had Loshak called it earlier? *The cavalry.*

She ran. And breathed. And listened to the upbeat murmur of her heart banging away in her chest, squishing and thumping.

Something clicked and echoed down the long stone chamber. A sharp sound. Metallic.

Darger froze. Feet stopping short beneath her. Both hands retracting toward her chest.

She listened.

The clinking sound whooshed and shuddered around her. Bounced off every curve and angle of the rocky walls.

She couldn't tell which way it was coming from.

She opened her eyes. Looked behind her through squinted eyelashes, as though slitted eyes might help her see something in the total darkness.

Black nothing stared back. The void an open thing before her. A vacancy.

She turned around. Looked that way.

Still nothing. That gaping abyss.

She swallowed. Waited. Kept her breathing as silent as she could, her chest barely moving.

And then she saw it.

A flashlight beam pushed into the dark tunnel before her, lifting up over a rise — a circle of light piercing the gloom.

Darger couldn't breathe. Couldn't move. Her mind tried to

perform some reassuring calculus to verify that the light was coming from the opposite way of the lake.

It was. Wasn't it?

The glow swayed back and forth along with the gait of the person carrying the light. Stretching where it crawled over the ground. Elongating.

Then the shaft of light rose up and lurched toward her.

CHAPTER 73

Another flashlight beam sheared away a cylinder of darkness, rising like a lightsaber alongside the first. It shot through the cave, pulling up a few yards shy of Darger's feet.

And then voices rang down the cavern, the echoes making them too sibilant to be understood, all esses and lip and mouth noises. She could tell by the timbre that they were male, but that was about it.

A lump formed in Darger's throat. Bobbed there like a golf ball when she swallowed.

It has to be SWAT. Has to be.

The lurching cadence and sizzle of radio chatter all but confirmed it.

She moved that way. Jogging toward the tubes of light.

"FBI!" she said, her voice sounding dry and thin even as she raised it. She held her hands good and high.

The voices cut out and the flashlights stopped moving. She couldn't see the officers, couldn't even really see silhouettes beyond the lights. But she heard the rasping of hands settling onto the grips of assault rifles, the metallic ticks and clacks of the weapons being handled, being raised.

She stepped fully into the light, eyes stinging from the brightness.

"Agent Darger?" a man's voice said from the dark behind one of the flashlights.

The two SWAT team members stepped closer, coming into view at last. Bulky Kevlar vests. Helmets. Goggles. Behind their face shields, big smiles curved the corners of their mouths upward.

"Holy shit. What are you doing down here?"

The SWAT officer studied her face, seeming to understand that she didn't recognize him. He pulled his helmet off, that blond movie star haircut spilling out from under the shell. He smiled and tucked the helmet under his arm, standing up straighter.

"Hendrix," Darger said. She turned to look at his partner. "And DeBarge?"

"Affirmative," the other said, leaving his helmet on. "So wait. This is the cavern you pursued your, uh, additional suspect down?"

Hendrix clapped his partner on the shoulder.

"Told you this tunnel was hot, didn't I? Fuckin' told you there'd be action."

Darger explained enough about Worm for them to understand, and DeBarge radioed it in. Hendrix gave Darger a bottle of water, and she drank long and deep before handing it back. She felt tingly, overwhelmed to be back in the light, back around human beings, but the cool water seemed to help.

"Backup is waiting at the address you gave 'em as we speak," DeBarge said, tucking his radio back into his belt. "Nowhere left for this asshole to run now."

Darger felt a touch of the tension in her shoulders melt away.

"Well…" Hendrix said. "We've got the sucker penned in pretty good, yeah? Surrounded. Seems to me like we ought to work that way. Try to flush him out of his hole like a groundhog, you know?"

He held his helmet in both his hands, ready to put it back on.

"And if he sticks his head out?" DeBarge said.

"Why, that's when we go and blow it off for him."

They both chuckled at that.

And then a gunshot cracked somewhere behind them. Crashing. Roaring.

The bullet pelted Hendrix's forehead. Made a neat hole there above his right eyebrow.

A surge of blood and goop flung out of the back of his skull, tilting his head forward before he even started to fall.

CHAPTER 74

Hendrix's body fell to the cave floor in slow motion. His eyes blank. Vacant. Jaw going slack. Mouth falling open.

His flashlight plummeted alongside him. Slipping from his limp fingers. It clattered to the floor and spun, the light swirling around and around, making oblong shadows shift and dance over the cave walls.

He belly-flopped to the cold stone. Lay there face down. Utterly inert.

That red gorge gaped up from the back of his skull, partially covered by a loose flap of his scalp. It looked like a tattered piece of parchment covered with blond hair.

Everything held still for two breaths as Darger gazed into the black hole of the wound. Her heartbeat seemed to count down to the deadline.

In that quiet moment, she saw that Hendrix's assault rifle had been pinned under his torso on a diagonal. Tangled awkwardly in his arms. She thought she should shift his bulk and grab it.

But more shots rang out. Bullets whizzing past. Ricocheting off the rocks.

She tore her gaze away from Hendrix's body and ran for cover, climbing the small rise she'd watched the flashlights spill over. Instinct wanted to put a barrier of rock between her and the gunfire, shuffled her legs that way.

Gunfire screamed and echoed in the enclosed space. The steady pop of the semi-automatic rifle clashed against the erratic reports from the Glock. Stone cracked into shards where the bullets hit, powdery bits pattering and swishing to the ground.

Anguished voices tangled over each other behind her. Already she couldn't really tell who was who and where either of them were, the sounds getting jumbled, echo tails smearing over everything so she couldn't make out the words.

She didn't think. She just ran. Blind panic taking control. Twitching her legs in rapid flurries. Moving her into the dark once more.

The ground dipped beneath her. She skidded down the slope, and the murk pulled her under its veil, shifted her out of view of the lights behind her.

She waited a second in the thick gray of this sheltered space. Blinked. Held her hand up, barely able to make out the outline of it here.

And as she stared at those faintly grayscale fingers, the events of the past few seconds caught up with her all at once.

She pictured Hendrix's eyes again as he fell. The light was out in them, even before he touched down.

He was gone.

Her skin prickled at the thought, chest going strangely hot and cold at the same time. She backpedaled a few more paces.

Maybe she should keep moving. Keep some distance between her and the firefight. In case DeBarge went down, too.

She turned around. Skimmed her fingers along the wall again. Jogging deeper into the cave.

And slowly she picked up speed. She'd eventually find help this way. Better to catch up with DeBarge later with reinforcements, if she could. There was nothing to be gained by lingering here, that was for sure.

She didn't see the faint silhouette of the stalactite until it was too late. The black protrusion jutted down from the cavern ceiling, just a little blacker than all else.

She ran into it face first. At speed. Her whole body shuddering and buckling at the moment of impact.

Bright stars burst inside her skull again, and the world ripped itself out from under her. Tilting. Fading. The blackness lurched once and swallowed her whole.

She, too, was out before she hit the ground.

CHAPTER 75

Loshak peered down the hole in yet another basement floor. His toes edged up to the broken concrete borderline. Even with the lights on down there, he saw it as a black hole, a void, something unknowable.

How many goddamn tunnels are there? When does this case end? Does it?

Does it fucking ever end?

He felt cold sweat trickle down his back, droplets streaming from his collar, tickling all the way down. It wasn't just paranoia, he knew. The case did keep getting weirder, every step of the way.

Finally, he looked away from the pit. Stepped away from that cratered place in the concrete.

A few other officers milled around the basement with him. Ambrose paced among them, speaking into a cell phone.

They were waiting on a second SWAT unit to arrive. Waiting while Darger wandered around somewhere down there.

Loshak paced back over to the hole in the floor. Gazed down into it.

He wanted to go in now. Pursue Darger and Worm. But task force orders meant he had to wait for the backup unit to get here. The SWAT team would lead the raid.

Of course, if this tunnel connected to the others, the SWAT officers already down there would come upon them sooner or later. Backup armed with assault rifles.

"Agent Darger said he was unarmed, so…" Ambrose said.

Loshak turned to see the detective holding his phone against his shoulder for the moment. His eyes flicked from Loshak to the hole and back again like he knew what the agent was thinking.

He had been unarmed. That was true.

Well then… It would all work out for the best. Wouldn't it?

Excited voices erupted upstairs, interrupting Loshak's thoughts. All eyes in the basement tilted toward that doorway at the top of the stairs.

"Sounds like they've got something up there," Ambrose said, his voice so low it sounded more like he was talking to himself.

Loshak could muster no enthusiasm for the development, just two words sounding inside his skull.

Now what?

CHAPTER 76

Darger woke facedown on the cold rock, snuffling for breath like a hound, the scratchy feeling of dust in her throat. She coughed. Turned her head and sucked in a lungful of cool air. The chill of it reminded her of where she was.

Before she even opened her eyes, a rapid fire montage of those ridged cave walls flashed through her head, the camera in her mind zooming down the center of an endless tunnel.

Then she remembered Worm leaping for that box on the wall and shutting off the lights, remembered the clatter of gunfire ringing up and down the rock corridor, remembered the bloody jelly of brain and blood vacating the back of Hendrix's skull, his limp body tipping toward the cave floor like a felled tree.

It all seemed distant now somehow. Buried back in a past she couldn't touch anymore, whether it'd been minutes or hours ago. Part of her suspected it hadn't been so long.

At last, her eyelids fluttered and opened. Blinked a few times.

The darkness had returned. Total blackness hung up in all directions.

She sat up. Peeled her body away from that cold rock slab. Propped her arms behind her to support her weight.

Her head throbbed, felt wobbly atop her stiff neck, the steady whooshing noise of her pulse loud in her ears. She just sat there for a few seconds, breathing and letting her head get steadier.

Then she crawled back the way she'd run. Climbed that sloped section of cave on hands and knees. Staying light and quiet.

When she got to the top of the rise, the faintest glimmer shone on the floor ahead of her — a trickle of light spilling out from a deep black contour.

A smothered flashlight, she thought. Hendrix's most likely. She half-remembered it slipping out of his fingers as he fell, clattering down alongside him. She couldn't help but wonder if the stifled lamp was being muffled against the rock or his corpse. Surely it was pressed tight against one or the other.

She listened for a long moment before she moved again, pushing herself upright on her knees like a meerkat standing on its hind legs and tilting her ears toward that sliver of illumination, one after the other. She heard nothing, not even so much as the dripping water she'd heard back toward the lake section of the cave.

She brought her hands back down to the stone and crawled toward the light. Palms pressing into the cold rock shelf below.

In the dark, the light almost seemed to be moving to her rather than the opposite. Floating. Gliding through the gloom. Drawn to her like a will-o'-the-wisp.

When she reached it, she fumbled a hand toward its half-halo shimmer. She felt something soft and cold — something wrong — her hand jerking back like she'd touched an electric fence.

Words flashed in her head one at a time:

Cold.

Dead.

Flesh.

She heaved a few breaths before she tried again. Wetness sizzling between her teeth. It took a second for her fingers to find and grip the body of the flashlight, and then she picked it up.

Hendrix's shattered head came into view as the light ascended. That red canyon still yawning out from behind that flap of papery scalp, all the shadows in the crevasse shifting as the flashlight moved.

The small tactical flashlight had been jammed tight against the frigid flesh of his neck.

She swept the light around. Found only empty cavern stretching away in both directions, all those swirling brown and gray minerals forming knobby growths that protruded from the floor and ceiling like rotting teeth.

DeBarge wasn't here. Was that good or bad?

Darger's mind whirred again. Tried to put these puzzle pieces together. Maybe DeBarge had given chase. Pressed Worm back toward the basement on Ash Avenue. Semi-automatic weapon fire had a way of being persuasive like that.

She swung the light back down toward Hendrix's corpse. Let it dance over him a second, keeping her eyes away from that pitted wound, and then she smiled faintly.

Laying the flashlight on the ground, she jammed her fingers under Hendrix's torso and shifted his weight. One hand hefted him at the hip while the other lifted his shoulder.

What she sought lay there, and she plucked it free, wiggling it to and fro to disentangle it from his arms.

She clutched the assault rifle in both hands for a second before she picked up the flashlight. The AR-15 felt light in her grip. Felt good against her skin.

Dark Passage

A line from *Die Hard* sounded in her head:
Now I have a machine gun. Ho ho ho!

CHAPTER 77

Darger clicked off her light. Crept forward in the dark, staying low.

It felt better to embrace the darkness. To join it instead of fighting it. She kept the flashlight at the ready, and she used it periodically to get a look around, but she didn't want it tipping her off from a distance. Stealth was everything in this place.

She moved back in the direction of the house on Ash Ave. The quiet seemed to grow as she proceeded, its hush swelling into something bigger, something reverent, something almost religious, something that smeared icy fingers at the back of her neck, made goosebumps plump all the way down her spine.

She traveled like that in the dark for what felt a long time. Feeling her way. Waiting for a noise or a glimpse of light up ahead. Something. Anything.

After going around a long curve that didn't seem familiar, she decided to try her light again, fingering the small rubber-coated button. Its click seemed louder now, something metallic and shrill stabbing at the silence, piercing that hushed awe for half a second.

The beam of light shot through the darkness. It took a second to make sense to her squinted eyes. Everything was blurred and jumbled for a second, and then the image came clear:

The natural rock walls stretched up around her to form the ceiling of the cave, closing in on themselves at the top where the lumpy stalactites clustered. The light glinted on the bare light bulbs as she swung it past the strand of them. She swished the light around in all directions a few times, somehow not satisfied, and then she swung it straight up toward the ceiling again. Craned her neck to look up at it.

She had no memory of this place. Didn't recall any section of the caves or tunnels where the ceiling had been that tall.

But this had to be the way she'd come. Had to be.

Didn't it?

Bubbles squirmed in her belly. Flitting everywhere. She imagined getting lost down here. Stuck wandering.

She shined the light down the cave both ways, looking behind her and ahead of her. Then she shut it off and kept going. She'd trust her gut. Press on.

The cave sloped down beneath her feet at a steeper angle now, and the air seemed to grow colder and thicker around her. The faintest tremor assailed the muscles in her shoulders and along the top of her back. She ignored it and kept moving.

Soon that dripping sound returned. The steady *tap-tap-tap* of water droplets slapping at wet rock. The noise was so small at first, delicate, nearly inaudible. But it grew with each step she took until it pealed out over everything, traveled great distances, almost rolling like thunder in this quiet place.

That was good, she thought, the familiar drip. Even if she found no comfort in thinking of the gleaming black surface of the lake somewhere ahead of her, she knew where she was now. Or thought she did, anyway. It was hard to stake all of her trust on the sound of dripping water.

She walked for what felt like a long time. One foot reaching out in front of the other on repeat, stepping down carefully on the uneven shelf of rock. Quiet breaths passed in through her nostrils and out over her lips, easier to keep them soundless that way.

And the sound of the dripping water changed as she advanced — the slap of the liquid hitting rock morphing into the plop of liquid hitting liquid. Each wet impact rang out a chiming tone like a struck xylophone instead of that clap against the cavern surface. Musical.

She came around another bend, and when she turned on her light again, the lake lay before her once more. The flashlight's glow glinted on the obsidian surface, the water as still and shiny as glass. Again, she recoiled at the sight of it, at the sight of the glistening moss hanging down in clumpy strands along one wall.

After another moment's hesitation, she edged into the vast chamber that contained this underwater pool. The thick air swirled around her once again, humidity brushing at her cheeks. It felt colder here, too. Open. Like she could feel the high ceiling yawning above, the cave opening itself wider here.

Her steps shortened, each leg taking a choppy stab at the ground, toes grinding down into the rock like she needed to make sure she was still on solid ground. She wanted to be quieter now, more careful. It felt like the water was watching her, rooting for her to fall in.

She eased down the sloped path along the water's edge. Swung her light down toward the lowest point, at the far end of this stagnant pool.

That was where the body lay.

CHAPTER 78

The louvered closet door had been pushed all the way open, the bifold panels pinched tightly together at the end of their track. Loshak shook his head as he peered into the cramped space beyond them.

The body lay there, positioned with its back on the floor, both legs jutting up at a roughly 90-degree angle and resting against the wall. Pinned in place more than anything, Loshak supposed.

This image was made all the more strange by the fact that the upper half of the body had been wrapped in what appeared to be the black plastic of garbage bags duct-taped tightly around the torso. The ratty cargo shorts looked incongruous protruding from that sheening black plastic veined with the silver of the tape. The whole thing was almost comical despite the morbidity. Absurd. Like not only did this corpse not fit into the bag, it didn't even come close.

The blood on the shorts had gone brown. Looked like coffee or tobacco stains now. The blood smears were plentiful enough to suggest that this person, too, had met a violent end.

"Figure this to be Cora's boyfriend. Chase, I think she said his name was," Ambrose said from somewhere behind Loshak.

"That's what I was thinking," Loshak agreed.

"Based on her location, it seems likely to me he would have been moved to this property. Any guesses on how this might fit in with the rest?" Ambrose said.

The agent didn't turn when he responded. His voice stayed

even, didn't betray the mounting frustration inside.

"Not really. Some kind of damage control, maybe. Seems like there was a lot to cover up, so…"

Loshak couldn't take his eyes off the upright portion of this body left in the shape of a capital L. Those legs sticking up, leaning against the drywall.

The skin of the calves looked pale. Milky white. Stark against the dark hair. Loshak supposed that being vertical would have drained the blood from the legs, sent it all down to settle in the lower back which probably looked dark and bruised as result.

Another house. Another body. Christ. How many more would they find? How would they ever make sense of all the moving parts in this case?

He shook his head again as he turned away. He couldn't dwell on it now. He needed to get back to the basement. The second SWAT team would arrive any minute, ready to plummet into yet another hole in the ground.

Darger and Worm were down there somewhere.

CHAPTER 79

Darger stopped. Stared into that circle of light where the dark bulk stretched out on the cavern floor.

The prone body nestled in an indentation in the stone. Like it was cupped in a rock bowl. Face down. Back and legs curved in a semi-fetal position. It straddled the place where the larger cavern narrowed down to the mouth of the tunnel leading out of this chamber, back toward that section of cave where the moss grew thicker.

Her eyes locked onto the torso, finding the faintly visible lines where the ribcage and abdomen connected. She watched for a twitch, a tremor, a hitch as breath sucked in, a subtle deflating as the wind vented its way out.

Nothing. Motionless.

A shiver climbed up the muscles in Darger's back. Cold feelings veining through her flesh.

From this distance, it was hard to make out details even with her miniature spotlight aiming right onto it, everything looking dark and indistinct. The angle of the face and positioning of the body, too, worked against her. Made assessing height or build impossible.

Was it him? Or was it DeBarge? He wasn't wearing a SWAT helmet, and she could see short, cropped hair bristling over the domed top of the skull. But that didn't tell her much. It looked like Worm's hair, but she hadn't seen DeBarge's.

Her mind darted through a panicked series of thoughts, mentally testing out scenarios, chaining together cause and effect explanations, crossing some out, backtracking, but none of the speculation did her any good. She wouldn't know anything for sure until she got closer.

She started that way, slow at first, picking out each step with care. She lifted the flashlight to her mouth and pinched it between her teeth as she moved. Wanted to have both hands on the gun now. Needed to.

Details began to come clear on that dark bulk ahead, the downed body sharpening into focus at last. A red collar emerged atop his black t-shirt, drew a thin slash there around his neck.

She swallowed. That was Worm's shirt. No question about it.

Then she saw the gun — her Glock — just beyond his outreached hand, the grip angled away from him.

Her heart leaped in her chest. She imagined him lurching for the weapon, turning it on her.

She stopped. Watched him for a second with the rifle aimed and ready. Her hands fidgeted against the AR-15. Felt suddenly sweaty. Clammy. Slick against the angles of the weapon.

The stillness was immense. Somehow more total here than she'd ever experienced. Even her movements and the sound of her breathing served only to strengthen the physical presence of it. Motionless. Lifeless.

This is a dead place.

Still, the sprawled body did not move, did not breathe from what she could see.

She took a deep breath and edged closer again. Those sweaty palms trembling slightly against her rifle.

Once more, her panicked thoughts raced through chains of

ideas, tried to come up with an explanation for what she was seeing. Maybe DeBarge got him and headed toward the house on Ash Avenue where the cavalry waited. That could make sense, though she didn't like it, wouldn't like it until she knew for sure.

Her eyes flicked from the gun to the body as she got closer. Two marbles set in her head, swiveling back and forth and back and forth. Gaze touching the Glock and then his hand, gut clenched tight, willing both of them to stay right where they were.

When she got close enough, she kicked the gun away from the prone figure. Watched it skitter deeper into the mouth of the cave, into the dark.

That felt a little better.

Then, keeping the assault rifle trained on the body, she backpedaled toward the weapon. Plucked it off the ground. Checked the magazine and found it empty. Tucked it into her holster.

Better still.

She took a few breaths. Crept back toward the body.

It hadn't moved in all this time. That seemed more plain, more real, now that she was up close.

She hovered over it a second. Felt faint breaths flutter in and out of her quavering chest.

She toed the sprawled figure. Sunk the front of her shoe into the lower back. No response. No movement at all. If he was breathing, she could detect no sign of it.

Maybe her guess had been right — DeBarge had got him and got out. It seemed more plausible now.

She knelt. Prodded the body with the barrel of the gun.

When that, too, elicited no response, she dared reaching out a hand.

She grabbed him by the shoulder. Rolled the torso up, the face peeling off the ground, angling into the light.

Except there was no face. Not really.

The visage was blown out. Cratered. One eye. No nose. Not much of a top lip or pallet left. Just a bloody chasm where the features used to be.

Darger gasped and shuffled back. That sharp intake of breath echoed around the room, sounding warbled as it rolled out over the dark water.

The body slumped out of her grip. Slapped down in a new position, his skull rolling to one side and going motionless again. And now the light touched some of the shadowed places on one side of his head — the entry wounds were revealed at last.

Two neat bullet holes punctured the flesh behind the ear. Both bullets had clearly exited through the center of his nose, each taking a scoop of head out with them. Venting. Leaving a pit where DeBarge's face had been.

Yes. DeBarge. She was sure of it now.

The black tactical pants and SWAT issue boots still adorned his legs and feet. Worm had killed him. Probably put two bullets into his skull at point-blank range after the fact to destroy his face, obscure his identity.

There was no puddle of blood here beneath the body. No bits of bone or brain or skin. He'd been moved here.

Still squatted down, Darger shuffled back a touch as the revelations kept coming.

Worm had slid his own shirt onto the corpse and laid him

out here on display, once again trying to obfuscate, trying to cover his tracks, buy himself some time.

Time for what, though?

There was nowhere left for him to go there, was there? Nowhere to run now. He must be nearby. Perhaps waiting around the corner in the next section of cave. Tucked back in a cluster of stalagmites, a spidery thing waiting for his next victim to come along.

Darger slowly stood, and her ears perked up. She listened to the screaming void beyond the steady dripping of the water, that immense stillness once again seeming to overwhelm this rugged cavern, swallowing it whole.

She took the flashlight from her teeth and thrust it into that gaping tunnel before her. Swung it around like a cutlass, slicing up the dark.

No movement showed in the flashlight's gleam, though. Only that chiseled rock face on all four sides. Barren.

Darger swallowed. Backpedaled a few paces toward the edge of the subterranean lake.

And then Worm burst out of the water behind her.

CHAPTER 80

Darger spun. Stumbled backward.

Worm's slimy figure rose out of the water. Looked black and shiny in the half-light of Darger's swinging flashlight.

She moaned.

He dove for her. Runnels of water drizzling down from the looted Kevlar vest strapped to his chest.

She swept the automatic gun in front of her. Elbow locked against her hip bone, forming a pivot point. Squeezing the trigger again and again. Gun stock battering into her as the weapon popped over and over.

The shots went high. A wild spray of them roaring over Worm's head. Pelting the surface of the water in the distance. Sending dark ripples and eddies in all directions.

His shoulders clubbed into her knees. Drove her straight backward, her legs pitching out from beneath her, tipping her forward.

And then his arms clutched around her calves. Wrenched upward. Helped gravity to rip her down, down, down.

The force laid her out flat. Arms going wide. Floating for a second.

And then she crashed down on top of him. Landed on his back. Their torsos pounding together hard enough that she felt her ribcage jolt and flex.

They struggled in the dark once more, taut things wriggling against each other like snakes. Limbs entangling.

The flashlight was pinned between them, its glow blinking

and shifting and mostly smothered by their heaving bodies.

Darger saw flashes of him. Writhing wet body parts visible in fits and snatches in the fractured light.

She didn't see the gun. Didn't feel it. She couldn't dwell on that now.

She fought to stay on top. Felt her way along his twisting form. Found herself face to face with him.

She swung. Clobbered him in the jaw with a short right hook.

His head snapped to the side, and he flinched hard.

But his eyes stayed hard. Stayed mean.

He tried to swing back, his fist thudding into the side of her neck, but he had no leverage. The shot connected cleanly, but it felt hollow.

When she caught him with another punch, a right cross that thumped the back of his skull into the stony floor, he changed tactics. Snaked his arms around her ribcage. Gripped her tight. Clenched her in a hug that squeezed the breath out of her. Tried to roll her. Wanted to pin her underneath him.

And then his fingers scrabbled at her jaw, climbed along her chin. A curved finger jammed into the corner of her lip. Ripped out hard in a fish hook.

Red flashed inside Darger's head. Pain, bright and hot. It felt like her cheek was being torn off, plucked away in one clean flap of skin.

An uncontrollable scream crawled up her throat and jetted through her clenched teeth. Raspy and shrill.

She twisted away from his finger. Jammed her face into his person as hard she could to keep her mouth safe from his roving hand. Worked her arms around him and clenched him back. Blinked hot tears down over her cheekbones.

They grappled like that for a while. Bodies mashed together. Arms and legs working. His crooked fingers still digging at her, seeking her mouth or eyes, searching for something soft to penetrate and destroy.

She slid her face away from his hand. Over and over. Mouth and nose gliding upward over his chest, over his collarbone.

She felt his skin against her lips, then felt the protrusion against the corner of her mouth. Something almost spongy.

She parted her lips. Sunk her teeth into that dangling bit of skin and cartilage. Biting hard and deep.

Then she wrenched her head away and ripped off most of his ear.

CHAPTER 81

Worm screamed.

His arms released her ribcage. That boa constrictor grip retreating all at once, letting her breathe freely again.

He scrabbled back. Slid out from under her. Kicking. Flailing. A wild animal now. Feral and fevered. Acting totally without thought.

Darger sat up. Fists bobbing to chin level. Ready to defend herself.

As he moved away, the flashlight came unblocked, tumbling down to the cave floor to light the scene once more. The grayscale smear around Darger slowly repopulated with color and detail, reality seeming to re-congeal into solid substance before her eyes.

Worm got to his feet in choppy thrusts. Both of his hands pawed at the tattered remnant of his ear, a ragged flap set over a dark hole that wept blood now.

His eyes were wild. Big and wet. The eyelids pulsing around them.

He bounced from foot to foot. Vaguely sidling back from her against the wall. It was like his whole brain was on fire. Idiot panic overtaking his limbs, moving him along without purpose.

Thrashing. Hysterical.

When he backed into the cave mouth, though, some shred of reality seemed to snap back for him at last. He turned and ran, disappearing into the circle of darkness. Faint whimpers spilled from his lips, the mewling sounds trailing away as he vanished into the murk.

Darger stood. Spit out the misshapen chunk of cartilage at last. Watched the flap slap down to the cave floor and go still. All of the lobe and part of that curled seashell outer ear stared up at her.

She smeared her sleeve at her lips. Took a big breath.

Then she gathered the AR-15 and the flashlight and followed him into the darkness.

CHAPTER 82

The bends and dips in the tunnel seemed to keep Worm just out of Darger's line of sight. She could hear his wet feet slapping at the rock floor, beating out a steady rhythm that echoed all around like a smattering of applause, but she never quite saw more than a snatch of his back before it ducked or swerved away again.

Finally, she wheeled onto a long straightaway, and he was there. A bobbing silhouette, a shadow moving beyond her flashlight's reach.

She dug in. Ran harder. Built speed. Gained on him.

And slowly the beam of her light crawled over the shadow. Lit him up. Reduced him from a menacing shape in the gloom to a man. A man running for his life.

She raised the rifle. Ready to fire.

Something glinted over his shoulder, something that almost looked skeletal in the half-light. It took Darger's eyes a second to make sense of the angular metal criss-crossing before her.

The ladder.

They'd reached the final straightaway — the place where the ladder led up into that hole in the basement floor. Darger felt an intense lightness come over her being at this realization. Excitement bubbling in her head like club soda.

Worm leaped for the ladder. Clambered up it. Arms and legs looking loose and monkey-like as they dragged him through that hole into the vast brightness above.

CHAPTER 83

Loshak paced the basement floor. Waiting. Impatient. Listening to the buzz of the fluorescent light bulbs, the sound of his own agitated breathing.

He'd made his way over by the steps where Ambrose and the others lingered, and the lead detective was starting to speak when the sounds began down in the hole.

"SWAT is pulling in now. They'll be—"

Loshak held up a hand, and Ambrose's words cut off. All heads followed Loshak's gaze, turning to the concrete hole across the room.

Gravelly footsteps pattered below. Faint rasps of the sandy floor being crushed. Quiet at first and growing louder.

Loshak drew his gun. Felt more than saw those around him do the same. Kept his eyes trained on that dark circle on the other side of the space.

He crept toward the hole. Slow steps. Careful and quiet. Gun extended before him.

Ambrose fell in beside him. Both of them slinking forward. Nobody spoke. Nobody breathed.

The crunch of the footsteps changed then. Replaced by the aluminum ping of weight hitting the rungs of the ladder.

Loshak stopped a few feet shy of the hole, and the others followed his lead. Fanning out at his sides.

He felt his arm steady. Felt his heart pounding. Felt a single bead of sweat glide down the back of his neck.

The sounds got louder and louder, bigger and bigger, closer

and closer.

Nothing stirred in the room above the tunnel. The stillness was absolute. The tension drawn so taut it couldn't even quiver.

A small man appeared in the opening. Skin wet and slick-looking. He hoisted himself up and out of the hole. Seemed to levitate there. Drifting upward in slow motion.

And then all hell broke loose.

Loshak lurched toward him first. Gun thrusting for Worm's face.

"Freeze! Down on the ground!"

The circle of law enforcement closed on him like jackals. The pack drawing tight around him. Right on top of him. Everyone screaming. Snarling. Growling. Barking. All the words made unintelligible.

Worm's eyes stretched wide. Pupils so black they looked like pits in his head.

He flailed his arms. Flopped forward onto his belly and sort of slid forward on the concrete like a seal doing a trick at Sea World. Skidding there.

Ambrose and Loshak leaped as one. Grabbed him. Yanked his arms up behind his back.

The cuffs fastened around his wrists with a percussive click and pop. Two metal loops that held him now. Restrained. Secured.

And then it was over, and Loshak could breathe again. His eyelids fluttered. He stared at the prone figure. Watched as the others lifted Worm to his feet, no more words passing between them. Just the scrapes and whispers of them sweeping him off the floor.

The little man's mouth quirked. Lips shaking. Chin

puckering and trembling. It wasn't until Loshak saw the tears drizzle down Worm's face that he understood what was happening. The piece of shit was crying. Silently sobbing like a child in trouble instead of a deranged murderer and rapist.

Loshak turned back to the hole then, and he heard more pings on the ladder. Slower this time. Confident.

Darger emerged from the tunnel. Lifted herself onto the concrete with a long stride that left her in a crouch, and then she stood. Her gaze went straight to Worm, locking onto the handcuffs pinning his hands behind his back.

"You OK?" Loshak said, drawing her eyes to his.

She blinked twice before she answered.

"Never better," she said.

She smiled about halfway then, and her teeth were bloody.

CHAPTER 84

Two days later, Darger and Loshak drove over to Penn
Presbyterian Medical Center to visit Cora and Lily. The
automatic doors whooshed open with a faint hiss as they
approached, revealing a lobby that looked more like a hotel or a
convention center than a hospital. They passed a gift shop, a
food court, and a huge wall of windows looking out on a lush
courtyard.

Ambrose intercepted them just before they reached the
elevators and guided them to the med-surg unit.

"I envy the two of you," Ambrose said as they rode up to
the fourth floor. "Your work here is almost done. But we're
going to be cleaning up this case for months. Agent Zaragoza
called her boss this morning and told him that if he didn't send
her more techs, she was going to quit on the spot."

"Did she get the techs?" Darger asked.

"Oh yeah." Ambrose chuckled. "The funny thing is, she'd
never actually quit. She thrives in this kind of chaos. And I bet
her boss knows that, but no one else wants this case."

"Understandable," Loshak said. "Nine bodies, if you count
the four we found at the dump. Five houses to sort through.
Four of them with tunnel access. Who knows how many linear
feet of manmade passageways there are snaking around down
there, let alone the natural cave system? Nightmare."

They went in to see Cora first, and the first thing Darger
noticed was the way the girl's eyes strayed to the window beside
the bed every few seconds. Darger recalled Danny telling them

he didn't like being in locked rooms or not being able to see a window nearby after being underground. She thought he'd sounded paranoid then, half unhinged. But she understood now, having been down there in the tunnels herself, dirt and stone coiling around her, pressing into her. At the very least, she didn't think she'd be venturing into any basements for a while.

"You're the experts from the FBI?" Cora said, turning to face them after they'd introduced themselves. "The ones who study killers?"

Darger nodded.

"That's right."

"Then maybe you can tell me why," Cora said.

"Why?"

"Why this happened. Why someone would do this. Why Chase had to die."

Darger glanced over at Loshak and then back to Cora.

"I don't think there are any answers for that, unfortunately."

Cora's eyes flicked to the expanse of glass looking out over the city. She picked at the wristband encircling her arm.

"There was a part of me that knew we shouldn't have gone there. To that house. Knew that Chase was wrong to do it." Cora paused, and when she spoke again, her voice was barely a whisper. "Maybe this is our punishment."

"I don't think it works that way," Darger said. "Sometimes bad things just happen. Which maybe isn't any more comforting. But neither you nor Chase deserved any of this."

Cora inhaled deeply, letting her shoulders sag as she let the breath out. The girl's brow furrowed, and she went on.

"Maybe sometimes those cold feelings you get are worth listening to. When your skin prickles. When your hands go icy and numb. Maybe some part of you knows way down deep in your bones. And maybe if I'd listened to my skin, listened to my bones, I could have talked Chase out of it, and none of this would have happened."

There was a knock at the door, and then a nursing assistant bustled in with a tray laden with food. Darger saw the way Cora's eyes lit up at the sight of her dinner and after exchanging a wordless glance with Loshak, decided it was time to go.

They wished Cora the best and exited the room.

"She seems in good shape, medically and psychologically," Loshak said, folding his arms over his chest.

Ambrose nodded.

"They're discharging her tomorrow. All things considered, I think she got out of this pretty lucky."

They moved three doors down to the room where Lily was being treated. Ambrose lowered his voice.

"This one, on the other hand..."

He let the sentence trail off.

Darger peered through the gap in the door, which stood ajar. Lily was a tiny, frail thing in the bed. Barely taking up space at all and so pale she practically blended in with the white sheets and pillow. Purplish half-circles marred the skin under her eyes.

"We've gotten bits and pieces out of her, but being down there that long did a number on her mentally, I think," Ambrose explained. "You can talk to her if you want, but I wouldn't expect to get anything very coherent."

The same nursing assistant who'd brought Cora her tray whisked past them with Lily's meal. No sooner had the tray been set down than Lily began to wolf down the food. Her motions were frantic, using the spoon to shovel some kind of porridge into her mouth. She ate as though she was afraid the tray might be taken away from her at any moment, like she had only moments to get as much of it down as fast as she could. But what disturbed Darger more than the compulsive, panicked eating was the haunted look in the girl's eye. The way she glanced up and around every few seconds, wary of her surroundings.

Lily finished the porridge. Licked the bowl and spoon clean. And then stared at the empty vessel, an expression of absolute misery on her face.

Darger had seen the tray they'd brought in for Cora. It had been full of all sorts of things: burger and fries, a cup of soup, mixed veggies, and a slice of what looked like cheesecake for dessert. It was easily twice as much food as what Lily had received.

"Why are they giving her so little food?" Darger asked.

Ambrose pursed his lips.

"The way the doctor explained it to me is that after prolonged bouts of starvation, they have to be very careful reintroducing food. Something about all the electrolyte imbalances that happen as a result of not eating, and how when the body gets food again and the metabolism kicks back into gear, it throws everything out of whack. They get abnormal heart rhythms and can go into acute heart failure. It's called refeeding syndrome." Ambrose thrust his hands into his pockets. "So she's on a very strict diet and will be for some time. That's one of the things that makes talking to her so difficult. She just keeps asking for food."

Darger's heart broke a little as she watched Lily pick up the spoon and begin licking it again, like maybe she'd left a morsel or two.

"I think any questions we have for her can wait for another day," Loshak said, turning to face her. "What do you think?"

"Yeah," Darger agreed. "They can wait."

CHAPTER 85

Their next stop was to interview Warren Francis Strass, AKA Worm. They followed Detective Ambrose over to the detention center, parked, and got in line to make their way through the security checkpoint.

The jail looked like any number of similar institutions Darger had been in before. Industrial and hard and antiseptic. Every sound echoing down the cavernous, windowless hallways. It reminded her of being underground. A shudder ran up her spine, and she had to glance back the way they'd come, back at the doors that led outside.

"So here's another little bizarro snippet for you," Ambrose said. "You know how Cora told us that Cowboy was the one who killed Chase and locked her in the cage?"

"Yeah."

"It wasn't Cowboy. It was Worm."

"But she described Cowboy to a tee. Hat. Mustache. Ponytail," Darger said, checking the features off on her fingers.

"That was a Worm in Cowboy clothing," Ambrose said.

"What? Why?"

Ambrose shrugged.

"We haven't got that far in his confession, so I couldn't tell ya. The DA is having him start at the very beginning to give us everything in detail, step by step. We've barely scratched the surface, to be quite honest. But if you want to ask him about it, go for it. I'd love to hear an explanation."

"So he is going to plead out after all?" Loshak asked. "We

heard there'd been some waffling."

"Oh yeah. He's gonna plead," Ambrose said, nodding. "Once we reminded him that Pennsylvania is a death penalty state, he got real talkative. He says he'll tell us anything, cop to anything, as long as that's off the table. Much to his lawyer's chagrin. Still, I don't know how much insight he's going to be able to offer you, at least in terms of your work in behavioral analysis."

"Why? Is he too nuts?"

Ambrose only smirked.

"You'll see."

CHAPTER 86

Worm was already waiting in the meeting room when they arrived — a small room with plain white walls. The only window looked out on the hallway. No natural light touched the space.

Darger wondered if Worm felt at home in this little cell, the way he'd seemed to feel at home in the tunnels.

She studied him as they entered the room. He wore a brownish jumpsuit with a zipper that ran from the crotch to the neck. When she saw the way the legs of the jumpsuit had been rolled up to keep them from bagging around his ankles, she realized how short he was. Shockingly so. She'd forgotten that, somehow. He'd seemed bigger in the eerie underground lighting. Bigger when she'd fought him for her life.

The second thing she noticed was the pack of cookies in front of him. The kind Sandy had mentioned when they'd interviewed her. The small elf-shaped sandwich cookies. As they sat down across the table from him, Worm pried the two cookies comprising the sandwich apart and scraped the chocolate filling off with his front teeth. When he'd swallowed that, he stuck the two cookies back together and shoved the whole lot into his mouth.

Loshak gave her a look that indicated she should take the lead.

"Hello, Warren," Darger said.

"Warren." He snorted. "Call me Worm, man. Everyone does."

"OK, Worm. Let's talk about what you and Cowboy were up to."

"It was all Cowboy's idea. The whole thing." Worm paused with a cookie halfway to his mouth and looked thoughtful. "Always was kind of obsessed with digging, now that I think about it. Like this one winter, way back, we got all this snow. So much that it drifted all the way up on the tall side of his deck. Then we had an ice storm, so it sort of coated the whole thing with a shell. We dug it out into a sort of igloo. It was pretty rad."

Darger thought this sounded like something children would do.

"When was this?" she asked.

"Oh, a long time ago. I think I was ten, so Cowboy woulda been fifteen or sixteen."

"You've known Cowboy since you were ten?"

"No." Worm's gold tooth glinted when he grinned. "I've known Cowboy since I was born. He's my cousin. Shit. *Was* my cousin now, I guess."

That was interesting. Serial killing cousins, like the Hillside Stranglers.

"Anyway, Cowboy always did like girls. Had a way with the ladies, I suppose you could say. Sometimes had two or three girlfriends at once, though I don't think any of them ever knew that. I envied him for it. Looked up to him, you know? He was, like, the coolest dude I knew." Worm crunched a cookie between his molars. "But he got kinda weird after he left the Marines. Was convinced we were heading for *Armageddon,* which I thought was just the name of a movie, to be honest. But he said that we had all the tools to survive it. And that it was the responsibility of someone like him, who sees the world for what it is, to remake the next version of civilization."

"And that would entail what, exactly?" Darger asked.

"Well he said that everything really got messed up when we let women, like, start doing man stuff. Said we never should have allowed women to be soldiers or doctors or cops." He gave her a pointed look as he swallowed another cookie. "Said that men were made to be the ones in control. Making decisions. Having the power. That women were supposed to have the babies and take care of the men. That's how it works in nature right? It's the order of the natural world. What we have now? That's unnatural."

Darger wanted to ask if he was familiar with the order of the natural world when it came to the praying mantis but let him talk instead. His eyes flicked over to Ambrose.

"Hey, can I get another thing of cookies?" he asked, flicking at the empty package on the table.

"Maybe later," Ambrose said. "How about something from the vending machine?"

"Is there candy?"

"Sure. I think it's got Skittles, peanut M&Ms, Starburst."

Worm's head bobbed once.

"OK."

"Which one?" Ambrose asked. "Starburst?"

"All of them."

Ambrose raised an eyebrow.

"You want something to drink with that?"

"More Hawaiian Punch."

Darger caught an expression of mixed disgust and disbelief as Ambrose exited the room. A surge of anger rose in her chest at the notion of Worm sitting here stuffing his face, while Lily could barely eat more than a few morsels without running the risk of dying.

"Anyway, I'm not always the best at explaining it," Worm went on. "But the way Cowboy would say it, always made sense."

"So you were preparing for Armageddon? How did the girls fit into that?"

Worm lifted his arm and scratched his armpit.

"Well… that's how it started. The apocalypse or whatever. But Cowboy could be kind of an impatient dude. Especially when it came to putting his plan into action. So after we were digging for a while, he said we needed to test it out."

Ambrose came back in, dumping an armload of candy and a can of punch in front of Worm.

"Test it out, how?"

Worm ripped open the bag of Skittles.

"He said we needed to get a couple of girls as like, guinea pigs."

Darger felt nausea roiling in her gut as Worm poured Skittles into his mouth. The small candy-coated spheres rattled against his teeth.

"Because part of his plan was that eventually the girls, well, they would kinda be into it. He had a theory that if you kept 'em down in the dark long enough, isolated like that, that they'd *want* to come out and do stuff. Cook and clean and well… other things."

Darger squeezed her hands into fists. Stay calm, she thought. Let him keep yapping himself into a life sentence.

"So we got the cages set up down in the tunnels, and we

grabbed Trinity and Amaranth one night when Bo and Puck were working down in the tunnels."

"They were the," Darger swallowed back her revulsion, "guinea pigs?"

"Yeah. And that part was easy enough. Drugged their wine, loaded them into the truck, and took them over to the test site."

"That would be the house on Finch Lane?"

"Yup. Cowboy decided that would be our beta testing grounds." Worm pawed at the bandage that concealed the remnants of his ear. "Put the girls in the cages. Easy peasy. That part anyway. The thing was, it didn't go exactly as Cowboy thought it would. He was dead wrong about how they'd react. He thought they'd be dying to be let out of those cages, so that they'd basically do anything we wanted. But it didn't work that way, see? They were pissed. I think maybe it was the dark. Made them kinda crazy. They fought."

Worm tugged at the neck of his jumpsuit, revealing a nasty looking bite wound on his chest.

"One of them did that?"

"Fucking Amaranth. Not sure what it is with you bitches and the biting. But then Cowboy says that's part of the current insanity with the world situation. Makes all the women a little crazy."

Darger felt a strange pang of pride that Bailey Harmon had fought back. *Good for you, Bailey.*

"Why did you starve them?"

"Well, Cowboy said we needed another variable. A way to show them who had the power. And he was right. It made them more docile. It was easier too. Not having to haul food up and down the damn ladder all the time. We'd give them just a little bit, if they were good. A fresh jug of water and some crumbs, basically. And they'd lap it up. And beg for more. And we'd tell them there was much more where that came from, if they did exactly what we said."

Darger felt ill again.

"What about Stephen Mayhew and Bo Cooke," she asked. "Why starve them?"

"Well they were the betas for the betas. Cowboy said we wouldn't know how far we could push it with the girls, so we used the guys as experiments. Had them in a different section of the tunnels altogether. Man you shoulda seen how the fight went outta them. Bo, see, I knew he didn't like me on account that me and Amaranth had kind of a thing going on. But three days without food, and he was a different man. 'Please, Worm. Please, man. Just give me something to eat. I'll do anything.'"

Worm's imitation of Bo was high pitched, whiny.

"I used to go down there with a sandwich or some chips, and I'd eat it right in front of him." He cackled and ate another handful of candy. "Drove him fucking crazy."

Darger waited for him to go on. He tore into the bag of M&Ms, glancing around.

"I probably shouldn't admit this because it would piss Cowboy off, but I guess he's dead so it hardly matters. But I let Bo out, eventually. When he was real weak. Could barely move. I opened his cage and let him crawl out on his hands and knees. Told him I was taking him to a big feast." Worm snickered. "I led him all around the caves like that until he collapsed. Just kinda keeled over. Ended up being kind of a pain because then I had to drag his ass all the way back to the cage so Cowboy wouldn't figure out what I'd done. He was kind of a dictator that way. Always wanted things done his way."

"And Stephen Mayhew?"

Worm scratched at one of the scabbed over places on his cheek.

"Eh, he just kinda faded away. He was always cool to me so I had no interest in messing with him. He was a means to a end. Wrong place and shit."

"Is that what ultimately happened with Bailey and Courtney?" Darger asked. "Or Amaranth and Trinity, as you knew them? Did they just fade away like Stephen?"

"Yeah. We thought we had it worked out. Exactly how much food to give the girls to keep them going but not to ever, like, give them enough energy to fight. But I guess we took it too far. Cowboy was pissed. Raged for like a full hour. Kicking those dumb ass boots against the cages. He broke his toe doing that. Hobbled around for a few days."

"Is that when you decided to get rid of the bodies?"

"Yeah. I said we should just bury 'em somewhere in the tunnels. Lotta hidey holes down there. But Cowboy said he didn't want that rotting corpse stench. Or to run the risk of any of the other workers stumbling across any of it. So he had me take them into the city and dump them."

"Let's back up. Before that, you grabbed Lily?"

"Well yeah. Cowboy was determined to make this work." Worm shook his head. "It'd become his life's work. That's what he called it. Lily, she was a trooper."

"Where'd you find her?"

"Oh she was a friend of Eddie's girl."

"Edward Swensen?" Darger asked. "He's the one currently missing a face?"

Worm tittered. A raspy, high-pitched sound that made the hair on Darger's neck stand on end.

"Yeah. Man. That was so crazy! Have you ever seen the Hostel movies? They show a guy getting his face peeled off. And it comes off like… like an orange peel, you know? Just kinda—" Worm made a suctioning noise with his mouth "—pops off in one piece. I always wanted to know if it was really like that, in real life. It's not quite so clean. Like it kinda sticks to the skull a little. But it still did come off mostly in one full piece with a little knife work on my part. So crazy!"

Darger had the sense that none of this was quite real to Worm. That the things he'd done, the atrocities he'd committed and taken part in, were not much different than the fictional version he'd once seen on TV.

"And Cora and Chase," Darger asked. "Was selling him drugs just a ploy to get her?"

"Well yeah. We were running low on workers, and Cowboy wanted a second girl, like, pronto. Took us a while to find someone to come up and happen to have a girl with him, but it worked eventually."

"And it was you who killed Chase? Dressed as Cowboy?"

Worm's eyes were alight with intrigue.

"Yeah. Did she buy it? I bet she did. I looked *good*. Got that idea from *The Usual Suspects*." He nodded his head and shoveled more candy into his mouth. "Great movie."

"But why?" Darger asked. "Why dress as Cowboy to fool a girl you were going to lock in a cage?"

"Well, to be honest, I think Cowboy was starting to lose it a little. He started getting paranoid. Convinced you all was onto us. Which I guess was sorta true. He kept talking about going on the run."

Darger shook her head.

"I thought you said he wanted to continue the experiments. His life's work or whatever."

"That's the thing. He was back and forth. One minute we had to start packing. Figure out where we were gonna go. What we were gonna do. And then he'd calm down and say that we'd worked too hard. Gotten too far. And we had to see it through. So then we'd start making plans again. I started having to slip him some of the sleeping pills we kept around in his bourbon. A little nightcap to calm him the fuck down. Anyway, he was kinda conked out when Chase came over with his girl. And I figured it was up to me to see the plan through."

"You weren't perhaps trying to tie up loose ends?"

Worm chewed and stared at her blankly.

"In what way?"

"Set it up to make it look like cowboy did it all."

Worm pursed his lips.

"Now why would you think that?"

"Why else mutilate Edward Swensen? Because you wanted us to think he was you, and that you were dead — at least for a while. It wouldn't work for long, but probably long enough for you to get out. Meanwhile, Cowboy would be left holding the bag."

"I appreciate that you think I'm some kind of mastermind, but the truth is, Cowboy was always the brains behind everything." Worm shrugged. "He was the one with the big ideas."

Darger decided to move on.

"Do you know what remorse means?"

"Do I know what remorse means?" he scoffed. "Jesus, lady, I'm not a idiot."

Darger said nothing.

"You wanna know if I feel bad?" Worm emptied the last of the peanut M&Ms into his mouth, chewing as he spoke. "Cowboy said that guilt and shame are for suckers. But I seen some of the families on the news. They seemed sad. And that made me feel kinda bad. Like if I coulda waved a magic wand and brought their daughter back, I woulda. But I can't right? Like that happens in movies sometimes, but it ain't real life. Cowboy always said we shouldn't fret about what we can't control. And I can't control that, right? Life goes on."

Darger considered the irony of Worm making such a statement. Life wouldn't go on for Bo Cooke or Bailey Harmon or countless others. And while Worm sat here stuffing his face, Lily could barely eat more than a few morsels without running the risk of dying.

She stood.

"We done?"

"Yep," Darger said.

He put out his hand, as if to shake.

Darger ignored it and moved to the door. She glanced back once. Saw Worm still pigging out on his junk food. And she silently wished that one of these days, he would choke on it.

EPILOGUE

"So is he a genius or an idiot?" Darger asked as she and Loshak drove back to the hotel. "It sure seems like he was trying to wrap things up there at the end, the way he impersonated Cowboy. If we'd stormed the place even a few hours later, Worm might have gotten away."

"Maybe it's both," Loshak said. "Maybe the most conniving scheming part of him is sort of subconscious. Something he does without thinking. Something almost beyond his outward abilities. He improvises the whole way through, and his intuition is sort of smarter than he is."

"Like a… sociopathic savant?" Darger asked.

Loshak huffed out something resembling a laugh.

"For lack of a better term, sure. I mean, there are a fair number of low IQ serial killers who got away with their crimes for a shockingly long time. Henry Lee Lucas. Gary Ridgway. Arthur Shawcross."

"I thought you said that IQ tests are a load of manure," Darger said.

"They are. But my point is that these aren't bright guys on any level. And I don't really need a test to tell me that." Loshak held up a finger. "But maybe they have a sort of… genius lizard brain that does all the calculating for them. Without them even being aware of it most of the time."

"Or maybe he's a pathological liar," Darger said. "Maybe Worm wants us to think he's dumber than he is so we underestimate him."

"I don't think the ideas are mutually exclusive. He can be a liar and be stupid at the same time. Maybe he overestimates his own intellect."

"I guess that's true." Darger gazed out the window as the city flits by in a blur. "I know one point we can definitively agree on, at least."

"What's that?"

"Dude's a fucking creep."

☾

Darger got to her room and started to pack. She and Loshak had originally planned on staying overnight before agreeing that they'd rather sleep in their own beds tonight, even if it meant getting back to Virginia late.

She had her suitcase half-filled when she remembered that Luck had called while they were staking out Cowboy's house.

She checked her call logs and noticed the date. Had that really only been two days ago? It seemed like weeks had passed, most of them underground.

She found that Luck had also sent a text in the meantime. It just said two words: BIG NEWS.

Darger had a feeling that Luck's desk duty was coming to an end. She looked forward to being able to say, "I told you so."

She dialed his number.

"There she is," Luck said. "I've got news."

"So I've gathered. Spill it."

"I got engaged!"

Luck's voice was giddy.

"Engaged?" Darger repeated, stunned.

"To Irma, my physical therapist!"

"Oh. Wow," Darger said. "Congrats."

The glee in Luck's voice had vanished.

"Sheesh. Don't get too excited, Violet." He paused for a second. "What's up?"

"No, it's just…" Darger wondered how to put the question. Figured it was best to just ask. "How old is she?"

"Twenty-eight. Why? You're not going to give me a speech about how she's too young for me, are you?"

Darger let out the breath she'd been holding.

"No. The opposite actually."

"What?"

Darger swirled a lock of hair around her finger.

"Well, I only know her by her name. Irma. And I had a great aunt named Irma, so I… guess I couldn't help but picture my great aunt Irma in her mechanical chair and her walker and her big white hair."

Luck let out a burst of laughter.

"Oh, she's gonna love when I tell her that."

"Don't tell her!"

"No, really. She'll think it's funny," Luck said.

"Well, congratulations again. And more genuinely this time."

"Congrats to you, too. You closed another one, huh?"

"Yeah."

"And you managed to not almost die this time?"

Darger had a flash of fighting Worm in the cave. The feel of his ear cartilage snapping under the pressure of her teeth.

"Yep."

"Nice work. Anyway, I'll let you go. I'm sure you're still busy wrapping things up."

They hung up, and Darger let herself fall into a sitting position on the end of the bed.

Casey Luck was engaged.

She was genuinely stunned, and… something else. Disappointed? Maybe?

She sat with it for a few moments, and then she let out a silent chuckle. Was she being serious?

So she'd talked to Luck on the phone a lot lately. And they'd become close. Was she really imagining there was more to it than that? He was two thousand miles away.

And the more she thought about it, the more she wondered if she'd gotten a little fixated on him *because* he was out of reach. She'd been that way as a teenager. More interested in imaginary crushes on boys she'd barely ever exchanged a word with than the messy reality of dating.

Jesus, she thought, half amused, half annoyed with herself.

She needed to get laid.

She sat there for a few seconds, listening to the quiet in her hotel room. And then her phone rang.

"Hello, Violet."

Darger didn't recognize the number, but the voice on the other end was familiar. The touch of a Georgia twang that softened the first syllable of her name. *Vah-let.*

"Owen?"

"I need a favor."

COME PARTY WITH US

We're loners. Rebels. But much to our surprise, the most kickass part of writing has been connecting with our readers. From time to time, we send out newsletters with giveaways, special offers, and juicy details on new releases.

Sign up for our mailing list at:
http://ltvargus.com/mailing-list

SPREAD THE WORD

Thank you for reading! We'd be very grateful if you could take a few minutes to review it on Amazon.com.

How grateful? Eternally. Even when we are old and dead and have turned into ghosts, we will be thinking fondly of you and your kind words. The most powerful way to bring our books to the attention of other people is through the honest reviews from readers like you.

ABOUT THE AUTHORS

Tim McBain writes because life is short, and he wants to make something awesome before he dies. Additionally, he likes to move it, move it.

You can connect with Tim via email at tim@timmcbain.com.

L.T. Vargus grew up in Hell, Michigan, which is a lot smaller, quieter, and less fiery than one might imagine. When not click-clacking away at the keyboard, she can be found sewing, fantasizing about food, and rotting her brain in front of the TV.

If you want to wax poetic about pizza or cats, you can contact L.T. (the L is for Lex) at ltvargus9@gmail.com or on Twitter @ltvargus.

LTVargus.com

CPSIA information can be obtained
at www.ICGtesting.com
Printed in the USA
LVHW090906240723
753027LV00093B/285/J